THE ΩMEGA ACCORD

America Withers...Freedom Dies

STEVE EDWARDS

THE ΩMEGA ACCORD

America Withers...Freedom Dies

STEVE EDWARDS

Durham, NC

The Omega Accord: America Withers...Freedom Dies
Steve Edwards author
sncedwards@yahoo.com
www.perrinafbhistoricalmuseum.org

Published 2022, by Torchflame Books
an Imprint of Light Messages Publishing
www.lightmessages.com
Durham, NC 27713 USA
SAN: 920-9298

Paperback ISBN: 978-1-61153-472-6
E-book ISBN: 978-1-61153-473-3
Library of Congress Control Number: 2022917282

Dedicated to God the Father.

Also, to my ever-amazing wife,
whose love and support
throughout the tedious writing process
never wavered.

ACKNOWLEDGMENTS

A special thanks to Perrin AFB Historical Museum Directors Tom and Laura Longmire and Attorney Matthew C. Aycock for their timely and valued contributions.

PROLOGUE

Thursday, December 17

As the morning's radiance illuminated idyllic Victoria, the man with piercing dark eyes and thick black beard enjoyed a rare moment of tranquility. Scanning the pastoral setting from the balcony of his Fairmont Empress suite, he felt the crisp and refreshing northwest air.

Three stories below, the intimate harbor teemed with activity as holiday tourists flocked to the endearing crown jewel of British Columbia and pride of Western Canada. Street vendors mesmerized shoppers with innovative wares. A single-engine pontoon plane glided smoothly into the narrow harbor leaving frothy wakes of white-topped waters. In the distance, a three-deck ferry from Port Angeles meandered into the channel packed with revelers, vehicles, and supplies. Piercing the din was a lone bagpipe. The hauntingly shrill notes were harbingers of good times and evil tidings. Glancing at the black face of his stylish Movado, the traveler noted the hour. There was ample time for an early lunch, gift wrapping, and careful preparation.

Mimicking a Renoir masterpiece, the nearby park was a pleasant walk from the hotel district. Towering firs, massive trees, and bulging bushes dotted the sculpted grounds.

Stripped of brilliantly colored leaves, a cluster of red maples appeared stark and out of place as their spindly branches reached ominously to the heavens in a desperate plea for new life. With a cloudless sky, winding sidewalks, and ample seating, the setting was both charming and disarming.

Arriving early for a 1 p.m. meeting, the gift bearer previewed the area with a practiced eye. The oft bustling park was empty, a victim of holiday shopping and winter chill. Catching his eye was an isolated bench framed by a tight row of evergreens aping cathedral spires. Taking a seat, he placed a brightly wrapped gift box on his lap. The glossy green paper trimmed with silver ribbon was a beacon to his contact.

As a distant church bell tolled the hour, an ecru man with leathery skin, moussed hair, bushy mustache, and crackling eyes approached at a deliberate pace. Stopping at a safe distance he nodded. Though strangers, they were brothers emerging from their shadowy profession into the glorious Canadian sunlight.

"Why am I here?" As spittle hurtled from the enraged lips of Juan Ramirez's twisted mouth, his face turned dark. "You know this meeting is extremely dangerous."

"Like you, I too was summoned." Mimicking the weariness of a preoccupied tourist the gift bearer's unchanged pitch was soft and detached.

"But why? And who the hell are you?"

"Who I am is irrelevant. Just call me Mr. B. Your diablo earring is very distinguishable."

"So, you have my picture. Why have I been summoned?"

"You executed the messenger."

"What are you talking about? My only killing was that scumbag Lupe Gonzalez."

"He *was* the messenger. You eliminated Mr. A."

"But...this meeting isn't safe. Jorge Gonzalez is also in Victoria celebrating the winter holiday. The master knows our location. Why am I here?"

"You've been summoned to hear a message and receive a gift."

"The message?"

"The hierarchy has grave concerns. You were ordered to stop Venezuelan-based Chinese triads from entering Mexico. Yet you have stupidly ignored the directive and created a blood feud. Jorge has vowed revenge."

"Lupe had to die. That greedy bastard was infringing on my territory. How was I to know that he was *the messenger*"? Arrogantly defiant, the stocky drug lord fingered an unfiltered cigarette from his coat pocket. Flaming the tobacco, he nervously sucked the acrid smoke into his blackened lungs.

"Your foolish action has distracted Jorge and forced a decision." The curt declaration was greeted by a guttural gasp and nervous silence.

"Mexico can no longer be ruled by two kingpins."

"Meaning?"

"You are now *numero uno.* Jorge Gonzalez has a date with the devil."

"How? When?"

"That is my business. Your concern is simple. Prevent the triads from overrunning Mexico. *Comprende?*"

With piercing eyes, the gift bearer studied the pleased but puzzled drug lord. The furrows on Ramirez's brow were deep and straight like plowed rows. His black eyebrows were astonishingly thick, untrimmed and arching high above both watering eyes. The thick mousse in his jet-black hair was greasy like a recent lube job. As acrid smoke spiraled upward in tiny trails of white vapor the new messiah flashed a wry grin and nodded approvingly. An unwritten murky agreement had been negotiated.

"And the gift?"

"The surprise celebrates your ascension to *el jefe.*"

In a fluid motion, the weary traveler passed the glossy package to Mexico's new kingpin. Salivating like a crazed Christmas child, Ramirez eagerly attacked the bow and glossy paper. With eyes blinking in anticipation, he peered into the opened box. Suddenly his expression soured.

"What the hell? A bobblehead? But the damn thing doesn't bobble."

"Mr. Ramirez, this gift is priceless. A *shabti* denotes kingship. Carved from rare wood and painted with an artist's exactness the figure represents a perfect likeness."

"Well, I'm honored and amazed. I now possess my own Juan Ramirez statute. It's a mantle masterpiece."

"But there's more. The gift comes with a sparkling surprise, an upgrade for that ruby in your diablo earring. Hidden within the shabti is a rare chocolate diamond to partner with your white diamond."

"Where?"

"It is cleverly concealed within the hard plastic abdomen. The wood finish hides the invisible seams."

"How does it open?"

"Just rub the figure's head. The heat from your fingers triggers a spring-loaded cavity. With this jeweler's loupe, you can examine the flawless diamond with an expert's aplomb."

Consumed with avarice, the Mexican messiah vigorously massaged the wooden head. Suddenly eagerness turned to agony as his eyes widened and his face twisted, the only notable signs of physical distress. Penetrating the skin from miniscule pricks was a newly formulated and highly lethal cyanide derivative.

Immune to the throes of death, the gift bearer contemplated the newly altered landscape. Mexico now belonged to Jorge Gonzalez. Exuding an air of indifference, he reached into his bag and removed a stainless steel tool. Flashing a devilish grin, he clamped the razor-sharp shears around the kingpin's earlobe and squeezed. As blood oozed from the open wound, the vaunted diablo earring fell harmlessly into an unfolded handkerchief.

Rearranging the limp body into a sleeping position, the killer of many casually packed his props and exited the park. As if on a Sunday stroll, he ambled nonchalantly toward the Empress for a refreshing spot of English tea.

As dark shadows frolicked across the Saanich Sea's frigid black-blue waters, Mr. B drove the scenic route to nearby Sidney-by-the-Sea. Easily locating the immaculately groomed city park, he navigated the Land Rover into a postcard picnic area and shut down the purring engine. A fortress of Douglas firs formed a natural amphitheater and temple of repose. With the area clear of prying eyes, he heard the deep growl of a turbocharged Jaguar.

The arrival of Jorge Gonzalez was imminent.

Accompanied by a pair of fawning minions, the slender drug lord walked toward Mr. B with the quiet confidence and ease of a lurking puma. Though physically unimpressive, his mannerism radiated a quiet menace. In Sidney's temperate climate, both guards wore tight-fitting black tee shirts, bodies toned and biceps bulging.

Ambling nonchalantly toward the new arrivals, the gift bearer readied the harnessed violence stored within his lithe frame that could instantly ape a Cat Five tornado: howling, destructive and deadly.

"*Feliz Navidad*, Senor Gonzalez."

"And you are a dead man, *amigo.* Why have I been summoned from my holiday? And who the hell are you?"

"My identity is unimportant. I bring a message and gifts."

Tamping his explosive Latin temper, Gonzalez's scowling face relaxed. In a flash of lucidity, he remembered the pecking order. Master trumped kingpin. Puzzled, he stroked his trimmed black mustache.

"The message?"

"The Venezuelan-based Chinese triads must never enter Mexico. *Comprende?* Fail and you die a miserably slow death."

"Si," muttered the drug lord in a resigned tone. "The gifts?"

"Both have been wrapped especially for you." As Mr. B casually reached into his bag, the larger of the guards stepped forward. He flashed a knife, the eight-inch blade glistening like a freshly caught silver tarpon. Amused by the veiled threat, the killer of many chuckled and nonchalantly removed a bloodstained handkerchief.

Suddenly Jorge's petulant expression turned fierce, his eyes ablaze with anger. "You are not funny, *amigo*. I was expecting a surprise, not a bloody rag."

"Ah, but this is a gift. Do you recognize the significance?" The unfolded cloth revealed a withered piece of purplish human flesh.

"That is Juan Ramirez's diablo earring...and ear."

"You have a keen eye."

"But how did you get it?"

"I did a little pruning after his demise in Victoria. The execution was payback for your murdered brother."

"*Muchas gracias.* But what does this mean?"

"You are now *numero uno*, the newly anointed Mexican messiah."

"I am pleased."

"The master also sends you this present." With an easy motion, the gift bearer reached into the bag and produced an ornate package decorated with glossy red paper and a large green bow. Lusting in eager anticipation, the kingpin eyed the serendipity.

Magnifico.

Mimicking a frenzied piranha, Gonzalez savagely attacked the wrapping. As scraps littered the ground the vaunted surprise was unveiled. Suddenly his jubilant expression turned dark as his scruffy eyebrows arched in confusion. Then a sly smile appeared on his razor-thin lips.

"A bobblehead? But the head doesn't bobble."

"Amigo, the gift is priceless. A *shabti* denotes kingship. Carved from rare wood and painted with an artist's precision it represents a perfect likeness."

"Yes, it *is* a miniature me. It's exquisite."

"But there's more. Awaiting you is one hundred million dollars. The treasure is offshore and stored within a container."

"Money?"

"No. Fentanyl."

"Ah senor, you play games. A lock requires a key. Where is this surprise?"

"It's right before your eyes. You see but don't see. The key is hidden within the shabti's belly. The wood finish hides the invisible seams."

"How does it open?"

"Rub the figure's head. The heat from your fingers triggers a spring-loaded cavity."

"The master is most generous. But he is well aware of my propensity for caution." Instantly the lurking puma barked an order to the smaller guard. "Carlos, rub the wooden head. Bring me good fortune."

Flicking a half-smoked cigarette from his mouth, the ecru man with arms of rainbow tattoos vigorously massaged the wooden head. Suddenly eagerness turned to terror as his eyes bulged and face contorted, the only outward signs of physical distress. Emitting a guttural gasp, the minion slumped to the ground. Watching in horrified fascination, Jorge and the knife wielder stood transfixed.

A blink later the kingpin reacted with an icy fury. "What the hell?" Reaching for the Beretta tucked in his belt, he was a nanosecond too late. Mimicking a cobra's lightning strike the gift bearer drove a knuckle punch into the Latin's throat, crunching the cricoid cartilage. With a ghoulish howl the Mexican messiah tumbled to the ground, his eyes locked in death.

Enraged, the knife bearer lunged and slashed at the betrayer. Hindered by a muscular upper torso his choppy movements were predictable. The clumsy lunges were met by hard chops and effortless sidesteps.

With the attacker off-balance, Mr. B's perfectly timed, cocked elbow slammed into the Hispanic's ribcage. The blow was followed by a steeled palm to the left temple. With the guard disabled, the killer of many pivoted with a bullfighter's grace and unceremoniously snapped the exposed neck.

Relaxing on a nearby bench the weary traveler marveled at the waning afternoon light. The transformation of color was a daily miracle as millions of blood-orange emanations eclipsed the sun's blinding yellow. As the fiery orb inched toward the western horizon, a shimmering sunset concluded another glorious Canadian day.

CHAPTER 1

Monday, January 4

"Open caskets give me the creeps." The whisper was barely audible. "Daniella's face looks like rubber."

"Shhh! Father Mooring is about to pronounce the benediction."

"As we honor the life of Daniella Kirby and conclude this service of celebration the real question is not why we die... but why do we live? We live because of God's amazing grace given freely to each of us. Now may the Lord bless you and keep you until we meet again. Amen."

As the overflow crowd of grieving friends and colleagues exited the sanctuary, Dallas police officer Nick Crosby and FBI Special Agent Mackenzie Fallon remained seated.

"Her death was a real shame," uttered the veteran cop in a hushed tone. "Hell, Daniella was barely thirty. And you're right about those funeral bastards. They mutilated her beautiful face."

"Too many innocent cops are being targeted. We've got to stop these killings."

"But how? We chose this profession."

"I say fight fire with fire," bristled the bureau veteran. "Quick trials. Life imprisonment. No pardons. That should raise some eyebrows. Every time I pass the pictures of dead officers lining our halls, I seethe at the sight."

"I agree, but..."

"Nick, look!" The interruption was commanding. "That stained glass is ablaze with color. The morning light is making Christ's hands come alive. It's like an expression of hope."

"That's the Irish in you. Hope springs eternal." Peering into Mackenzie's teary eyes, Nick hesitated. "Mac, I need to say something."

"What?"

"I think this moment is *our* wake-up call."

"How so?"

"For ten years we've been career slaves. As a result, our relationship has tanked."

"Has it been that long?"

"Yep. But things have changed. Your travel days are over. And I've been reassigned to safer neighborhoods. I think Daniella's death was an omen that we should finally get married. Hell, we're both pushing forty."

With a surprised but delighted expression, Mackenzie peered at the athletic five-foot-eleven hockey enthusiast with deep-set, dark brown eyes. Two inches taller and strikingly handsome, Nick Crosby possessed a quick smile and charismatic personality.

"Are you proposing to me?"

"I am. It's about time. What do you say?"

"I think it's wonderful. But there's an issue."

"Meaning?"

"You have to work daylight hours. Otherwise, our marriage has zero chance. Chemistry has never been an issue."

"That's it? Then I agree. When's the date?"

Pleased with the decision, Mackenzie reached for his hand and gently squeezed. "I suggest June."

"That's perfect. A summer date gives us time to reserve a great venue. Plus, I know a special someone that might conduct our ceremony."

"Great. I can't wait." Scanning the empty sanctuary Mackenzie suddenly waxed philosophic. "Strange, isn't it? Out of death comes life. It's appropriate that we should spend our best years together."

"C'mon, let's head to your place and toast Daniella."

Ominous puffs of gray clouds hung low over the ritzy New Orleans neighborhood, proffering a threat of rain. On cue, a jagged streak of lightning electrified the ebony night followed by a rumble of thunder. A foul odor of mold and decay penetrated the musty air courtesy of the nearby Mississippi River and stagnant bayous. Cloaked in the shadow of a massive cedar, the man with dark eyes waited patiently. Squinting at his black Movado, he flashed a sadistic grin. Five o'clock somewhere was about to take on a whole new meaning.

Suddenly, he noted movement. As anticipated, the retired Fed Governor and his poodle "FiFi Midnight" were enjoying their customary evening stroll. As the financial icon edged closer, the gift bearer gripped a replica of an ancient weapon. Crafted from lightweight wood, the arc-shaped, aerodynamic boomerang with razor-sharp silver inserts was perfectly balanced. Positioning the throwing stick in his right hand he waited for William Wilson, Jr., to close within sixty feet, well within the perfect killing zone.

With a cocked right arm, the killer of many forcibly hurled the convex weapon at a forty-five-degree angle. The blurring disk generated a high-pitched, distinctive whirring. Yet the partially deaf banker was clueless. Starting right and veering left, the silver-edged killing stick tracked toward the exposed head. Aping a streaking missile, the projectile slammed into Wilson's neck at a thirty-degree angle, slicing the soft tissue and lodging against the spine. The carotid artery severed, death was instantaneous.

Emerging from the shadows, Mr. B casually flipped a wooden token next to the body and vanished into the night. Ever loyal, "Fifi Midnight" whimpered and settled into an eternal wait.

Tardy for a hastily called 6:15 p.m. meeting, Morgan Nash sheepishly eased into Mackenzie's spacious office and settled into a side chair. With pugnacious eyes, fiery cheeks, and fierce scowl, the Special Agent glared at her tardy agent. Noted for her apocalyptic temper, the physically toned daughter of Irish immigrants from Dublin was in a surly mood.

"Dammit, you're late again. Did you drag your ass just to aggravate me? The New Orleans killing has the Director in a frenzy."

"I was updating Jennings on the Warren kidnapping."

"Victor needs to step it up."

"Give him a break. Hell, he's just a rookie."

"Screw that. The man is facing suspension. What's your take on the murder?"

"Take? Mac, the killing was just reported. Details are skimpy."

"Dammit, I *should* have summoned Victor. I was expecting more."

"Jameson must have really reamed your ass."

"Like he gives a damn. This case is high profile."

"Screw the Director. Tell him the truth. Weddings trump murders. Hell, after three divorces, the guy should toss you a bone."

The flippant response was met with a wry smile. The attractive thirty-eight-year-old Dubliner with ivory skin, auburn hair, narrow cheeks, and thin lips had been with the bureau for fourteen years.

"By the way, I think you should invite half of Ireland."

"Hah. My heritage links to poor potato farmers." With the welcomed diversion, Mackenzie's crackling green eyes softened but remained intelligently vigilant and alarmingly deceiving.

"Mac, your people have to come. Hell, they're Gaelic."

"Meaning?"

"They're fun. You Irish are blessed with an amazing sense of humor, no doubt a gift from some magical Leprechaun."

"Extravaganzas cost big money, which is beyond my pay grade. And Nick's a cop. Our wedding is going to be simple, elegant, and inexpensive. By the way, my minister is performing the ceremony. Reverend Osborne is nationally recognized and a great guy. Cheap beer may top the menu but not the vows."

"Well, you have my humble blessing. Dawn predicted your marriage. I just wish she was still alive to witness Mackenzie Fallon *finally* getting hitched."

CHAPTER 2

Wednesday, January 6

"Mac, how is your morose agent?"

The caller's tone was curt. On the line with Mackenzie was her no-nonsense, ruddy-faced, cigar-chomping boss FBI Director Sean Jameson.

"Any progress?"

"He's distraught but hanging."

"Meaning what? That's pretty damn ambiguous."

"What do you want me to say? Hell, he is my partner. Morgan's functional but not himself."

"Which continues to drag your career into the muck, burying you in kidnapping and trafficking. It's a waste of your talents. I need you in homicide. I need you on this case. But can your guy handle the pressure? Or does it hit too close to home?"

"Honestly, I don't know. At times Morgan is brilliant. A blink later he's lost. His wife's murder and daughter's disappearance just gnaw at him."

"Dammit, can you count on him? I need to know?"

"Director, the guy puts in eighteen-hour days. He's a workaholic with amazing instincts. Morgan sees what others miss. Yet he's different, often aloof. It's those damned demons."

"Can you trust him? Or is he your Achilles heel? Mac, I need to know. Maybe I should assign Murphy to your team."

"What about Morgan?"

"He'll be reassigned."

"Look, I like Michael. Like me, he's Irish to the core. But the charmer lacks vision. Thinking outside the box is not his thing. Morgan creates on the fly. Yeah, he's eccentric as hell and unpredictable, yet so insightful. Hell, the man's a legend for saving the Texas Governor. Out of nowhere he leaps across a table and tackles a waiter in the midst of a Texas-Mexico summit. Then he grins, bows, and totes the assassin from the room."

"That was pretty gutsy…and disgustingly theatrical."

"Like a court jester." Mackenzie smiled as she recalled the incident. "An irritated eye caught his attention. In the shadows, the waiter removed a false eye, squeezed the rubbery center, poisoned the Governor's soup, and proceeded to serve. But in his haste, he didn't adjust the deflated eye. Morgan knew the staff. None of the servers had allergies. As he reacted, the rest of us just watched in stunned silence. My first thought was: "Oh hell, his ass is toast."

"But he was right."

"Yep. That's my partner. The man possesses a sixth sense. He trusts his gut and reacts."

"Then we sit tight. Loyalty is admirable, but don't let your Texas bias cloud your judgment and sink your career. If another Fed murder hammers the headlines, your team is up. Any questions?"

Hearing no response Sean Jameson grunted a sigh of disgust. The die was cast. A blink later the line clicked silent. Expunging a sigh of relief, Fallon tossed her cell phone and relaxed.

As the graying shadows of twilight morphed black, a waxing half-moon peeked over the horizon, unveiling a frigid night. Scenting the winter stillness was oak and pine as tiny wisps of white smoke spiraled upward from numerous chimneys. Residents in the upscale neighborhood were huddled around cozy stone fireplaces enjoying rounds of expensive liquor and commiserating over hastily uttered New Year's resolutions.

Disregarding the moonlight, the man with dark eyes scaled the estate's brick retaining wall and meandered through countless stately pines standing erect and at attention as if guarding Atlanta's social elite. Invisible in the shadows, he waited until 6:30 p.m.

With key in hand and security code stamped in memory, Mr. B cautiously entered the backdoor. Hearing a familiar chirp and thinking his wife had returned early, the pear-shaped financial icon added a piece of wood to the study's fireplace, moseyed to the wet bar, and paid scant attention. In the well-guarded, gated community nothing sinister ever happened.

Like a big cat stalking his prey, the harbinger of evil moved stealthily toward the walnut-paneled office. His cutting-edge rubber soles created an aura of silence. The pristine two-year-old ranch-style house smelled of expensive perfume and Cuban cigars. As anticipated, the diminutive banker was pouring his legendary evening scotch, an eighteen-year-old Glenfiddich single malt at one hundred and twenty dollars per bottle. Flashing a wicked Jack-O-Lantern smile, the widow-maker waited until the icon reached for a cigar. With perfect timing, he triggered the taser.

Struck in the center of his back, the renowned banker arched in agony, instantly releasing the vintage drink and unlit stogie. As he crumpled awkwardly to the carpet his privileged expression quickly morphed to unmitigated terror.

Rolling the financier onto his back, the weary traveler stared into a pair of horrified and pleading eyes. The financier was panting wildly as rivulets of sweat trickled down his obese cheeks.

Sexually aroused by the pathetic cries, Mr. B smiled derisively before thrusting his dagger deep within the soft abdomen. With a hard twist, the steel point pierced the heart. Exhibiting zero remorse, he slid the body from the pooling blood and squishy carpet. From his utility bag, the artisan selected a cordless hand-held oscillating saw custom designed for cutting bone and muffling sound. Ignoring precision, he savagely mutilated the chest cavity and removed the oozing heart.

Aping an artist's flair the Carlos protégé carefully wrapped the head with red strips and adorned the lips with blue. Precisely at 7 p.m., he toted the corpse to the front porch, doused the lights and carefully positioned the body to face east. Pleased with the arrangement, he placed a portable scale of justice next to the victim. On one scale was the banker's wrapped heart. Taped to the other was a white feather. A note and two tokens completed the theatrics.

CHAPTER 3

Thursday, January 7

"Well, if it ain't the infamous Morgan Nash. How is your well-documented boozing problem? I'm surprised to see you, really amazed given your "sit-u-a-tion."

His beady eyes crackling with hostility, venom spewed from the animated lips of Special Agent Devonta Richardson. An Atlanta native, the African American's short black hair was flecked with gray. His skin was speckled with sunspots and deeply wrinkled. Bags of puckered flesh hung limply beneath the veteran's fatigued eyes.

With a furtive glance, Morgan ignored the taunt, refusing to engage in a pissing contest. Assigned as lead agent, he was taking charge. Emboldened, Richardson pressed the jibes. "Now why on earth would the Dallas office send its highly acclaimed 'cartel buster' to the Peach State? You don't think we 'Georgia boys' are perceptive enough to weave traces of evidence into crime-solving theories?"

The sarcasm was met by a granite glare and clenched jaws. Hounded by the Director, Mackenzie Fallon had brokered the emergency 9 a.m. Atlanta meeting. The savage killing of Gerald Winston had rocked the nation. As Chairman of the Atlanta Federal Reserve Bank, the financial icon wielded immense national power.

With a grisly murder on his home turf and a stymied career, Richardson desperately needed the case. An arrest and prosecution represented his golden ticket to D.C., maybe to a Deputy Directorship. There was no way in hell a junior agent would steal his glory. Bristling with hostility, the barbs spiked.

"You ain't capable of leading this case. It's too personal. Hell, it's likely the same bastard that murdered your wife and kidnapped your daughter. Thirsting for revenge you might go ape-shit, ignore the law and start chugging again."

"Shut the hell up!" The Texan's explosive command was reinforced by an angry scowl and hard-set eyes. "I was ordered here because mystic symbols have suddenly replaced logic. And according to my boss, you're not real creative. Got any tangible leads, Richardson... or *theories?*"

"No."

"Then stuff the smugness and tell me about Wilson's murder."

The electrifying rebuttal startled the Atlanta native, instantly deflating his puffed-up resolve. "According to the NOLA M.E., the financial guru was killed by a lightweight wooden boomerang fitted with silver blades. The damn thing was a replica of an ancient Egyptian throwing stick."

"That type of weapon requires a specific skill set. This is no ordinary assassin."

"Yeah. But who in the hell uses a boomerang? And why *pure silver?*"

Listening but not responding, Morgan's grim expression and pursed lips remained unchanged. Unnerved by the silence, Richardson tensed. The stoic Texan was not the unstable drunk he was rumored to be.

"What about the gold etchings on the surface of the boomerang?"

"A snake's head and 'Allahu Akbar' were legible. The letter 'B' and number '12' were also noted, plus the grouped letters "RE."

"Any ideas?"

With a limp shoulder shrug, Richardson's response was tepid. "Not really. The snake could symbolize cults, gangs, or numerous things. "RE" could indicate initials or link to the Egyptian Sun God. 'Allahu Akbar' is a common extremist chant. The letters and number mean zilch at this point."

"What about the token?"

"It's puzzling as well. The stylish crown points to Osiris, Egyptian god of the underworld."

"Interesting. What's the latest on Winston?"

"The early reports are mystifying."

"Why?"

"The man's head was wrapped like a mummy. His body was carefully positioned to face *east*. But why? Hell, Atlanta ain't Mecca. And why call attention to a justice scale fitted with an oozing heart and a white feather?"

"Given the weight disparity, why didn't the damn thing tip over?"

"That was my initial question. Agents said the scale was customized. The wide base was crafted from *pure silver*."

"So, a precious metal becomes the common denominator. But why? Describe the new tokens."

"The jackal likely represents Anubis, the Egyptian god of embalming and cemeteries. The bizarro figure is definitely Ammit, an underworld goddess with the head of a croc, chest of a lion, and butt of a hippo."

"What was her purpose?"

"The goddess gobbled the hearts of pharaohs that didn't pass judgment."

Instantly Morgan tensed. "Winston was symbolically damned. But the man was a revered saint. Or was this a message to the Federal Reserve?"

Nervously wringing his hands, Devonta shook his head. "I'm clueless."

Scratching a patch of unshaven whisker stubble, Nash pondered the baffling report. "Is this one elite killer or two? But from where? And what's the motive?"

"Personally, I think it's a hate crime. Nothing else makes sense. 'Allahu Akbar' indicts Islamic radicals."

"Possibly. But there's nothing definitive."

"So, what's next?" Flashing a smug expression, Richardson hoped the Texan was stymied.

"I'm not sure...at least not yet." As he walked to the window, Nash's mind was racing. Abruptly, he pivoted. "Each murder is conceptually Egyptian but uniquely different. Could this indicate a copycat?" Hesitating, he quickly backtracked. "No. My gut says one killer. The murders connect."

Fingering the cold security of his Glock, Morgan began to pace. With a quizzical look, he stopped. "Do these symbols actually link to ancient Egypt? Or is this a staged deception? The killer could be American or Hispanic, not some Islamic radical. What's your take on the wrapped head? Do the red strips mean anything?"

"If linked to ancient Egypt, the color indicates male gender."

"What about the justice scale?"

Glancing at his notes the Special Agent read the report. "According to research, the scale played an integral role in Egypt's mythical 'Weighing of the Heart' ceremony. Apparently, the Sun God was judged during his nightly underworld journey. I have an Egyptologist on call if needed."

"One is on his way to Dallas."

The unexpected response caught Richardson by surprise. The drunk was both savvy and well prepared. Continuing, Nash barked an order. "Read the Atlanta note."

"Gerald Winston...Die Satan...Allahu Akbar...In the name of RE." The letters 'BA' and the number '11' were also printed."

"So, you add a letter and subtract a number. Does "BA" represent the killer's name or initials? Is the contract for twelve murders? If so, we need to move fast or watch the case spiral out of control."

"But how? With no leads, we're stymied."

Ignoring the comment, Morgan peered out the window. Two small children were hopscotching down a sidewalk. It was their moment of innocent bliss and pure joy, but not for him. His wife was dead, and his daughter was kidnapped.

Lucky bastards.

With another glance, he saw nothing but glee. The kids were without a concern in the world, at least not yet.

Good for them.

Refocusing, his mind calibrated the possibilities. "The words 'Die Satan' could link to radicals. Angry Islamic fundamentalists frequently chant the phrase. Or they could tie to the Federal Reserve. Big-time investors vehemently complain about the Fed's abuse of power."

Irked by the theorizing, Richardson exploded. "Dammit, you are not qualified to lead this investigation! Wall Street has zero bearing on this case. Our killers are two glory-seeking jihadists spewing hate and creating a frenzy. They're screwing with us by using ancient symbols."

"You definitely think *two* killers?"

"Yeah. That's my belief. These radicals salivate to attack the 'Great Satan.'"

"I disagree. But that could change. Switching topics, Mackenzie noted your friendship with President Hyatt."

"I've known Robert for years."

"Is there any connection between these barbaric killings and his globalist policies?"

"Are you serious? Robert Hyatt has absolutely no tolerance for extremism. These murders are the work of Islamic radicals. They are definitely not linked to the President."

"What about angry conservatives? Many believe Hyatt's liberal policies juxtapose socialism. They despise his open border initiatives."

"Dammit, that hooch did pickle your brain. You think Republicans are orchestrating these murders?"

"It's plausible."

"That's crazy talk."

"Is it? Infuriated by leftist ideologies, they retaliate and force Hyatt into a centrist position. Anyone can stage Egyptian killings, even conservatives."

"Personally, I think the rumors are true. You're still a boozer. The bureau has no use for you. Other than Mackenzie Fallon, you have zero support."

"Yet here I am, leading this national investigation. Ironic, isn't it?" With a wry smile, Morgan ignored the bait and politely bowed. The anticipated verbal barrage was not forthcoming. Unhinged, Richardson's tightly tamped ego erupted in a fury.

"Dammit, this is *my* case. I'm calling Robert. No junior drunk is going to steal my glory. By tomorrow your ass is toast. Enjoy your administrative leave." Enraged, the Special Agent flashed a sadistic grin.

"Playing politics, Devonta? Maybe that's why Jameson bypassed you and assigned me. So shut the hell up. Otherwise, take up knitting as you stumble and bumble into retirement. Tell me about the Vice-President."

With a defiant nod, the humiliated Georgian acknowledged the underlying message. Intimidation was not going to faze Morgan Nash.

"Richard Anderson has been an ardent supporter of the President's global vision. Young and charismatic, he was well-liked as Virginia's Governor. Yet Richard was considered too inexperienced to run against Robert. But the party needed his charm and voting base. This man has the potential to be another Jack Kennedy."

"So, he's another career politician," mused Morgan, flashing a sarcastic grin. "But is he a killer? Maybe *he's* orchestrating the murders to fast-track his career."

As Richardson fumed and fumbled for a response, Nash quickly continued. "Is he colluding with the President to blame conservatives? You could make the case. Both crave power and the spotlight. In D.C. anything goes, even murder. Hell Devonta, our suspect list seems endless. Anything else?"

"No."

"When were the victims killed?

"The murders occurred at 6 and 7 p.m."

"Given sequential times the next hour becomes critical. But where? Who?" Peering into Richardson's eyes, Morgan noted a blank look. "Describe Winston's dagger."

"The double-edged blade was approximately ten inches in length with a slight curvature near the tip. The weapon was definitely not military."

"What about the taser?"

"It was likely an X26 which fires two barbs at a rate of one hundred and eighty feet per second. With a range of five yards, Winston didn't have a chance."

"But he did have time to express fear before dying. We're dealing with a hard-ass, sadistic killer. How was the heart removed?"

Eager for his unwelcomed intruder to exit, Richardson flipped several pages. "The assassin used a cordless, handheld oscillating saw to savagely mutilate the chest. No other organs were touched."

"It takes strength to kill, cut, and tote a body. Our artisan is likely male." Pausing, Morgan glared at the belligerent Special Agent. "Any last word?"

"No."

"Then I'm off to Dallas for a crash course in Egyptian history. Keep me posted."

And go screw yourself, Mr. Asshole.

CHAPTER 4

Friday, January 8

Shortly after 10 a.m., Morgan sauntered into Mackenzie's executive office and plopped into a side chair. Noting the Dubliner's sulky scowl and pulsating cheeks, his flippant spirit quickly quailed. In a dour mood, his boss was all business, expecting facts, not supposition. Dark circles sagged beneath her puffy eyes as sleep had been near impossible since Monday's murder.

"Well, you're back. What have you got?"

"Other than a boatload of questions I have precious little. Richardson was a prick. Atlanta's M.E. was AWOL. And the food was awful. So, I flew back last night."

"Prick?"

"Yeah. He kept insisting that I was invading his playground. Like I was going to steal his manly balls or something."

Unexpectedly the Special Agent flashed a wry Irish grin. The tongue-in-cheek remark was pure Morgan. On good days unexpected spews of dry humor and sarcasm flowed with alacrity from his lips. Yet those days had been rare since his family's demise. Moroseness had replaced humor.

"Suspects?"

"None. The assassin could be American, Hispanic or Islamic. It's a crap shoot at this point. Cartels, terrorists, or politicians could be pulling the strings. Richardson leans toward two killers. I think one."

"What about the symbols?"

"They're theatrical, baffling, and Egyptian. Richardson was clueless."

"What about you?"

"I'm stymied as well…for the moment."

"Dammit, Morgan, that's not going to cut it. Look, I stuck my neck out for you. I need something tangible."

The curt retort triggered an irate response.

"And I need a straight answer. Mac, is this the same bastard that murdered Dawn and kidnapped Erin?"

Ambushed by the unexpected rebuff, the Dubliner carefully weighed her words. "The Egyptian tokens found at your home were common tourist items. Any killer could have left them."

"Any? Dammit, you're playing games. For two fricking years, I've been consumed with guilt. I failed my family. I failed you. I failed everyone. I have every right to know."

"Look, what you seek is revenge. Empty that hatred and listen. This case is explosive. It's not about you."

"Then who is it about? For God's sake, it's my family. So, it *is* about me. It's personal."

"Partner, I get the anger. But this investigation goes far beyond you. So, don't turn rogue or play vigilante. Richardson thinks two killers. You disagree. Why?"

"It's the professionalism. The staging points toward one elite assassin. But what's the motive? Who's footing the bill? And why target the Federal Reserve? Nothing about this case feels right."

"I agree with Richardson. A duo of jihadists makes perfect sense. Mummified heads and voodoo magic create sensational stories. An oozing heart incites public outrage. Everything points to radicals spewing their hate."

"Mac, I'm not buying. My gut says one killer. My killer."

"You and that damned gut. It's going to get you whacked someday. But for now, keep it in check. I need your insights."

"Yes ma'am. But if the shoe fits, he's dead. No remorse."

With a parent's understanding, the Dubliner knew her partner's hard-ass attitude was a survival mechanism. Dawn's death and Erin's kidnapping had been devastating. Returning to work as an avowed loner, Morgan had refused to trust anyone. Fanatically driven, his work had been acceptable but not exceptional.

Peering into his smoldering eyes, the Special Agent made a gut-wrenching decision. The truth finally had to be revealed.

"You're leading this investigation for two reasons. You have amazing instincts. And your wife's symbols *are tied* to this case."

"Then it *is* the same bastard."

Scrutinizing her partner's hard lines and clenched jaw, Mackenzie noted the wrinkles. The past months had been a living hell. Like most combat vets there was a hollow, sunken look to his eyes. Though he was impossible to read, she knew he was listening.

"Possibly. But you have a job to do. If you're hell-bent on ignoring orders expect zero support. Understood? You're toast if you step out of line."

Robotically, he nodded. Losing the case was not an option. Ever the obedient soldier, Nash stood and aped a mock salute. Hastily exiting the room, he knew it was time to meet his savior.

Perplexed by the pushback, Mackenzie added a double touch of Irish elixir to her coffee. For the first time in two years, she had seen a playful response from her eccentric partner.

"Yet can I trust him?" she wondered. "Morgan's still masking everything. And he's damn good at it."

As a hallway clock tolled the one o'clock hour, a stylishly dressed cosmopolitan academic quietly entered the Spartan-like office and took a seat. Quickly assessing the Egyptian's diminutive physique and Bohemian bowtie, Morgan sat stunned. At six-foot-three he dwarfed the renowned Egyptologist by almost a foot.

Pushing sixty-three years of age, Dr. Razemi Adbul Fawarzi was spry and deeply tanned. Archeological digs in the Valley of the Kings had served him well. Sporting a hawk nose, black mustache, playful eyes, and graying hair, the academic had split time between the University of Cairo and Columbia University.

"Thanks for coming to my rescue. Hopefully, you can shed light on the perplexing symbols."

"Please call me Dr. Raz or Raz. That's the moniker given to me by my students." Privately, the Egyptian was proud of the nickname. The badge of respect was a professor's highest honor.

"Then call me Morgan."

"Oh no. That would be a sign of disrespect."

"As you wish."

"You're very trusting to request my assistance. Ghoulish skulls and decaying mummies have been my only investigations." Chuckling, the academic beamed.

Unamused, Nash ran his gaze up and down, completing an in-depth look. The teacher's surprising appearance and cavalier attitude cloaked his mind with doubt. "Okay, you've studied both files. Are we dealing with a single killer or two?"

The tone was unwelcoming, flat, and frosty. The initial test of truth was underway.

"That's easy." The unexpected arrogance was accompanied by an impish grin. "The answer is one. Your killer is male and *Egyptian."*

"That's bullshit. There's no evidence."

"Ah, but there is. The archaic language conveys an apocalyptic story."

"What story?"

"Agent, to your untrained eye and myopic thinking the trio of tokens appears disconnected. But that's incorrect. To the enlightened, these specific deities form the dreaded "*omega accord*."

"I've never heard of it."

"Think '*holy trinity of the damned.*' In Christianity, Father, Son, and Holy Ghost signify hope. Correct?"

"Yeah. That's my belief. The threesome represents life, death, and resurrection to both faithful and sinners."

"Such was never the case in ancient Egypt. There was no forgiveness or redemption. Sin equated to *death, damnation, and dissolution*. That was the accord's feared trifecta. Extinction awaited any unworthy pharaoh."

"Did many rulers pass judgment?"

"Doubtful. Most were tyrants. The underworld's "Weighing of the Heart" ceremony made a heavenly afterlife virtually impossible. During judgment, a pharaoh was either condemned or vindicated. His heart was weighed against a white feather of truth. If the scale balanced, the deified mortal ascended to the stars. If it sank, the underworld god Osiris rendered a guilty verdict. Immediately, Ammit gobbled the heart. Anubis consumed the remains."

"Those were Winston's tokens. The scale was badly tilted."

"The Fed didn't make the cut. Dissolution was the verdict."

"But why?"

"That is to be determined."

"Did extinction alter royal behavior?"

"No. The effect was just the opposite. Clever pharaohs ordered priests and scribes to create amulets and magical spells. As if paying penance, they tried to buy or trick their way into eternity. But the magic was not foolproof."

"Why?"

"Egyptian judgment was as real as the rising sun."

"That's very enlightening. But why is someone targeting the Federal Reserve and aping an ancient accord? It makes no sense. Plus, there's the baffling emphasis on silver. Why?"

"Agent, you see but don't see. The precious metal connects to the trifecta and conveys an apocalyptic prophecy."

"I'm not following."

"In ancient Egypt, silver represented *divinity*. Using the precious metal inappropriately was absolutely forbidden. The guilty were tried, executed, and damned to extinction."

"That's the accord's trifecta."

"Correct. Now, switch your thinking to the Federal Reserve. Does a recent decision come to mind?"

"Yeah. The Feds prioritized *bitcoin...over...silver."*

"And in retaliation, two Feds were murdered. *Silver* inserts decapitated Wilson. A *silver* blade pierced Winston. A *silver* scale rendered judgment. This particular killer has an affinity for history and vendetta against the new currency."

"That's quite a convincing story. But it's pure conjecture. Give me something tangible."

"Agent, heed what I say or fail. I see and understand. You see but don't see. To catch a ghost, you must open your mind to new realities and venture far into the unknown."

"But that smacks of mysticism. Don't jack with me."

Unexpectedly, the academic's thin lips morphed into a Cheshire grin. Seated across from him was another obstinate student. "Agent, *together* we solve this case. Alone, you cannot."

Irked by the pomposity, Morgan's fists tightened as his knuckles turned bone white. But the diminutive professor was maddeningly right. His scholarly insights were needed.

"You're probably right, which leads to a question. Why was Winston's heart *physically* removed? Hell, the mythological ceremony was purely *symbolic.*"

"The extraction underscored dissolution. In ancient times a pharaoh's embalming took a minimum of one hundred and fifty days. Internal organs were carefully preserved and stored in canopic jars. *But the heart was never removed. Never.*"

"Why?"

"An intact heart was essential for the pharaoh to pass judgment. That was critical."

"What about the brain?"

"It was irrelevant. The heart represented both mind and soul. If judged righteous, the pharaoh lived eternally. Winston failed the test. Agent, this barbaric act was not staged for the media. Nor was it about theatrics. It was a cataclysmic warning to reverse policy."

Peering at the diminutive teacher, Morgan faced a monumental moment of truth. "You're quite the spin master. If right, you've shed light on motive and narrowed our suspect list. But what if you're wrong?"

"What if I'm correct? Sometimes you must travel the unknown road."

"That is an understatement."

Chuckling, the academic flashed a wry grin. "Agent, let me be less esoteric. The assassin possesses an Achilles heel."

"Meaning?"

"New tokens work in your favor. Once a pattern forms you can leapfrog and set traps."

"But that implies more deaths. Plus, I'm not Egyptian. I don't think like the killer."

"Then you must learn."

Instantly, Nash hesitated. "Fine. But summarize only the basics."

Flashing a wry grin, the academic immediately accepted the challenge as a stream of historical background spewed from his razor-thin lips.

"In ancient Egypt, there were no laws. There was only a code of conduct established by the gods. Everything was orderly until a jealous Seth killed Osiris and sliced his brother into fourteen pieces. Isis and Nephthys collected the scattered parts. With the help of Anubis and Thoth, the sisters stitched Osiris back together. Magically, they restored his life by taking the form of kites and rapidly beating their wings. Alive but blind, Osiris headed to the underworld."

"That's an amazing story and actually helpful. The recreation parallels the Federal Reserve."

"Explain."

"In 2008 and 2009, the Feds magically restored the American economy. But they were blind to human suffering. Their harsh policies and solvency requirements forced many companies and institutions into bankruptcy. Countless individuals were compelled to forfeit homes. Revenge has always been a compelling motive, even today."

"It was certainly the demise of many pharaohs."

"Can your mythology determine future murders?"

"Not yet. It's too early."

"What's next?"

"Assuming the form of a mummy, Osiris became "Judge of the Dead." His son Horus removed an eye and gave him sight. The orb became known as the "Eye of Horus."

"What was the eye's purpose?"

"The all-seeing eye restored life. Eternity was every pharaoh's dream." Pausing, the academic stretched and yawned. "Agent, I 've had very little sleep. This trip was rush-rush. I have to leave."

"Not yet. Give me five more minutes."

Noting Morgan's desperation, the archeologist reluctantly acquiesced. "Five minutes. No more."

"Please continue."

"Eons before the Israelites worshipped Yahweh, my ancestors acknowledged Amun as their creator. Yet there was a problem. Surrounded by universal waters, the King God was lonely. Thus, he procreated the Sun God RE. Emerging from the primordial ocean RE birthed Shu, God of Air, and Tefnut, Goddess of Moisture."

"Your people were henotheistic?"

"Yes. Amun was supreme followed by lesser gods. The King God's fluid contained male and female elements. Both were essential for creation. The union of Shu and Tefnut produced Geb, the Earth God and Nut, the Sky Goddess. In time, Geb and Nut produced Isis, Osiris, Seth and Nephthys."

"Did this mark the beginning of Egypt's pantheon?"

"Correct. The gods were ranked according to power beginning with Amun. RE came next and so on. Created prior to humanity, the eight lesser deities were known as the "*Ogdoad.*"

"The letters 'RE' were noted at both murders. Was this a reference to the Sun God or someone's identity?"

"That too is to be determined."

"Anything else?"

"A pharaoh's journey into the underworld always began with the setting sun. Yet Winston's body was carefully positioned to face '*east.*'"

"Why?"

"The placement was to guarantee damnation and dissolution. A pharaoh's mummy had to face '*west.*' Otherwise, there was no hope for eternal life."

Unexpectedly Morgan flashed a concerned look. "Look, I get the symbolism and theatrics. But something's amiss. What's the end goal? Is it revenge or something greater? I'm really struggling."

"That is obvious. You seek definitive answers in a case devoid of certainty. Welcome to your maze of unknowns."

Irked by the mocking tone, biting sarcasm, and smug gamesmanship, Nash's expression hardened. In utter disgust, he slammed his steeled palm against the desk. Startled by the crude violence, the diminutive professor jumped.

"Dammit, teacher, fantasy cannot drive a murder case!"

"Oh, but it can. In which direction does your urine flow?"

"Huh? It flows straight down."

"Then go with the flow."

Surprised by the simple logic, Morgan hesitated. "Explain."

"At sunset, RE began his nightly twelve-hour journey through the underworld. Sixty minutes were allotted for each west to east increment. When were the first two murders?"

"The times were 6 and 7 p.m."

"Then the next hour becomes crucial assuming the killings remain sequential. Stop swimming against the current. Let the symbols guide you."

"That's easy for you but not for me."

"Agent, quit bracketing your mind. You win by embracing the unknown. You win by interpreting RE's journey through the underworld."

"Then I've got a shitload to learn." Unhinged, the newly-christened student directed the academic to the infamous cafeteria. "Eat and get some rest."

Glancing at his wall clock, Morgan lamented the passing of time and muttered a not-so-quiet profanity.

Shit! Five freaking hours and I've got nothing.

Unexpectedly, an imposing shadow hovered in his doorway. The Dubliner's rosy cheeks were ashen.

"Mac, you don't look so hot."

"Hell, I'm about to puke."

"What's up?"

"Our killer has struck again… and nearby. A body with a wrapped head was discovered in the narthex of St. Maria's Catholic Church."

"Father Rivera?"

"That's uncertain. We need to leave ASAP."

"I'll call Raz. We'll pick him up on the way."

Shortly after 9 p.m. Fallon's team and a slew of authorities enveloped the low-income neighborhood church. Arriving early, the Dallas M.E. had carefully unwrapped the victim's head. Surprisingly the deceased was Antonio Luis Delgado, the first Hispanic Federal Reserve Governor. The iconic priest was also dead, but not mutilated.

Eying the grisly scene Morgan's words were terse. "Mac, you've got to muzzle the media before this butchery stuns both the Hispanic community and Wall Street."

"I'm on it. We don't need riots and a sell-off."

Uninvited, the M.E. interrupted. "You're too late. A '*Herald*' reporter snapped pictures and busted his ass to leave. The prick was lurking when I arrived."

"I'll talk to the editor. Given the complexities, maybe he will cooperate." Abruptly, the Special Agent jogged to her car.

Studying the theatrics, Morgan stood puzzled. The staging was similar yet different. Standing next to him the academic appeared unfazed, casting a smug expression.

"Raz, Delgado's mutilation smacks of a serial killer. It's ruthless and undisciplined. Can you decipher the token?"

"Meet Montu, Theban god of war. The orb atop the falcon's head symbolizes the Sun God RE."

"So, the letters remain consistent. But the silver scale is much smaller. The killer couldn't tote a large bag into a crowded church without attracting attention. What's your take on the black wrapping and silver strips?"

"The combination is ominous. A specific individual is marked for death."

"Who?"

"Fed Chairman Martha Ramsey is the likely target. Black symbolizes death. Silver signifies abuse. The Chairman's bitcoin policy damns both her life and the Federal Reserve."

"Are you sure?"

"Absolutely."

The pomposity caught Morgan by surprise. "If correct, suspicion shifts to Wall Street. Numerous investors vehemently oppose the new policy. Bitcoin creates uncertainty which destabilizes the markets. Outraged, they collaborate and orchestrate the murders."

"Bravo!" Clapping his hands, the Egyptian beamed. "Welcome to your new world of illogic progressions."

"Screw the rhetoric. Fed leaders need protection ASAP."

Inwardly amused at the agent's reaction, Raz hesitated before posing an obvious but poignant query. His myopic student desperately needed schooling on the cataclysmic effect of linchpins.

"If more die, what happens?"

"That's easy. The markets bleed red." Suddenly Morgan hesitated as his off-the-cuff response triggered a deeper thought.

"Is that...the answer?" His broken cadence reflected uncertainty. "Is destabilization the end goal? But that can't be right. Dammit, Raz, nothing makes sense."

As his anger simmered, Nash stepped away and tried to refocus. Several blinks later he meekly turned to the academic. The pleading in his eyes was telling. "Does the latest note mean anything?"

"Not yet. "BAB-10." It's another subtle change, a letter added and number subtracted."

"Crap. The bastard is screwing with us. Let's head back to the office. The is going to be a very long night."

CHAPTER 5

Saturday, January 9

Shortly after midnight, Mackenzie tapped on Morgan's door and entered. With her was a tall, disheveled-looking stranger.

"I want you and Raz to meet Alexander Fulton, President of the Dallas Federal Reserve Bank. He's here to assess Delgado's murder."

Visibly rattled, Fulton paused to gather himself. "Agents, let me begin with the obvious. You must stop these killings. Otherwise, the Fed's financial stability is totally at-risk. But why is this happening?"

"Right now, we can only speculate," surmised Nash. "Islamic fundamentalists or Mexican cartels could be the culprits. But the killings could be personal or political."

"So, you have nothing. I was expecting more."

As Morgan tensed, the Dubliner quickly intervened. "Mr. Fulton, how can we help?"

"You can start by protecting Fed Governors, Presidents, and Chairman Ramsey. We must work without fear to monitor financial conditions and adjust monetary policies."

"Recently, you imposed strict monetary regulations and solvency requirements on banks and investment firms. Many failed the new tests. Have your people received any threats?"

"Agent Fallon, we've been bombarded. Numerous companies *and* individuals have been affected by the mandates. But we weren't surprised. Our confidential data has been an accurate predictor of bankruptcies. This secret has never been shared with the public."

"Did you also calculate the number of poor souls that would lose jobs and homes? I've known a great many."

Insulted by Morgan's biting criticism, Fulton bristled. "Little credence has been given to behavioral outcomes. Decisions are never based on emotion. Results are determined solely by statistical analysis."

"In other words, you don't give a damn about suicides or lost income?"

"Agent Nash, worrying about individuals has been an unaffordable luxury. The Federal Reserve has a sole focus, the financial well-being of America. To some, we've been heartless. But we have a job to do. Numbers, not faces, have been our focus."

With angry eyes fixated in a chilling stare, Mackenzie countered. "Mr. Fulton, you're coming across as robotic and non-caring. Hell, every Fed Governor has to be in grave danger. You've made a lot of enemies."

"Look, it's an impossible job. When we implement changes, shit happens. If we increase rates by a quarter or half-point, people and businesses catch hell. That uptick could decimate industry sectors and eliminate thousands of jobs. That's why we carefully weigh our final decisions. But policy always outweighs collateral damage."

"Well sir, your lack of empathy has certainly opened Pandora's Box," chirped Morgan. "Our list of possible suspects has multiplied tenfold."

"Hey, anyone connected to the Federal Reserve has caught hell. I've received death threats. But we've made the right decisions. Regardless of the human factor, our first priority has been to stabilize the financial system and contain any systemic risks that threaten the markets."

Unexpectedly Raz intervened, easing the tension. "Could a foreign group be responsible for these attacks? You control the national payment system."

"That's possible. But the timing is confusing. As of late, our economy is trending upward. However, additional murders could lead to an equity selloff. If so, America could return to 2008 recession levels or lower. If that happens, we might not be so lucky."

As Fulton prepared to leave, his parting words intensified the angst. "You must end the carnage. Otherwise, we face a financial abyss. Investors cannot live in dread and uncertainty."

With the Fed's departure, Morgan peered at his partner. "Have you received any updates on Delgado?"

"Yep. And the preliminaries were damned explosive. Three punctures were noted on the body. Two were from a taser. The third was from a needle. Blood samples revealed a potassium solution used by cardiovascular surgeons to stop the heart. To put it bluntly, Delgado was butchered while still alive."

"Mac, that tidbit can never be publicized. What about Father Rivera?"

"The holy man was stabbed by the same dagger that killed Winston. His body was not mutilated."

"Can you assign protection details to all Fed Governors and the Chairman?"

"Definitely. Hey, your guest looks exhausted. Hell, it's after 1 a.m. Return him to the hotel and reconvene before lunch. That's not much rest but it's the best we can do." Eager to adjourn, the Dubliner exited the room and headed to the snack bar. A strong cup of Irish coffee was sorely needed. An unpleasant pre-dawn call to the Director was looming.

Weary from a short restless night, the Egyptologist reluctantly trudged into Nash's office. The noon hour was fast approaching.

"Hey man, you're late. How ya hanging?"

"Truthfully, I'm toast. Please begin softly and no fist banging."

"That's a deal. Look, I owe you a favor. You need coffee. I need food. Let's head to the cafeteria."

"Great."

Following a solemn lunch, the duo returned to Morgan's office. Unexpectedly, an ominous figure stopped in the doorway. With unabated tears and a surreal look, Mackenzie Fallon appeared traumatized. Unnerved by the Hadean expression, Nash tensed, a sense of dread blackening his mood and bastardizing his mind.

With sunken eyes and a grimace on her face, the Special Agent's lips trembled. Slowly gathering herself, she spoke in a hushed tone. "Partner, I bring horrific news. It's about Erin."

"Is my baby dead?" Cloaked in a shroud of gloom, Morgan sat pale-faced and stony-eyed.

"Yes. Her little body was found a short time ago. Wrapped in yellow linen, she looked like a small mummy."

"Was she mutilated?"

"No. According to the M.E., she appeared fatigued but healthy."

"My Erin's dead?" With blank eyes and slumped shoulders, Morgan's words mimicked a dead man walking. He quivered as a first tear appeared, followed by rivulets. With bluish lips frozen in grief, he tried to form a syllable but couldn't.

"Remain here until we know more. A chaplain is coming to pray with you."

"What about Raz?"

Mackenzie hesitated. "I sent him to his office."

—~~—

For two excruciating hours, the widower and grieving father sat with a faraway look. During the eerie silence, no words were exchanged with the holy man. This was not the time to sing God's praises or listen to an uplifting message about "the good news."

"Why, God? Why did you desert me? Why did you let my Erin suffer and die alone? Why not me?"

His fixed expression aped a mourner's sorrow. For two long years, he had willed himself to become mentally and physically steeled, earning a coveted master's level black belt in Okinawan karate. Yet, with only two words, Mackenzie's kryptonite had shattered his Superman resolve.

"Erin, dead."

In excruciatingly slow motion, the desk clock ticked off the cruel seconds. Shortly after 4 p.m., the Special Agent reappeared and softly tapped his shoulder. "Let's go to my office."

Mimicking a zombie, Nash trailed the fast-walking Dubliner. Slumping in a side chair, he robotically buried his head in both hands. Reluctantly, she conveyed the findings.

"Erin died around 7 a.m. Her body was intact. The only marks were two punctures. At first, the M.E. thought the wounds were from a taser."

"Taser! What bastard would taser an innocent child?"

The veteran agent steeled herself. The worst was yet to come. "No, partner. The punctures were from a *snake."*

"No! Oh, hell no! My Erin was bitten by a fricking snake?"

"It wasn't just any snake. The punctures were from a Nile asp. Erin died instantly."

With emotions spiraling wildly out of control, Morgan's face contorted into a hellish anguish. Shaking uncontrollably;

his listless eyes morphed pasty white. For some unknown reason, the merciful God of Jesus had damned his family.

"Dammit Mac, she suffered. My baby..."

Suddenly, his pent-up volatility erupted. Reeling wildly out of control, he snatched the Dubliner's heirloom lamp, ripped the plug, and hurled it forcibly against the wall. The powder-blue porcelain shattered into hundreds of tiny shards. Mentally shredded, he drifted into a black void of hopelessness. Locked in a hypnotic trance, he fingered the Glock and moved the barrel ominously ever closer to his mouth. Transfixed, the Dubliner watched in fascinated horror.

One blink. Two blinks.

Suddenly, her paralyzed mind awakened with a fury.

"What the hell?"

Diving at her suicidal partner, she knocked the 9mm from his trembling hand and screamed for help. Quickly responding were two nearby agents. One grabbed Morgan's legs. The other pinned his torso. Struggling fiercely but clamped tightly, the grieving widower slowly relaxed. The nightmarish drama was over for the moment. Dejected and deflated, he sat motionless on the floor and wept. Dismissing the agents, the Special Agent gently put an arm around her morose partner.

With an empty look, Nash brushed away the tears and spoke in a hushed tone. "Dammit Mac, Erin was scared and alone. Every night, I saw her in my dreams. Why did she have to die? My heart has been shredded."

Like a parent caring for a traumatized child, Mackenzie held him tightly. No words were spoken, or appropriate. After several agonizing minutes, she peered into his lifeless eyes and whispered softly.

"Promise you won't do that again."

The sacred covenant was met by a blank stare. Seconds later a hint of recognition appeared. "Morgan, you scared the hell out of me. If you're dead the killer wins."

"That's not going to happen. His sorry ass is mine. Whatever it takes, I'm going to avenge my family."

Easing her sidekick into a nearby chair, Mackenzie quickly returned to her desk. Reluctantly, she spoke. "There's more, but would you rather go home?"

"And do what? Stare at pictures of my dead wife and daughter? Stare at a forever reminder of my failure to protect? Just the mention of Erin's name triggers uncontrollable anguish. Go ahead, I need to know."

"She was wearing a rearing cobra headband. A beetle token covered her heart. Two wooden figures were placed nearby. Other than fatigue, Erin looked beautiful."

"That's bullshit. My little girl is dead!"

Trapped in the same emotional hell as all parents that traumatically lose a child, Morgan tried to picture his precious four-year-old. When last seen, Erin's hair was golden like the radiant rays of a glorious Texas sunset. Her teal eyes danced with joy as she giggled and laughed. Because Erin was always the charmer, Dawn had nicknamed her "Sparkles." Her memory was forever etched in his heart and mind. But that was two years ago. Two fricking miserable, long years.

"Should I stop?"

"No. I want every detail. I want to know my killer. When can I see her?"

"We can leave now."

Ravaged by the sight of his daughter, Nash wept. With a silent goodbye, he returned to Fallon's office. As both took seats, the Dubliner hesitated and then spoke quietly.

"We need to talk."

"Dammit Mac, this is not the time. Not when my precious baby lies stone cold in that morgue. Not when guilt is ripping my soul. You can fire me later."

"Look, I'm sorry about Erin. But..."

"NO!!!" The interruption was curt, commanding. "Look, I've heard your little speech. You're sorry about my loss. You're sorry about dumping my pathetic ass. But dammit, these murders *are* connected. Of all people, you should have some empathy."

As fresh tears streamed down both cheeks, Morgan wrestled with his foremost demon. *Fear.* Fear of being replaced. Fear of another failure. "You think I'm suicidal. But that's over. Look, a huge part of me is gone. There's nothing's left but revenge."

"Partner, your sorrows are my sorrows. Look, I've always cared about you. But you're facing a father's worse nightmare. A decision has to be made."

"Dammit, you've got to wait. I've known this could happen. For two fricking years, I've lived with guilt, panic, and dread. Now I have nothing but this case."

"Morgan, it's a tough call."

"Then let me quit begging and rephrase. You need me. Otherwise, you fail."

With piercing eyes, the Dubliner acknowledged the obvious and nodded sagely. "That's true. But I need a clearheaded Morgan Nash to decipher the symbols. Can I trust you?"

"You can."

"Fine. But a profiler *will* work with you."

"A shrink? That's not going to happen."

"It's not your call. Either cooperate or walk. The D.C. office is sending Dr. Meredith Lindsey. An analyst for five years, she comes highly recommended."

Blindsided by the betrayal, his quads and calves tensed like tightly wound springs poised to skyrocket. But then he hedged. Accepting the order, Morgan flashed a huge scowl and abruptly exited. The case was his lifeline.

Irked by the decision, he stopped in the hallway and slammed a fist into the wall. In pain but satisfied, Morgan entered his office and took a seat. Glaring at Raz his words were chiseled. "Tell me about Nile asps."

"Agent, I'm sorry..."

"Dammit, I don't need sympathy. Tell me about the fricking snake."

"As you wish. The asp is a small but deadly cobra found along the Nile."

"The bite? How long did Erin suffer?"

"Death was practically instantaneous. According to Cleopatra, an asp bite was the least terrible way to die. Victims simply fell asleep without spasms or convulsions. The viper was a sign of royalty."

"Royalty my ass. Did the bastard leave a note?"

"Yes."

"Read it."

"Erin Nash...Allahu Akbar...In the name of RE." The signature was "BAB."

"But that's wrong. There should be a new number and letter."

Hesitant, Raz carefully weighed his response. Sitting across from him was a volatile volcano hell-bent on physicality. "Agent, in my opinion the killer did not want this assignment. The funerary tokens were placed as a sign of respect."

"Respect? That's bullshit!"

"You asked."

"Describe the symbols."

"There were several, including a shabti."

"A what?"

"A shabti is a carved likeness of your daughter. The wooden statuette was always placed in a pharaoh's tomb. Inscribed on the back was an inscription from Chapter Six of the 'Book of the Dead.'"

"Was the inscription relevant?"

"Absolutely. It was an insurance policy. In the afterlife, the shabti performed any hard labor, not the king. The figure was placed in Erin's honor."

At the mention of his daughter's name Morgan bristled. Noting his expression, Raz paused. "Would you like to stop?"

"No. What were the other tokens?"

"There was a cow, beetle, and cobra headband. All were common funerary amulets to protect the dead. The cow symbolized Hathor."

"Explain."

"The goddess was a nurturing mother figure and guardian of the necropolis. As the righteous entered the underworld, Hathor offered love and protection. The Nile's west bank symbolized the entrance. Your daughter's care has been assigned to her."

Hearing nothing but gibberish, Morgan blocked the words. Jesus was the shepherd of little children, not some Egyptian deity. Erin was in His loving care.

"Explain the beetle."

"My ancestors were fascinated by the novel and unexplained. A dung beetle was often seen pushing a pile of mud along the ground. To their surprise, new life emerged from the muck. This simple phenomenon expanded their theology. A scarab pushed the sun across the sky and enabled rebirth."

"But how does this relate to Erin? Something's amiss."

"The beetle was also a guardian of the heart. Khepri was the god of resurrection. Inscribed on your daughter's token was an inscription from Chapter Thirty of the 'Book of the Dead.'"

"Was it the same?"

"No. This writing was heart-specific. The notation protected the deceased when brought before Osiris and his tribunal."

"How?"

"The covenant forbade the heart from confessing any sins or wrongdoings committed during an individual's lifetime. It represented a clever way of escaping judgment."

"What about the headband?"

"Cast from divine metals, the rearing cobra was poised to spit venom against enemies. The dreaded viper was Egypt's protector. Royals wore the headband with great pride."

"But Erin was no elitist. Nor was she a threat. Dammit, why was she targeted?"

With piercing eyes, the Egyptian responded. "They wanted you to suffer. And you have. For two long years, you have grieved and floundered. Now they're out to break you."

With his mind focused on his beloved Erin, Morgan heard nothing but gibberish. As he visualized two years of captivity in cages and chains, his simmering anger erupted.

"Why didn't the bastard come after me?"

"He did. But you weren't home. Her death was a prophetic warning. Agent Nash, *you* are a dead man walking."

"That's good. Those bastards know where to find me." Aping the hideous scowl of a Howler monkey, Morgan promptly rose and silently exited the office.

CHAPTER 6

Sunday, January 10

In the blackness of a Sabbath morning, the grieving widower faced a parent's worst nightmare. His precious "Sparkles" was cremated. Trembling uncontrollably, Morgan's knees buckled when her ashes were handed to him in a hastily customized urn. Saying goodbye to the physical presence and sheer joy of a precious child was virtually impossible.

Mentally numb and physically unstable, he was driven home by colleagues. With a promise not to harm himself, the accommodating agents slowly disappeared. Mercifully, no new murders had been reported. Yet it didn't matter. His once joyful, energetic home was forever shrouded in sorrow.

Fittingly, Dawn's urn was painted burnt orange. In white were the block letters "UT." Both represented the proud colors of her beloved Texas Longhorns. Her eight-by-ten-inch picture sat next to the ashes. Taken during a game, the photo showcased Dawn's beauty, smile, and passion.

The new urn was pastel yellow. Appropriately, "Sparkles" was creatively written in brightly colored glitter. Erin's last picture sat nearby. Laughing and happy, the four-year-old was joyfully playing in a field of Texas bluebonnets.

Staring at the mantle, Morgan allowed himself a moment of reflection. A UT cheerleader for three years, Dawn had been a huge crowd favorite. Her contagious enthusiasm, back flips, and high energy always ignited the 100,000 faithful fans. Plus, she was engaged to Morgan Nash. The Longhorn's popular safety was a three-year starter and second-team All-American.

With one violent collision, his dream of playing in the NFL vanished. But he still had Dawn. In his time of utmost pain, she had stood with him. During their ten-year marriage, her irresistible charm never wavered. Then came Erin. The beautiful baby with golden hair captured their hearts.

Overwhelmed by a flood of memories, his sense of failure intensified. In his family's greatest time of need, he was out playing cops and robbers. With a vow never to forgive himself, he said goodbye. Gently kissing both photos, the widower and grieving father headed to the office.

As his office clock chimed 3 p.m., Nash fingered the cold steel of his Glock. The suicidal demons were bastardizing his mind. Focus was impossible. Unexpectedly, an unwelcomed surprise appeared in the doorway. The intruder was Mackenzie Fallon, accompanied by an attractive woman. Irked, he steeled himself to be upbeat and civil.

"Hey boss, any news?"

With a furtive glance, he scanned the stranger's face. The strawberry blonde's sapphire eyes were piercing and perceptive. Her thin smile was alluring and disarming. A spattering of pale freckles danced lightly across the bridge of her nose.

"Nope. It's been quiet."

"Who's your guest?"

"I want you to meet Dr. Meredith Lindsey. A profiler, she *is* going to be working with you."

"Thanks. But I prefer to work alone."

Stung by the rebuttal, the stranger's rosy cheeks flashed crimson as her ice-blue eyes crackled with a not-so-veiled hostility.

"That is not your decision. Meredith *is* your new partner."

Irked, Nash's lips quivered, then clamped. The Dubliner's dire warning reverberated in his mind. Anxious to leave, Mackenzie sugarcoated the introduction.

"An astute psychologist, Dr. Lindsey has worked numerous cases. A graduate of Michigan, she earned advanced degrees at Yale. Your new teammate also ran cross country in college."

Inwardly impressed, Nash peered at the tall runner. Obviously blessed with an elite athlete's power and purpose, the shrink was in her early thirties, or about his own age.

With no further comments, the Special Agent placed a file on the desk and exited the increasingly frigid office. Her partner's granite glare and defiant posture were telling. Clearly, the analyst was not welcome. Ambushed by the hostile reception, Meredith tensed. With the daunting task of initiating the conversation, she focused on his boots.

"Gator?"

Stunned by the ridiculously stupid question, Morgan choked back a snicker. A blink later he caught himself. The disarming query was a distraction. The profiler was a gamer.

"What difference does it make? By the way, profiling lacks validation. I'm not a huge fan."

Angered by the jibe Lindsey's eyes morphed dark and cold. The pissing contest was underway. "Maybe I'm contracted, an analyst on loan."

"Maybe you should just leave. And don't let the door hit you in the ass."

"Funny man, but I'm not playing. Enlighten me about the boots."

"They're snake."

"What kind?"

What a freaking idiot.

"In Texas, there's only one variety. Playful, it hisses. Angry, it rattles."

"A rattlesnake? A city girl, I've never seen one."

"Maybe it's time. But don't turn your back. It's liable to bite you in the butt."

Blindsided by the witty sarcasm, Lindsey's expression hardened. Noting her snarled lips and angry eyes, Morgan did the unexpected. Winking, he grabbed the classified file and exited. Stunned by the abrupt departure the profiler sat perplexed. The grieving, tightly wound agent was an enigma.

Desperate for solitude Nash ambled to an empty room. Time alone was desperately needed to study the analyst and reflect. Thumbing through the file he marked a footnote. The five-foot-ten athlete was still participating in half-marathons. Suddenly his jaw dropped in surprise.

What the hell? The shrink runs with a Glock?

Scratching a patch of unshaven whisker stubble, Morgan pondered the revelation. The weapon was a constant companion. Reading deeper into the file, he noted another shocker. The attractive analyst was still single. Circling the information, he questioned why someone so alluring wasn't married. Suddenly his fortress of solitude was shattered as Mackenzie barged into the small office and plopped into a side chair.

"Sorry about the interruption. But there's a bombshell not listed in her file."

"Let me guess," quipped Nash. "The woman eats men for breakfast."

"No. Tragically, Meredith was raped in college by a gang of frat boys."

"Wow. I didn't see that coming."

"Morgan, this confidential tidbit makes her extremely dangerous. Our analyst may look and act like 'Miss America' but do not be deceived. Emotionally, she's scarred and tough-minded. Super smart and intuitive, the D.C. office thinks Meredith Lindsey walks on water. Be very careful. With the stroke of a pen, your ass is toast She's assisting with the case but also analyzing you. Do not mess with her."

"Thanks. I noted the arrogance. But that pent-up anger has to work against her. It's been my worst enemy."

"You're probably right. Yet the bureau has big plans for her."

"What was the outcome?"

"Only one attacker was convicted. The others received a slap on the hand. Mentally, Meredith has to be one very distraught woman."

"Well, this is going to be most interesting."

An hour later the petulant profiler reentered Nash's office and quietly slid into a side chair. Anticipating a verbal onslaught, she was astonished. An easy smile had replaced the agent's adversarial scowl. With a quick scan, she noted his chiseled frame. According to the file, Morgan Nash stood six-foot-three and weighed a solid two hundred and ten pounds. Curious, she flipped a page and reread a paragraph. Physical punishment had replaced alcohol as a new addiction. The grieving widower was a black belt in Uechi Ryu.

Anxious to jettison the unwelcomed intruder, Morgan shattered the awkward silence. "So, you're a Wolverine? We hammered you pretty good in Austin."

"Your wife was a cheerleader. Correct?"

"Yeah. Dawn was a three-year favorite. She was first on the field when I got hurt."

"Your shoulder was pretty messed up. And didn't you suffer a concussion?"

"Yep. X-rays revealed a snapped collar bone and numerous tears. But the surgeries were successful."

"Your fans named your vicious tackle '*Double Shot.*' Why?"

"It was a play on words. It looked like I hit the receiver twice."

"Did your dad ever hit you? According to my notes, your homelife was pretty abusive."

Angered by the remark, Nash tensed. "Look, I'm not going to talk about my past or family. Maybe it's a strike against me. But that's too bad. You can peddle your psychobabble elsewhere."

Sidetracked by the pushback, Meredith found herself in a quandary. The agent's volatile history was critical to unlocking his troubled soul. "What was your major in college?"

"Accounting."

"But you became a cop."

"Being high-profile at UT opened doors. After graduation, I worked for a computer company. But the job was boring and non-physical. That was my wake-up call. Later, I learned Uechi Ryu."

Having studied his file, the profiler was well aware of Morgan's martial arts proficiency. But she needed him to talk. Flashing a surprised look, she blurted: "What?"

"It's a form of Okinawan karate, graceful but lethal. The physicality tamps my inner demons."

Intrigued, Meredith thumbed to page eight. "In time, you earned a black belt. You must have a real hankering for pain."

"I do."

And I deserve every blow.

"Why did you leave Austin?"

"I wanted more. A friend had contacts. Eventually, I was accepted by the FBI and assigned to Dallas."

"Colleagues have dubbed you the "cartel buster." Supposedly, you have some sixth sense. Are you leading this case because of that innate ability?"

Easily deflecting the question, Nash chuckled. "Maybe, if you believe the rumors." Suddenly the lighthearted response turned serious. "I'm spearheading this investigation for one reason. The killer links to my family."

"Is that what you believe?"

"Yeah. I think it's the same bastard. But there's nothing concrete. Hell, it could be the cartel seeking payback. Or maybe some 'coyotes' seek revenge. Numerous drug traffickers want me dead. Look, this interrogation is going nowhere. I need a break." Flashing a faux smile, Morgan grabbed a handful of files and abruptly exited. Angered by the departure, Lindsey jogged to Fallon's office. Observations needed to be shared.

"How is my eccentric agent? Is he behaving?"

"Mackenzie, your partner is one petrified onion. The first layer is proving difficult to peel. Mr. Nash is compartmentalizing everything and shutting down all emotions."

"Can he lead the case?"

"That's questionable. Scared shitless, your man works day and night trying to outrun a host of inner demons. Grieving is not his thing. Right now, physical pain is his savior. It's his way of maintaining emotional balance. If off the case, I think he shoots himself."

"With that granite look, he's unreadable. What's going on in that thick skull?"

"Unfortunately, his mind has become a raging battlefield. Riddled with guilt, Morgan has a classic failure complex. He failed his family. He failed you. He failed himself. Your partner has tremendous protective instincts. Yet he wasn't home in Dawn and Erin's greatest time of need."

Nodding, the Special Agent sighed. "It's a real pickle. No revenge equates to self-destruction."

"That's my take. Your man is really hurting. But payback is a great motivator."

"I've known Morgan Nash for five years. He is instinctive as hell. But anger has offset consistency. First it was his childhood. Now he has zero family."

"Tell me about his wife."

Cracking a wry Irish smile, the Dubliner chuckled. "That woman was simply amazing. Blessed with a genuine smile and the brightest of blue eyes, Dawn captivated anyone that gazed upon her. Charismatic as hell, she was fun but intellectual. Her wisdom, wit, and grace were uncanny."

"You're describing the perfect woman."

"That was his beloved cheerleader. Dawn possessed the perfect mixture of beauty, laughter, talents, and strengths. Ever the charmer, her presence had a calming and stabilizing effect on his inner demons."

"She was his rudder."

"Yep. Will he be able to focus?"

Instantly, Lindsey hesitated. "Mackenzie, that's unanswerable. In my professional opinion, he either implodes or avenges. There's no middle ground. Instinctively, Morgan senses this. That's why he's terrified."

"Him? That's difficult to believe."

"It's true. Uncertainty ravages his mind. What if he can't eliminate the killer? What if he lets you down? What if he fails again?"

"That's tough. But it's also good. Morgan knows what's at stake. But blocking those inner demons is going to be tough."

"It's going to be extremely difficult if not impossible. That rugged persona is a protective shell. Inside he's a frightened little kid."

"Are you sure about this?"

"Absolutely. Doubt gnaws at him like an aggressive stage four cancer. Plus, this case is beyond his expertise. So yes, he's mortified. Is another failure looming?"

"But Morgan has always risen to the occasion. He's been a take-charge guy."

"Look, your man is trying to lead. But the combination of demons and distractions makes it very difficult."

"Can he succeed? Yea or nay? I need to know."

"Mackenzie, he has a slim chance if his memory reverts back to football. At UT, Morgan Nash was able to deflect the cheers of 100,000 screaming fans and slow the game. Your partner has to regain that mindset in order to function at a high level."

"Assuming success, what's his prognosis?"

"That's another unknown. Maybe he's good for several months. Maybe not. If distracted, he dies."

"That's razor thin. Going forward, what can I expect?"

Instantly Lindsey hesitated, searching for the right words. "Expect the opposite of what you might think. Do not expect him to grieve. Do not expect him to show remorse. Do not expect his old self. Either the killer dies, or he dies. It's that simple, yet complex. If Morgan somehow survives, maybe he can make peace with the demons and move forward."

"So, it's all or nothing. How can I help?"

"Be supportive. Give him a little slack. But set boundaries. The mysticism presents a huge challenge. With everything jumbled, he's likely to wander."

"Dammit. This is going to be a frigging nightmare."

CHAPTER 7

Monday, January 11

"Agent Nash, why are you here? My practice is limited to high-risk patients. The bureau provides excellent therapists."

The flippant response triggered an immediate reaction. "Is suicide a good enough answer? Every fricking day I put a gun in my mouth. Then something happens. The phone rings or I get a text. But I'm getting closer and closer to pulling that damn trigger."

"Why do you want to harm yourself?"

"It's my only option. Death frees me."

"From what?"

"The gore."

"Describe what you're seeing."

Instantly Morgan hesitated. The mental images were vividly horrific and beyond description. As tears welled in both eyes, his lips moved but no words emerged.

"Agent, this may be too painful. Do you want to stop?"

"No. Just give me a second. I see my wife's terror-stricken eyes and bloodied face. I see my daughter's sheer panic and helpless agony. I see both alone, quivering in fear and pleading *for me* to save them."

"Are the images real or imaginary?"

"YOU RAT BASTARD! READ THE FUCKING FILE! Dawn is dead. Erin is dead. Is that tangible enough for you? Inside, I'm dead. I'm here for help, not some psychobabble."

"Describe their deaths."

"Both were savagely murdered. My wife was stabbed repeatedly. Her face was a shredded mess. The killer kidnapped my daughter. For two years, I have languished in absolute hell. Recently, her little body was discovered. My precious baby was bitten by a Nile asp and wrapped like a mummy."

"Did they apprehend the killer?"

"No. There's been no justice."

"Is that what you seek? Or is it revenge?"

"What difference does it make? The bastard needs to die."

"Life imprisonment is not enough?"

"Hell no! Only a slow agonizing death can erase the images."

"Agent, listen to yourself. Payback is your *fixation*. It's your best friend but your worst enemy. Thus, your dilemma continues. The pictures remain indelibly locked. Look, I can prescribe meds to help you function. But you need to relax and sleep."

"Dammit, I don't want pills. I want this fricking nightmare to end. I want this bastard dead. I want to see my wife and daughter alive again."

"Have you thought about leaving the FBI?"

"No."

"Then your journey is going to be long, winding, and painful."

"Why?"

"It's simple. Anger trumps guilt. You face two major obstacles which cannot be simultaneously resolved. I suggest you schedule another session."

"What if I kill the prick?"

"Then your nightmare ends. Your images disappear. Your anger fades. At that point, we focus on guilt."

"So, it's either a long journey or a dead assassin? Hell, that's an easy decision. I don't need another session."

"But you have unresolved issues."

"Look. I'll make a deal. We'll talk again if I survive."

"So, it's all or nothing."

"Yep. The man needs to die a thousand deaths."

Wearied from the incessant crisscrossing travel, the gift bearer noted the bleakness of the frosty night. Ever vigilant, his trained eyes scanned the gravel road and rural countryside. Cloaked within the shadows of mature cedars, he was anxious to finish the job. The overpowering stench of formaldehyde was impairing his focus.

The metal disk clutched in his right hand felt perfectly round and flat. On both sides were etchings, harbingers of evil. Suddenly his face twisted, mimicking a silent scowl of righteous indignation. The assignment was a joke. With eyes ablaze, his countenance darkened. Eying the malignant silver object, his rage intensified. Squeezing mightily, he tried to mangle the projectile. Yet his vice-like fingers lacked the thrust of a hydraulic press.

Sudden movement caught his attention, snapped the ire, and brought a flash of lucidity. With a sigh of resignation, Mr. B placed the small missile into a grooved leather pouch. Aping a pitcher warming in the bullpen he slowly rotated his right arm. Hitting the perfect rhythm, the arm arced faster and faster until it became a windmill blur. At full speed, the leather pouch made a distinctive whirring that could be heard within fifty feet. Yet the elderly victim at forty feet heard nothing. Tone deaf, the icon was totally engrossed in his thoughts.

With a flick of the wrist, the gift bearer released the high-speed projectile. The polished silvery disk slammed into the Fed's forehead with alarming brute force. As the financier crumpled to the ground, a purplish-red splotch spread minuscule death veins. Emerging quickly from the shadowy darkness, the killer of many unwrapped a slimy package and crammed a well-preserved green frog into the icon's gaping mouth. Overcome by the stench, he instantly vanished into the inky night.

The incessant shrill triggered an all-too-familiar sense of dread. Glancing at the clock Morgan noted the ungodly time. The caller had to be Mackenzie Fallon.

"Did I wake you?"

"No. I prefer cleaning at midnight."

"Are you serious?"

Sometimes the Dubliner didn't get it. Maybe it was an Irish thing. "I couldn't sleep. What's up?"

"Another Fed has been theatrically assassinated. Jackson, Tennessee was the location."

"Details?"

"Sketchy. I'm waiting on reports. Meet me at 8 a.m." As Mackenzie terminated the call, Morgan attempted to sleep but couldn't. Irked, he grabbed a rag and began dusting.

CHAPTER 8

Tuesday, January 12

As a hallway clock pinged the hour Nash joined Meredith and Raz in Fallon's office. As anticipated, the Special Agent was in a gruff mood.

"Our latest murder occurred in Jackson, Tennessee. The victim was retiree Randolph Macon, former President of the Chicago Federal Reserve Bank. A well-preserved green frog was stuffed into his mouth. Time of death was approximately 9 p.m. The rural setting delayed discovery of the body."

"Add another soft target to the list," quipped Nash. "Our ghost seems hell-bent on destabilizing the economy."

"But that's impossible," countered Mackenzie. "No individual can destroy our financial system."

"That's likely true. But destabilization *can* force policy changes that weaken the U.S. and embolden Russia and China."

"I'm not buying. Something's amiss."

"What about the weapon?" Suppressing a giant yawn, Meredith interrupted and then reached for her triple-shot latte. Like Morgan, her night had been difficult. "On the phone you mentioned unique."

"Indeed, I did. A Davidic slingshot was the culprit. But a simple rock wasn't good enough. The bastard hurled a silver disk. But why? Accuracy had to be risky at best."

"That's an erroneous assumption," corrected the Egyptologist. "Ancient slingshots were extremely accurate at close range. Even children were adept. The weapon was used for hunting, war, and revenge. Pharaohs often..."

"DAMMIT, THIS IS SO WRONG!" yelped Morgan. "Forget slingshot. Forget frog. Forget theatrics. Focus solely on *time.*"

"Why?"

"Mac, *the hourly sequence is* the crucial connector. The ticking clock links the Sun God's nightly journey to the dreaded omega accord."

Instantly, Mackenzie bristled. "Forget it! Fantasy cannot and will not drive this case."

"But it is."

"How?"

"The accord was the underworld's holy trinity of evil. Overcoming the trifecta of death, damnation, and dissolution was the Sun God's nightly challenge."

"So?" As the Dubliner's mercurial temper simmered, her hard, questioning look spoke volumes.

"Only death and damnation have been highlighted to date."

"Which obviously leaves *dissolution*."

"Correct," answered Morgan. "The trifecta's third stage is the eight-hundred-pound gorilla which *expands the case.* That explains the elaborate staging. RE wants us distracted, focused on theatrics and not the end goal."

"Which is?"

"That is to be determined."

Immediately the Special Agent's countenance darkened as the simmering anger exploded. "Dammit, that's not going to cut it. I need facts, not jibber-jabber."

"But..."

"Look, we're done with this mythological crap. Without suspects and motive, we've got nothing. Are there any other idiotic comments?" As the room grew eerily silent, the Dubliner continued. "A frog token was also found next to the body. Other than a letter added and a number subtracted, the message was the same. Raz, are you any closer to an explanation?"

"What was the letter?"

"It was "a" as in alpha."

"Bravo! That completes the circle. *BABA* is the killer's symbolic name."

"Important?"

"Think of it as his calling card, Agent Nash."

"Like Carlos the Jackal?"

"Yes. Aptly depicted as a baboon, BABA was Egypt's god of aggression."

"Does the name offer any insights into future killings?"

"Agent Fallon, that is unanswerable. It's too early to tell. You must be patient."

"PATIENT?" Addled by the scholarly indifference, Mackenzie's rosy cheeks pulsated scarlet as her apocalyptic temper erupted. "Dammit, that word does not exist in my vocabulary. Delay means death. Folks, I need answers, not bullshit. Right now, a fricking baboon represents our only shred of evidence. That's my report to the Director."

"That's it?"

"Morgan, stop! Without something tangible, we're hopelessly mired in a state of confusion."

"What about the cartel killings in Victoria? Do they link to the case?"

"The Director says no. Nor is there any connection to your family."

With the curt ending, the Dubliner abruptly exited the room. Trailing closely behind was the profiler. With Mackenzie's departure, Morgan sat puzzled and dismayed.

Begrudgingly, he trudged to the snack bar accompanied by the Egyptian.

Twenty minutes later, the pair returned to Nash's office. With flecks of glaze crusted on his black mustache, the archeologist was riding a sugar high.

"Agent, I may have something to lift your spirits. The Sun God's nightly journey was broken into twelve increments beginning at 6 p.m. Each hour represented a *challenge* for RE."

"Why didn't you mention this to Mackenzie?"

"My words would have fallen on deaf ears. Agent Fallon has no tolerance for mythology."

"Neither does Jameson. Okay, explain the challenge."

"The Sun God's perilous journey was made *without significant allies.*" Enunciating the final three words, the academic watched in fascination. Four blinks later, a slight hint of understanding appeared in Morgan's eyes. Suddenly his face twisted as the words connected.

"Is that the answer? Does destabilization trigger a *global reset?*"

"Explain."

"A loss of allies both weakens and isolates America. It renders us incapable of policing the world. Hell, it's an open invitation for adversaries to seize territories and resources."

"But would European and Asian allies abandon the U.S.?"

"In a heartbeat. Whenever our economy tanks and military shrinks, they broker new deals. A loss of allies absolutely benefits a number of bad characters including China, Russia, Iran, and North Korea."

"You must warn Agent Fallon."

"Mac won't..." Abruptly, Nash's brows arched in consternation as his lips contorted in agony. "Dammit, Raz, we've been blind, deaf, and dumb. We've fallen headfirst into BABA's trap."

"I'm not following."

"Our fixation has been on those damn symbols. As a result, we've overlooked the obvious. Was there a famous Egyptian dagger?"

With a blank stare, the archeologist hesitated and then flashed a wry possum grin. "Oh yes! One belonged to Queen Nefertiti. Replicas are sold everywhere."

"Describe."

"With a winged hand guard, the original version bore Nefertiti's likeness on the hilt. The silver blade was eight inches in length."

"Was there a slight curvature at the tip?"

"Yes. It was an exquisite piece."

"Bingo! That's BABA's dagger."

Buoyed by the discovery the pair scurried to Mackenzie's office. In a humorless mood, the Dubliner winced when seeing the unwelcomed intruders.

"Mac, we've uncovered our first piece of concrete evidence."

"Well, it's about time." Punching several buttons, Mackenzie summoned the profiler. During their wait, Raz posed a troublesome query.

"Agent Fallon, should these murders continue who benefits?"

Pleased by the logical query Mackenzie flashed a wry grin. "Finally, a man who thinks. That's a very legitimate question. Morgan, what's your take?"

"Defense contractors would be the big winners. It's a no-brainer."

"Why?"

"Mac, it's the historical and predictable answer. More murders would create confusion and instability. Sniffing weakness, our adversaries rattle sabers and threaten action. Invariably our politicians overreact and pour billions into defense contracts. Industry titans reap huge rewards."

Clumsily interrupting was Lindsey as she dropped several files and eased into a seat. "Sorry, but I overheard every word."

Intrigued by her partner's response, Mackenzie's dubious expression slowly morphed to concern. "You make a valid point. But without hard evidence, there's nothing for Jameson."

"I wholeheartedly agree," purred the analyst. "No bureau analyst is going to heed a single word." Unexpectedly her silky tone turned snarly as the pretended innocence dissipated. "That's why I recommend Morgan's *immediate termination.* Mystic symbols and wild speculation cannot drive this case. We need someone more polished and effective, like a seasoned veteran."

Blindsided, Nash instantly reacted. "Like some D.C. crony or lover? Meredith, that's pure bullshit and you know it. Cut the smugness. In your eyes I'm just some vile and abhorrent lowlife. Isn't that the truth?"

"Look, I've tried to be objective. But you're about to implode." As her piercing Judas eyes crackled with hostility, the profiler's facial expression reflected one of privilege. Lacking was any trace of sincerity. "You aren't capable of handling the increased pressure. This investigation has to have someone with more expertise. I have no choice but to make the recommendation."

As his volcanic anger glowed white hot, Morgan physically tensed and defiantly glared at his betrayer. Noting her vengeful expression, he knew a verbal onslaught was only seconds away. Unwilling to play the role of patsy, he decided to sucker punch and run.

"With all due respect, I think this firing is more about your ego than my ability. It's another glowing report for the swamp rats, a perk for some special buddy. Well, you can take this case and shove it where it's very dark." Storming out of the office, he was trailed by the diminutive Egyptian.

Infuriated by the ambush, Mackenzie fumed. "Was that necessary?"

"Yes. That's my report."

"Look, we're all feeling the pressure. Are you sure?"

"Absolutely. Your man is a porcelain doll. Unfortunately, he's cracking and ready to shatter at any moment."

"But this case is unique. It demands his insight."

"Mackenzie, each new death makes the situation more complicated. Right now, he's trying to shoulder the load. But he's scared. Can he silently grieve, decipher codes, and save America all at the same time? Inside that thick skull he's fighting powerful demons."

"Can he continue? Yea or nay?"

"No. In my professional opinion, Morgan Nash is drowning. I recommend his immediate reassignment. You cannot count on him."

Faced with a monumental decision, the Dubliner weighed the assessment. After a long moment of reflection, she shook her head. "Not yet. I'm overriding your recommendation. Things need to play out."

With her career on the line, Mackenzie hastily exited the office. A nip of the Irish was desperately needed.

CHAPTER 9

Thursday, January 14

Shortly after midnight, a hellish shriek shattered Nash's restless slumber. The irate caller was barely audible.

"Mac, slow the hell down. What's up?"

"You are. As you predicted, the case *has* exploded."

"BABA?"

"Yeah. Scratch the Secretary of Finance. Move your ass for a 6 a.m. briefing."

In a brittle mood, Morgan arrived early. Instantly, he tensed. Seated comfortably and sipping coffee was his Judas shrink. Acknowledging her clout, he tamped his anger and flashed a faux grin.

"Morning."

"Your face looks puffy. Lack of sleep?"

"I'm making it. Look, this case demands unity regardless of personal feelings."

"I agree." With a wide-eyed look of disingenuous innocence, Lindsey's sapphire eyes sparked in silent protest. "Your boss supports you. So, slip on your big boy pants and take a seat."

Accepting the jibe with equanimity, Nash slid into a chair and politely posed a question. "What's *your* take on the case?"

"Obviously, the bad guys are winning. Taking advantage of your inexperience, they're creating havoc." Pleased with the chiding retort she sipped the vanilla latte. Like a coiled viper, she toyed with her prey.

"That's just bullshit. You should get the fu..."

"That's quite enough!" With glowering eyes and scowling expression, the Dubliner entered the office and squashed the profanity-laced tirade. In a foul mood, her cheeks pulsated an angry shade of red. Lagging several steps behind was the donut-munching academic.

"Morgan was right about RE expanding the case. Finance Secretary Roger Swisher was the latest victim. The time was sequential."

"But why? According to reports, the financial icon was nearing retirement. Didn't he have some fancy estate in Virginia?"

"Chantilly was the murder site, Meredith. An aide tried to reach the Secretary but got no response. This particular killing was both gruesome and unique."

"How so?"

"Like Delgado, his head was wrapped with black tape. But white strips were artistically layered around his mouth giving the impression of immensely protruding lips. A narrow beard of carved wood was attached to the chin. The single token was a snake. The message was identical except for a subtracted number."

"Weren't false beards the rage in ancient times?" Casually sipping her drink, Lindsey flashed her squinty eyes to the Egyptian.

"Oh yes," squealed Raz. "The beard was an outward sign of transformation. Pharaoh had become Osiris the 'Living King.'"

"What about the snake?"

"Agent Fallon, the token was likely Apophis. The underworld's giant serpent symbolized chaos, which seems very appropriate at the moment."

Unexpectedly, the Dubliner's priority fax machine chattered and churned out a single page. With a quick scan, her face turned apoplectic. "Dammit, panicked investors are demanding answers and liquidating. Massive losses are projected at the opening bell."

"Mac, that's to be expected," reflected Nash. "Hell, the Dow is down nearly three thousand points since Christmas. Each new murder destabilizes our markets and increases concerns."

"True. But something's not right. You view the theatrics as pure distraction. Right?"

"Yeah. They hide RE's real intent."

"Which is?"

"REBIRTH."

"Rebirth?" Glowering at her eccentric partner, Mackenzie instantly erupted into apocalyptic anger. "Dammit, Morgan, what the hell? Earlier, you said greed. Are you certain about anything?"

"Yeah. The two intersect at the apex."

"Apex? Dammit, that makes zero sense."

"Au contraire. If our economy tanks, two things happen. *The world changes form. And our adversaries enjoy an economic rebirth*. The same interlocking scenario takes place during the Sun God's underworld journey."

"Dammit, there you go again. Mysticism is not going to drive this case."

"Ah, but it is. Mac, hear me out. As dawn approaches the Sun God *symbolically dies* and *changes form* before living anew. But that's at the *very end* of the twelve hours."

"So? It's a frigging story. Make a point."

"Okay, something hideous awaits America at sunrise. Is that definitive enough for you? More explosive than 9/11, it foreshadows our demise. The end result is global reset."

Stunned by the speculation, the Dubliner slowly shook her head in disgust. "Do you actually expect me to believe this crap?"

"Heed what I say or fail. *Death* debilitates economy. *Damnation* destroys allies. *Dissolution* redefines world power."

"That's bullshit. This omega accord is pure make-believe. It's mythological nonsense."

"Mac, listen. *Greed is the overriding factor*. But it's on a much broader and grander scale. An altered world creates untold wealth for RE and his shadowy partners. But subplots twist the narrative." Pausing, Morgan searched Mackenzie's fiery green eyes for any semblance of enlightenment. Yet none were forthcoming, only white-hot flames from her riled lips.

"Dammit, Meredith was right. You are drowning. You've become a fricking Brahman mystic."

"Maybe. But I know one thing. These people *relish* symbolism. The Sun God's nightly journey points to a cataclysmic event. Picture it as America's "Sword of Damocles." Dissolution hovers just waiting to be unleashed."

With pursed lips, the Special Agent pushed back and reflected. "When busting cartels, you made some really outlandish calls. But you were right. Once again, you're teetering on the edge. Worse, you're deeply committed. Have you uncovered anything specific?"

"Yeah. Raz and I have discovered a symbolic code that unlocks RE's underworld journey. We've deciphered the first four hours."

"Meaning?"

"BABA replaces the Sun God as our 'Guide' or 'Pathfinder.' The Mississippi River equates to the 'River of Wernes.' 'Boat' indicates location. 'Dawn' designates time. Modern RE apes mythological RE."

"Interesting. But your little theory has major flaws. Swisher's death occurred in *Virginia.* Plus, your ominous event has no definitive date or location. Unless BABA magically reappears in Tennessee, we're done with this rebirth crap. The Director has every right to fire you."

"Fine! Let's fiddle while Rome burns. Plus, the news gets worse. The Sun God's journey symbolically points to a lurking traitor."

"Who?"

"A D.C. mole. RE has him on the payroll. Mimicking the Egyptian God of Wisdom, this individual has both influence and clout."

"Hell, that describes most D.C. politicians. Screw the symbolism." Noting the early hour, the Dubliner barked an order. "Eat breakfast. Then find something. Morgan, you stay."

As the others exited, Nash sat dejected. The abysmal meeting had ended in utter failure. "Obviously, you're not done with me."

With a sagacious nod, Mackenzie tamped her frustration and took a deep breath. "Look, you're smart. Your theories are borderline brilliant. But the Director has never accepted fantasy. Plus, you have me worried."

"I'm fine."

"Talk to Meredith. Get help before you implode."

"Mac, you're..." Abruptly, he stopped. The Dubliner's terrified expression was telling. Bridling his anger, Morgan obediently nodded, flashed a faux smile, and exited the office. Walking down the hall, he defiantly shook his head and yelled a late response.

"Now is not the time for shrinks...especially Meredith Lindsey!"

And may God smile on fools...and foolish utterances.

Fast walking to the cafeteria, he sought out the Egyptian. Weighing on his mind was a single question.

"Teacher, were pharaohs terrified of Osiris?"

"Absolutely! Without his approval, they couldn't pass judgment, ascend to the heavens, live like gods, or influence the world. Osiris and his tribunal represented a huge barrier."

"Is that what this is about? Symbolic gods at play? Influencing the world?"

"That is yet to be determined."

"Fair enough. Let's eat and head to my office for another session."

CHAPTER 10

Friday, January 15

Shortly after midnight, an all-too-familiar shriek shattered the ebony silence. Furious at being awakened, Nash growled into the receiver. "Dammit Mac, what now?"

"BABA has struck again." The feminine voice was commanding. "We have a huge problem."

With a death grip on a triple shot coffee Morgan sluggishly flopped into one of Fallon's side chairs. The ungodly time was 4:20 a.m. Notably missing were Meredith and Raz.

In a dour mood, Mackenzie quickly summarized the murder. "Richmond, Virginia was the location. The victim was President of the Philadelphia Federal Reserve Bank. 'Allahu Akbar' was highlighted on the note. Public outrage toward Muslims has spiked."

"That's not good. The race card pressures Hyatt to break a campaign promise and retaliate. A regional conflict in the Middle East represents a huge win for the defense industry. RE keeps upping the ante."

"A military buildup is highly unlikely," countered Fallon. "The President doesn't want us involved in feuds involving Kurds, Sunnis, and Shiites."

"Mac, you can't believe a word. In D.C., truth shifts like the wind. Politicians lie. Look, avarice breeds strange bed partners. Hawkish generals, ambitious Senators, and desperate contractors could easily orchestrate these murders. The message to Hyatt is clear. Either reverse policy or forget reelection. Lurking in the shadows, some powerful group wants war. It's dirty, hardball politics that pays handsome rewards. The death of a few innocents means nothing to them,"

"Morgan, that's crazy talk. Yeah, groups can pressure. But that's it. The President is too well insulated."

"Then RE moves to Plan B."

"Which is?"

"*Robert Hyatt's elimination*. Hell, it makes sense. The end justifies the means."

"That's just bullshit. In a blink, you pivot from benefactors to assassination."

"Mac, think it through. A presidential assassination ends Act One with a thunderous bang. These random murders cannot continue indefinitely."

Striking a nerve, Mackenzie hesitated. "If correct, what's Act Two?"

"The omega trifecta comes to fruition. Think of it as a Greek tragedy. Dissolution follows death and damnation."

"Dammit, stop. I'm not buying. There's nothing to support your twisted theory."

"But..."

"Look, killing Hyatt makes zero sense. The Vice President is a clone. Hell, Richard Anderson *is* Robert Hyatt. A Presidential assassination changes nothing. Go shave and get something to eat. Then find me something useful."

With the damning rebuttal, Nash fumed out of the office. A refill of high-octane coffee was sorely needed.

As the brilliant rays of sunlight peeked above the horizon, Raz and Meredith lethargically trudged into the Dubliner's office. Deliberately tardy by seven minutes, a clean-shaven Morgan defiantly eased into a side chair. In a grouchy mood, Mackenzie's tone was flat, frosty.

"Richmond, Virginia, was the location of our latest Fed murder. According to the local M.E., time of death was around midnight. The victim was President of the Philadelphia Federal Reserve Bank. John Robert Davis was impaled by an ancient Egyptian spear fitted with a silver blade. For good measure, the killer bludgeoned his head with an Egyptian throwing stick or wooden barbell. The note read "BABA-7."

"Where was security?" Irked by the savage killing, the profiler fumed. "I thought Fed leadership was under twenty-four-hour protection."

"Davis had a detail. Once inside the condo, he waved them away. Folks, this rampage has to stop. You're authorized to use every bureau resource."

Energized by caffeine and pastries, the two men reconvened in a small conference room. Desperate for connections, Morgan posed an instant query. "Raz, did all pharaohs worship the Sun God?"

"Oh, yes."

"Why?"

"They were terrified of *syncretism.*"

"I'm not following."

"Syncretism was the merger of the Sun God with lesser deities. The result was a supernatural powerhouse that terrified the people, especially around Heliopolis. RE was forever identified with the Ogdoad."

"Ogdoad?"

"Remember? They were the eight lesser gods birthed by Amun and RE."

"Yeah, I recall. Tell me about Heliopolis."

"The Nile city was dedicated to the god Ptah and located approximately *thirty miles north of Memphis."*

Unexpectedly Morgan rocketed to his feet. "Memphis and Jackson are about thirty miles apart. Was Heliopolis east or west bank?"

"East."

"Jackson is also east bank...on the *Mississippi River*. Coincidence? I think not. This could be our major break."

"Possibly. But BABA is in Virginia."

"A Memphis return changes everything. Do you possess an ancient map?"

"Yes. It's in my temporary office."

"Please retrieve it. We need to plan for BABA's arrival."

"How?"

"We juxtapose the Nile and Memphis deltas. We identify target cities from New Orleans to St. Louis."

"I'll be right back."

Within minutes the Egyptian returned with a badly tattered map. Carefully, he aligned the document with Morgan's U.S. southeastern map. Unexpectedly, the archeologist flashed a wry grin. "Look, New Orleans parallels ancient Thebes."

"Important?"

"Possibly. New Orleans was your first murder. Thebes was the worship center of Amun, the 'King God' or 'Hidden One.' The Sun God was often referred to as 'Amun-RE.'"

Buoyed by the discovery, Nash quickly eyed other river cities. "There are numerous targets if BABA returns. I've got to update Mackenzie."

As the academic ambled to the snack bar, Morgan jogged to Fallon's office. After he pleaded his case, the Dubliner reluctantly agreed to contact Memphis authorities. "I'll make the calls. But with BABA in Virginia, few will listen."

CHAPTER 11

Saturday, January 16

Shortly after 3 a.m., a satanic shrill shredded the tranquil night. Awakening in a panic, Morgan fumbled for the nearby Glock. A blink later, he sighed at the ungodly hour. "Dammit Mac, can't it wait?"

"No. Apparently, you *are* a Brahmin mystic. BABA has circled back. Two are dead in Tennessee."

"Location?"

"Bartlett. It's a Memphis suburb. Meet me at 5 a.m."

Arriving late, Morgan's half-shaven, disheveled appearance spoke volumes. Sagging beneath both eyes were plump, dark circles. Sitting quietly were the analyst and academic. Both appeared exhausted. Observing her weary team, the Dubliner flashed a hideous scowl and summarized the murders.

"The location was Bartlett, Tennessee. The victims were a retired Fed Governor and his wife. Both were stabbed. William Bishop's heart was removed and his head wrapped. Attached to his chin was another false beard. The woman was not mutilated. The time of death was sequential. The note was the same minus a number."

"Tokens?"

"There was one, Meredith. It was a mummified man wearing a funny-looking crown."

"That's Osiris," blurted the Egyptian. "The 'Atef' was the underworld god's trademark. Conical in shape, the crown was white with a small disc on top. Plumes adorned each side symbolizing royalty."

"Interesting. There were new props as well. A shepherd's crook and small flail were carefully positioned on the Fed's chest. Raz?"

"The crook symbolized authority and protection. The flail represented judgment and punishment. The dreaded lash featured three beaded strands. Almighty pharaoh held the power over life and death."

As the bizarre array of symbols cast an ominous shroud of silence, Nash calibrated the possibilities. Suddenly, he flashed a sly Leprechaun grin. "Mac, substitute "king" for "pharaoh."

"Why?"

"RE wants us fixated on a person. It's another distraction."

"Meaning?"

"Ignore the Fed. Ignore the theatrics. Focus solely on *kingdom.* Egypt's northern kingdom juxtaposes our Mississippi delta."

"Relevance?"

"The symbolism points to Memphis as the epicenter. Each Tennessee murder lies within a thirty-mile radius."

"Dammit, Morgan, there is no epicenter!" Irked by the flimsy theory, the Dubliner's eyes crackled with fury. "Give me something tangible."

"Mac, listen. Bartlett juxtaposes ancient Cairo. Jackson overlays Heliopolis. BABA's next city is definitely Memphis."

"May I interrupt, Agent Nash?"

"Sure, Raz."

"You see but don't see. Passion often blurs one's vision."

"What do you mean?"

"Examine the ancient map. Show me Memphis." Studying the frayed sheet Nash pointed to the historic city.

"Does ancient Memphis reside on the Nile's east or west bank?"

"Oh hell!" As if sucker punched Morgan's eagerness morphed into agony. "It's west bank. Today's Memphis doesn't work."

"Why?"

"Boss, BABA's killings have all been east bank."

"But Memphis, Tennessee, is east bank. It is the right side."

"It's not if RE sticks to the ancient map. Dammit, everything points to a river. But what river? Something's amiss."

Unexpectedly, Raz flashed a sly grin. "What about the *underworld?* The river guides the Sun God on his nightly journey."

Instantly, Nash's eyes darted to the academic. "That could work. But there's no link. Does anything significant occur during the seventh hour?"

"At midnight, RE sailed past the decapitated adversaries of Osiris. Suddenly the Sun God was ambushed by Apophis. The gigantic serpent was a mortal enemy."

"What was the snake's purpose?" Puzzled by the scenario, Meredith interjected the query.

"Apophis had two assignments. The harbinger of evil was charged with swallowing the sun *and* plunging the world into darkness."

"That's it," yelped Morgan. "That's the connection. Who represents modern RE's mortal enemy? Is it the Fed Chairman? Is it the Treasury Secretary? No. His greatest adversary is the *President of the United States.*"

"Dammit, Morgan, that's bullshit. It's speculative without a shred of evidence."

"I disagree. What happens if RE eliminates Hyatt?"

"As previously stated, the answer is absolutely nothing. The Vice President *mimics* Robert Hyatt. It's a smooth transition. The policies remain unchanged."

"I vehemently disagree," argued Nash. "Young and inexperienced, Richard Anderson creates enormous uncertainty. His presence plunges America into uncharted waters and sets the stage for a reallocation of world resources."

"Fine. Show me the proof. Every fricking word is hypothetical."

Stymied, Morgan's eyes darted to the Egyptian. "Raz, how did the Sun God evade Apophis?"

"The serpent was disabled."

"How?"

"RE's entourage of knife-wielding protectors slashed the giant snake. Working in tandem, the "Scorpion Goddess" gripped the head while the "Director of Knives" secured the tail."

"That's it!" blurted Nash. "Mac, the seventh hour underscores two critical points. It describes a coordinated effort and identifies RE's shadowy accomplices."

"Are you referring to Batman and Superman? Both were fiction. Morgan, these protectors were make-believe. You're toast if Jameson gets word of this crap."

Ignoring the veiled threat, Morgan pressed his argument. "The seventh hour references two *identifiable* partners. The 'Scorpion Goddess' is RE's D.C. informant. The "Director of Knives" is a defense contractor. The underworld symbols link to today's reality."

"You may actually have a point," muttered Mackenzie begrudgingly. "Meredith, the capitol is your haven. Can you identify a rogue arms dealer?"

"No. There's too much oversight. An industry titan is not going to betray America."

"What about small caps? Many are suffering from Hyatt's military reductions. They're not diversified or cash-rich like the big boys."

"Only two have made recent headlines. Baker-Smith Missile Systems and Adams Advanced Weapons have lobbied for government bailouts."

"Scratch those names," barked Nash. "Traitors don't beg. They perform personal services."

"Well, that's a start," sighed the Dubliner. "Maybe Jameson can uncover some Judas contractor. Break for breakfast. Then find me something relevant."

Sated by five donuts, the Egyptian steamed into Nash's office and plopped into a side chair. Anxious to separate fact from fiction Morgan eyed the sugar junkie. "Raz, am I right? Is the Sun God's nightly journey the key?"

"You can certainly make the case. The tokens point to the underworld."

"Are you positive?"

"Absolutely. But certainty is often porous."

"That's an understatement. Okay, here's what we know. Dawn is the trigger. The plan is global. And something apocalyptic is looming."

"Agent, you see but don't see. I concur only with sunrise. The five o'clock hour marks the end of RE's journey. But that's it."

"Then we focus on dawn. The sun rises in the east. Does direction link to RE's shadowy accomplice?"

"Possibly. But you must narrow the scope. Does direction reference America's east, Middle East, Eastern Europe, or Far East?"

"I'm not sure. I think he's a global leader. But there's no definitive proof."

"Then we keep searching. How do you plan to proceed?"

"Honestly, I don't know. I just don't know. For the first time in my career, I'm stymied."

Meandering to the snack bar, Meredith deviated down a side hallway. The detour allowed her to keep tabs on her explosive patient. Slowing her pace, she peered into Morgan's office and abruptly stopped. Something was terribly wrong. With his head buried in his hands, the grieving widower was slumped in his chair.

"Are you okay?"

"I'm fine. Go away." The muffled tone was soft, garbled. Embarrassed, he didn't look or move.

Instinctively, she pulled a chair next to him. Her soothing tone was reassuring. "Hey, it's okay. The weight of the world can get heavy. You need to take some time off to grieve and rest."

"I can't."

"Morgan, you can't save others or even yourself with everything locked inside. Talk to me. Open the floodgates."

"Go. You need to leave."

"No. I can help."

"How? Look, I've got nothing. I've got no feelings. I've got no family. I've got no case." The pathetic words were telling. Morgan Nash's soul was empty. Any semblance of joy had been stripped from him.

"Look at me. I'm here to help."

As Nash's face slowly emerged, his electric green eyes were dull, lifeless, and moist. Mired in a personal hell, he was noticeably missing that passionate fire. Studying his face, Meredith noted the purplish-black circles ringing both eyes.

Etched along the forehead were deep worry lines, seemingly one for each murder. His sandy brown hair was matted and askew. Broken by repeated failures, Mackenzie's partner was a portrait of a living man with a dead heart.

"Look, I'm here for you. You need a friend. You need someone that can listen and understand."

"Friend? Hell, you tried to fire me. I've got no reason to trust you."

"Then let me simplify. Trust me or lose the case."

"That sounds like Raz."

"Morgan, you desperately need support. Either work with me or I report this incident to Mackenzie. You need help."

Uncertain, he scanned her face. Surprisingly, the hard lines and crackling eyes were gone, replaced by a soft and caring expression. Acknowledging the truth, the widower made a gut decision.

"Okay, I need support. But am I beyond repair?"

"It's never too late." Pleased with the decision, Meredith gave him a hug. Oblivious to the caress, he didn't move. As his sobs waned, the pair sat in a prolonged and nervous silence. Finally, she gave him a playful nudge. "Go home and get some sleep. That's the only way to outwit BABA."

"Do I have a choice?"

"Nope. With rest, things will get better. We'll keep this conversation strictly between us."

CHAPTER 12

Sunday, January 17

Unnerved by a Hadean shriek, Morgan awoke in a surly mood. Fumbling for the phone he responded tersely. "Mac, what the hell? It's 4:50 a.m."

"You were right. Memphis *was* the target."

"I knew it."

"But you were only half-right. The victim lived in *West* Memphis, Arkansas."

"But that's wrong."

"It doesn't matter. Scratch another retired Fed. Throw on some clothes and meet me in my office."

"But..."

Abruptly, the call terminated. With zero sleep, the Dubliner was in a brittle mood. Puzzled, Nash pondered the revelation.

West bank? It doesn't fit. Unless...

As the first rays of sunlight frolicked along the eastern horizon, Fallon scanned her weary team. In a battle of attrition, the bad guys were winning. "Okay, our latest murder occurred in West Memphis, Arkansas. This atrocity was particularly grisly and troubling. Johnathan Gruber's mutilated guts and vital organs were stuffed into large jars. Time of death was around 2 a.m."

"That describes a serial killer," yelped Morgan. "It's not BABA's style. Is there a second assassin?"

"No. According to the M.E., BABA was the killer."

"You highlighted 'troubling.' Why?"

"Meredith, the staging was totally different. There was no porch. There were no tokens. Gruber's remains were found in a small fishing boat. Four containers rested next to his wrapped head. Raz, have you an explanation?"

"Yes. The retired Fed did not pass judgment. The theatrics underscored his death and damnation."

"What about the jars and boat?"

"Agent Fallon, a pharaoh's internal organs were always stored in *canopic jars*. But the heart remained intact. These steps were critical for the righteous to board a *solar boat* and sail into the heavens."

"But solar doesn't mesh with fishing. Something's missing. Why pick a remote city, rickety boat, and isolated location? Is BABA saying goodbye?" Hearing no response, the Dubliner barked an order. "Break for breakfast. Then find me some answers."

In pain from a pounding migraine, the Special Agent headed to her secret elixir. Coffee laced with Irish whiskey was a family remedy.

Invigorated by caffeine and pastries, the exiled threesome reconvened in Morgan's office. Sipping a triple shot Nash eyed the Egyptian. "Can you explain Gruber's murder?"

"No. It's virtually impossible."

"Why?"

"The staging could be literal or symbolic. The boat could be river or solar. The jars could be ordinary or canopic. I could add more but it's useless."

"Then we're stymied," growled Meredith. "Gruber's death hasn't changed a thing."

"Then we look elsewhere. Raz, does anything significant occur during the eighth hour?"

"No. The Sun God encountered more enemies. But they were eliminated by RE's entourage of knife-wielding protectors."

Frustrated by the response, Morgan rapped his fingers and muttered an unintelligible profanity. "Then we focus on what we know. Hours seven and eight spotlight boat and accomplices. The plot thickens when you add river and dawn. But who's the target? And where?"

"I checked upcoming river events," chirped Lindsey. "There are no major happenings from Memphis to New Orleans in the next sixty days."

"Are you positive?"

"Absolutely."

"Dammit. The clues should form a pattern. But nothing fits. Is the Mississippi delta even in play?"

"Agent Nash, you seek validation. Yet that is virtually impossible at this moment."

"Why?"

"It's simple logic. You may be *ahead* of BABA's schedule. You must exercise patience."

Instantly Morgan exploded. "That's a hell no! People die if we don't act. Plus, the team is toast. The Director wants our ass."

"Hang on," proffered Meredith. "Raz may be right. To remain alive, BABA must stay a step ahead."

"But there must be a way to short-circuit the bastard. Otherwise, the case is non-ending."

"Agent, is it more important to catch a little fish or big fish?"

"What?" Addled by the philosophic query, Nash glared at the Egyptian. "Playing games, teacher? The fish cannot be separated. BABA and his master must perish at the same time."

"Then you will fail. Pursuing collateral damage will cost you the case."

"That's bullshit." As Morgan's smoldering angst edged toward eruption, Meredith unexpectedly draped a comforting arm around his shoulder.

"Hey, you're making progress. The pieces are connecting." The tone was quiet and consoling.

Acutely aware of the Texan's physicality, the Egyptian quickly added a word of encouragement. "Like Horus, your mind is cunning and wise. BABA senses your presence. Press him until he errs."

As the tension ebbed, the trio strolled to the snack bar. An extended break was badly needed.

A short time later, the threesome reassembled. Unexpectedly, Morgan flashed a sly possum grin. "Get packed. It's showtime. With Mac's approval, we fly to Memphis this afternoon."

"Agent, you're playing a fool's game." The academic's rebuttal was vehement and curt. "Without new symbols, you're chasing the wind."

"That's the plan. We determine direction and pounce." Abruptly exiting, Nash trotted to the Dubliner's office. As he plopped into a side chair, his beaming face aped a mischievous child.

"Dammit, I know that stupid-ass look. It means trouble. If factual, I'm listening. Otherwise, get the hell out of here."

"Mac, I need your approval. It's important."

"Regarding?"

Given an opening, Morgan quickly outlined his bodacious plan. Stunned by the bold initiative, the Special Agent sat perplexed. "You're right about being proactive. We've got to do something. But BABA's whereabouts are unknown. Likely, he has fled the area."

"That's not my thinking. With unfinished business, our ghost hovers near the epicenter."

Suddenly, Mackenzie hesitated. "Have you weighed the outcome? If BABA vanishes, you're gone."

"Mac, I know the consequences. Is the trip a go?"

"I'm not sure. The delta is a huge area. And desperate trips usually don't end well. Can't you be more specific? Personally, I think BABA returns to New Orleans. It completes the circle."

"Boss, listen. New tokens give us a huge advantage. If nearby, we can nail his sorry ass and prevent a catastrophe."

"Well, I like the boldness. That's the old Morgan. But can you deliver? Honestly, I should say no. But this case is unique."

With the Dubliner's reluctant approval, the team exited to pack. Takeoff from a nearby corporate airport was at 3 p.m.

Landing in the ebony chill of early evening, the FBI Gulfstream taxied to an isolated hanger. Greeted by obsequious Memphis agents, the visitors were escorted to a downtown hotel. Foregoing supper, the team opted for room service and quickly vanished. An early morning call was expected.

CHAPTER 13

Monday, January 18

The clamoring was deep-throated, unfamiliar, and maddening. Fumbling to answer the hotel phone Morgan growled. "Mac, it's 4:10 a.m. What the hell?"

"Your hunch was right. Fulton was the location."

"Is it nearby?"

"Yeah. A local cop discovered a wrapped head, portable scale, and oozing heart. The tape was yellow."

"The victim was a woman?"

"Yep. But gender didn't matter. Her body was carefully positioned to face east. The note read BABA-4."

"So, another Fed was damned. Was there a token?"

"A black bull. Hopefully, Raz has an explanation."

"Anything else?"

"Yeah. There was a bizarre drawing on the victim's abdomen."

"When do we leave?"

"Meet in the lobby at 8 a.m. The hotel is arranging breakfast and transportation. The Memphis bureau is providing office space. Go back to sleep."

As the team huddled in the cozy confines of a small conference room, the Dubliner's dour mood was telling. "Our

Fed was retired and in poor health. Tased and stabbed, Lucy Wainwright's heart was removed and her head wrapped. Her frail body was found shortly after 3 a.m. The lone token was a black bull. The M.E. also noted a bizarre drawing on her abdomen. She sent this picture."

"Mac, this killing makes zero sense," blurted Morgan. "Fulton is an unknown. Wainwright is an unknown. The drawing is an unknown. Why?"

In unison, three sets of eyes darted to the Egyptian. Suppressing a giant yawn, the diminutive academic was struggling to remain awake.

"Raz, can you explain the drawing?"

"Agent Fallon, the image was a deliberate misrepresentation of the "Eye of Horus." As stated, the eye restored life. However, this drawing depicted death. The dreadful artwork was intentional."

"But why? Morgan's right. Something's not Kosher. What makes Fulton so damn important?"

"That is for you to decide. The river city parallels ancient Cairo. It's east bank and *north* of Memphis."

"But that's impossible!" Rocketing to his feet Nash glowered at the diminutive Egyptologist. "North can't be right."

"Agent, I can read maps. The answer is correct."

Instantly, Mackenzie intervened. "Morgan, what the hell? What difference does it make?"

"The location should have been south or east of Memphis. A pattern was forming that foretold BABA's next move."

"Well, you guessed wrong. Likely, he's vanished."

"No. There's still unfinished business. Raz, does Fulton offer any hint regarding the next location?"

"Agent Nash, it's not that easy. Numerous towns in Tennessee, Mississippi, *and* Louisiana juxtapose the ancient Nile. BABA could pop up anywhere."

"Does any Egyptian pharaoh offer a clue?"

"Which dynasty? Which period?"

Angered by the bickering, Mackenzie immediately barked an order. "Dammit, that's enough. There is no obvious pattern. Meredith, is the President heading south anytime soon?"

"No. Hyatt has nothing scheduled. I checked the major cities and along the Mississippi River."

"Then we're stymied. Unless something changes, we are returning to Dallas."

Following a much-needed break, the Special Agent rebooted the meeting. "Jameson called. Barring a minor miracle, we're finished as a team within twenty-four hours. His tone was less than cordial."

"I concur," parroted Lindsey. "Our ghost is like the wind... impossible to catch."

"That's bullshit, Meredith. Even BABA makes mistakes. Raz, explain the bull."

"Agent Nash, that too is virtually impossible."

"Why?"

"In ancient Egypt, there were numerous bulls. Did the token reference the 'Apis'? Was it the 'Mnevis'? Was this the 'Jubilee'? There were many others as well."

"But that token had to convey something."

"It does. '*Catch me if you can.*' The symbol is a taunt. Like the bull, BABA is an enigma. He's impossible to predict, locate or understand."

"Dammit, Raz, that attitude just chafes my ass. Nothing is impossible. Does the ninth-hour help in any way?"

"That is for you to determine."

"Just summarize the fricking hour. And cut the mocking. It is so damn irritating."

"As you wish. With the approaching dawn, the Sun God encountered Osiris's twelve alarming guardians. These fire-breathing cobras feasted off the blood of their captives."

"Mac, that's the missing piece," yelped Morgan. "RE must overcome a significant danger to achieve his end goal. Underscore '*significant*.' Who represents his final enemy?"

"Obviously, you want the President to be the answer. But I disagree. So does Jameson." Refusing to open Pandora's Box, the Special Agent barked a new order. "Meredith, come with me. Raz, go with Mr. Nash. Untangle this mess. The clock is ticking."

Huddled in an unused office, Nash glared at the sugar junkie. As the academic munched on pastries, his anger simmered. The dots were frolicking but not connecting.

"Teacher, was a particular bull revered by the people?"

"Oh yes. The Apis was sacred in Memphis. In life, the bull represented the local god Ptah. In death, it identified with Osiris. Infused with godlike abilities, the Apis cured disease and ensured virility. Black in color, the Apis was easily recognizable and always pictured with a disk residing between the horns."

"Was the bull celebrated or feared?"

"It was adored. The Apis symbolized new life. The god-calf had distinctive markings. The cow was never able to birth again."

"What were the markings?"

"A white diamond was emblazoned on the calf's forehead. Hidden under the tongue was a scarab. An eagle's image was imprinted on the back. Double hairs on the tail concluded the markings. The bull's life span was short. After fifteen years, the Apis was sacrificed and mummified."

"But why kill a god-like bull? That makes no sense."

"The Apis had a singular purpose. It was sacrificed once

the pharaoh became a living god. This sacred deity ruled the animal kingdom."

"Anything else?'

"Possibly. After thirty years of rule, an aging and often frail pharaoh held a 'Royal Jubilee' or 'Heb-Sed.' This festival was designed to showcase his physicality and impress the people. The newly anointed god-king ran with the Apis."

"That sounds like Pamplona. Young Spaniards risk their lives running with the bulls. But where's the connection? That token means something. Spain equates to southern Europe. Is there a significant city immediately *south* of Memphis?"

"No. Only tourist stops juxtapose the ancient Nile until you reach Thebes or New Orleans."

"Then we focus on the Tennessee names. Mackenzie and Jameson can run checks. Maybe some small town houses another retired Fed. We need something to pop ASAP."

With list in hand, Morgan hastened to the Dubliner's office and presented his meager findings. "Mac, I think the token references direction. If so, BABA is moving south. Can you alert authorities in Southhaven, Horn Lake, and Walls?"

"I can. But it's a long shot. Does Raz agree?"

"No. He thinks it's a waste of time."

"That's my thinking. BABA could easily head north. St. Louis seems more plausible."

"Possibly. But only southern cities juxtapose RE's ancient map. Eventually, our ghost meanders to Mississippi, but not yet."

"Morgan, is there anything tangible to sway Jameson? We need to buy some time."

"No. Everything's speculative."

"Then it's over. We return to the hotel at 3 p.m. The team needs rest. Though unlikely, another dawn murder is possible."

Mired in depression, Nash relaxed in bed and stared at his notes. To his dismay, the case was ending with a whimper. Unexpectedly, the hotel phone clamored. Noting the 4 p.m. hour he sighed. Likely the caller was Mackenzie coordinating dinner.

"Agent for hire. May I help you?"

"You are not funny. We've got a huge problem. Meredith has been tased."

"Is she alive?"

"Yeah. Her injuries are minor. EMTs are bringing her to the hotel accompanied by a doctor."

"Any details?"

"She was ambushed while jogging in a nearby park. Tased from behind, Meredith was left helpless on the trail."

"Was BABA the shooter?"

"Locals are puzzled. But it was his signature. Either he didn't have time to kill or simply passed on the opportunity. Other runners were nearby."

"Dammit. The bastard knows our every move."

"That's an understatement. Meet me in Meredith's room."

Shortly after 5 p.m., the pair huddled with the victim. Shaking uncontrollably, the analyst was conscious but pale. Her immaculate strawberry blonde hair was tangled and matted after plunging headfirst into the hardpan. Numerous abrasions dotted her face and torso. Adorning her right cheek was a dark purplish bruise. A jammed right shoulder created pain with every movement. Refusing meds, she doggedly tried to provide details. Hovering nearby was an impatient doctor.

As Morgan gently caressed her hand, Meredith eagerly responded. Leaning close he whispered softly. "Hey, you're going to be okay. You're safe."

"Don't leave me."

"Never. Can you tell us anything?"

"I was jogging in the park. Nearing a cluster of trees, I felt a horrible sting in my back. A step later, I was writhing on the ground. The pain was excruciating."

"Did you see anything?"

"No. It was a hit and run ambush."

"Other runners sprinted to your rescue," added Mackenzie. "But they were fifty yards away. The wooded area was clear when they arrived. The police have no suspects."

"Mac, was there a token?"

"Yeah. There was one."

"Then it had to be BABA. The bastard shot, tossed, and vanished. What was the symbol?"

"Oddly, it was another pharaoh. But why?"

Rudely interrupting was the doctor. "Your time is up. Please leave. I need to remove bits of gravel from the abrasions. Plus, your colleague needs rest."

In the hallway, Fallon fumed. "Dammit, this is so frustrating. BABA appears and disappears at will. To him, it's a fricking game. Let's go to my room."

With Raz in attendance, the trio huddled in the Dubliner's suite. Impatient, Morgan was quick to speculate. "Boss, BABA did *not* want to kill Meredith."

"But why? Hell, he had the opportunity."

"The tasing conveyed a message. But other than attracting attention, what did he gain?"

Flashing a wry grin, the Egyptian floated a response. "Agent, you've just answered your own question. Hey, I haven't left Memphis."

"But that makes no sense," growled Mackenzie. "Neither does the token."

"Agent Fallon, this particular symbol has real significance. Like a modern-day pharaoh, BABA had the power to give life or take it. In a merciful act, he spared Dr. Lindsey."

"I agree," added Nash. "But there's more. The token references both life *and* death. Mercifully, Meredith still lives. Unfortunately, a symbolic pharaoh soon dies."

"Are you referencing Hyatt? Two hours ago, I would have reamed your ass. But things have dramatically changed."

"Mac, the President *is* in grave danger. That's the underlying message."

"Possibly. But there's nothing definitive for Jameson. There's nothing that links Meredith to Hyatt."

"That's not my assessment," countered Morgan. "The dots connect."

"How?"

"The underworld journey ends at 5 a.m. This final hour is critical for RE to dissolve and evolve into a new orb. But the deity must get past a final hurdle."

"Meaning?" Dubious about a mysticism connection to reality, Mackenzie eyed her partner.

"Today's RE faces the same challenge. The President poses a real threat to his plan. Hyatt's death marks the beginning of America's demise."

"Morgan, I don't know. It's pure conjecture. But if true, what's next?"

"Dissolution juxtaposes *rebirth*. As the sun rises, RE's shadowy partner finally emerges. His dawning signifies a shift in world power and economic rebirth for adversaries. You must warn Jameson."

"That's not going to happen. Look, it's a damn good story. But without something concrete, I'm helpless."

"Fine. Let the Director explain Hyatt's death."

CHAPTER 14

Tuesday, January 19

The incessant clamoring was relentless. Startled by the predawn call, Nash responded curtly. "Mac, it's pitch-black outside."

"Get your ass out of bed. Our ghost bleeds red. Meet me in five."

"Where?"

"My room. I've ordered coffee."

Ten minutes later, two bedraggled figures trudged into the Dubliner's room and robotically poured coffee. The Special Agent's white-knuckle look was telling. "BABA has struck again. But this was no easy kill. Our ghost was wounded. Morgan, your delta warning nearly saved a life. The Fed was sleeping with a gun."

"Location?"

"The murder occurred in Germantown, a Memphis suburb. There was a single token. The message read BABA-2."

"But that's wrong. Three is the correct number. BABA doesn't make mistakes."

"Well, he screwed up this morning. Our ghost made a sound, got wounded, scribbled a wrong number, and vamoosed. The victim's wife was sleeping upstairs. Awakened by the shot, she immediately called 911. The Fed was relegated to the couch because of a snoring problem."

"Token?"

"There was one. A black man was wearing an odd-shaped, plumed crown."

"That was Arensnuphis," yelped Raz. "The victim had to be African American. The token represented a *Nubian* pharaoh."

"But that doesn't tie to Egypt. The skin coloring is wrong."

"Agent Fallon, Nubia, located near the southern border, was Egypt's sworn enemy. Nubians were often conquered and enslaved. Centuries later, the country grew stronger and invaded. Numerous Nubian kings became Egyptian pharaohs."

"That's it," cried Morgan. "Ignore the color. The pharaoh points to leadership. What about time of death?"

"The M.E. estimated 4 a.m. The police arrived shortly thereafter."

"That's also wrong. It's an hour later."

Unexpectedly, the deep clamoring of Mackenzie's hotel phone interrupted. Within seconds her face was aghast.

"Partner, you were right. Another murder occurred in Piperton. Time of death was 3 a.m. Given the rural setting, the Fed's body wasn't discovered until a short time ago."

"Mac, that confirms it. Memphis *is* the epicenter. BABA is combing the suburbs."

Agent Fallon, may I interject a question?"

"Of course, Raz."

"Are these murders of *equal significance?"*

"Equal? That's impossible to answer. Logically, I would say yes."

"What about you, Agent Nash?"

"I concur. What's your point?"

"Archeologists view things differently. I see these killings as both *weighted and symbolic*. The first victim carries greater weight than the second. That explains the altered time. These deaths symbolically pose a dire warning. Not only is the President in grave danger but also the Vice President."

"Or you could modify the symbolism," countered Morgan. "One *or* the other is the target. Mac, you must warn Jameson. BABA is down to his last victim."

"That's out of the question. Without a confirmed date, target, or location, the Director isn't going to listen. Plus, BABA's wound may change everything. Hell, he could rehab in Miami or disappear forever. Slap on some decent clothes. We leave at eight. More dots need to connect."

Irked by the dismissal, Nash huffed from the room. Trailing several steps behind, was the academic.

As a hallway clock chimed the nine o'clock hour, Morgan and Mackenzie sat dejectedly in the small conference room. Even the talkative Raz was quiet. Uncertainty tamped the next move. Unexpectedly, a haggard figure quietly entered and took a seat.

"Meredith, what an unexpected surprise," beamed Morgan. "Your presence brightens a rather grim morning."

"I've been released for limited duty. Any news?"

"We're mired in the muck," growled the Dubliner. "We have a wounded killer and two murders. Yet, we're stymied."

"Maybe not," replied Raz. "BABA needs to heal. Mississippi is not real populated."

"South would be logical. Does he deviate from the river?"

"Hell no," blurted Morgan. "The bastard hugs the Mississippi before returning to New Orleans."

"Why?"

"A NOLA return symbolizes RE's rebirth and perfection. It completes the circle."

"But neither the President nor Vice President is traveling to Louisiana," countered Mackenzie. "A short drive to Mississippi makes sense but only for rehab, not murder."

"I respectfully disagree."

"Why?"

"RE has a timetable, Mac. Healthy or not, our assassin has to be in position to fulfill the contract or face death. Look, presidential trips are often secretive. We've got to warn officials in Greenville, Vicksburg, and Natchez. The Memphis alert almost saved a life."

"I can make the calls. But who's going to listen? Is there anything else?"

"What about Mississippi's leaders? Have you received any itineraries?"

"The Director faxed a few. But none have been helpful. The bigwigs are huddled in D.C. State officials are headed to Jackson."

"When?"

"This weekend. They're attending an evangelical conference."

"Dammit," muttered Morgan. "We're drowning with no lifeline. Has Jameson received any updates regarding White House travels?"

"No. We've been blackballed for weeks. But I did contact a confidential source. He has promised to call at the first opportunity."

"Does that mean hours or days?" The surprising query came from Lindsey. "Our time is short."

"I expect to hear within twenty-four hours. Okay, we split up, head south, and hopefully catch a break. Morgan, you and Raz take Greenville. Meredith and I get Jackson. Locals can cover Natchez and Vicksburg. If BABA reappears, we move fast."

Completing the Greenville trip in a shroud of silence, the two men stopped for supper at a local diner. Dominating Morgan's mind was Hyatt's demise. Nervously rapping his fingers on the table his faraway look was telling.

"Agent, you haven't spoken for hours. Are you okay?"

"No. My gut says the prelude ends with a thunderous bang. Yet a critical piece is missing."

"You see but don't see."

"Exactly."

Unexpectedly, the Egyptian's face tensed and then twisted. Appearing in great agony he sat transfixed.

"Hey man, do I need to call 911?"

"No. My pain is purely psychological. I must apologize for my myopic thinking."

"I'm not following."

"Agent, you were absolutely correct about a missing piece. Queen Nefertiti has been in plain sight since day one."

"But you identified her dagger."

"The weapon was a mere tool. The real story was her *husband.*"

"Explain, but keep it simple."

Buoyed by the discovery Raz flashed a wry grin and continued. "Pharaoh Akhenaten shattered Egypt's conventional paradigm. It was a vital connection that I overlooked."

"Meaning?"

"Akhenaten was an extraordinary thinker. An avid sun worshipper, he shocked the nation by radically shifting to *monotheism.* The worship of a single god was theologically unthinkable. In a blink, Egypt's long-standing pantheon of gods was officially destroyed."

"What prompted the change?"

"Akhenaten believed the Sun God RE created life by warming the earth. There was no other explanation. In gratitude, he ordered the paradigm shift. Both Egyptians and conquered Mediterranean nations were forced to worship RE as their singular god."

"That was radical," interjected Morgan. "The priests had to be furious."

"They were outraged and quickly eliminated. But the youthful pharaoh wasn't finished. As a tribute to RE, Akhenaten erected Sun God monuments, created a new art form, and built a new capital. In effect, he fostered a religious and cultural revolution."

"Bingo! That's the missing piece. Ancient RE links to modern RE. With the dawning of each new day, the sun changes form as darkness morphs to light. Understanding this particular symbolism is critical. It's the linchpin that triggers RE's actions. The bastard is aping Akhenaten, attempting to create his own enlightened, altered world. Let's eat and get to the hotel. I need to update Mackenzie."

"Will your pragmatic boss listen?"

"With nothing tangible, that's laughable. But I can try."

CHAPTER 15

Wednesday, January 20

Annoyed by the deep clamoring of the hotel phone, Morgan refused to budge. Nestled under a mountain of covers, he felt warm and secure. Noting an array of dancing sunbeams, he finally answered. "Sorry, Mac. What's up?"

"Our ghost must be a rapid healer. But his latest murder makes zero sense. Meet us at the Greenville police station at 9 a.m."

Delayed by heavy traffic and road construction, the harried female twosome arrived a half-hour late. In a surly mood, Mackenzie summarized the surprise killing. "BABA's final victim was a *retired postal carrier and widower*. The Greenville murder occurred around 5 a.m. After he was tased and stabbed, the mailman's head was partially wrapped with red strips."

"But that's impossible," blurted Nash. "A postal carrier sends our elite assassin into retirement? The time is right. But the target is all wrong."

"There were new theatrics as well," grumbled Fallon. "The body was positioned to face *west,* not east. And the heart was *not* removed. Instead, BABA placed a *small plastic heart* on a portable scale of justice. The lightweight toy balanced perfectly with the white feather of truth."

"The widower passed judgment," chimed the academic. "BABA's previous victims were damned to extinction. But mercifully, he wanted the mail carrier's soul to ascend into the heavens."

"But why? BABA's a fricking killer, not some guardian angel. And this whole underworld business is pure make-believe." As her frustration flared, Mackenzie's fiery eyes glowered at Raz.

"I know," interrupted Morgan. "Let me answer."

"Okay. Impress me."

"Mac, the widower, was *not* his final target. Nor was this a mercy killing. Instead, this was another taunt. Like Meredith's tasing, BABA did the unexpected."

"I actually concur," quipped Lindsey. "Like Carlos, he loves the chase. The thrill fuels his ego and manhood. No doubt he's rewarding himself with some whore. What about a token?"

"There was one. But it too was absolutely bizarre. The woman had an elongated neck and a weird headdress. Two horns cradled a round orb."

"That's Queen Nefertiti," yelped Raz. "The royal headdress represents Hathor, goddess of love and nurturing. The postman is reunited with his wife."

"But a heavenly ascension makes zero sense. There's no connection. What makes an ancient queen so damn important?"

"Agent Fallon, Nefertiti's relevance was her marriage to Akhenaten. The young pharaoh was Egypt's most revolutionary and forward-thinking leader. His singular worship of the Sun God RE triggered a true paradigm shift."

"That's enlightening. But it doesn't answer my question. What's the tangible connection?" Tamping her volatile temper, the Special Agent barked orders. "Morgan, you and Raz find the link. Meredith, come with me. We need to calm the locals. Apparently, this part of the Deep South doesn't appreciate Feds."

With their abrupt departure, Nash peered at the cosmopolitan academic. "Forget the paradigm. Forget monotheism. Focus on Akhenaton. What single characteristic stands out?"

"Agent, you're asking the impossible. This revolutionary thinker changed the culture of an entire society."

"Give it a try."

"If pressed, *dedication* was his shining characteristic. The king never wavered in his belief about the Sun God or radical new order."

"That's the..." Suddenly, Morgan hesitated. "Wait. That's too obvious and likely another trap. We need to *reverse* our thinking. BABA wants us focused on the revolutionary ruler. Like the postal carrier, the token is a ruse. The bastard wants us preoccupied while plotting Hyatt's demise."

Unexpectedly, the academic flashed a wry grin. "I actually agree. To him, it's a game. It's best against best. That's the Egyptian way. If BABA wins, Hyatt dies. If you win, he dies."

"But how do we stop him?"

"You outwit him. Think of Nefertiti as a chess piece. The queen marks BABA's move."

"If so, what's my play? How do I counter?"

"You check with the missing piece."

"Which is?"

"*Location*. Remember, this is a match of wits. With my assistance, you possess a huge advantage." Flashing a thin smile, the academic unexpectedly winked. "I know the location."

Suddenly Morgan's eyes brightened with excitement. "That's it! The modern location marks the assassination. Raz, this *is* a test. Find the city. Save the President. But we need your ancient map. Otherwise, BABA wins."

"Agent, slow down. The final act is just beginning. *Vicksburg* is your answer. The river city juxtaposes Akhenaten's ancient capital."

"But according to Meredith, there's nothing scheduled in Vicksburg. It's not in play. Plus, there's no definitive date or target."

As uncertainty shrouded his mind, Morgan hesitated. He stared blankly at the wall, his mind racing. Several minutes later, a faint grin appeared on his lips.

"However, when you add Vicksburg to boat, river, dawn, and RE, a pattern begins to form. I can sense it."

"Agent, your imagination is impressive. But, reality paints a different picture. A thick labyrinth protects BABA. Each move allows him to remain a step ahead."

"Okay, location explains the latest token. But I'm curious. The queen's elongated neck is absurd. It's badly deformed."

"Agent, Akhenaten was an extremist. Revolutionary art was the centerpiece of his new empire."

"But why? Hell, he had everything."

"The youthful king thrived on controversy. Thus, he and Nefertiti were always depicted with alien-shaped heads, full lips, snaky eyes, long necks, pendulous breasts, paunchy stomachs, spindly limbs, and swollen hips."

"You're describing an ancient Picasso. Weren't most pharaohs portrayed as mighty warriors?"

"Oh, yes. They wanted to be physically imposing. But Akhenaten was unique. Futuristic thinking was his strength. Thus, every aspect of his kingdom had to be radical."

"Did the people ever revolt? Hell, their entire culture was being obliterated. Plus, their god-like king was depicted with feminine qualities."

"The story didn't end well. Akhenaten and his revolutionary dreams were obliterated from Egyptian history. In the eyes of most historians and scholars, the Pharaoh never existed."

"That's my worst fear. Is extinction Hyatt's fate?"

~

As the team regrouped, the Dubliner's cheeks pulsated a fiery red. Her meeting with the locals had not gone well.

"Boss, you look livid."

"Meredith and I have been dealing with village idiots. Hopefully, you've made progress."

"Possibly," uttered Morgan. "But the answer is mixed. The token points to Pharaoh Akhenaten. If correct, it references an altered world. But there's no tangible proof."

"What triggers the global reset?"

"*Dissolution.* Act One ends with a tumultuous bang. The President's assassination triggers a series of apocalyptic events that seal America's fate and changes the world."

"If true, where's the location?"

"Vicksburg. The river city parallels Akhenaton's revolutionary capital."

"What about date? A Vicksburg stakeout could be a waste of time. Hell, it could be forever."

"A definitive date remains unanswered. Hell, even Hyatt is questionable. There may be a mystery target. RE is the master of surprises."

"Dammit, Morgan, that's enough. I need a straight answer. Is there anything concrete for Jameson?"

"No. Vicksburg represents a best guess."

"Then it's a dead issue."

"Fine. Hyatt's blood is on your hands. Proof or not, I think he's the target."

"You seem pretty adamant. Why?"

"It's the dawn prophecy. The Sun God eliminates his greatest obstacle before morphing into a new image."

"Okay. Let's say Hyatt gets whacked. RE continues…"

Instantly Nash interrupted. "Mac, that's incorrect. There is no continuation. The deity *evolves or changes form*. This new figure is not RE. It's his shadowy partner. With Hyatt eliminated a powerful eastern figure emerges with the clout to reshape the world."

In total disbelief, the Dubliner slowly shook her head. "Partner, I don't know. You spin a story with no substance. Committing our limited resources to some mythological prophecy is too much."

As Morgan tensed, Meredith quickly intervened. "What are you picturing? Are you seeing a symbol or face?"

"Neither. My mind flashes two unshakeable words."

"Which are?"

"*Radical change.*" These people are hell-bent on unleashing the omega accord and redefining the global roadmap."

"But that's virtually impossible," growled the Dubliner. "It's not going to happen. Convince me with something real." Eager for an aspirin and a nip of Irish whiskey, Mackenzie barked a new order. "We remain in Greenville until I hear from the Director. This hell-hole is our new home."

CHAPTER 16

Thursday, January 21

As morning sunbeams flickered through the curtains, an all-too-familiar clamoring shattered the tranquil setting. Noting the time, Nash was surprised. It was well past 7 a.m. "Boss, what's up?"

"Absolutely nothing. It was a blessed, peaceful night."

"That could be good or bad. A BABA disappearance leaves us hanging."

"We shall see. Meet us at the Greenville station."

~

Arriving early, Morgan isolated himself in a small cubicle. Overwhelmed by numerous unknowns; depression gnawed at his soul. Unexpectedly, a familiar figure appeared in the doorway. The Dubliner's grim expression was telling. "I ran your theory by Jameson. As expected, he was livid."

"The man's a damn fool. Forget the handbook. The tokens connect. A tsunami of pure evil is slowly building."

"That's possible. But forget Hyatt. The Secret Service is keeping him under wraps."

"Mac, frayed blankets have holes. JFK was killed. Reagan was shot. I'm convinced that Hyatt has a date with death within the next few days. Have you heard from your source?"

"I'm expecting a call this afternoon. Keep digging." Abruptly, the Special Agent vanished down a long corridor. Irked by the intrusion, Nash meandered to the snack bar. Dominating his mind was a daunting question. Spying the academic, he pulled up a chair.

"Raz, is Vicksburg the right call?"

"Does it really matter? BABA is a ghost. The President is safe. The case ends with a whimper."

"What do you mean?"

"According to Dr. Lindsey, we're returning to Dallas this evening. Director Jameson issued the directive citing our lack of progress. Plus, Agent Fallon has no desire to remain in Mississippi."

As a hallway clock tolled the two o'clock hour, Morgan's solitude was rudely shattered as a harried figure barged into the room. Mackenzie's frenzied expression was revealing. "We are *not* returning to Dallas. Things have dramatically changed. We're headed to Jackson."

"Your source?"

"Yep. And it's getting very interesting. The President *is* secretly flying to Jackson. At dawn tomorrow he's addressing southern evangelical leaders. The trip is strictly hush-hush. There's no press or publicity. Flying military, Hyatt is staying at a downtown hotel."

"Where's the meeting?"

"First Baptist is the host."

Suddenly, Nash hesitated. "Mac, that's not right. Jackson *isn't* a river city. It *doesn't* fit the pattern."

"Then your logic is flawed."

"But..."

"Zip it. There's more. The President is traveling with a minuscule Secret Service detail. He does not want to attract attention."

"But that's insane. The damn fool towers over most agents. If exposed, he's dead."

"The Secret Service is confident. Other than a few steps fronting the church, Hyatt is inside."

"But even a short walk exposes his head and shoulders. It's an easy shot for a sniper."

"Sniper? That's not BABA's style. It's too impersonal."

"Mac, forget analytics. RE thrives on the unexpected. We need to leave. An early arrival gives us an opportunity to pinpoint shooting locations."

"That's doable. We travel in thirty minutes."

"What about the stakeout? Can your forty-year-old ass handle an all-nighter?"

"That's an insult. And yeah, my cute little butt can survive four or five hours. Plus, the Jackson office is providing extra agents. We can take positions before midnight."

"Good. That gives us extra time. BABA knows his spot. I doubt he shows until 4 a.m. or later."

"Morgan, listen. Tamp the excitement. This trip is a huge risk. A failed stakeout ends your career. Jameson wants you ousted."

"I get the picture. Is the assassination fact or fiction? Am I sane or crazy? Screw the Director. Let's roll."

Arriving in the blackness of early evening, the team zoomed to the Jackson office. Within minutes a contingent of agents was headed to nearby First Baptist Church. Armed with preassigned locations, six teams scurried in different directions. As they cautiously approached their assigned target, the Dallas duo stopped and gaped. The dilapidated three-story antebellum structure was abandoned and badly damaged. It was also a mere two-hundred yards from the church entrance. Clear of obstruction, several corner windows represented a sniper's dream.

"Let's peruse the third floor," whispered the Dubliner. "The corner office seems perfect."

Moving in unison, the pair sprinted the grimy stairs. As anticipated, the dusty office was littered with needles, shards, and trash.

"Mac, even a half-blind BABA could make this shot. Hyatt is six-foot-four."

"Forget it. This location is too close. Personally, I think our ghost is a no-show. It's too risky. Let's canvas the area and return to the Jackson office A miserable night awaits us."

As a distant church bell chimed the bewitching hour the black-clad teams returned and took positions. Jacked with adrenalin, the Texas twosome created a makeshift position fronting the corner window. Assigned as housekeeper Nash diligently policed the filthy concrete floor. Within minutes his bag was filled with needles and trash.

"My butt is going to ache like hell tomorrow," moaned Mackenzie. "This is likely a fool's mission. Hey, is that glass in your hand?"

"Yeah. I'm going to sprinkle a few shards around the doorway and stairwell. If BABA crunches, we shoot."

CHAPTER 17

Friday, January 22

Shortly after 2:30 am, Morgan nudged his shivering partner. "We've got company downstairs."

"Get ready."

With weapons primed and pointed at the door, both listened and waited. Several minutes later, the movement stopped.

"Check it out," grumbled the Dubliner. "This is your show. I'm frozen."

Bypassing the glass shards, Nash moved stealthily out the door and down the stairs. Gripped tightly in his right hand was the imposing Glock with a chambered round. A check of the second floor proved fruitless. Nearing the first floor, he heard shuffling to his right. The corner office was obstruction-free. Peering into the dimly lit room, he let out a disappointed sigh. The intruder was a homeless man wrestling with a tattered sleeping bag. Positioned nearby was a cheap bottle of wine. Tamping his frustration, Morgan retraced his steps and plopped next to his quivering boss.

"Our visitor is a vagrant. The all-nighter may be a waste of time."

"Forget it," quipped Mackenzie. "A BABA no-show keeps Hyatt alive."

"I still think the President is taking a huge risk. That minuscule detail isn't about to leave him to canvas the neighborhood. This rush trip cloaked in secrecy is a joke."

"That's why we're here. We're his backup. The Secret Service has no knowledge of our presence."

"Well, I hope the man survives," admitted Morgan. "But failure ends my career. I'm not ready to leave."

"Hell, ranching might be fun. You might enjoy it."

"That's not going to happen. There's still unfinished business."

"Morgan, listen. BABA is already the winner. Yeah, you can blow his brains out. But you can't resurrect your family. Revenge is going to destroy your soul."

"What soul? Hell, my feelings were destroyed a long time ago."

"Fresh air could prove therapeutic."

"No. It's either BABA or me. The bastard needs to die."

Aching from a shivering body and sore butt, Mackenzie glanced at her watch. The time was 5:20 a.m. Something was terribly wrong. The President was a no-show. Suddenly she felt a hard nudge. A procession of five SUVs was approaching the well-lit entry to First Baptist Church.

Peering through the open window, both watched as Secret Service agents departed vehicles and scrambled into position. In a practiced motion, the minuscule contingent surrounded the middle SUV. Seconds later, a stately Robert Hyatt emerged from the vehicle and ascended the flight of steps. He paused to shake several hands before entering the church; his head and shoulders were clearly visible.

In abject frustration, Morgan threw up his arms in disgust. "Well, that's it. Hyatt lives. And I'm toast. When is he leaving?"

"The conference ends around 9 a.m."

Suddenly, both heard crunches on the stairwell. Pivoting, they aimed their weapons at the doorway. To their delight, the relief team entered the room. The long, hellish night was finally over.

At 7:30 a.m., the Dubliner reconvened the team in a small conference room. The update was brief and somber. "We've been ordered to Dallas. The stakeout was an utter disaster. We're leaving late this afternoon." In a dour mood, the exhausted Dubliner exited.

As the eleven o'clock hour approached, Mackenzie located her male counterparts. "I bring good news. The President is safely back at the hotel."

"That's great. When is he leaving?"

"Morgan, I neither know nor care. Hyatt is no longer our concern. I suggest we break for an early lunch. It's likely our last meal together."

Reconvening after a quiet meal, the foursome met for final instructions. Unexpectedly, a highly animated agent burst into the conference room.

"Agent Fallon, I have news. An unidentified body was dumped near the M.E.'s office."

"So? How does that concern us?"

"The victim's head was wrapped with red strips. There was also a note. Apparently, your killer has reappeared."

Rocketing to his feet, Nash fist pumped and yelped excitedly. "I knew it. BABA has unfinished business."

As her fiery green eyes crackled with anticipation, the Dubliner instantly barked orders. "Agent, we need prints, pictures, and blood samples ASAP. Hell, we need everything."

As the rookie sprinted from the room, a golden cape of exoneration nestled around Nash's shoulders. *His* killer was lurking. "Hey, we're back in business."

"Not yet. It's Jameson's call. The victim could be another mailman."

"Mac, this is classic BABA. Emerging from the shadows he does the unexpected. Call the Director. Plead our case."

"I'm not..."

Rudely interrupting, a second agent barged into the room. "Agent Fallon, you've got to see this photo. The tattoo was emblazoned on the victim's massive arm."

"Impressive. What's the significance?"

"The mountain man belonged to a deep-south paramilitary group. Stabbed multiple times, he retaliated before dying. The M.E. noted lots of blood on the clothing. Your ghost likely sustained a major injury."

"Dammit! We finally catch a break, and BABA disappears. Fresh wounds finish our team."

"Maybe not," interrupted the agent. "This particular tattoo has history. Members of this elite group have served as mercenaries in numerous hot spots. They've been trained by a Captain B.J. Forrest. The former Army Ranger was seriously wounded in the Gulf War."

"Who was his commander?"

"General Mark Robison."

"That's interesting but not relevant," growled the Special Agent. "Anything else?"

"Maybe. As of late, their focus has been Africa and the Middle East. The operators are paid well to protect...and kill." Flashing a satisfied grin, the young agent abruptly exited.

With his departure, Morgan wasted no time in posing the obvious. "What prompted BABA to kill a mountain man?"

"I don't know. You tell me."

"There can be only one logical explanation. The killing is a distraction while BABA stalks Hyatt. Our ghost wants us fixated on Forrest. But I suggest we focus on Robison while keeping an eye on the President."

"But that makes zero sense. Robison is a four-star and the Army's number two man. Plus, he's tight with top dog General Riggs."

"Mac, that resume makes him the perfect mole. Hawkish, he's well-positioned and no fan of Hyatt."

"But there's no proof," flamed Mackenzie. "There's nothing to change Jameson's mind."

Unexpectedly, Raz interrupted. "Agent Fallon, may I pose an *inverted* question?"

"Sure. A different perspective might be good."

"Did BABA *kill* in order that Hyatt might *live?*"

"Interesting. But your logic is confusing."

"Was the President ever a target? That has always been our assumption. But what if we were wrong? Perhaps the covert operator was BABA's final kill."

"That's bullshit," blurted Nash. "Hyatt *is* the final target. Nothing else makes sense. BABA is simply waiting for the right opportunity. Boss, read the note. Maybe something pops."

"It doesn't."

"Why?"

"Morgan, there is no message. It simply reads: "*The Fourth D*."

Suddenly Nash's mouth gaped as if jolted by a thunderbolt. "Mac, the wording is extremely relevant."

"Why?"

"D" implies *distraction.* It's another taunt. The bastard wants us mired in confusion. But we deviate and outwit him."

"But how? Robison isn't a lead. Neither is Forrest. And Hyatt is safe."

"He's not if you add a fifth 'D.' *Disinformation.* That's BABA's game...a clever mix of distraction and disinformation. Mac, keep the focus on Vicksburg. Hyatt dies if we ignore the threat."

"Maybe. But it's out of my hands. Jameson is making the calls. Vicksburg is likely a non-factor."

"Fine. But hear me out. There's also another scenario."

"Does it involve General Robison?"

"No."

"Is it feasible?"

"Definitely. RE's D.C. mole works for the Secret Service. It's the perfect set-up. The minion relays the President's every move."

"I actually agree," chimed Lindsey. "But there's more. The plant works in Hyatt's *protection* detail."

"Interesting. But there's nothing concrete to sway Jameson." Scowling, the Special Agent anxiously rapped her fingers. "Look, I want to act. But I'm helpless. Let me call Jameson and beg for more time. Afterward, we break for an early supper."

"Can Agent Nash drive me? Columbia needs an update on my schedule. It shouldn't take long."

"Sure, Raz. Meet us at Aunt Jessie's Café. Supposedly, it's a popular haven. Morgan, check out a car and get cracking. Hopefully, I can sway the Director."

Twenty minutes later, the Dallas men meandered to the rear parking lot. The seldom-used loaner was located on a back row. Nearing the dusty sedan, they were approached by two men in dark suits. Sensing trouble, Nash instinctively reached for the Glock.

"Release the weapon or die." The unseen command was harsh, confusing, and eerily familiar. "My gun is aimed at your back."

The tone was cruel. . Unexpected.

"Raz... is that you? What the hell?"

Flashing Berettas, the two strangers quickly relieved Morgan of his weapon. Stunned by the Egyptian's betrayal, his mind twisted in confusion. "Dammit, I thought we were teammates."

"That is a rather flawed assumption. What you think is irrelevant. What you see is real."

"But..."

"Shut the hell up!"

"Just who are you?"

"I'm Apophis."

Ignoring the danger, Nash choked back a chuckle. "Hell, you're no giant snake. You're just a piss-ant little prick."

"I may be small but deadly. I'm like the asp that bit your daughter."

"You son-of-a-bitch!" Enraged, Morgan whirled. But his movement was quickly stopped by the suits.

"Agent, it's your choice. Your pathetic life ends now or later. No help is coming."

"Get in." The Middle Eastern accent was steeled. Robotically Morgan slid into the backseat, his mind a tangled web. For weeks he had trusted, even befriended, the academic.

"So, nothing was real?"

"Only my acting was genuine." Riding shotgun, the Egyptologist turned and smirked. "For weeks, I have led you on a merry chase. BABA was never in any real danger."

Bristling, Nash sat defiantly. "Hell, you're just another traitor with a funky name. No doubt you're making lots of money. But you are never going to spend it."

"Unfortunately, you'll never know. After tonight a third urn will reside on your mantle." Flashing a sadistic Cheshire grin, the academic beamed.

"You bastard! I'll get..." Unexpectedly, Morgan felt a prick. In a blink, his bastardized world went black.

As the café overflowed with enthusiastic customers, Mackenzie grew impatient. Irked at the delay, she contacted the Jackson office. Two minutes later, her counterpart returned the call. "Mac, your partner signed for a loaner and left a while ago."

"Jim, check security cameras. Something's not right."

A short time later, the veteran agent returned the call. "We've got a huge problem. Morgan has been kidnapped."

"Kidnapped? By whom?"

"It was your Egyptian buddy plus two pals. The smug bastard was holding a gun. Your partner was forced into the back seat."

"Dammit." Seething at the betrayal, Mackenzie uttered a curt response. "We're headed your way." As the line clicked silent her volatile temper erupted. Slamming her palm against the table, plates, and utensils scattered in all directions.

"Mackenzie, what the hell?"

"Morgan's been kidnapped."

"Who?"

"It was our academic and two buddies. Did you see this coming?"

"No. I thought Raz was part of the team. I've never been more shocked."

"That makes two of us." As her fiery emerald eyes crackled with fury, Mackenzie canceled the order and requested coffees to go.

"Dammit, Morgan was right. The pieces *were* coming together. Panicked, Raz must have contacted his master."

"Our Judas played us like chumps and orchestrated every move."

"Were there any signs? Was Raz any different today?"

"No. He was riding a sugar high un…"

"Until that young Jackson agent barged into the room and underscored BABA's wound." Rudely interrupting, the Dubliner completed the sentence. "Then he grew extremely quiet and aloof. His whole demeanor changed."

"They likely knew each other. Both were Egyptians recruited by RE."

"That makes sense. But the timing is off. Why kidnap Morgan when Jameson is dismantling the team? Something's amiss."

Unexpectedly, the Dubliner's phone buzzed. Answering immediately, she listened intently. Thirty seconds later the call ended.

"Well?"

"Jim's people located the car. As expected, it was abandoned. There was no sign of blood. Morgan must have been drugged."

Shaken by the grim news, Meredith wept. "Mackenzie, what are we going to do? Kidnap victims have less than twenty-four hours before vanishing."

"We drive to the office and wait. Look, Morgan is smart and tough. With luck, he escapes and contacts us. Maybe Raz calls and demands money. Either way, we search for a crumb that saves our man."

"Will we ever see him again? Alive?"

"I'm hopeful. Maybe we catch a break. This just chaps my butt."

Leaving a twenty-dollar tip, the Dubliner grabbed the double-shot coffees and headed to the Jackson office.

As the drug effects ebbed, Morgan stirred. Glancing around the room his eyes locked on a lone figure. His betrayer was grinning.

"You smug bastard. I'm going to kill you."

"That's highly unlikely. The tape is very secure. Welcome to one of RE's many safe houses."

"You are going to suffer a very slow and painful death."

"Threaten all you want. But it's useless."

"What time is it?"

"It's rather late, shortly past 10 p.m. No doubt Agent Fallon is missing your charming company."

With darting eyes, Nash noted the smallish barren room. Likely it was the third bedroom in an older house. The two ecru men were standing watch.

"You are one arrogant prick. But why was I kidnapped? Hell, you knew everything."

"The master was concerned. You were linking pieces faster than expected. You understood the assassination. You connected General Robison. You dissed the distraction. You were edging ever closer to the truth."

"But we were finished. The team was returning to Dallas. Hell, I was unemployed."

"But you were not about to quit. Your obsession forced RE into a decision."

"So, there is a timetable?"

"You've been right all along. All remaining obstacles are to be eliminated."

"Does that include BABA?"

"Sadly, our assassin extraordinaire has become a liability."

"When?"

"Soon. My master has no eagerness to kill the best."

"Then I'm right. Hyatt's assassination triggers a string of apocalyptic events that guts America and reshapes the world."

"See, you are most perceptive."

"But you helped me. Why?"

"Agent, that was always the plan. RE wanted you to enjoy limited success. But your relentless probes were becoming problematic. You were sensing a much larger picture."

"Talk to me about your network. I'm curious."

"That's a no-no. Just know that it's thriving and well diversified."

"Look, I'm powerless. Give me something. Talk strategy."

"Unfortunately, that particular topic is off the table."

"Hey, I'm a dead man. Toss me a bone."

"Okay, think global. Like Akhenaten, the master's plan is all-encompassing."

"Interesting." Morgan glared at his Judas, his mind racing. Additional time and answers were desperately needed. Suddenly, his face twisted as several dots connected. "You are one greedy son-of-a-bitch. BABA *has* to die. You're getting his paycheck."

"The master has always rewarded his best assets. I've been a loyal servant for years."

"But why? Hell, you're a highly acclaimed academic and archeologist."

The compliment triggered a snicker. "Agent Nash, you have one investigative flaw. Your Achilles heel has always been the *obvious*. Since day one, you have overlooked the most critical clue of all."

"Meaning?"

"Bloodline. My DNA links to BABA's."

"Does that lineage also include the master?"

"That too is another mystery in a series of mysteries."

"Whose bloodline?"

The query triggered a chuckle. "The answer is so blatantly obvious. You see but don't see. My veins flow with the royal blood of Akhenaten."

"You're right. I didn't see that coming. Why didn't you kill me in the parking lot?"

"That would have been both risky and problematic. The FBI would have swarmed the area. Their interference would have altered Hyatt's assassination."

"Then I was right. When?"

"Tomorrow."

"Where?"

"Vicksburg."

"Bingo!"

"See, your gut was right. Only the date and time escaped you."

"But 5 a.m. *is* the time. The dawn hour fits the underworld's sequence."

"That too was a very clever ruse. Sunrise was merely a distraction. Hyatt has a date with death at *noon*."

"But that's impossible. The President is back in D.C."

"Agent, like soft clay, you've been so easy to mold. Hyatt delayed his return for a quick stopover. For weeks, I've misled you. The Sun God's journey and rebirth were never relevant. Yet you bought into the story. Desperate people are so easy to manipulate."

"You're right. I was foolish."

"Which concludes our little talk."

"Wait. Are the generals and the Vice President also traitors? Are they part of RE's inner circle?"

"See, even in death you probe. Your mind is relentless. The master's network is powerful, diverse, and widespread. But like BABA, a few loose ends need pruning."

"Does D.C. control the network?"

"That too is unanswerable."

"Why?"

"What difference does it make? Your life is ending."

"Dammit, I deserve to know. My family is dead. I'm dead. Why would leadership betray the American people?"

"Agent, the answer is so blatantly obvious. But again, that is your weakness."

"Okay, I see but don't see. Enlighten me."

"Since the dawning of time, aristocrats have lusted for power and control. Their thirst has been unquenchable. Today's political elitists are no exception."

"That sounds inclusive. Bingo! The network is a *global cabal.* RE's tyrannical partnership extends far beyond the U.S., Right?"

"That too is confidential."

"Do these narcissistic bastards embrace Akhenaten's vision?"

"Ah, the student progresses. Yes, the plan is both revolutionary and radical. Encompassing the Vatican, London, and Beijing the beacon of change glows brightly."

"Vatican? But Pope Anthony would never betray his people. The Holy Father is a religious icon."

"Did I mention *Anthony?*"

Stunned by the revelation, Nash's eyes darted to the doorway. With the Holy Father also in grave danger, Mackenzie had to be alerted.

"Well, I've enjoyed our little conversation. But your shifting eyes are searching for an exit. And orders are orders. Things are about to get somewhat unpleasant and messy."

On cue, the larger suit stepped from the shadows and anchored the back of the chair. In unison, his smaller partner edged forward and slammed a gloved right fist into Morgan's jaw. The blow was followed by countless jabs and hooks. Dripping with sweat and gasping for breath, the ecru man finally stopped. His target was unconsciousness.

From the doorway, Raz flashed his trademark Cheshire grin. *Fists tonight. Drugs tomorrow. Game over.*

With nary a word the two men sliced the bonds and toted the limp body to a small bedroom. Working quickly, they retied his hands and feet. Unexpectedly, the larger suit slammed a steel-toed boot into Morgan's exposed ribs. To his delight, a distinct crack was heard. Abruptly, the pair exited.

Beaten unmercifully, Mackenzie's cartel-busting sidekick didn't move.

CHAPTER 18

Saturday, January 23

Shortly after midnight, Nash's right eye opened to total darkness. His left eye was swollen shut. With a throbbing head and barking rib, Morgan felt the agony that quickly suppressed panic as he assessed the dire situation. Movement was restrictive if not impossible. Both wrists were tightly bound behind his back. Cord secured his ankles. Only a lateral roll was theoretically feasible. Worse, it was his only option.

Dammit, I've got to move. Mac has to be warned.

An attempted left roll proved disastrous. The cracked rib created a firestorm of unbearable pain. A right roll generated tears and an abrupt stop. But the agony was manageable. Executing a double roll, he felt his feet touch a wall. Repositioning his body, he pushed to sit upright and instantly gagged. The broken rib was creating a searing, white-hot pain. As the burning subsided, Morgan slowly twisted onto his stomach. Angling his hands clockwise and forcing his head hard left, he noted the time. The luminous display read 1:17 a.m.

Panicked, he executed a series of exploratory rolls. A short wall revealed a small, empty closet with a partially opened sliding door. Blocking the pain, Nash wormed his way into the tight enclosure. The depth was shallow, less than three feet. Slowly, he twisted and maneuvered until his neck, head, and lower back were firmly positioned against the closet wall. Nauseous from the pain, he ceased all movement. His fragile world was spinning.

As anger slowly trumped suffering, he willed himself to stand. With jaws clenched, knees bent, and feet planted, he forced himself upward, managing a hunched position before thumping his head against the top shelf. Inching along the wall, his eager hands explored for anything sharp. After several squirms and wiggles, all movement stopped. Fighting blackout, he was unable to sustain the stooped position. Suddenly, his wandering digits miraculously touched metal.

Bingo! Security panel. Flimsy door.

Manipulating his fingers, he reached for the plastic latch but came up short. As his strength waned, Morgan repositioned his stance for one climatic push. Ignoring the rivulets of sweat that blurred his good eye, he arched onto his toes and fingered the insert. Tugging on the latch Nash opened the ultralight metal door ever so slightly. Doggedly he strengthened his grip and pulled at the panel with repeated up and down movements. With multiple attempts, the hinges loosened. A final jerk ripped the thin door from the panel.

Gagging, Morgan maintained control of the door, slid to the floor, and vomited. As the heaving eased, he wiggled away from the stench. Fueled by sheer hatred, the revenge seeker braced himself against a wall and tediously rotated the panel. Finally, he felt a jagged edge. Working methodically, he relentlessly scraped the sharp point against his bound wrists. After countless attempts, the cord unraveled and severed. Ignoring the dripping blood and excruciating pain, he quickly untied his feet. With the dawn hour quickly approaching, time was needed for preparation and sleep.

Cloistered at the Jackson office, Mackenzie fretted. Unable to focus, her eyes darted from the computer and fixated on the wall clock. The time was 4:05 a.m. Any hope of finding her partner alive was quickly dissipating. Unexpectedly, a dark shadow appeared in the doorway. The interloper was Meredith.

"Any news?"

"I've heard nothing."

"Can I help in any way? I'm a techie."

"Thanks, but no. Just sit tight and pray. Hopefully, something pops."

With the analyst's abrupt departure, the veteran agent willed herself to be proactive. Aided by her shadowy contact, she hacked into the Secret Service's personnel files. Twenty minutes later, Mackenzie sat dismayed. The shotgun approach was too broad.

Refocusing, she remembered Hyatt's minuscule protection detail. Intrigued, the Special Agent scanned the current roster, yet nothing popped. The records were spotless. Relentless, her efforts continued. Suddenly the Dubliner's eyebrows arched in eager anticipation. According to his bio, Agent Walter Jocko Melewski had been an aide to General Matthew Riggs during the Iraqi war.

Though insignificant, the crumb was a link to the Army's top dog. Fascinated, her mind calibrated the possibilities.

Would Jocko accept a bribe, ignore his duties and collude with Riggs? Was he connected to Robison?

Frustrated, she closed the file. The grassy knoll theories were pure conjecture. Plus, the agent was low on the pecking order. The pharaoh tokens pointed to leadership. The illegal hack was a bust.

With the dawning of a new day, Morgan shuddered. The all-too-familiar shroud of dread was bracketing his mind. His sight and mobility were limited; death was the predictable outcome. His one hope of survival resided in the disciplines of 'Uechi Ryu.'

Originally called 'Pangai-noon' for half-hard and half-soft, the focus of 'Uechi Ryu' was self-confidence and inner harmony. The rigid training emphasized steeled toughness, instant strikes, and hard blows. A black belt with two gold stripes, he had achieved the ranking of 'Nanadan.' The accomplishment was equivalent to a seventh-degree Master's Title. Any chance of survival depended on the rigid training.

Slowly a simple plan began to emerge. Satisfied, Nash edged to the closed door and waited. Within minutes he heard a distinctive sound. Hard-soled boots were headed his way. With a death grip on the panel, the trap was set.

As anticipated, the smaller suit cautiously opened the door and peered into the darkness. The room was eerily still and silent. Satisfied, he leaned forward and fumbled for the light switch. Instantly reacting, Morgan stepped from behind the door and slammed the sharp point into the ecru's temple. Stunned by the ambush, the second suit reached for his Beretta. The reaction was too slow as the black belt's toe kick hammered his groin. Yelping in pain, the Middle Easterner stooped. Grabbing a handful of hair, Nash shattered the exposed nose with a palm punch. Unconscious, the minion slumped to the floor.

With the pair disabled, the Texan flashed a sadistic grin. Payback was sweet. With no remorse, he unceremoniously snapped both necks. Next on the list was his Judas partner.

With Beretta in hand, he crept down the hall and scanned the family room with his good eye. Unexpectedly, a shot rang out. Winching in pain, Morgan returned fire. The off-balance shot snapped the Egyptian's collarbone. Writhing in agony, the cosmopolitan academic released his weapon and surrendered.

Grimacing, Nash stepped toward his betrayer. As anticipated, the Egyptologist was a coward. Unexpectedly, Raz flashed his trademark Cheshire grin. "Agent, your side is bleeding. I apologize for the accidental shooting."

"I'm happy to return the favor. Undress, you little bastard. Let's see if you possess any more surprises."

Leering, the minion slowly removed every stitch of clothing. Totally exposed, he winked. "Like a Leprechaun, I'm wee but magically delicious. Care for a sample?"

"You are one smug bastard. Even naked, you're defiant."

"And your face has been pulverized. Obviously, my men disobeyed orders."

"Both paid dearly for that mistake. Now I have a score to settle with you."

"I'll talk if you guarantee my safety. You will need my testimony."

"That's unlikely."

"I know names and dates."

"And I have unresolved issues."

"You need me."

"Why?"

"Look, you're bleeding profusely. You have but minutes to live."

"That's good to know. It gives me ample time to blow a hole in your left shoulder." In a fluid motion, Morgan raised the Beretta and fired. Instantly, the Egyptian screamed in pain.

"Update me on RE's plan. Otherwise, say goodbye to your left knee."

"Go ahead. Others stand ready to take my place."

"Give me something or..." Suddenly Nash's face twisted in agony as pain sapped his strength. Fighting blackout, he staggered several steps, lost eye contact, and slumped into a chair.

Buoyed by the distraction, Raz triumphantly edged toward the door. After several steps, he stopped. Bleeding profusely from the shoulder wound, his life was ebbing. As blood dripped to the floor, he uttered a hasty prayer to Allah and pressed his tongue against a faux molar. Instantly, a tiny pill fell into his mouth. Crushing the cyanide capsule, he yelled: "Praise RE and the Aggh...."

A throaty gurgle silenced the outburst as foam bubbled around his lips. Crumpling to the floor, the betrayer landed awkwardly on his back. Enraged, Morgan exploded. "Damnit, you needed to suffer. I wasn't finished with you." Irked, he pumped three additional shots into the lifeless body.

That's for my family. Texas roadkill.

With the threats eliminated, Nash glanced at a nearby clock. Suddenly, his eyes popped in panic. The time was 7:10 a.m. Mackenzie had to be warned. Locating Raz's phone, he entered the Egyptian's favorite password and promptly passed out.

As sunlight filtered through the curtains, Morgan finally awoke. He was writhing in pain, his mind spinning. Scanning the room, he fixated on the clock, yet nothing registered. Minutes later, the relentless ticking rocked his memory. The time was 10:40 a.m. Frantic, he entered Mackenzie's number. With caller ID flashing Raz, the Dubliner's response was curt.

"You bastard. How much do you want?"

"Mac... it's... me." The tone was soft, garbled.

"Morgan? Is that you? You sound awful."

"Hurt."

"Bad?"

"Come. Hyatt...dies."

"When?"

"Noon."

"Where?"

"Vic..."

"Vicksburg? I'm calling the police."

"No. Spook...BA."

Instantly the line went silent. Panicked, the Dubliner screamed into the receiver. "Morgan, talk to me. Dammit, talk to me. It's not your time to die."

Anxious to rescue their fallen colleague, the Jackson office quickly accessed the Egyptian's GPS. Within minutes a convoy of FBI vehicles was slashing through streets at high speed; lights flashing and sirens blaring. Fallon's car was in the lead.

"Is he okay?"

"Meredith, I don't know. He's really weak. Hell, I could barely hear him. Hopefully, Morgan stays alive."

As tears tracked down both cheeks, the profiler sobbed.

"You really care, don't you?"

"Yes. Your partner is unique."

"That's an understatement."

"What about Raz?"

"There was no mention. Likely, the bad guys have been eliminated."

"Mac, I didn't see this coming."

"Neither did I. The arrogant bastard was a great actor. He fooled all of us."

Eight harrowing minutes later, Mackenzie's unmarked sedan skidded to a stop at the safe house. With Glock in hand, she sprinted to the front door. Lagging two steps behind was the analyst, toting a first aid kit. Blowing away the lock with two quick shots, the Dubliner cautiously entered the eerily silent hallway. Peering into the spacious family room she was stunned. The hellish scene was a Dante masterpiece.

The centerpiece was the academic's naked body. Spread eagled on the floor, he wore a ghastly death mask. Sporting a purplish hole in the forehead, the traitor had been shot in both shoulders and knees. The outline resembled a five-point star.

Off to the right, she noted Morgan slumped in a chair. His feeble body was badly battered. Blood seeped from a waist wound and numerous facial cuts. One eye was swollen shut. Ignoring the grotesque scene, Meredith rushed to his aid.

"Hey, I'm here for you. But you need a doctor."

"No. Go."

"That's bullshit. We stay," growled Fallon. "I'm calling an ambulance."

"Hyatt. Noon." Slurring the words, Morgan gasped. Swelling around his mouth made speech difficult.

The dire prediction forced Mackenzie into a hasty decision. "Meredith, check his side. Is there an exit wound?"

Pulling up his shirt, the analyst noted entry and exit wounds. "It's clean. There's no slug."

"Then slap on a bandage. We need to go."

"Absolutely not!" Flashing an angry scowl, Lindsey's guttural response was curt. His face is an oozing mess. Give me a minute."

"Rib," uttered Morgan in a soft whisper. "Tape."

Ignoring Mackenzie, Meredith dressed the facial cuts, patched the waist, and bound the rib cage.

Irked by the delay, the Special Agent checked the rooms. Two Middle Eastern suits were disfigured with broken necks. The academic aped a pin cushion.

"Morgan, did it take five shots to kill the bastard?"

"Yep."

"Why?"

"Star. You don't..."

"You don't mess with Texas?"

"Yeah."

Exhibiting a wry grin, the Dubliner understood. The Lone Star state's motto was payback. Refocusing, her eyes darted to Lindsey. "Ready or not, we're hauling ass."

Aided by a bevy of agents, Morgan was hustled to the sedan's backseat. With seatbelts fastened, the Dubliner set the GPS and accelerated toward nearby Vicksburg.

"Mac, is there time?"

"Not likely. It's going to be tight."

"Can't you contact the Vicksburg police?"

"No. Morgan was right. The locals are clueless about the secret visit. Plus, they have zero authority. Hopefully, Raz was lying to save his ass. The prick was a great performer."

"But we need backup. Get Jackson agents to help."

"No. The FBI is out. So is the Secret Service. Too many cars attract attention. Our best chance is to move quickly and quietly. We can beg for help if needed."

Anxiously eying her watch, the Special Agent calculated the odds. A noon arrival was virtually impossible. The river city was a good fifty-minute drive.

"Meredith, grab that shit handle. I'm fixing to fly."

Ten miles later, a garbled word floated from the backseat. "Real." Hearing the soft utterance, Mackenzie glanced in the rearview mirror. "What's real?"

"Shift."

"Dammit, that makes no sense. You need a doctor. Where's BABA?"

"Bui..." In mid-word, Nash passed out.

Driving straightaways at ninety and taking curves at seventy-five, the Dubliner concentrated, her forehead beaded with sweat. A miraculous arrival didn't mean squat without pinpointing the shooter. Peering in the mirror, she winced. Her partner's pasty hue mimicked a ghost.

Seconds later a piercing cry shattered the silence.

"Boat!"

"What kind?" The analyst's yelp was frantic, pleading. "Fishing? Leisure? Guide?"

"Ste..." Unable to complete the babble Morgan blacked out.

"Dammit, he's gone again," bitched Fallon. "More muttering. Anything?"

"Something about ste... Mac, that's it! *Steamboat!* There's a Civil War replica docked at Vicksburg."

"That's got to be it. A long walk makes Hyatt an easy target."

Minutes later, another disjointed but chilling word floated from the backseat. "Shoo."

Glancing at her watch, the Dubliner pressed the accelerator. "Meredith, get on that damn phone. Pinpoint the boat. Check for nearby buildings and shooting positions."

With fingers working at warp speed, the analyst entered the data. In a blink, the smart device flashed an apocalyptic answer. "Damn, the dock is wide open. It's a clear shot from numerous structures."

"Shit. Research buildings with multiple stories."

"Give me a distance."

"Try two thousand yards. Wait. That's too iffy. Enter seven hundred yards or less."

Working feverishly, Lindsey panicked. "Oh hell, eight buildings feature multiple stories."

"Check topography. Check five hundred yards. Focus on downhill."

Frantic, Meredith recalibrated the calculation. "Six buildings are within five hundred yards. We're stymied."

"Fis..."

Hearing the garbled slur, the analyst shook her head in dismay. "Morgan, that's gibberish. Talk to me."

"Barr."

"That makes no..." Suddenly the mumbled words connected. "You mean barrel? It's like shooting fish in a barrel?"

Buoyed by a slight nod the profiler recalibrated the smartphone. "Mac, there are three buildings within three hundred yards of the dock. Fronting the river, they've been abandoned for years. All are three stories and in the same block. They have a penthouse view of the river."

"What about obstruction? Check the layout."

Enlarging the pictures, Meredith stared in disbelief. "Each corner window offers a perfect shot. But the location is too close. Secret Service is blanketing these buildings."

"Dammit. Morgan, are you sure about the time and boat? Was Raz screwing with you?"

"No...secu..."

"There's no security?" Shocked by the revelation Lindsey's eyes bulged in dismay. "That can't happen. It's a long walk to the entrance."

"Meredith, he's delirious. This trip is a crap shoot at best."

"But what if he's right? Screw their fragile ego. The Secret Service needs backup. I'm calling the Sheriff's office."

"Get deputies to search two buildings. We can take one."

"Me."

"Dammit, you're not going anywhere," barked Fallon. "You're staying in the car."

"DAWN."

Unnerved by the yelp, the Dubliner hesitated and then recanted. "Meredith, make the call. Beg for help. Deputies can check the most obvious location. We take the next. And God help me, Morgan searches building three."

"But he's in no condition. Why?"

"I made a promise. Plus, he has help."

Irked at the response, Lindsey noted the time. Instantly, her face scrunched in agony. In four minutes, Hyatt was dead. Panicked, she contacted the Sheriff's dispatcher and requested help. Less than a minute later, the call terminated.

"Mac, that fricking woman was clueless about Hyatt's visit. As a courtesy, she's rerouted two deputies."

"Shit. They may be a no-show. How much longer?"

"A couple of minutes or so. Look, there's the boat."

Accelerating, Fallon blitzed the back streets. Suddenly, the analyst's voice crackled with terror. "Mac, there's the procession. But it's slowing. We can't make it."

"That's bullshit. Hang on!"

"You're crazy!"

"Likely."

"Look, the buildings are dead ahead."

Twenty seconds later, the unmarked car rolled to a halt. As the front passengers checked weapons, the rear door swung open. Emerging into the sunlight was the backseat ghost. Gripped tightly in his right hand was the betrayer's Glock.

With flashing lights, the Sherriff's unit pulled up. As Fallon barked orders, teams one and two hustled to their assigned positions. Grimacing with each step, Morgan moved steadily but slowly. Approaching the front entrance, he paused to pick up a large round object. Stopping near the entrance, he tried to yell a dire warning.

"Taser!"

But no one heard the shout, barely above a whisper.

Stepping into the building, Nash hesitated. His prophetic utterance had been right. Secret Service was notably absent. Dodging the litter trap of discarded cans, glass, syringes, and paper, he disregarded the first floor and slowly ascended the stairs. Each agonizing step induced searing, white-hot pain. As he glanced at the time, his angst spiked. It was ninety seconds *past* noon. Yet no shot had been fired.

Shit.... silencer. Or, his Judas had lied again.

Suddenly, a distinctive clap shattered the stillness. Limping toward the sound Morgan noted recently disturbed dust. The third-floor corner office fronted the river and offered a perfect shooting position.

Uncertain, he cautiously approached the closed door and abruptly stopped. Behind that wooden barrier was *his* killer. Yet, with objects clutched in both hands, twisting the knob was impossible. As pain blurred his thinking, Morgan stared at the obstacle. Mired in indecision, he reexamined the knob. To his surprise, the door was not firmly shut. Buoyed by the discovery, he executed a hard leg kick. As the door swung open, his rubbery legs defaulted. Stumbling hard right, he noted movement to his left.

Corner!

With head down, BABA was busy dismantling his custom Lapua rifle. Instantly shock engulfed his face. The meddling agent was supposedly dead. Instinctively, he grabbed the taser and fired.

Tracking the motion, Morgan instinctively ducked behind the round object. The metal lid from an old trashcan created a perfect shield. With a loud clang, the dual barbs ricocheted off the impenetrable disk. Lowering the barrier, he blindly returned fire. Emitting an angry yelp, BABA glanced at his wounded left shoulder, grabbed the Nefertiti dagger, and bull-rushed his enemy.

Panicked by the unexpected, Nash triggered another round. The wild shot slammed into BABA's left forearm. Wincing but not stopping, the Egyptian rammed into his adversary at full speed. As the pair tumbled to the floor, the assailant landed on top, pinning his rival's right shoulder and arm. Pressing the advantage, he jabbed repeatedly at the exposed left side. Ignoring the searing pain, Morgan twisted and hacked with his left elbow. The sharp raps knocked his lighter opponent off balance. With a freed right hand, he blindly triggered the Glock. The badly angled shot ripped into the assassin's left hip. A second round shattered the left kneecap.

Writhing in pain, BABA released the dagger and rolled to the floor. Mired in the dust and grime, he lay bleeding from shredded stitches and multiple wounds. Driven by an innate will to live, the killer of many grabbed the dagger and inched toward the Texan.

Unnerved by the movement, Nash fingered three wild shots. The badly aimed slugs peppered the far wall. A fourth round hammered BABA's right side. With his killer vanquished, Nash lowered the weapon and stared at the ceiling. His fragile world was spinning and darkening. As blood dripped from numerous gashes, he never saw the minion's movement. Twisted in an awkward position, the Egyptian slowly removed a hidden ankle revolver and squeezed the trigger. The misaimed slug slammed into Morgan's left shoulder. Yelping in pain, he instinctively returned fire. The off-target shot ripped into the assassin's right bicep. Hopelessly maimed, the killer of many released the weapon. As both men oozed blood, the grimy floor waxed crimson.

Seconds later, BABA doggedly scooched toward the nearby ankle revolver. Sensing danger Nash fixated on the movement, but nothing registered.

Suddenly an inner voice clamored.

"SHOOT! FOR GOD'S SAKE, SHOOT!"

With her angelic face contorted in sheer terror, Dawn's shrieking cries rocked his mind, growing louder and louder.

"DAMMIT, MORGAN SHOOT!"

Guided by the telepathic message, his finger twitched. The round struck BABA squarely in the forehead. Uncertain, he squeezed off two more shots. The first blew away the Egyptian's right eye. The second shredded his right ear.

With his world blurring, Mackenzie's cartel-busting sidekick passed out.

Hearing the shootout and fearing the worst, Fallon and Lindsey sprinted into the archaic building. Ascending to the third floor, they noted fresh tracks and an eerie silence. With guns in firing position, they barged into the corner office and abruptly stopped. The ghoulish scene was beyond description.

"Oh hell," cried the Dubliner. "Oh God, no!"

With staring eyes, a clearly dead BABA lay sprawled on the floor. Riddled by multiple bullets his body revealed the ferocity of the shootout. Noting her partner's limp body, she grimaced. His face was buried in the grime. Blood seeped from numerous wounds.

Fearing the worst, Meredith checked for signs of life. Finding none, she felt bitter bile surging into her throat. As tears riveted down both cheeks, she cried in anguish.

"Mac, I can't find a pulse. I think he's dead!"

"Try CPR. Help is coming. Don't let him die."

As the analyst worked feverishly, the Dubliner's eyes locked on the Egyptian. Mentally, she tried to recreate the scene. *Morgan couldn't see. That wall is a mess. But the bastard is dead. How?*

"Mac, there's a pulse. It's faint."

"Keep working. I need him alive."

Kneeling next to her battered partner, she caressed his hand and whispered. "If you die RE wins. There's no justice for Dawn or Erin."

As a howling north wind underscored the bleakness of a wintry night, Morgan's good eye opened and blinked. Groggy from surgery he scanned the room.

"Where...?"

"You're in a Jackson hospital," quipped the Dubliner. "Meredith and I have been stuck in this hell-hole for hours."

"Bad?"

"Nah. Other than a few hundred stitches you're fine. Surgeons have upgraded your condition from hopeless to critical. Hell, I was hoping for a new partner."

"BABA?"

"Satan's disciple has officially crossed the river Styx and descended into the murky depths of Tartar."

Attempting to shift position Morgan winced in pain. "Damn, that hurt. Even a twitch is agonizing. What time is it?"

"Look outside," laughed Meredith. "The night is pitch black and frigid. It's bedtime."

"Hyatt?"

"The President is dead. Richard Anderson is his successor."

"Dammit Mac, it's my fault. I couldn't see. I couldn't run. If only..."

"Morgan, stop. You are not at fault. It was Hyatt's awful decision that led to his demise. That minuscule detail was sheer idiocy, as was his impenetrable veil of secrecy. In D.C. there are no secrets."

"What about the Secret Service?"

"Those bastards didn't arrive for *eight* fricking minutes. There was a huge lapse in security. Now they're pointing fingers at us."

"Pricks."

"Hey, your work is done," interrupted a cheerful Meredith. "Let's lighten the mood. The villain is dead. No more killings."

"What about RE?"

"Our phantom remains a mystery...and off your radar," answered Mackenzie. "You need to rehab and clear your mind. Everything's going to be copacetic."

"Yeah, good insurance. Thanks for coming. I'm a bit tired."

"Well, you gave us a good scare. Thankfully you're going to survive." Turning to leave, Mackenzie hesitated. "Partner, I have to ask. You were blind, beaten, shot, and stabbed. How in the hell did you kill BABA?"

Dawn.

As he faded, the Special Agent glanced at Meredith. "God bless that woman. She's his guardian angel."

"But that's impossible. His wife is dead."

"Yet Morgan survived. You saw his condition. You saw the room. Dawn telepathically guided him."

"Has this divine intervention ever happened before?"

The incredulous query brought a wry smile to the Dubliner's lips. "Yeah. His protector has intervened numerous times, which made me a believer. Dawn has always been his savior in times of need. Their love affair was one for the ages."

CHAPTER 19

Wednesday, January 27

Airlifted to Dallas late Tuesday evening, Nash awoke in a suburban hospital. As the morning sunbeams brightened the room, he was pleasantly surprised to see two familiar faces.

"Hey there. It's great to see you. What's up?"

"Meredith and I wanted to check on our hero. Plus, we have news."

"Regarding?"

"BABA. His real name was Hussan Nefari. His bloodline actually traced to Pharaoh Akhenaten."

"Parents?"

"Both were killed by American air raids while visiting Iraq. Vengeful, BABA joined the Iraqi army and fought against us. Captured, he was released near the end of the Gulf War. Blessed with unique skills, he became an elite assassin."

"That man was one tough son-of-a-bitch. BABA refused to die."

"Was he part of RE's inner circle?"

"No, Meredith. According to Raz, our ghost was simply a killer extraordinaire."

"I agree," chirped Fallon. "Scratch one minion. What's your take on the new President?"

"Mac, Richard Anderson has zero experience. Moderates and conservatives have to be shocked."

"Well, investors are certainly spooked. Markets of late have been bleeding red."

"Personally, I think he fails. The guy is arrogant and shallow. His presidency is great news for our adversaries."

"Jameson agrees. In fact, Russia is already testing the waters. The Kremlin is pouring troops and equipment into northern Syria and along the Ukraine border."

"That's no surprise. But it's likely a bluff. Moscow enjoys testing the manhood of new Presidents. Expect Beijing to do the same."

"Speaking of China, they've just brokered a deal with India. They're planning joint maneuvers in the Indian Ocean. Both are relocating troops and transports to deep water ports."

"But they're bitter enemies. The Pentagon has to be concerned."

"According to my sources, they're baffled."

"Is there any good news?"

"Yep. The case is officially over. I'm planning a June wedding. And Meredith is flying to D.C. Hey, our time is up. Is there anything else?"

"Yeah. Did BABA leave anything of interest in that room? Key pieces are still missing."

"We found a small card in the corner window. That was it. Evidently, the bastard wanted credit for the assassination."

"Did you take a picture?"

"Yep. It's on my phone." Reaching into her bag Fallon retrieved the device. "Take a look. It's the same message."

Intrigued, Nash scanned the note. Suddenly, his eyes did a double take. "Mac, the ending letters are different. They've been altered."

"Morgan, the message is vintage BABA," blurted Meredith. "Give it a rest."

"I disagree. There's a subtle difference."

"Meaning?"

"'A' has replaced 'E.' R-E has become R-A. Likely, RE has an accomplice with these initials."

"Dammit, partner, it doesn't matter," grumbled Mackenzie. "The case is over. There's no BABA and no meaning. Enjoy your rehab." Irked by the unexpected pushback, the Dubliner's fragile temper flared.

"Mackenzie's right," echoed Lindsey. "It's time to relax. Carpe diem."

"But something's not right. The pharaoh tokens reference power. These new letters could indict Richard Anderson. Maybe they point to new V.P Roger Allday or Senator Rashard Alton. We need to investigate."

"No, we don't. Dammit, you want this case to continue. But it's over. I'm off to Aspen to plan a wedding."

"Mac, you have to alert Jameson. This change has meaning."

"Fine. What's my message?"

"Urge him to reopen the case. Explain the lettering. Tell him about possible accomplices."

"Forget it. The Director's new priority is damage control. The Secret Service is pointing fingers and inciting the press."

"Look, BABA didn't plan on dying. That note has significance. Was there anything unusual about his capture or release in Iraq?"

"The military records were sketchy. Hussan Nefari was captured, interrogated, and released in the northern sector." Suddenly, the Dubliner tensed as several dots connected.

Noting the subtle change, Nash flashed a wry grin. "I see those eyes. There's more to this story."

"His imprisonment triggered a connection. Colonel Richard Anderson was the interrogator. A short time later, Hussan was granted an early release."

"Did the records indicate a reason?"

"No. The findings were heavily redacted."

"What about Allday? What was his military background?"

Irked by the repeated questions, Fallon's simmering angst erupted. "Dammit, Morgan, we're done with the questioning. We are not venturing down this rabbit hole."

"Fine. At least tell me about Allday. Hell, I deserve something."

"Don't press it. Our V.P. was on General Robison's staff. He delivered messages to General Riggs. Are you happy?"

"Yeah. That gives me something to ponder. If the case ever reopens, we focus on these four suspects."

"Don't count on it. Jameson wants you reassigned to Alaska. Get well. Then buy some heavy coats. Anchorage gets a tad chilly."

"That's real funny. I'm buying a ranch."

"God help us." With a devilish smirk, the Dubliner abruptly exited the room. On her heels was the analyst.

CHAPTER 20

Thursday, January 28

Granted an early release, Morgan made a beeline to his office. A short time later he sat dejected. With BABA dead and no leads, the case was officially over. Depressed, he strolled into Fallon's office and suddenly gasped. The somber workplace was abuzz with festivities.

"Hey, our conquering hero has finally arrived," yelled the Dubliner. "You're just in time."

"For what?"

"We're celebrating a new beginning. These past days have been wonderfully peaceful and quiet. Have some cake."

"It's really good," purred the profiler. "The icing is yummy."

"No thanks. Isn't this shindig a little premature?"

"Nope. Case file 180388B is history."

"But critical pieces are missing. Questions have to be answered. Like, how *did* BABA get so damn close?"

As humor morphed into seriousness, Mackenzie eyed her rehabbing patient. "Jameson posed the same question. Where *was* the Secret Service? Those buildings should have been blanketed."

"Was it a breakdown in communication or a mole? Somebody had to be responsible for that area."

"The Director and I did a little digging. Walter "Jocko" Melewski was assigned to the three buildings."

"Did you check his service record?"

"Yep. It was spotless. But there was an interesting coincidence. Melewski served in the Gulf War as aide to Robison and Riggs."

"So, the plot thickens. Everything points east."

"But that's where the story ends and our celebration begins. Meredith is heading to D.C. I'm flying to Colorado. And Jameson is targeting human trafficking."

"That's great. But dammit, I deserve some answers. Who is this mysterious RA? Do the letters link with RE? Is the Secret Service compliant? Mac, you can't leave me hanging."

"Look, it's out of my hands. According to Jameson there's no evidence to reopen the case."

"Morgan, just relax and enjoy the moment," chirped Meredith. "Let's party before scurrying in different directions."

"Thanks, but there's still plenty of unfinished business. Mac, I need your approval."

"For what?"

"An experiment."

"Why?"

"So, I can gain closure and sleep at night. Unlike yours, my mind races with doubts and questions. A colleague can help."

Instantly, Mackenzie hesitated. "Partner, I know that squirrely look. Who is this person?"

"He's an unknown techie specializing in the dark web."

"Oh really? How does the netherworld link to closure? I'm a little dubious."

"Screw the skepticism. Just hear me out. I want my buddy to place a simple headline. There's no content or names. Within hours the one line vanishes without a trace."

"Partner, that makes zero sense and serves no purpose. Plus, the dark web is rather suspect."

"But it's a global pipeline. That's why I want your permission. The wording simply reads: "SECRET SERVICE LINKED TO PRESIDENTIAL ASSASSINATION."

Instantly, the Dubliner exploded. "Dammit, no! That headline cannot appear."

"Why? There's absolutely no risk. Nothing can be traced to us."

"Forget it. Never underestimate the Secret Service or DOJ. This little stunt is likely to create a firestorm."

"Mac, that's my end goal. The headline simply appears and disappears. According to my quirky genius, it's safe."

"Morgan Nash, you're screwing with the wrong people," countered Lindsey. "You're likely to be arrested and imprisoned."

"Look, the headline simply pops and vanishes. If it creates havoc the case reopens. If not, it's over. I can live with that. There's nothing to lose and everything to gain. Mac, I need your approval."

Expunging a guttural sigh of disbelief, the Dubliner sat dismayed. Her healing wild-child was on the prowl, determined to make something happen. "Okay, contact your slimy buddy. Let's see what happens. But I disavow any knowledge of your activities. We break for lunch in ten minutes."

Sated by an enjoyable meal, Morgan, Mackenzie, and Meredith meandered to their unmarked car. Engaged in playful bantering, they paid scant attention to a nearby black sedan with darkened windows. Blinking on and off were the emergency flashers. Unnoticed, the front passenger window was open.

Suddenly a glint of reflective sunlight caught Morgan's eye. Emerging from the window was a silvery object. Instinctively reacting, he dove at Mackenzie, creating a domino effect. As the trio tumbled off balance, two shots rang out. With bystanders gaping in disbelief, the idling car sprinted toward a busy intersection and instantly disappeared into a sea of traffic.

Springing to her feet, the Dubliner attempted to return fire but stopped. There was no shot. With a quick scan, she noted blood oozing from Morgan's left arm.

"You're hit."

Retrieving a small knife from her purse, she quickly cut away the sleeve. Sighing in relief, Mackenzie grinned. "Hell, it's just a graze. It's bloody but with little damage. Maybe a stitch or two. Let's get you to a doctor."

Returning to the privacy of the Special Agent's office, the trio sat shaken and glum. The ambush was an ominous omen. Wincing from a new set of stitches, Nash assessed the situation. "Well, my little ruse worked. RE reacted."

"You damn near got us killed," lamented Lindsey.

"Yep. But now we know."

"That was close," growled the Dubliner. "Beginning tonight, you're staying with me. Nick has the graveyard shift. Your little headline created a firestorm. Jameson has agreed to reopen the case but on a limited basis."

"Are we included? Wait! What about your travels?"

"Sadly, they've been put on hold. We're leading the investigation."

"Then we need to track our one lead. It's time to pay Jocko Melewski a neighborly visit."

"Partner, that's not going to happen. Kidnapping a federal agent is taboo."

"Did I mention kidnapping?"

"It was implied."

"Mac, hear me out. "Jocko" is our only hope. Look, I just want to talk. The trip is a quickie."

"When?"

"Tomorrow." Mimicking a possum on steroids, Morgan unexpectedly flashed an impish grin. To everyone's surprise, a rare mischievous twinkle danced in his eyes.

"Dammit, I hate that stupid-ass look. There's more. Spill it."

"Have you told anyone in the office about today's shooting?"

"No. My only call was to Jameson."

"Good. Circulate a memo about the ambush. Underscore the seriousness of my wound. I'm rehabbing at an undisclosed location."

"Then what?"

"I stay out of sight, charter a private jet, and hire a couple of buddies. We visit Jocko and leave. According to today's news Anderson is cloistered at the White House."

"Who pays for this trip? What about arrangements? A 'visit' requires preparation including Melewski's schedule."

"Mac, trust me. A close friend can make arrangements. And there's no cost. His company owns a jet."

"Aren't you a wee bit concerned?" Dubious about the outcome, Meredith voiced the sarcastic query. "Morgan, you're about to commit a felony."

"Look, we have to act. Otherwise, we're sitting ducks. Jocko and I are just going to have a friendly chat. He has to be interrogated...but not kidnapped."

"Are your buddies trustworthy?"

"Mac, they're ex-teammates and honorably discharged vets."

"But they're likely to get arrested."

"Look, no one is going to get hurt or put in jail. We should return before dawn. Just keep the trip hush-hush."

"Is there an actual plan?"

"Yeah. We knock on the door, gain valuable information, and fly home. No one is in danger including Jocko."

~

As the wall clock rhythmically pinged the six o'clock hour, the Dubliner smuggled Nash from her private office and drove home. Eager to watch college basketball, the pair kicked back, ate pizza, and guzzled beers. Shortly after 9 p.m. the widower headed to bed. His return to work had been long and hazardous. Within minutes he was sound asleep.

~

Ninety minutes later, he awoke in a frenzy. As beads of sweat streamed down both cheeks, Morgan sat gasping. A pleasant dream had morphed into a hellish nightmare. On the UT sideline, a radiant Dawn was enthusiastically leading cheers to the approval of a sell-out crowd. Suddenly the festive image turned black as her face locked in sheer terror. Hysterical, she kept pointing and screaming.

"MORGAN LEFT! LEFT! LOOK LEFT! DAMMIT, LOOK!"

The frenetic cries were unrelenting.

Unnerved by the horrific image, he switched on a bedside lamp and took several deep breaths. Suddenly, Nash noted movement to his left. Ten feet away, a small serpent was slithering rapidly across the floor and toward the bed. With his eyes fixated on the viper, he calmly reached for the Glock and fired. The slithery motion instantly stopped.

Awakened by the gunshot, Fallon grabbed her weapon and barged into the room. Abruptly she halted. Her guest was calmly sitting in bed and holding a smoking gun.

"What the hell? I thought you had committed suicide. You scared the living hell out of me."

Uttering nary a word, Morgan pointed to the floor. Edging toward the bed, the Dubliner froze, her eyes bulging in disbelief.

"A snake? But how?"

"Boss, meet Cleopatra's asp. It's small but lethal."

" "It was your daughter's killer... a real tragedy."

"RE has us in the crosshairs."

"Dammit!" snapped Mackenzie, her mind flooded with questions. "How in the heck did a snake get into my house? Better yet, how did you know? Hell, you were asleep."

"Dawn woke me. In a dream, she was cheering. Suddenly the image turned ugly. Frantic, she kept screaming "LEFT." It was the same telepathic message that saved me from BABA."

"God bless her. True love transcends into the afterlife. But it's impossible to explain."

"Mac, we both believed in Christ and eternal life. But her faith went further. Like the ancient Romans, Dawn believed a person's soul remained active and alive. It assisted loved ones in dreams, revelations, and crises."

"Obviously, your guardian angel was right. But how did a viper get into my house?" Suddenly, the Dubliner's jaw gaped. "Wait. My Nick left a note. A repair man made an unscheduled visit. For years I've had a maintenance agreement. After an inspection, he left."

"The asp was another RE surprise. Did you mention my stay to anyone?

"Unfortunately, I did. I told my fiancé. And I told some guys in the break room. They weren't buying your hospital story."

"Have each man checked out. One has to be a mole. Did you mention my trip?"

"No. That was forbidden."

"Good. Trust no one. Do you mind if I relocate to the couch? This day just keeps getting better and better."

CHAPTER 21

Friday, January 29

With a mid-morning arrival at a North Dallas corporate airport, Morgan greeted three men. Two were tall and physically imposing. The third was short and thin, the son of a Texas billionaire. After they exchanged pleasantries, his eyes darted to Robinson Wilson III. The stylishly dressed businessman served as a D.C. lobbyist for his dad's international operations. "Robby, I thought we were using one of your dad's private jets."

"This *is* his jet...and very private."

"But I was expecting something smaller, like a Gulfstream."

"It was his decision."

"But there are only four of us. A Boeing?"

"Oh, this baby is much more. Featuring unmatched luxury and extra fuel capacity, this reconfigured 737 can fly non-stop from Dallas to Paris. With limited seating, every recliner reclines into a plush, comfortable bed. The amenities make international travel a breeze. Dad and I zip to Europe on a regular basis."

"But a ride like this is not warranted."

"Dad wanted to express his thanks. Your mansion heroics saved the Governor and crushed the cartels. They're good friends and riding buddies. My old man has a ranch just west of Austin."

An hour into the flight, Morgan huddled with his newly formed team. With nary a word, he handed his ex-teammates thick cash envelopes. Both men stood six feet four and weighed a chiseled two hundred and fifty pounds. At UT, the pair had been wild, crazy, and tough. After graduation, both served as Army Rangers.

Robinson Wilson III was President of a privately held integrated oil company. Avid rancher Quentin Wilson Senior was his father and Chairman of the Board. The pair owned sixty percent of the company's stock with plans to launch an IPO. Never a jock but a stellar student, Robby had become one of Morgan's closest friends.

"Our mission is simple," stated Nash. "While Robby attends to D.C. business, we handle the Georgetown target."

"Does the guy have a set routine?" Luke's bass voice matched his rough demeanor. On his left cheek was a half-moon scar, a forever reminder of combat.

"Our target is always prompt. Like clockwork, he arrives at 6 p.m. and parks in front of his townhouse. This evening we screw with him. Our vehicle occupies the spot. Parking in the next block is his only option. Once he's on foot, I tail him."

"What's our role?"

"It's simple. Luke douses the porch light. Shawn dismantles security cameras. Afterward, you disappear into the hedges. Once the agent unlocks the door, I trigger the taser and rush to catch him. To bystanders, he looks inebriated. Together, we lug him inside. Questions?"

With three shoulder shrugs, the flimsy plan was approved.

Landing in mid-afternoon, the customized Boeing taxied to a private area. The corporate airport was small, efficient, and discreet. As anticipated, security was notably absent.

The old man and influential friends had cleared the way. As Robinson departed for nearby D.C., the trio headed to Georgetown.

~

Eager to relax after a grueling day, Jocko noted the obvious. His assigned space was occupied. Irked, he parked in the next block and hiked to the front door. An angry call to a towing service was pending. Robotically, the veteran agent inserted the key. Suddenly he felt a horrific sting in his back and collapsed like a drunk. Rushing to his aid, Morgan was joined by his invisible colleagues. Within seconds Jocko was seated at the dining room table and tightly bound. A hood covered his head.

"Agent, the decision is yours." Standing several steps behind, Nash spoke in a steely tone. "You can either live or die. RE wants information."

Instantly, the veteran tensed. Addled by the adduction, he sat erect, defiant and still. Watching intently, Morgan noted his demeanor. The mention of RE had zero effect.

"Melewski, you screwed up. You're a fucking Benedict Arnold."

"Hey, I'm no traitor. I love this country. What do you want?"

Unexpectedly, Nash slapped the back of his head. Inflicting pain, the hard blow spun the agent's neck.

"Hyatt's sniper was in *your* area. You betrayed America."

"You're wrong. Our minuscule detail obeyed orders and covered assignments."

"But the shooter found a perfect position in *your* zone. Why didn't you search the building?"

"I was told the area was clear. The locals checked it out."

"Liar!" A punch to the right shoulder inflicted more pain. "Talk Iraq. Identify your commander."

"What?" Baffled by the question, Melewski hesitated. Another hard blow got his attention. "I was an aide to General Riggs. Later, I was transferred to General Robison's staff."

"What was your rank?"

"Captain."

"What was your role?"

"I delivered messages."

"Location?"

"My assigned area was the northern sector."

"Who was your point of contact?"

"Major Richard Anderson. Sometimes it was Riggs or Robison."

"Are you referring to the current President?"

"Yeah."

"So, you betrayed Hyatt to help Anderson?"

"No. I didn't betray anyone."

"Were the messages written or oral?"

"They were always written on a slip of paper but enclosed in an envelope. Nothing was ever typed or printed. I presented the envelope to Major Anderson and stood at attention. After a quick read, he burned the sheet."

"Were all messages one page?"

"No. Others received thick packets. Only Anderson, Riggs, and Robison received the single sheet."

"What was Anderson's assignment?"

"The major was an interrogator."

"How often did you visit him?"

"I made deliveries several times a month."

"Weren't you a wee bit curious? Hell, the message was just one page. Did you ever peek?"

"Once. But the scribbling was coded and confusing."

"Did you understand anything?"

"No."

"Think hard. Your life depends on the answer."

"Look, the coding was bizarre. There was a letter followed by a dash and then more letters or numbers."

"Give me an example."

As Jocko hesitated, Morgan pummeled a fist into the back of his head. Writhing in agony, the newly engaged agent shook his head in defiance.

"Talk. Or I inflict more pain."

"Wait. There were two coded sequences. They read something like N-g-br-5 or Is-s-n-6. Different headings started with O, H, or Ak. Letters, numbers, and dashes were all over the place. Honestly, I thought the codes were about prisoner transfers."

"Think harder. Otherwise, you suck water."

"I noted three columns. But they were uneven. There were more sequences under the S and AS columns. Only three lines were under E. The coding was something like H-iv-st-7 or At-g-ne-8."

"Did you bump into Roger Allday?"

"Briefly. The major was a messenger for Riggs and Robison. Roger worked the southern sector."

"Why south?"

"That was his assigned area."

"Did Allday ever peek at messages delivered to the generals?"

"No. Roger was very secretive about his work." Suddenly, Melewski tensed. "Wait. There was a moment. He was drunk and babbling. Roger said Robison burned every message. Like me, he thought it was odd. That was it."

"Did Allday visit others?"

As Jocko hesitated, Shawn hammered his arm. Playing off his teammate's unexpected violence, Morgan's taunt was cruel and icy. "Last chance. In five seconds you'll be sucking water and praying for mercy."

"Wait. Roger mumbled something about a *desert phantom*."

"Name?"

"Uh, it was Rhodes. But the colonel didn't exist."

"That makes no sense. Say goodbye to your bride."

"Wait. The mysterious colonel was linked to some secretive mission. It was hush-hush."

"Was the colonel stationed north or south?"

"Neither. According to Roger's ramblings, the post was west and far away from any fighting. The ghost camp was tabbed "XZ."

"Did the camp exist on a map?"

"No. I checked repeatedly but there was nothing."

"Okay, you might make it after all. Think hard about "XZ." Your life hangs in the balance."

"Supposedly, Riggs's Rangers were preparing a special surprise for escaping Iraqi units. But these elite troops never saw any action."

Intrigued, Morgan tamped his angst and removed a syringe from his pocket. Additional interrogation was useless. Melewski was a minion at best and not a traitor. With a quick jab, he sank the needle into the agent's shoulder. A blink later he was out for the next six hours. Working quickly, the team relocated Jocko to the couch and headed to the corporate airport.

CHAPTER 22

Saturday, January 30

With a smooth descent into the North Dallas corporate airport, the reconfigured Boeing touched down in the pre-dawn blackness. With little sleep, Nash sat frustrated and exhausted. Transfixed in his restless mind were the bizarre codes. Yet nothing connected. As the former Rangers deplaned, both nodded but said nothing. Minutes later, Morgan accompanied Robinson to his nearby luxury townhouse. Though Austin was home, the Wilson's owned numerous properties in America and worldwide.

Eager to unravel the baffling mystery, Nash arrived early at his office. To his dismay, Fallon and Lindsey were lurking in the hallway. Uninvited, both entered his domain and took seats.

"Well, you're not dead or in jail. How did it go?"

"Mac, Melewski was extremely cooperative. But the information was coded and vague. Plus, there was a ghost colonel and a mystery camp."

"Was Jocko tortured during your 'cordial' visit?"

"Nope. The trip went as planned. The agent was sleeping like a baby when we left."

"What was his role in Iraq?"

"Like Allday, he was a messenger. Both delivered secret reports to Anderson, Riggs, and Robison. The mystery camp was located in General Riggs' sector."

"Are the codes decipherable?"

"No. They're confusing as hell."

"Did Melewski describe the outpost?"

"Meredith, Camp 'XZ' didn't exist. According to Jocko, elite Rangers were building a secret defense parameter. Colonel Rhodes was the commander. There was no fighting anywhere in the sector. Nor was the camp listed on any maps."

"Okay, we keep digging," barked Mackenzie. "Morgan, stay put and update Jameson. But don't mention your sources or Melewski. Meredith, run background checks on our four suspects. We need something to pop."

Famished, the trio agreed on lunch at a nearby café. Exiting the bureau's front entrance, they walked a narrow sidewalk toward Fallon's unmarked SUV. Parked cars lined the busy four-lane thoroughfare. Fast-walking ahead of the agents was the long-striding analyst. Unexpectedly, Morgan noted movement to his left. A black sedan was slowing with open windows. As if tossing trash, the front seat passenger casually flung a rock-like object in their direction. Clunking on the sidewalk, the hard projectile ricocheted wildly off the building and spun toward Lindsey. Accelerating, the harbinger of evil switched lanes and vanished in the flow of traffic.

"GRENADE!"

Screaming the warning, Morgan lunged left and jammed his shoulder into a parked car. Diving right, Mackenzie slammed into the brick building. Confused by the yell, Meredith froze. A click later, the grenade exploded. Propelled backward, the analyst landed hard on the sidewalk. She writhed in agony as trickles of blood oozed from numerous wounds.

Dazed and in shock, Nash attempted to stand but quickly lost balance. The ringing in his ears was unbearable. Glancing right, he noted Mackenzie. The Dubliner was struggling to sit upright. Blood seeped from her left side. Reacting to the explosion, numerous agents poured from the front entrance and formed a protective shield. One contacted medical assistance. Others aided their fallen comrades.

Braced against the car door, Morgan fought to stay coherent. Fresh wounds to his arm and leg induced horrific pain. Staring at Lindsey, he grimaced. A pool of blood was forming on the sidewalk. Aided by colleagues, he staggered to his feet and hobbled gingerly toward his boss. In the distance numerous sirens were blaring.

"Mac, how bad?"

"I'm not sure. That metal sticking out of my side can't be good."

"Medics are on the way. Poor Meredith was shredded. The damned grenade bounced in front of her and exploded. Her torso saved our lives."

As a bevy of emergency vehicles screeched to a halt, paramedics scurried to the wounded. Working feverishly, a team attempted to slow Lindsey's bleeding. Dubious about the outcome, they rushed her to an ambulance. Within seconds the flashing lights vanished into a sea of traffic. Minutes later, the wounded agents were hustled to the same undisclosed hospital.

Shortly after 4 p.m. Morgan was moved from recovery to a private room. The ringing in his ears had dissipated. His overall condition was good other than numerous stitches. Standing guard in the doorway was a familiar face.

"Hey John, is there any word on Mac or Meredith?"

"Our fiery Irish boss is stable and in recovery."

"Anything serious?"

Suppressing an urge to utter a glib remark, John's eyes drifted to his friend. "Morgan, you and Mac were damned lucky. The shard in her side was thin and intact. Stitches were required in a few other places."

"Meredith?"

"The shrink's prognosis is grim. I think she's still in surgery."

"That damn grenade was meant for us, not her. It just bounced the wrong way." Grimacing, Nash felt sorry for the beleaguered analyst. After a rocky start the pair was finally getting along. The thought of losing her was traumatic.

"The Director has ordered round-the-clock protection. We've got your back."

"What about our office mole?"

"The rat was arrested but never made it to jail."

"Why?"

"Suicide. The bastard chomped on a hidden cyanide capsule."

"That's good. A little justice goes a long way."

Shortly after 7 p.m. an unexpected surprise rolled into Morgan's room. Pushed by an aide, the pallid Special Agent managed a weak smile. Pleased by the appearance he flashed a heartfelt grin.

"Mac, is that really you? No makeup. And your hair is a mess. I feel bad for Nick."

"And you're still alive. Dammit, I was hoping for a new partner."

As the bantering dissipated, Morgan turned serious. "Mac, we were both real lucky. Meredith caught the brunt of the shrapnel. That damn thing could have easily bounced our way. Doctors aren't sure about her outcome."

"I noted the blood. That poor soul has really suffered. For some ungodly reason RE has upped the ante."

Instantly, Morgan tensed. "Mac, it was the trip. I've got to warn Melewski."

"Are you sure?"

"Yeah. That grenade was retaliation. Now the bastard has Jocko in the crosshairs."

"I'll contact my source and get a number."

Twenty-minutes later, a hospital aide rolled the Dubliner into Nash's room. Aping the grim reaper, she provided a brief update. "You're too late. Jocko died a short time ago from a hit and run. Police are searching for the suspect. According to witnesses, the incident was deliberate."

"Dammit Mac, Jocko's death was my fault. The poor guy was about to get married." As tears welled in both eyes, he sat in disbelief.

"That's nonsense. Blame RE. Those codes must be damned explosive."

"But they're undecipherable," countered Morgan. "The prick has to know."

"Does he? Your ability to solve puzzles creates doubt. RE wants you dead at all costs. And by implication, that includes me."

"Well, the shit has certainly hit the fan. We've got to get the hell out of here."

"Tomorrow, we're moving to a safe house," muttered Mackenzie. "We are not going to die in a hospital."

CHAPTER 23

Sunday, January 31

Shortly after 8 a.m., Nash hobbled to intensive care. As he peered into Meredith's room his jaw gaped. The analyst's hue was a pasty white. Easing next to the bed he caressed her hand and whispered softly.

"Hey, doctors are pleased. You're doing well."

"Hooray for me. Can you stay?"

"No. We're headed to the office. Our wounds were minor."

"Be careful." Ever so lightly, she squeezed his fingers. "I don't want to lose you."

"Likewise. I'll check back later."

With a mid-morning arrival, the agents sipped coffee in the Dubliner's office. Weighing heavily on their minds was a single question. "Was there a next move?"

"Mac, travel is our only option. It keeps RE off balance and us alive. The mysterious Colonel Rhodes is our best lead. We need to locate the desert phantom."

"But he's military. You can't waltz into a base and coerce him like Melewski."

"Contact the Director. See if his people can locate Rhodes. I can check with my sources. Hopefully, the guy is retired."

"Make your calls. Let's reconvene at noon."

Eager for lunch, Nash hobbled into the Dubliner's office. Busy at a computer, the Special Agent flashed an irritated scowl. "Any news?"

"Mixed. Colonel Mark Rhodes retired with a spotless record. Inquiries about Camp 'XZ' were fruitless."

"Jameson ran into the same problem. Army brass was not cooperative. The location was likely destroyed by the military. Are you hungry?"

"I could eat. But I'm not leaving the building."

"Then we take our chances downstairs. Hell, the cafeteria poses a greater risk than RE."

Shortly after 2 p.m., an ominous shadow appeared in the Dubliner's doorway. Morgan's harried expression was telling.

"Partner, I don't like that look. Is it Meredith?"

"No. It's our desert ghost. He's dead."

"Colonel Rhodes?"

"Yeah. Depressed about retirement, the guy shot himself. Details are pending."

"Morgan, that's bullshit. RE seems to be everywhere."

"Including my computer. I must have triggered a flag when researching our mystery man."

"Dammit, we're boxed into a corner. Even these offices aren't safe. Suggestions?"

"Yeah. Forget safe houses, Mac. Too many agents know the locations. The hospital remains our best bet."

"I agree. But even that safety net expires in a day or so."

"Likely. That's why we take the fight to RE. We do the unexpected."

"Meaning?"

"We focus on our four elitists. We dig until something pops. If so, we move fast."

"Anyone in particular?"

"Allday has my interest. The new V.P. has contacts, clout, and a low profile."

"What about the codes?"

"I'll keep working. A break zooms us to the top."

"Then let's head to the hospital. Nick wants me alive for our June nuptials."

Arriving in late afternoon, the pair headed directly to intensive care. Given a brief update by an accommodating nurse, both grimaced. The analyst was back in surgery.

"Nurse, what happened?"

"Her fever spiked, Agent Nash. Shrapnel peppered her torso. Jagged pieces were everywhere. They're still being located."

"How long will she be in surgery?"

"There's no telling. My guess is one to three hours. The procedure is somewhat exploratory. But your colleague is young and fit. Infection is the greatest risk."

Downtrodden, the duo ambled to the waiting room. Ninety minutes later, the nurse reappeared. "We're returning Dr. Lindsey to intensive care in an hour or so. The surgery was successful."

With the nurse's departure, Mackenzie glanced at her watch. The time was approaching 6 p.m. "Well, that sucks. I suggest we eat, get some rest, and start early."

"That sounds good."

Bored with television reruns, Nash limped to intensive care. Halted by the lead nurse, he was reminded of the late hour and directed to a nearby waiting room. He was thumbing through a "*Star Power*" magazine when his eyes suddenly popped.

Well, I'll be damned.

Transfixed, he carefully studied pages forty-six and forty-seven. Mesmerized by the pictures, he didn't notice the abrasive nurse. A brief visit with Meredith was approved. Ripping the thin sheets from the tabloid, Morgan stuffed them into his shirt pocket.

"Agent, you get two minutes. Dr. Lindsey needs rest."

"What about fever?"

"It's declining. That's a good sign."

Stepping into the room, he choked back a gag. The profiler's pasty white hue had morphed to an ethereal gray. Lightly touching her hand, he felt no response. Leaning close, his words were heartfelt. "Take care. I don't want to lose you."

Hobbling to the Dubliner's spacious suite, he rapped on the door. "Dammit, go away. I need sleep." The anti-social response was curt, aping a guttural growl.

Peeking into the room, he waved. Clad in purple silk pajamas, Mackenzie's head was buried in a book. Noting her partner's dumbass Cheshire grin, her mood instantly soured.

"That idiotic look means trouble. Now is not the time."

"Mac, we need to talk."

"Can't it wait?"

"No. We need to prep for a secretive trip."

With a reluctant nod, the Special Agent listened to Morgan's bodacious plan. At the conclusion, her eyes were bulging in disbelief. The proposal was sheer idiocy. Stunned, she merely shook her head. "Partner, this trip is not only outlandish but a waste of time. Hell, it's suicidal...a death wish."

"Do you have a better option? We're dead if we don't act."

Reluctantly she nodded. "You make a valid point. Make your calls. And may God take pity on fools."

"I'm on it."

"Wait. I'm not calling Jameson. This idiocy is strictly off the record."

Returning to the Spartan-like quarters, he quickly made two calls. The first was a no-brainer. Luke and Shawn were always available for a generous payout and new adventure. Robinson's billionaire father was the critical unknown. The daring scheme required his aircraft, global connections, and a hefty investment.

Forty minutes later, the flimsy plan was green-lighted. To Morgan's delight, the old man agreed to handle all arrangements and costs. Heaving a huge sigh of relief, he packed for the trans-Atlantic flight.

A round of high-stakes poker was looming.

CHAPTER 24

Monday, February 1

As "code blue" reverberated down the hallways, frantic nurses rushed Morgan to critical care. At 7:10 a.m., he was pronounced dead. A short time later, his body bag was placed in a waiting hearse. With a quick signature and friendly nod, the muscular funeral attendant drove the black harbinger of death away from the hospital's prying eyes. Several miles later, the vehicle rolled to a stop at a nearby mall. Idling nearby was a gray limousine with darkened windows. Bounding from the front seat of the hearse, Mackenzie, Luke, and Shawn ripped off their funeral attire and entered the limo. Flashing a wry grin, a suddenly alive Morgan exited the rear door and joined the group. To his surprise, Robinson was missing.

Noting his confused look, Wilson Senior chuckled. "Robby's back at the ranch playing cowboy. Hell son, you need bravado to sell this idiotic ruse. That's me. I'm rich. And I can bullshit with anyone."

A lifetime of ranching in the South Texas sun had weathered the old man's face and hands. A cowboy at heart, the sinewy seventy-three-year-old billionaire was well-respected for his savvy investments and business acumen. In a festive mood, the former Marine officer stood an erect six-foot-one with silvery hair and a pencil-thin mustache.

"Sir, I'm deeply grateful. But I don't want you kidnapped or killed."

"Look, this ain't my first rodeo. I can take care of myself."

"So be it. Meet my boss. This is Special Agent Mackenzie Fallon."

"Howdy, ma'am. It's a pleasure."

A half hour later, the stretch limo entered the sprawling acreage of the Dallas-Fort Worth International Airport. Diverting to side roads, the chauffeur navigated to an isolated hangar. Noting Mackenzie's confusion, the old man laughed. "Agent, our billionaire's club has special access to hangars, security, and customs. Plus, the Governor has pulled a few strings."

Winking at his boss, Morgan immediately noted the rancher's value. The oil baron had the clout and bluster to make things happen. Plus, his international experience was vital to their Cairo success.

"What about Egyptian customs?"

"That's not a problem, Mackenzie. We trade perks and grease palms. Their dignitaries often borrow our planes. Plus, the Governor can cover our butts when needed."

"What's the flight plan?"

"We fly to Madrid and refuel. After an extended break, we mosey over to Cairo." Suddenly, the billionaire's nonchalant expression turned serious, his words candid. "Agents, we have to talk. We're headed into a hostile country with a flimsy-ass plan. Have you added any details?"

"Nothing has changed, sir. Contacting the Director or other credible sources was too risky."

"Hell Morgan, this whole trip is a crapshoot. Kidnapping two renowned archeologists in a foreign country is pretty damned dicey. What's their story?"

"The father and son are curators at the Cairo Museum of Antiquities. The Egyptians are linked to our four suspects. If things go bad, they're dead."

"What makes you think they're involved?"

"It's because of these pictures." Reaching into his pocket, Morgan quickly unfolded the tabloid photos. "Take a look."

"Hey, these shots are from Anderson's dinner party a few days after the swearing-in ceremony. The shindig was a rush job. So, I was a no-show. Our new President has a real hankering for the spotlight."

"Sir, look closer."

Peering intently, the rancher grinned. "Those two women are toting some mighty fancy ornaments."

"A journalist questioned Anderson about his wife's cobra pendant. But the President refused to comment about her jewelry *or* his golden scarab cuff links."

"That's pretty fancy stuff and extremely rare."

"Look at General Robison's wife. Her miniature pendant is a golden woman adorned with a headdress. Likely, it's Isis."

"Son, I was a Marine interrogator for several years. Plus, I have experience with artifacts. These babies have to be black market purchases. Or, these guys are involved in some illegal dig."

"Exactly. We think the jewelry was stolen from western Iraq. If so, Dr. Ari Heri and son were the lead archeologists. Army Rangers under Riggs and Robison provided the labor and security. We're headed to Cairo to find answers."

CHAPTER 25

Tuesday, February 2

Refueling in Madrid, Morgan peered at the yawning billionaire. "Sir, are the Cairo accommodations set?"

"Affirmative. The six-bedroom presidential suite at the Nefertiti Hotel can easily accommodate our team. It's near the City Stars Mall and River Nile casino."

"Is there a fashionable restaurant nearby? I need to isolate the elder Heri."

"The Fayruz Restaurant has great atmosphere, privacy, and Middle Eastern delicacies."

"That sounds perfect. We can spend the afternoon touring the museum and then break for dinner."

"Good. A trustworthy friend can reserve a table."

"Was Heri eager to host you?"

"Are you kidding? Once my office dangled the cheese, he salivated."

"I assume the bait was large."

"Son, to attract greedy rats, you have to sweeten the pot. I authorized a fifty-million-dollar payout. The curators are most anxious to fleece the naïve, free-spending American billionaire."

Noting the twinkle in his eyes, Nash knew the old man was thirsting for adventure. "Sir, I'm most grateful. That old adage is true. Money talks, opens doors, and coerces loyalties."

Anxious to finalize plans his eyes darted to the Dubliner. "Mac, I suggest we split up at the museum. Mr. Wilson and I tour with the elder Heri. You take Luke and Shawn and accompany Apries."

"Sounds good. What about later?"

"That's easy. Show Apries a good time. Shower him with Mr. Wilson's money. Treat him to dinner and gambling. We reconnect at the airport before midnight."

Unexpectedly, the billionaire interrupted. "Morgan, the Fayruz is a posh restaurant. It's a favorite locale for high rollers. A kidnapping could prove disastrous."

"Fayruz is perfect. I want a public place. Dr. Heri is going to appear rather tipsy."

"What about Apries? Won't he call the police if daddy disappears?"

"Mac, he's the least of our worries. If the old man vanishes, he wins. Apries becomes sole curator of a world-class museum. According to my research, he loves fancy cars, luxury houses and lots of money."

"Morgan's right," quipped the rancher. "The son is not a concern. We kidnap the elder Heri, force him to talk, and then jettison his ass over the Atlantic."

"That's my thinking. No remorse."

"That's not acceptable," countered the Dubliner. "The curator could be innocent."

Instantly the old man flashed a devilish grin. "Mackenzie, Heri's money comes from the black market. The man is guilty as hell. This is going to be wickedly entertaining."

With a mid-afternoon landing in Cairo, the customized Boeing taxied to an isolated hangar. Obsequious agents quickly stamped passports and waved the team through security. Idling nearby was a black limo with darkened windows. The world-class Nefertiti Hotel was but a short drive away.

CHAPTER 26

Wednesday, February 3

Succumbing to the long trip, no one stirred until mid-morning. At 1:30 p.m., the team was driven to the famous Cairo Museum of Antiquities located near Tahir Square. Containing the world's most precious collection of Egyptian art, the museum featured five thousand years of history and one hundred and twenty thousand artifacts.

As anticipated, the overly accommodating curators agreed to divide the group. Led by Apries, Fallon's team headed upstairs. As the elder Heri pontificated about the museum Wilson posed a surprising question.

"May I request the origin of your names?"

Pleased by the unexpected courtesy, the curator immediately responded. "Ari translates as "guardian." Apries means "the sun enlarges his heart."

"What about your family name?"

"Heri means "sacred scribe and priest of Ptah." As the chief god of Memphis, Ptah was worshipped as creator and protector."

Fascinated by an array of stunning displays, Nash's group toured the lower floor. Mimicking the Louvre, the museum was massive. As the two groups reconnected, the curators agreed to the planned evening. Enticed by Wilson's two hundred thousand dollars, Mackenzie's foursome, including Apries and Morgan's ex-teammates, eagerly anticipated a fun evening of dining and gaming. Morgan's trio was headed to the Fayruz for a quiet meal and intense negotiations.

Sated by a fabulous dinner, the three men ordered coffee and another round of drinks. As Heri lusted in anticipation, the billionaire bided his time. Slowly the leisure conversation morphed into serious business.

"Ari, I collect rare artifacts. I'm here to spend fifty million dollars on Egyptian antiquities."

"Oh yes!" Unable to contain himself, the narcissistic curator squealed with delight. "I would be happy to supply your needs."

Controlling the tempo, the rancher slowly sipped his strong coffee. The rat was sniffing the cheese. "At the museum, I noted numerous Tut antiquities crafted from pure gold. Are they for sale?"

"Oh no! Pieces from the Cairo Museum are off the table. Sacred, they represent our fabled heritage."

"Then my trip is a waste of time. I'm leaving." Toying with the curator, the old man watched with a keen eye.

As smugness morphed into uncertainty, Heri's facial muscles tensed. "Wait. I have other artifacts. Precious and unlisted, they are in my private collection."

"Are they legit? I have no intention of getting arrested."

"Sir, these pieces have been rejected by the museum. They're duplicates and fragments. I've purchased many unsuitable items."

"Are the authorities aware of your private collection?"

"No. Corruption and greed are rampant in my government. I have retained certain things because of my valued contribution."

"If they're not museum worthy why the hell would I want them?"

"My private artifacts *are* worthy. They're priceless." Panicking, beads of sweat dotted the Egyptian's brow.

"Look Ari, I'm not spending fifty million U.S. dollars on a bunch of tourist crap. I need to know the origin of each antiquity."

"These particular artifacts come from a dig in western Iraq."

"Iraq? What are Egyptian antiquities doing in that hell hole?"

"For centuries there was a caravan route between Baghdad and Cairo. Numerous pieces have been discovered in western Iraq."

Patiently waiting, Morgan intervened. "How were you able to obtain artifacts from a war zone?"

"Your military recruited Apries to lead the dig. Many relics from ancient Egypt, Syria, Babylon, and Assyria were discovered."

"How did your son remain safe? Furious battles were being fought."

"Apries was guarded by elite Army Rangers. The dig was west of the fighting. There were no incidents."

Nodding at the confirmation, Wilson Senior flashed a faux smile. "Did you find gold among the relics?"

"Oh yes! Gold, ivory, onyx, lapis, and silver were all discovered. The ancient artisans crafted beautiful headbands, bracelets, rings, and other fine jewelry. I have a priceless collection of artifacts."

"Then why are you selling?" The billionaire's tone was chilling. "These antiquities are irreplaceable."

"My collection has become rather crowded."

"Why don't you sell to other museums? Hell, they would pay a fortune. Let the public enjoy your history."

"My preference is private collectors. The appreciation level is much greater."

"Did you bring an inventory and pictures?"

"Most certainly." Beaming, the Egyptian's tone was celebratory. "But the materials are in the limo."

"Then please fetch them. I want to conclude our business. My time is short."

As the curator vanished Morgan casually poured the contents of a small vial into the Egyptian's coffee. The tasteless drug was fast acting. Returning in a near sprint, Heri proudly promoted his inventory and pictures. With eyes locked on the billionaire he nervously sipped coffee. As his speech slurred, the rancher bitterly reacted for all to hear.

"Oh Ari, you're drunk again. We have to get you home."

Quickly reacting, Nash snatched the materials and assisted Heri from the restaurant. As the limo motored toward the airport he peered at the rancher. "Sir, Ari has no passport. My plan was to interrogate him in Cairo."

"That was too risky. The driver has a fake passport."

"What about security?"

"Agents have been generously compensated to cooperate."

"Look! There's the other team. We can be airborne by midnight. What's the flight plan?"

"We leisurely cruise to Paris and refuel. Haste often brings attention." Puffing a Cuban cigar, the old man grinned. The adventure had been a hoot.

CHAPTER 27

Thursday, February 4

Two hours later the curator's grogginess instantly morphed to fury. Noting his angst, Shawn quickly alerted the team. Closing ranks, Mackenzie flashed her Irish charm. "Good morning, Ari. Or should I say it's a pleasant day for us."

"Who are you? Why are you treating me like a criminal?"

"We're friends of RE. You are being flown to an undisclosed location."

"But why?"

"It's simple. The master demands answers. If pleased, you live. Otherwise, you vanish without a trace."

"But I've done nothing wrong. What do you want from me?"

As Fallon nodded, Luke's fists hammered the archeologist's face, opening cuts along both eyebrows and cheeks.

"Why are you liquidating a priceless inventory?"

"I had no choice. The locals were snooping. I was selling through back channels."

"Were these artifacts from western Iraq?"

With his eyes locked in terror, the curator squirmed and squealed. "Oh yes! They come from Iraq. Oh, please don't kill me. I can open many doors for you."

"Breathe deeply, traitor. Appreciate your last breaths."

"But I haven't betrayed the master. Only a few items were sold."

Edging closer, the Dubliner's fiery green eyes were hard-set and cruel. "That is for RE to determine."

"But I haven't divulged secrets. I wasn't at the dig."

"But you knew every detail. How?"

"Apries kept me informed."

"What did he tell you? You have fifteen seconds before plunging thirty thousand feet into icy water."

"Wait! Rhodes ran the operation."

"Colonel Rhodes?"

"Yes. Are you going to kill Apries? My son has done nothing wrong."

"That is for RE to decide. His life depends on you."

"The dig was located on an ancient trade route. Every week Apries listed new finds."

"Were the artifacts coded?"

"Yes."

"Who else was involved?"

"No one. My son spoke only to Rhodes."

"Liar! There were other American contacts. The master has zero faith in you."

"Allday!" The curator's yelp was high-pitched and panic-stricken. "Apries met with Allday! Once he met with Anderson and the generals."

Toying with the curator, Mackenzie nodded to Luke. "Hit him again."

Vehemently, the archeologist shook his head. "No! Please, no more. I detest pain. That's all I know."

Unexpectedly, the curator's eyes blurred as his body convulsed uncontrollably. With all eyes fixated on the frenetic movement, no one noticed his subtle facial change. With a hard flick of the tongue, Ari popped a false molar.

Crushing the cyanide capsule, he shrieked defiantly. "Allahu Akbar...Alla..."

As the Egyptian twisted in the throes of death, tiny bubbles crusted around his thin lips. Seconds later, the renowned curator slumped in his seat.

"Dammit, I didn't see that coming," growled Fallon. "Morgan, you were right. These bastards are terrified of RE. This trip was a bust."

"I disagree," countered the pragmatic billionaire. "This little venture was a goldmine. Heri validated Colonel Rhodes and Camp XZ. And unknowingly, he unraveled the codes."

Following a smooth Parisian landing, the luxury Boeing rolled to a stop inside a private hangar. Within minutes fawning contacts quietly and efficiently removed the curator's lifeless body. With a hundred thousand dollars exchanging hands, the corpse was headed to the deep waters of the Atlantic Ocean.

CHAPTER 28

Friday, February 5

Arriving in the predawn blackness of a Dallas morning, Luke and Shawn exited the Boeing and disappeared. Accompanied by Wilson Senior, the two agents returned to the protective confines of the hospital. By sunrise, they were sipping coffee in the Dubliner's temporary office.

Unexpectedly, a trusted agent barged into the room and handed Mackenzie a message. Scanning the note, her face registered shock. "Dammit, Apries was found dead in Cairo. Cause of death was an apparent heart attack. Morgan, you've pegged this RE from day one. The prick has moles everywhere."

"Apries was a marked man. But I didn't expect such a quick retaliation. We're running out of time and options."

"What about the codes, Morgan? Have you made progress?"

"Sir, the pieces are slowly coming together. The weekly reports listed origin, artifact, and material. For example, the column heading "E" represented Egypt. Artifacts included necklaces, headbands, rings, and so on. Next came a description regarding the type of metal, stone, or ivory. The ending number indicated weight. Br-g-10 signified a gold bracelet weighing ten ounces."

"That's good detective work," beamed Fallon. "Finally, there's something concrete for Jameson."

"Hang on," snorted the rancher. "Those gala ornaments sure as hell weren't replicas. They're priceless and likely stolen. Are you going to arrest these bastards?"

"Mr. Wilson, it's not that simple. With dead curators and nothing written, everything is circumstantial. Our suspects would lawyer up and deny charges."

"Forget theft," chirped Nash. "One or more is a traitor."

An hour later, Nash headed to intensive care. Expecting the worst, he was stunned. The analyst's pasty hue had undergone a miraculous transformation.

"Hey, you look great. It's actually amazing."

"I'm making progress. But it's slow going."

"What's the prognosis?"

"Good. Once the fever stabilizes, I'm home free."

"What about trauma?"

As if deflating a balloon, the smile instantly faded. "That's another story. Horrific nightmares create uncontrollable trembling."

"That's to be expected. Care to share?"

"The thought of being stalked or targeted is too much. It's unnerving."

"That's normal. Fear is a rough customer."

"Look, I should know these things. Hell, I'm a shrink. But now, it's me. It's scary."

"Time heals everything. My humble advice is to take baby steps. Live in the moment, nothing else."

"What about work?"

"It's been peacefully quiet."

"You haven't visited for several days. Were you gone?"

"Nope. We were obliging your surgeon. Plus, we've been busy chasing leads. Our suspects have been dying rather quickly."

As the analyst faded, Nash squeezed her hand, said goodbye, and silently exited the room. Another session with Mackenzie and the old man was looming.

Returning to the temporary office, Morgan immediately noted the Dubliner's grim expression. Acknowledging the rancher, he took a seat.

"Mac, you don't look so hot."

"Jameson called. You were spot-on. Hyatt's assassination has created worldwide uncertainty."

"Russia?"

"Yep. But it's Russia *and* friends. The Kremlin is continuing its military buildup in northern Syria and along the Ukraine border. India is doing the same along the Pakistani border. China is relocating troops and heavy armor to coastal cities with deep water harbors. The Pentagon is preparing for multiple small-scale incursions."

"Dammit. That was my worst fear," lamented Morgan. "Our weakness has them salivating. Mac, how has our glamour boy reacted?"

"According to the Director, Richard Anderson's manly balls have shrunk. Feeble warnings have been issued, but nothing else. Sanctions and military action are off the table."

"The man's a puss," snorted the rancher. "Like Hyatt, he's all talk and no action. Diplomacy only works if you carry a big stick. This guy wants to save the world with apologies."

"Maybe there's another reason." As Morgan flashed a wry grin, the billionaire reacted.

"Son, I know that look. Something's percolating in that twisted mind. What's the risk?"

"Less than ten percent."

"Does it include Robby?"

"Yep."

"Will it expose our suspects?"

"That's my hope."

"Then let's hear it."

"I agree," chimed a curious Fallon. "State your case."

"Okay. Right now, we're stymied. Our four suspects are all high profile. Anderson and Allday are political and well-insulated. Riggs and Robison are noted generals and virtually untouchable. In my thinking, we have but one option. We have to lure them into the open."

"But a trap requires the right cheese," countered the old man. "Otherwise, your plan is dead in the water."

"Sir, you and Robby *are* the bait. No one else has the clout to pull this off."

Intrigued, the oilman gave Morgan a jagged look. His piercing eyes were deep-set and rock-hard. "Look, I took an oath to defend this country. I've got no tolerance for flag burners or traitors. What have you got?"

Flashing another wry grin, Morgan outlined his bodacious plan. "I want your billionaire's club to host a black-tie event in D.C. The fancy shindig needs to include our suspects."

"When?"

"ASAP. But the gala needs to be a ballbuster extravaganza. Washington's elite must be in attendance."

"That could prove difficult," uttered Mackenzie. "What's the attraction?"

"The event honors the new President. It's the only way to ensure Anderson's presence and expose the guilty."

"But scheduling could take weeks or months. There's no time."

"I disagree," countered the billionaire. "When my friends throw a shindig, everyone attends. My staff can handle the arrangements. Honoring Anderson is smart. You can anticipate a robust gathering."

With the rancher's blessing, Morgan breathed a sigh of relief. With wealth came influence and power. The old man had the clout to make things happen, and fast.

"Thank you, sir."

"What's my role?"

"It's amazingly simple. I want you and the Texas Governor to approach the President. If he's wearing those scarab cufflinks, pay him a compliment. Then add this sentence. "I know the origin."

"That's it?"

"Yep. Hopefully, he's wearing those 'lucky bugs.' If not, my plan falters."

"And you want Robby to do the same?"

"Yeah. Instruct him to mingle with Allday and the generals. Compliment the women on their fancy jewelry. Then add the one sentence."

"Morgan, wait. There's a huge flaw. High-profile ladies don't wear the same attire to fancy galas. It's a social embarrassment."

"We take that chance, Mac. Any artifact springs the trap. Our traitor panics and calls RE."

"Then pray for success. I don't like being a target."

As predicted, Wilson's executives worked their magic. The gala extraordinaire was scheduled for February 12. Exhaling a collective sigh of relief, the team addressed their most pressing need. To remain alive, they had to vanish for a week.

"There's only one option," quipped the oil baron. "We head to desolate West Texas and disappear. A friend owns an untraceable hunting cabin in a remote and isolated area.

There's nothing but rolling hills, sparse vegetation, and pronghorn antelope. My buddy can make the arrangements. Mackenzie, the FBI must be excluded. That includes the Director. It's too risky."

"That's not a problem."

"Okay, we separately exit the hospital, rendezvous, and drive to the cabin. Like Robby, we simply vanish. There's no communication for a week unless my executive secretary sends an urgent message."

Agreeing to the simple plan, Morgan relaxed. Dubious, the Dubliner fired a final question. "What happens when our sabbatical ends?"

"Robby and I will join the Austin contingent and fly to D.C. One of my men will drop you at a friend's ranch. You'll be safe until after the gala."

CHAPTER 29

Friday, February 12

As lethal reality trumped restful solitude, the two agents relocated to the designated ranch. Accompanied by a host of Texas dignitaries, the Wilsons boarded the billionaire's customized Boeing and departed from Austin International. Relaxing in a plush recliner the old man glanced at the invitation and flashed an ironic smile. The posh gala was to be hosted by the infamous Watergate Hotel.

By 7:30 p.m., the oil baron was actively engaged in social exchanges. The grand ballroom was immaculate with stylish crystal chandeliers, colorful wall décor, and elaborate flower arrangements. A bevy of waiters roamed the audience serving chilled champagne and light hors d'oeuvres. The billionaire had spent a considerable fortune to create the perfect atmosphere.

Thirty minutes later, the President and his wife arrived to a tepid ovation. Trailing close behind were the suspect generals. A short time later, the Vice President and his wife joined the festivities.

Working the room, Robinson III greeted Allday. The V.P.'s stunning young wife was wearing a sleek, low-cut evening gown. Worn fashionably around her slender neck was an exquisite necklace crafted from gold and silver threads.

Dangling from the showpiece was a golden pendant featuring a small circle sitting atop a capital "T."

"Ma'am, let me compliment you on the gorgeous pendant. The Ankh is an ancient Egyptian symbol for life."

Flashing a gracious smile, the twenty-eight-year-old socialite appeared bewildered. "It's a gift from my generous husband. That's all I know."

Peering at Allday, Robinson artfully baited the trap. "Sir, your wife's trinkets are truly magnificent and rare. I've recently purchased some off-market antiquities. They're likely from the same dig in Western Iraq."

As if he had been hammered in the groin, his faux smile instantly vanished. A blink later, the politician's charm returned. "Rare? No. The necklace is a tourist item." Adept at deflecting comments, the Vice-President switched subjects and cautiously stepped away.

Mesmerized by the star-studded gathering, Richard Anderson eagerly sought out the Texas Governor and Wilson Senior. After the customary exchange of impersonal greetings, the billionaire smoothly transitioned topics.

"Mr. President, you're wearing those lucky cufflinks. Those babies had to cost you a pretty penny. They're exquisite and rare."

"Actually, they're tourist items. But they've brought me good luck. I've always been superstitious."

"I've done some dabbling in antiquities. Recently I purchased some black-market stuff from a dig in Western Iraq. Did your 'tourist items' come from the same site?"

Rocked by the explosive query, Anderson's face twisted, his eyes dark and steeled with hate. A split second later, the charm returned. Stepping away, he mingled with other guests.

With darting eyes, the oilman noticed General Riggs and wife. To his disappointment, the woman was showcasing a pearl necklace. Standing nearby, was General Robison and his petite bride. Her stunning necklace was crafted from wound gold, copper, and lapis lazuli. Introducing himself, he graciously complimented the youthful beauty.

"That's an exquisite piece, ma'am. That dig in western Iraq produces some amazing artifacts. My wife just loves our shopping sprees."

Overhearing Iraq, Robison froze. Two seconds later, the faux charm returned. "Sir, you're mistaken. This necklace was crafted by Tiffany artisans. It was a pleasure meeting you."

Enjoying the festivities, Wilson Senior and the Texas Governor renewed old friendships. As the gala waned, he rejoined Robby. Surrounded by trusted security the pair retired to their suite.

"Son, the pot is simmering. But who's in the kitchen?"

CHAPTER 30

Saturday, February 13

Following an uneventful return to Austin, the Texas contingent exited the luxury jet, boarded separate cars, and departed in various directions. Leery of an ambush, the Wilsons lagged behind. Blanketed by security, the pair was driven to their sprawling ranch. An hour later the billionaire eased into a leather recliner, acknowledged the agents, and flamed a Cuban cigar.

"How did it go, sir?"

"Mackenzie, the event was smashing. All four suspects were strutting around like royal peacocks."

"Did you learn anything?"

"That is to be determined. The ball is in their court."

"Was Anderson wearing those ridiculous cufflinks?"

"Morgan, that pompous ass was flitting around like a Hollywood rock star. When I mentioned Iraq, he panicked. General Riggs's wife was a non-factor. However, Robison's blonde honey was wearing a gold necklace interlaced with lapis."

"Allday's wife was flashing a gorgeous Ankh," added Robby. "When I mentioned Iraq, the Vice President scurried."

"How would you assess the evening?"

"The trip was definitely worthwhile, Mac. Three are definitely thieves. Riggs was the only unknown. But who are the traitors?"

"What's your take on Anderson?"

"Morgan, he's young, privileged, and arrogant. That's it. America's glamour boy is no Jack Kennedy."

"Was he cordial?"

"Hell son, he had to be. I was the host. But that half-ass smile was forced."

"Is he a minion?"

"That's debatable. The moronic prick comes across as God's gift to mankind. But he could be innocent. My gut says no. For the right price, I think Richard Anderson dances with the devil."

Interrupting was Fallon's ringtone. Listening intently, she flashed an expression of utter disbelief. Something horrific had happened.

"Boss, what's wrong?"

"That extravaganza opened the gates of hell. The caller was Jameson. Four murdered women were discovered with wrapped heads. The killings occurred in Seattle, Los Angeles, Kansas City, and San Antonio. All were linked to the Federal Reserve and murdered shortly after midnight."

"Well Mr. Wilson, you were right," quipped Nash. "One of the suspects panicked and contacted RE. Based on the suddenness of the killings, the bastard must have a target list on speed dial."

"Dammit, partner, I can't take another BABA. I'm getting married. Does this signal another killing spree?"

"No. I think it's a crystal-clear message. *The four women symbolize us*. RE is coming *and* fast."

"That means he knows about the ranch," snapped the old man. "We need to relocate. Time is our enemy."

Disheartened, Mackenzie wiped a tear from her eye and peered at Morgan. "We're not safe anywhere. And we're out of options."

"Unless we fight fire with fire. We take the initiative."

"Meaning?"

"We travel to Virginia, break into two estates, expose traitors, and disrupt schedules. We vanish before RE can react."

"Who owns these properties?'

"Allday and Anderson."

"But that's insane. We would never get past security."

"Son, I agree with Mackenzie. It's the wrong play."

"But we have no choice. Right now, we're sitting ducks."

"Dad and I are fine," quipped Robby. "We're relocating to the Governor's Mansion. Plans were finalized on the return flight."

Suddenly an unexpected call halted the quibble. Listening but not speaking, the Dubliner's lips curled in dismay. As the line clicked silent, her cheeks were a pasty white.

"Morgan, you were right about RE trimming loose ends. General Riggs died early this morning. Supposedly intoxicated, he rammed his SUV into a tree. According to the Director, the death was suspicious, likely a homicide."

"Well, scratch one suspect," barked the rancher. "Who's his replacement?"

"General Robison. This is fricking unbelievable."

"Mac, Richard Anderson is RE's weak link. The prick is pompous and sloppy. We need to search his estate."

"Son, you're thinking with that little head. My god, you're talking wealthy, powerful people with military surveillance."

"That's why I need Mackenzie. Security is her expertise. Plus, there's a caveat. Our disappearance buys time."

"When would you leave?"

"Tomorrow."

"Then may God smile on fools. If Mac approves, let's detail this idiotic plan."

CHAPTER 31

Sunday, February 14

Opting for an early morning breakfast, the team argued logistics. Dubious about the flimsy plan, Wilson Senior remained non-committal. "Son, my thinking is the same as yesterday. This venture is a disaster waiting to happen."

"I concur," added the Dubliner. "There must be other options."

"Mac, vanishing is our only hope. But we can't hide forever. A trip to Virginia exposes one or two traitors."

"How?"

"Sir, that depends on you and Mackenzie. If approved, we fly from Austin this afternoon."

"That's impossible. My Boeing is off-limits. So is Austin International. RE is just waiting."

"Is there a Plan B?"

"Yeah. A friend has a small jet in nearby Georgetown. I've made arrangements."

"Mr. Wilson, I'm grateful. You always stay a step ahead."

"That's why I'm still alive. Watch your six. You leave at 2 p.m. with Mackenzie's approval."

"Boss?"

"The answer should be hell no. But it's a reluctant yes. There's no other choice."

As the Georgetown Gulfstream rocketed through layers of puffy white clouds, Nash studied the topography of the two Virginia estates. The rolling hills and dense woods made perfect cover. Glancing at Mackenzie, he was startled. The Dubliner was quivering.

"Mac, are you okay?"

"Hell no. Since childhood, I've dreamed of a June wedding. The odds of surviving this insane adventure are slim to none."

"Relax. We'll be in and out in no time."

"Are we looking for anything in particular?"

"That's to be determined."

"You don't know?"

"We'll know when we find it."

"Morgan, that's pretty damn flimsy."

"I'm kidding. We look for the unusual."

"Do you anticipate Secret Service?"

"No. Chantilly is rural, crime-free, and asleep at dusk. It's a numbers game if anyone appears."

Landing in the chilly bleakness of early evening, the Gulfstream taxied to an isolated hanger. Located adjacent to D.C., the corporate airport was a beehive of activity. Peering out the window, Morgan flashed a wry grin. Their ride was a non-descript, dusty black pickup. Within minutes the pair was headed to Virginia.

Passing through Chantilly, they veered onto a country road and meandered to Allday's estate. Hiding the truck in a grove of trees, Mackenzie took the lead. With darting eyes, she searched for hidden wires and invisible beams. To her relief, none were noted. Morgan was right. Security was non-existent in the rural area. Other than a few outside lights the interior of the colonial two-story house was pitch black.

"Wait here while I disarm cameras and security."

A short time later, the Dubliner reappeared. "We're good to go. The system was standard grade."

Jogging to the back door, Nash easily picked the lock and entered the darkened kitchen. Guided by pin lights, they headed to Allday's wood-paneled study. Massive two-tiered bookshelves adorned both sides of the room.

Instantly, Mackenzie barked a command. "Search the desk and right side. The left is mine. But hurry. It's almost eleven."

Scanning the highly polished desk, Nash noted family pictures but no files. On an adjacent table were military and political photos. Noting nothing of interest, he searched the two-tiered bookshelf. Ten minutes later, he shook his head in disgust.

"Mac, this area is clear. Find anything?"

"Nope. The guy likes to read. Let's split up and peruse the house. Take the upstairs while I search the living area."

Twenty minutes later, they reconnected in the dining room. To their dismay, nothing damning had been discovered.

"Mac, I don't think Allday is our man."

"Or he's extremely clever. D. C. may be his lair. Let's get the hell out of here."

Fast walking, the pair retraced their steps and vanished into the winter blackness.

CHAPTER 32

Monday, February 15

Arriving at the President's estate shortly after midnight, they hid the truck and edged toward the sprawling ranch-style house. Taking the lead, the Dubliner methodically sprayed fine particulates to identify hidden wires and invisible beams. Unexpectedly, she stopped and held up a hand.

"Note the beams. I count three. Memorize the spacing."

Wiggling under the invisible fence, the pair edged closer to the darkened house. As anticipated, no guards were patrolling the grounds. Scanning for cameras the Dubliner barked a soft command.

"Wait here."

After a lengthy delay, a dejected Mackenzie returned. "Partner, we had better scram. Anderson has a bitch of a security system. I tried but failed."

"That was the old man's concern. Military?"

"Likely. It was definitely futuristic. Only an outside security pad was visible. The damn thing was attached to the rear door. There were no obvious cameras, wires or boxes. Worse, the door was steel."

"A wrong code must activate a shitload of trouble."

"That's my thinking. The pad is definitely a deterrent. It's obvious yet ominous. Punch the wrong digits and all hell breaks loose. That explains no guards. The system is definitely high tech."

"Well, the password can't be that difficult. Anderson isn't that smart. But I need a starting point. Can you recall similar prototypes?"

"Possibly. During training, we were shown various models. Though simple in appearance, the codes were tricky, no numbers or symbols."

"Okay, that helps. We focus on letters."

"Morgan, wait. It's not that easy."

"Why?"

"The systems varied. Codes were four, five, *or* six letters. If an entry was correct, the pad flashed yellow and then glowed green. Disarmed, the reinforced door automatically unlocked. There was no key. If the pad flashed red, you were in deep shit. Cameras blinked and alarms blared."

"Dammit. Those variations create a numeric impossibility. There's no way."

"Then we need to leave."

"Not yet. We need answers." Stepping away, Nash focused on Anderson's link with RE. Somewhere in the relationship was a critical clue. Locked in a trance, his mind raced.

Nervously glancing at her watch, Mackenzie noted the passing time. Their window of escape was rapidly closing. Unexpectedly, Morgan muttered three confusing words.

"Or is there?"

"What are you mumbling about?"

"Mac, the code is likely Egyptian. That's RE's mantra. But I need help."

"Forget it. Mythology is your baby. Think Raz."

"That's a bad idea."

"Why?"

"The bastard was the spin master of *disinformation*."

"True. But did he reveal anything?"

"Maybe. Let me think." Suddenly, Morgan tensed. "Mac, it's just the opposite. *Distraction* is the critical clue. It's the fourth "D."

"I'm not following."

"Think omission."

"What?"

"Raz jabbered at length about Akhenaten and other god-like deities. But when talking about a certain animal, the bastard was extremely evasive."

"Dammit, Morgan, this isn't the time for games. Look, that system is sophisticated. Death is real. You can't screw around with some stupid-ass theory."

"I needed a connection. Now I have it. The tabloid photos underscored Anderson's affinity for a special bull. The four letters are all lower case: "a-p-i-s."

"Ap...? Are you sure?"

"Enter apis. 'a-p-i-s.'"

"Look, this isn't the time for wild guesses."

"Trust me. Enter the letters."

Fully expecting the bowels of hell to explode, Mackenzie reluctantly entered the code. To her surprise, the pad flashed yellow and then glowed green. Both heard a notable click as the steel door unlocked. With Glocks in the ready position, they cautiously entered the darkened kitchen and moved toward Anderson's study. The custom-designed wood-paneled office aped Allday's.

"Morgan, take the desk and right bookcase. The left is mine."

Perusing the mahogany masterpiece, Nash noted a picture of Anderson's blonde wife and their three children. As his eyes darted right, a photo on a side table popped. The

President was posing with General Robison. But the photo had been clipped. A significant portion was missing.

General Riggs was literally cut out of the picture. That car wreck was no accident.

A second picture piqued his interest. Anderson was posing with Allday and Hyatt's widow. Scanning an adjacent wall, he fixated on a familiar sight. The framed picture featured the President standing next to a huge black bull. It was an artist's rendition of the photo featured in the celebrity magazine.

Raz was right. The 'apis' was no ordinary bull. That white diamond emblazoned on the forehead was special.

Buoyed by the circumstantial evidence, he eagerly searched the bookshelves but found nothing of interest. Suddenly an arcing pin light caught his attention. Waving frantically, Mackenzie was signaling that she had discovered something.

"Morgan, get your ass over here."

Moving quickly, he stepped close to his partner. Suddenly his eyes bulged.

"Scarabes sacer!"

"What?"

"That's Latin for sacred beetle, a symbol of new life."

"I think these bookends have a different meaning. They certainly got my attention."

"Why?"

"One is extremely valuable. The other is not."

"But they look identical," countered Nah. "I'm not following."

"Here, hold the left one."

"Okay, it's green and weighty."

"Now feel this one."

"It's also green and weighty."

"Wrong," grinned Mackenzie. "There's a slight deviation. The left beetle is pure jade. It's old and rare. But this baby is recent. Cast from plaster, it's textured to look and feel the same."

"Are you sure?"

"Positive. It's lighter around the edges but heavier in the middle. I think there's a battery tucked inside. The knockoff is a remote."

"Bingo. There *is* a secret room."

"Likely. But where's the contact point?"

"Mac, it's the painting. That's Anderson with the apis. The bull completes the circle. Aim the remote in that direction."

Acquiescing, Mackenzie pointed the faux beetle at the frame. Nothing happened.

"Try the forehead. Pinpoint the white diamond."

A split second later, they heard a muted humming. To their delight, a secret panel adjacent to the painting swung open. Entering a narrow doorway, both stopped in utter amazement. The brightly lit rectangular room was ablaze with color.

"What the hell?"

"Mac, welcome to pharaoh's tomb. The starry blue sky depicts a living king."

"But why would Anderson tinker in the macabre?"

"It's obvious. This room honors his master. The walls depict ancient signs and symbols. Like Raz and BABA, RE must be Egyptian."

Adorning the back wall was a floor-to-ceiling fresco. The upper tier featured a sky-blue background, brilliant yellow sun, and puffy white cloud. Peering from the cloud was an all-seeing, three-dimensional eye. The orb's rays radiated toward a man with an elongated neck, protruding lips, paunch stomach, and alien-shaped head. Standing erect, his long skinny arms and hands extended outward in a display of gratitude. Tightly gripped in his right hand was a circle sitting atop a block 'T.'

"Look, boss. Pharaoh is gripping an Ankh, a revered sign of life."

Featuring a skin tone of golden brown, the man was naked except for white linen wrapped around his waist. A white conical crown with a rounded top adorned his head.

"Who is he?"

"Akhenaten. Married to Nefertiti, the youthful king was Egypt's most revolutionary pharaoh. Raz and BABA were descendants. Most likely, RE and his inner circle are cast from the same DNA."

Baffled by the bizarre images, their eyes shifted to the cream-colored left wall. Painted in the center was a large clock. Eight of the Roman numerals were black. The numbers one, three, five, and ten were painted a dirty red. Adjacent to the clock, were two small men. Both were wearing powder blue conical crowns adorned with red stars. Nearby was a block letter 'T' sitting atop a circle.

"Morgan, note the 'T' image. The Ankh is inverted. That can't be good."

"According to Raz, *inversion* symbolized death and destruction."

"Damn. What's your take on the clock?"

"It must relate to RE's timeframe. The four dirty red numbers symbolize blood or dissolution. But I'm clueless about a meaning."

The right wall was equally puzzling. Frothy white tips from a foam green tidal wave were poised to smash a small eye. Riding the crest was a small fishing boat. The lone passenger was a stick figure clutching another inverted Ankh. Less prominent in the lower right corner was a man with brown hair and a blonde woman. Both were Caucasians. Gripping Ankhs, they were waving at the boat.

Adjacent to the doorway was a small desk displaying two framed pictures. Methodically, Morgan searched the drawers but found nothing of interest. Whipping out his cell phone, he snapped a series of pictures. The imagery was far too encompassing to commit to memory. Stunned by the revelations, the pair jogged to the pickup. A hasty retreat from Chantilly was in order.

With an early morning arrival in Georgetown, the duo headed to the safe confines of the Texas Governor's Mansion. Entering a small conference room, both were astonished. Sitting in a cushioned chair and casually sipping coffee was the analyst.

"Meredith, what a surprise," exclaimed Morgan. "It's great to see you. Welcome back."

"I had to be with you. My surgeon finally relented and granted me an early release. But you were hard to find. The Director hinted that you might be in Austin."

"We've been evading RE," quipped the Dubliner. "We're staying at the Mansion for the next week or so."

Sporting a huge scowl, Wilson Senior barged into the room. "Have you heard the news?" As three faces expressed blank looks, the billionaire reported the grim news.

"Anderson's wife was kidnapped late last night. Following a fundraiser, her security detail was ambushed. The Secret Service agents were killed."

"What about the First Lady?"

"That was the breaking news, Mackenzie. Authorities discovered her body a short time ago. The woman's head was wrapped with yellow strips. There were no ransom demands."

"Son-of-a-bitch," exclaimed Morgan. "Anderson's wife was a non-factor. I didn't see this coming. Sir, was there a note?"

"Yeah, but it wasn't much. The note contained a bright sun, small cloud, and large smiley face. The signature was RE.

But the First Lady wasn't the only victim. There were three others. Women linked to the Federal Reserve were murdered in Los Angeles, New York, and Chicago. A falcon symbol was placed at every scene."

"Dammit. Those killings were planned *before* we left," blurted Morgan. "The bastard was hell-bent on flushing us out."

"Where did you go?"

"We took refuge in a safe house, Meredith. Wilson's ranch was no longer safe."

"Well, the proverbial shit has certainly hit the fan," snarled the rancher. "You've got to leave ASAP. Hell, you're not safe in Texas."

Irked by the butchery, Mackenzie's cheeks pulsated a fiery red. "Morgan, you were right. RE has no intention of stopping. We've got to decipher those images and stop this madness."

"Obviously, your flimsy-ass plan was a success."

Unexpectedly, Nash flashed an odd expression "Mr. Wilson, it was both enlightening...and troubling."

"Is there an end in sight?"

"Possibly. But that's a question for Dr. Lindsey. Meredith, why don't you answer the man? You seem to know *everything.*"

"What do you mean?"

"It's simple. You owe us an explanation."

"About what? I resent that tone."

"You shouldn't. Nor should you be confused. The evidence is crystal clear."

"What evidence?"

"Why don't you tell us about Richard's secret room."

"What?"

"Better yet, why don't you tell us about *your relationship*."

Instantly, Meredith froze. "What do you mean?"

"AREN'T YOU THE PRESIDENT'S WHORE?"

With the damning accusation, the room grew eerily quiet. As her sapphire eyes crackled with hostility, the analyst sat rigid and still. Then like a coiled viper, she struck. "No! That's absolutely not true."

"LIAR! You've been his mistress for years. Now you're set to become the First Lady."

"You're wrong! Yes, there was a brief fling. But it was forced. I've never been anybody's whore. Richard was never going to divorce his wife. Nor was I ever in the picture. I've loved my time *with you*."

"Liar. You've played us, especially me. There wasn't any coercion. RE orchestrated everything, including your transfer to our team. Did that college rape really happen? Or was that another smokescreen? Like Raz, you've won an Oscar for best performance."

"Morgan, you're wrong. You've got to believe me. My feelings for you and the team are genuine."

"LIAR! You're supposed to be rehabbing in Dallas. Yet you're here. Why?"

"But..."

"Wasn't it because RE couldn't find us?"

Unexpectedly, Mackenzie intervened on the profiler's behalf. "Morgan, what the hell? Not one thing in that secret room indicted Meredith. Dammit, she's been attacked twice and made important contributions."

"Plus, she's in love with you," added Wilson.

"That's a joke. Our shrink is a great actress. Mac, do you recall that brown-haired man and blonde woman?"

"Vividly. They were standing next to the crested wave. It was Anderson and his wife. Both were holding Ankhs."

"Wrong. That blonde was Meredith. The President and his whore were celebrating RE's plan to reshape the world."

"But there were no faces. We saw only the backs of heads."

"Son, you've got to slow down and untangle some things.

Was the blonde actually Meredith? Hyatt's widow was blonde. Hell, there are numerous blondes in D.C."

"There was also a damning photo on the small desk. Unseen by Mackenzie, it was an intimate shot of Meredith with her lover. Why has RE always remained a step ahead? The bastard had *two moles*, not one. We didn't gain an advantage until Meredith was shredded and Raz died."

"Your make a valid point," snorted the former interrogator. "But other than a sordid romance, there's no proof of treason. Everything is circumstantial."

"Mr. Wilson, Meredith *knew* about the secret room. She *knew* about Anderson's relationship with RE. She *knew* our plans. We've been played from day one. That grenade was meant for us, not her. It just bounced the wrong way."

Motivated by years of pent-up anger, Morgan vehemently prosecuted the case. As Mackenzie and Wilson fixated on his vigorous rhetoric, the analyst effortlessly flipped a false molar. Raising her fist in defiance, she crushed the tiny cyanide capsule. As her body convulsed in death the trio sat silent as a hint of bitter almond scented the room.

Stone-faced, the pragmatic rancher posed the obvious question. "Son, was there actual proof? Yeah, the woman had an affair. But was she a traitor?"

"That was my question," barked the Dubliner. "There was no case."

"The picture was real but not damning. So, I rolled the dice. Prosecution was the only way to flush the truth. If innocent, Meredith would have reamed my ass. I would have apologized."

"You did well," muttered the old man. "You gambled and won. That double mole scenario was totally unexpected. RE has eyes everywhere."

"I'm calling security," growled the Dubliner.

As Mansion guards stoically removed the lifeless body the billionaire's darting eyes shifted to Morgan. "Obviously, the trip *was* successful."

"It wasn't initially. Allday's estate was a bust. But Anderson's study was an entirely different story."

"How did you locate the secret room?"

"I didn't. Mackenzie discovered a hidden remote within a bookcase. The damned thing was shaped like a beetle, sacred to the Egyptians. After several failed attempts she aimed the remote at a familiar picture. It was one featured in "Star" magazine. The apis bull opened a doorway to the secret room. I took these pictures on my phone."

Scanning the vivid frescos, the rancher sat baffled. "The images are definitely Egyptian. But they're confusing as hell. Why was an alien showcased?"

"Sir, that particular fresco honored Akhenaten. RE has an emotional tie to the pharaoh."

"But the guy looks deformed."

"Akhenaten was Egypt's most futuristic thinker and revolutionary ruler. Rather than competing with former macho kings, he created a Picasso-like art form. The elongated neck, alien-shaped head, paunch belly, protruding lips, and feminine appearance were his trademarks. The conical white crown represented Upper Egypt."

"What's in his hand? The damn thing looks like a toy rattle."

"Ankhs were a king's pass to eternity. Symbolizing new life, they were viewed as magical amulets and always depicted with a circle sitting atop a block letter 'T.' Yet on other walls, they're inverted."

"Inversion implies death. That blood on his Ankh symbolizes murder or war."

"That's our belief."

"What about that puffy white cloud with the strange-looking eye? It appears three-dimensional."

"Sir, that's by design. The "Eye of Horus" is all-seeing."

"That sounds god-like."

"It was. In Egyptian mythology, Horus donated an eye to his blind father. With restored sight, Osiris descended into the underworld. The magical eye has special powers."

"What about the clock? Those blood red numerals look rather ominous."

"We think the clock represents a double meaning. It symbolizes RE's timetable and America's demise. But that's pure conjecture. Most of the images remain a mystery."

"What about the two men in the lower right corner? Blue crowns historically symbolize war. Do those red stars indict Russia and China?"

"Possibly. But nothing's definitive."

Unexpectedly, Mackenzie intervened. "Sir, that secret room was akin to opening Pandora's Box. The frescos were amazing but baffling. It was like walking into a damn tomb. RE's plan was likely hidden among the hieroglyphics. But so far, the symbolism has been undecipherable."

"There's one other image," added Nash. "Note the foam green tidal wave on the right wall. It's about to crush a tiny eye. Riding the white-tipped crest is a wooden boat. The stick-looking passenger is holding another inverted Ankh."

"That's a rather odd depiction. Any explanation?"

"No. The tiny eye is different from the three-dimensional "Eye of Horus. The meaning is unclear."

"Well, I've seen enough," growled the billionaire. "Anderson is obviously guilty. But everything is circumstantial unless you can decode the images."

"That's my report to Jameson," chirped Mackenzie. "The arrogant bastard worships his Egyptian master."

"Mac, wait. Another desk photo changes everything. Give me a second to set it up. Take a look."

Peering at the grainy image, the Dubliner instantly reacted. "I don't get it. Lots of politicians pose with the Pope. It's just a photo-op."

"True. But most aren't connected to RE. Plus, Raz prophesied the Holy Father's demise."

"You've been holding back," grinned the old man. "You're onto something. I've seen that shit-ass look before."

"Possibly. But it's a longshot."

"Hell son, we've got to roll the dice before RE retaliates. Otherwise, we're dead."

"That's my thinking. But I need Mac's approval and your clout to pull it off."

"My support is no problem. Mackenzie?"

Dubious about another risky undertaking, the Dubliner listened and then nodded a reluctant blessing. There was no other option. A second trans-Atlantic flight was looming.

CHAPTER 33

Tuesday, February 16

Precisely at 3 p.m., five black SUVs exited the Mansion in a light drizzle. Six blocks later, the vehicles veered in different directions. One SUV made a beeline to Austin International.

At 3:15 p.m., three maintenance workers emerged from a service entrance, entered a commercial white van, and headed to the nearby Georgetown airport. A quick twenty-minute flight to Houston was looming.

With a smooth landing at the intercontinental airport, the sleek Gulfstream taxied to an isolated hangar. Peering out the window, Morgan beamed. Their overseas aircraft was another customized Boeing 737. The old man's billionaire club was amazing. As the Gulfstream rolled to a halt, the rancher made a surprise announcement.

"Agents, I've altered the plan. Two special guests are joining us."

"You wha...?"

Instantly, the oil tycoon bristled. "Son, that flimsy-assed plan was not going to cut it. You have to trust me."

As the team walked to the Boeing, a pair of unknown men emerged from a side room. The older of the two wore a suit and tie. His younger companion was clad in a golf shirt, khaki pants, and navy blazer.

"Agents, this distinguished gentleman is Samuel Livingston. A longtime friend, Sam owns a piece of this Boeing. More importantly, he's financing this little Vatican excursion. Pardner, introduce your special guest."

"Folks, meet Boston's beloved Cardinal O'Reilly. Timothy is responsible for our meeting with Pope Anthony."

Hearing the simple explanation Morgan relaxed. Once again, the old man was right. The two men were critical to their success. But Catholic's age was surprising. The youthful O'Reilly was fiftyish or younger.

Entering the re-configured jet, the team settled into adjacent recliners. In quick order Mackenzie oriented the newcomers but held back key points. Instantly, O'Reilly reacted.

"Your story is intriguing but not damning. That photo could mean anything. I seriously doubt any Vatican involvement. And please call me Tim."

Tactfully, Mackenzie countered. "Let me be clear. This is a fact-finding mission. Our goal is to separate fact from fiction."

An international lawyer, Livingston was also skeptical. "Personally, I think this RE is overrated. A global realignment is unimaginable. America is too strong. Yes, deals can be consummated, but that's it. I don't see world leaders buying into a fool's mission."

"Hold on," snorted Wilson Senior. "Don't underestimate this bastard. His network is unbelievably well funded and connected. Given the years of planning, anything is possible."

"Gentlemen, we're headed to the Vatican to find answers and eliminate traitors," interjected the Dubliner.

Instantly, the youthful Cardinal chuckled. "Well, you can scratch the Holy Father. The saintly man loves Christ and the church. Yes, he meets with world leaders. But he's in poor health. It's laughable to imagine his involvement with any conspiracy. Anthony only cares about the well-being of his people. That's it."

"Tim's right," echoed Livingston, his tone gruff and commanding. "Focus on the College. The Holy Father is livid about their lack of spirituality. It's being offset by materialism and political bias."

"Would any of the power brokers betray the Holy Church?"

"Agent Nash, the Vatican has a storied and questionable history. Even today, there are Cardinals with ambitious goals. But I have serious doubts about plots to kill Anthony."

"Sam anticipated an investigation. At his request I brought extensive research on my colleagues." Reaching into his briefcase O'Reilly clutched a thick packet. He handed it like a hot potato to Morgan.

"Thanks. Mac and I can pass the hours with some light reading."

"Don't look at me," chuckled Fallon. "This is *your* plan. I'm napping. Well, that's it. Let's agree to be informal and relax."

With all heads concurring the impromptu meeting ended.

Isolated in mid-cabin, Morgan eagerly opened the packet. Instantly, his enthusiasm quailed. There were over a hundred Cardinals to review. The task was Herculean.

Dammit! This is impossible. Where do I start?

With a deep sigh, he began with the obvious. To his surprise there was only one Egyptian Cardinal. The fifty-five-year-old Alexandrian was seemingly reclusive and small of stature but apparently well-liked. A vociferous German Cardinal was the complete opposite. Physically imposing,

Dietrich Franz was loud, pushy, and often rude. Highly respected was a youthful Brazilian Cardinal. Other notables included an Argentinian, a Spaniard, and two Italians.

Exhausted after two hours of intensive research, he invited O'Reilly to join him. "Tim, this little exercise is daunting. I need help. How frail is the Holy Father?"

"Is he approaching death? That's doubtful. A more apt description would be weak and frail. Only the Camerlengo knows the real truth. As an Irish American, I'm not privy to much confidential information."

"Let me rephrase. Would Anthony's demise benefit certain Cardinals?"

"Absolutely. I can name twenty or more not-so-holy men without blinking. Start with the Italians but be careful. The Vatican is a nest of vipers."

"What about others?"

"Focus on European and South Americans. And take a hard look at Xi Li from China."

"What about Americans?"

"That's laughable. No Yank stands to benefit from Anthony's demise. An American Pope is a pipe dream."

"What about Africans?"

"Realistically, they're fringe players. However, if voting extends into extra rounds any Cardinal has a chance. You have to account for that."

"Is there a favorite?"

"That's difficult to answer. Aggressive Cardinals often lose popularity. Given the cliques, constant lobbying, and power struggles, anything can happen. Expect the unexpected."

"Thanks. There's a lot to digest." As O'Reilly exited Morgan relaxed. Within minutes he was asleep.

CHAPTER 34

Wednesday, February 17

With a pre-dawn arrival at Rome's Da Vinci International, the customized Boeing taxied to a private hangar. Greeted by obsequious security, the team easily cleared customs and headed to a nearby hotel. Their appointment with Anthony was scheduled for early afternoon.

~

At 1 p.m. the group assembled in the hotel lobby. Four members were attired in dark suits. The lone exception was O'Reilly. Aping a colorful redbird, the Bostonian was clad in a scarlet cassock, cape and stockings. Clutched in his hand was a traditional galero, a broad-brimmed hat with tasseled strings.

"Okay, I look like a runaway choir boy. But beware, black sheep. In this fiery outfit I possess magical powers."

As the team chuckled Mackenzie posed a query. "Why is red your color? I'm curious."

"Scarlet represents my ecclesiastical order. The color symbolizes the blood of Christ and my readiness to sacrifice for the sake of the church. It also underscores the dignity of the office."

"You look like a man on fire," mocked Wilson Senior.

"Hey, I deserve a little respect. I'm a highflyer."

In a light-hearted mood the team entered the idling limo. A typical Irishman, O'Reilly did not appear to have a serious side.

Forty-five minutes later the group arrived at St. Peter's Square. Instantly Morgan noted the imposing obelisk. A centerpiece of Egyptian creation, the architectural masterpiece was a prominent symbol of new life. Escorted by blue-clad Swiss Guards, the American contingent navigated a maze of hallways and entered the office of the Camerlengo. As Tim chuckled, four faces registered shock. The executive assistant's physicality was stunning. The African stood six-foot-two and weighed a chiseled two-hundred and-twenty-pounds.

Irked by the Irishman's betrayal, the Camerlengo's granite expression hardened. Only two Americans were expected. With nary a word, the aide exited through a side door. As the group relaxed O'Reilly grinned. "Well, how do you like our Vatican bouncer? In private we refer to him as "Anthony's assassin."

"The man looks like a linebacker," quipped Nash. "What's his background?"

"The Camerlengo is Egyptian. Enzo Firelli is his name."

"That's Italian. Yet his skin is black."

"According to rumors, Enzo was discovered in a Cairo orphanage and adopted by a wealthy Italian couple. At age six he joined the family."

"That's a neat story if true," chirped Mackenzie. "Does the guy ever smile?"

"Not much. Intimidation is his game. And he's good at it. Make no mistake, Enzo Firelli is a very powerful figure. When a Pontiff dies the Camerlengo runs the Vatican while the Cardinals sequester."

"What about daily?"

"The man operates like an executive secretary. Anthony directs his schedules and activities. Fearful Cardinals avoid his company."

"I can see why. The chiseled beast is a scary man among choir boys."

"Morgan, he needs to be physical. A lot of bad stuff happens within these walls."

"That's my concern. Likely, the Holy Father is a target. But the suspect list keeps expanding. Oops, here he comes."

Flashing a hideous scowl, the Camerlengo directed the team to a small conference room. Seconds later the frail Pontiff entered. Unexpectedly, his cordial expression morphed into instant disdain.

"Enzo, you assured me this meeting was of extreme importance. Only Cardinal O'Reilly and a Mr. Livingston were expected."

"Holy Father, I was betrayed. Cardinal O'Reilly requested the urgent meeting. These others are an unwelcomed surprise."

"It was my fault," confessed the Bostonian. "I had to deceive. These Americans have delicate matters to discuss."

"So, I see." Caught in an embarrassing moment, Anthony paused and then acquiesced. "Introduce your guests."

Suddenly, O'Reilly hesitated. "Holy Father, Miss Fallon and Mr. Nash are the true messengers. They have words meant for your ears only. Mr. Wilson and Mr. Livingston are benefactors. Their generosity funded the trip."

Intrigued by the tangled web of deceit, Anthony paused. Strangers were never granted a private audience. Yet their presence pulsated urgency and authority.

"Enzo, Miss Fallon and Mr. Nash may remain. Please escort Cardinal O'Reilly and the benefactors to the waiting room."

As the door closed, the Holy Father's temper flared, his angst evident. "Miss Fallon, you have one minute. You have betrayed Vatican trust."

"Sir, Agent Nash and I are with the FBI. A plot against your life has been revealed. You are in grave danger."

"But the Vatican is secure. I'm surrounded by trusted Guards. There is no threat."

"That's uncertain. According to Director Jameson, the American murders link to rogue Cardinals. If correct, your demise is imminent."

With thinning silver hair and stooped posture, the Pontiff's appearance was haggard. His eighty-four-year-old face was badly wrinkled. Bags of loose skin drooped beneath both eyes. Though outwardly frail, his mind was razor sharp.

"Explain."

In a flow of words, the agents quickly outlined every aspect of the case. At the conclusion Anthony cracked a wry smile. "My picture with President Anderson triggered this trip?"

"Sir, we think it's relevant. Plus, other images point to the Vatican."

"Agent Fallon, I appear with many world leaders. However, a framed picture in a secret room adorned with Egyptian hieroglyphics *is* intriguing."

"Holy Father, may I ask a question?"

"Certainly, Agent Nash."

"Does the College embrace your recent initiatives?"

"No. Progressive Cardinals detest my feed-the-world initiatives. They desire a more secular agenda."

"Can you elaborate?"

"Absolutely. Six months ago, I initiated much-needed nutrition programs in Latin America, Southeast Asia, and Africa. As expected, there was opposition. Certain Cardinals lobbied for political alliances, ornate structures, and clergy benefits. To my chagrin, they've lost sight of the people."

"Feed-the-hungry ventures are costly. Did you liquidate tangible assets or properties to fund your initiatives?"

"No, Agent Fallon. God has provided. Miraculously, we've been blessed with monetary windfalls. Twelve months ago, my financial council recommended aggressive purchases of American equities. We've done amazingly well, even in this new year."

The timing caught Morgan's attention. "Sir, you should have lost money. Equities have plummeted in recent weeks."

"Our chairman has amazing instincts. Educated in America, Cardinal Xi Li has a PhD in economics. Last year he invested heavily in American equities. In December he liquidated and netted a billion-dollar profit. In early January Li reversed strategy and bet against the markets. Since that time, he's earned over five hundred million dollars. Cardinal Li has enjoyed perfect timing. The surplus money has been a godsend."

"Sir, who makes up your financial council?"

"Cardinals with a strong financial background are selected, Agent Fallon. The representatives are from Europe, the U.S., South America, Africa, and Asia. Are they suspects?"

"That is to be determined. One or more council members could be guilty of insider trading or traitorous activities."

"Your skepticism is deeply disturbing and difficult to believe. I'm dubious about any Cardinal betraying the Holy Church."

"Greed corrupts," countered Morgan. "Your demise offers RE a golden opportunity."

"I'm not following."

"With your death, corrupt minions can ensure the election of a short-term puppet. Meanwhile, RE grooms a future Pontiff. Lavish lifestyles and untold wealth can tempt even to the most faithful."

"If true, we must fight fire with fire. Show no mercy if any Cardinal is found guilty. The spirituality of the Holy Church is at stake. How can I help?"

"Sir, Mackenzie and I need access to the Vatican Library and a cover story. Additional research is desperately needed."

"That is not possible."

"Why?"

"Agent Nash, two Americans posing as researchers would overwhelm the Vatican grapevine. Nosy Cardinals would end your investigation. However, a single figure might fly beneath the proverbial radar."

Instantly, Mackenzie grinned. "Sir, my partner has just volunteered. Morgan has an affinity for detailed studies."

Flashing a wry smile Pope Anthony summoned the Camerlengo and guests. Quickly, he barked orders. "Cardinal O'Reilly, please make arrangements for Mr. Nash to lodge with the Swiss Guards. Escort him to the archives tomorrow at 8 a.m."

"What about my friends?"

"Return them to the hotel. Tomorrow they may tour Vatican museums at their leisure."

Abruptly, the weary Pontiff exited. On his heels was an irate Camerlengo. With their departure O'Reilly laughed. "Folks, we should toast the afternoon with a few rounds. Agent Nash, enjoy your last vestiges of freedom. I vote for pizza and beer near our infamous Spanish Steps."

~

With the team in agreement, a Swiss Guard was commandeered to escort them to the iconic attraction. In a celebratory mood, O'Reilly was pleased with the Holy Father's decisions.

"At supper let's toast Anthony. Afterwards, we can walk the Steps and grab a gelato. Just watch as the people shower me with adoration."

The Irish-American's prophetic utterances were understated. Obsequious waiters at the pizzeria provided immaculate service. Navigating the crowded Spanish Steps was akin to Moses parting the Red Sea. Enjoying a brief interlude from the mob-like atmosphere, O'Reilly grinned. "Next is the fabulous Trevi Fountain. It's just several blocks away. My adoring fans can open a pathway."

Arriving at the architectural masterpiece, they marveled at the sculpted images and flowing waters. Flashing his charm, O'Reilly volunteered a nearby bystander to snap pictures. As the team closed ranks, Mackenzie noted movement in the graying shadows. Isolated from the bustling crowd the area appeared foreboding. Straddling a fashionable Italian motorbike was a man wearing a black helmet with a dark visor and black leather jacket. Casually gripped in his right hand was a gun aimed in their direction. Instantly recognizing the Beretta, she screamed a dire warning.

"SHOOTER!"

Protectively reacting, she lunged at Morgan, creating a domino effect. Knocked off balance he tumbled into O'Reilly as two quick shots rang out. Revving the engine, the black-clad assassin roared from the darkness and into the crowded streets. Panicked by the gunfire, people bolted in different directions. Bounding to his feet Morgan fingered his weapon and scanned the area. With no clear shot, he shifted his gaze to Mackenzie. Unresponsive, his partner was face down on the cobbled stone and bleeding profusely from arm and shoulder wounds. Whipping out his cell phone, O'Reilly contacted Vatican security.

"Mac saved us," uttered Nash as the team formed a protective circle. "Those bullets were meant for Tim and me. Dammit, this shit has got to stop."

~

Within minutes a stream of flashing lights and blaring sirens appeared on the scene. Working feverishly, first responders slowed the bleeding and placed Mackenzie in an idling ambulance. Accompanied by her partner, the Dubliner was whisked to a nearby hospital.

Escorted by Vatican security, the benefactors and O'Reilly quickly joined Morgan in the waiting room. In undetermined condition, the Special Agent had been rushed to surgery. Angered by the ambush, Wilson Senior shattered the shroud of gloom.

"Dammit, even Rome isn't safe. Who's the frigging mole?"

"The Camerlengo has my vote," blurted Sam Livingston. "Dinner reservations weren't made until *after* the Holy Father dismissed us. That mean looking son-of-a-bitch must have eavesdropped."

"Well, the hotel is definitely out. Can we stay at the Vatican?"

"Sam, that's not a good idea," replied O'Reilly. "I suggest you remain at the hospital. This location is secure with Guards blanketing the area. Plus, you old guys can keep a close eye on Mackenzie."

"So be it," snorted the rancher. "But lots of innocent people unexpectedly die in hospitals. I want a gun and lots of ammo."

~

Seventy-minutes later a young surgeon provided an update. "Ms. Fallon has been moved to recovery. The arm wound was not serious but did induce bleeding. The shoulder wound was a little more involved. The slug ricocheted off the scapula and nicked the clavicle but missed the vital organs. There was substantial blood loss due to the bullet's irregular pathway. We are monitoring her very closely. Miss Fallon was extremely fortunate. Barring infection, we're optimistic about her recovery."

"When can she return to the states?"

"That's to be determined, Mr. Nash. Assuming no complications your patient can travel in several days. Right now, there's no timetable."

As the surgeon vanished, Tim peered at Morgan. "Agent, we need to leave. Our presence is endangering these fine men."

CHAPTER 35

Thursday, February 18

On the heels of a restless night, Nash met the Irishman for an early breakfast. At the appointed hour two Swiss Guards escorted the duo to the infamous Vatican archives. As Tim secured the documents, Morgan nervously scanned the room.

"Meet your worktable, Agent Nash. You can stretch but stay put. In my absence, the Guards remain with you."

Staring at the voluminous stack of files, he sat transfixed. The amount of research was overwhelming. Translated into English, each file represented a Cardinal's personal data and genealogy. Based on Tim's recommendation, the outspoken German was first on the list. Feverishly scribbling notes, Morgan paid close attention to Dietrich Franz's relationship with political and military leaders. When finished, he placed a bright red check by the name.

Next was the youthful Spaniard. After scanning the file, he underscored a key point. A native of Pamplona, Carlos annually ran with the bulls.

Interesting. Does this guy link to Anderson? Both love bulls and the spotlight. Could he be RE's transitional Pope or permanent successor?

Placing a red check by the name, Morgan turned to the Brazilian. Suddenly his eyes locked on the third paragraph. Arturo Francisco was a left-wing radical. Advocating Latin unification, the Cardinal was notably antagonistic toward Anthony. A bold red check was placed by the name.

As more suspects emerged, he noted the time. It was well past the noon hour. Emotionally drained, Nash motioned to the Guards. Walking briskly to the dining hall, he encountered an unpleasant surprise. The chatty and oft nosy Irishman was waving to him. Morgan's desire for a quiet lunch was shattered.

"Lad, you're a wee bit late," chuckled O'Reilly. "I've been watching for you." Pulling up a chair, the Cardinal immediately probed for information. "You've been gone for a while. Have you exposed the guilty?"

Munching on a sandwich, Morgan flashed a faux smile. The Irishman was a bit too curious. "Tim, it's been tough. My research is going to take time."

"What about the German? Now, there's a man you cannot trust. Plus, he comes from a bellicose nation."

"I placed a check by his name. But there are numerous Cardinals with interesting backgrounds, including you." Studying the Bostonian, Morgan felt uneasy. The opinionated Gaelic was cunning and nosy. Worse, he was likely a mainstay in the Vatican grapevine.

Flashing a sly grin, O'Reilly easily defected the barb. "Aye, lad, I have the squinty eyes of a traitor. Plus, I have connections. But most of us are satisfied with our rank. Plus, Americans have little hope of becoming Pope. That lofty honor has been reserved for Italians and Eastern Europeans."

Eager to rid himself of the distraction, Nash quickly excused himself and returned to the cavernous archives.

Uneasy, he glanced at his security blanket. The two Swiss protectors were reassuring. Suddenly, a cynical thought crossed his mind.

Why not Cardinal O'Reilly?

Curious, he grabbed Tim's file. After rereading several documents, Morgan grinned. O'Reilly's genealogy actually traced to the great "Potato Famine." Mired in poverty, his ancestors had migrated to America. Flipping several pages, a new document caught his attention. Mimicking numerous coastal elites, the Bostonian was an avid supporter of Hyatt's globalist policies. The Cardinal was also an acquaintance of Anderson and Allday. Sitting back, he reflected on the findings.

My glib Irish friend has some serious connections. Plus, he planned our evening itinerary. Coincidence?

Intrigued, he placed a bright red check by Tim's name. Next on the list were the Scottish and French Cardinals. Noting nothing of interest, Nash sat frustrated and overwhelmed. Too many suspects were emerging. Ravaged by indecision, he decided to focus on the obvious.

Is Anthony's financial whiz a trader or traitor?

As anticipated, Xi Li's financial credentials were impeccable. Yet, the Holy Father had frequently questioned the Asian's spirituality. Pushing back, he assessed the financial guru.

Could XI represent two of the blood red Roman numerals? If so, does he link to RE's timetable? Or do the numerals imply leadership? Is he the mysterious master planner?

Uncertain, he read deeper into the file. As rumored, Li was unpopular with Europeans and not Pope-worthy. Money seemed to be his almighty god.

Curious, he researched leading Italians. Most were powerful and well connected. Satisfied with his grueling inspection, Nash placed checks by several new names.

Pushing forward, he focused on Cardinals from smaller countries. By 7 p.m., his mind was reeling.

At his quick wave, the relieved Guards escorted him to the dining hall.

Grabbing a meager meal, Morgan ate in solitude. Unexpectedly, the Irishman appeared and plopped next to him. "Well, have you discovered the elusive pot of gold? Any arrests?"

"No. The College is impressive. The traitor is likely a world leader and not a Cardinal."

"Does your schedule permit a few beers?"

Tempted, Nash declined the offer. "No thanks. I'm making it a late night."

By 8:30 p.m., he was back at work and intrigued by a Mexican Cardinal. With strong ties to drug cartels, the Hispanic earned a red check. Over the next hour, Morgan focused on leaders from Central and South America. To his dismay, new suspects emerged.

Dammit. Obvious is too broad. I need a more defined approach.

What about slam dunks?

Scanning the Camerlengo's file, he fixated on background. Adopted from a Cairo orphanage at an early age, Enzo moved with his family to Milan. Growing up in Italy's financial center, the athletic youth excelled at soccer. Quietly, he rose through the ranks of the Catholic Church.

Okay, Mr. Jock, where is your birthplace? It can't be Egypt.

Then came a shocker. Enzo was Egyptian, born in Aswan.

But your skin tone is ebony not ecru.

Suddenly, it struck him. Aswan was located near ancient Nubia. Egypt's southernmost neighbor had been a mortal enemy.

Okay, your family name was Kukthe. Significant?

Suspicious of the adoption, Nash pushed back and reflected. Something wasn't right. Then he recalled a Raz session.

Enslaved Nubians were often brought to Memphis during the reign of Amenhotep III.

Suddenly his face tensed in anticipation. *Akhenaten's given name was Amenhotep IV. The family bloodline spawned Raz and BABA. What about Enzo?*

Suddenly a connection slammed his mind. *Bingo! The blood on Akhenaten's Ankh was literal, not symbolic. It underscored lineage.*

The bombshell revelation was quickly met with doubt. *But that can't be right. Nubians could never ascend to Egyptian royalty. Why would Bonito Firelli adopt a child from an enslaved country?*

Seeking clarity, he scanned new pages. Suddenly a small notation caught his eye. Pharaoh Akhenaten was a notorious playboy. Despite his marriage to the alluring Nefertiti, the king enjoyed intimate relationships with concubines.

That has to be it. Akhenaten impregnated one of Kukthe's daughters. Nine months later, she gave birth to a bastard son. The Firellis must have connected the dots. Their Nubian orphan was royalty.

Suddenly a series of vile thoughts flashed across his mind. *If so, RE knows about the Nubian's heritage. Is Enzo the Pope-in-waiting? No. A Camerlengo isn't eligible.*

A blink later discouragement morphed to eagerness. *But the landscape changes with Anthony's demise. Traitorous Cardinals could stage a coup and elect Enzo by adoration.*

Placing a bright red check by the name, the Vatican enforcer became suspect number one. Two others quickly emerged.

What if the Brazilian and O'Reilly were Enzo's partners? A radicalized Catholic Church would have the power to reshape Africa and Latin America.

Shaken by the sadistic possibilities, he forced himself to refocus. After scanning several European and Canadian files, Morgan decided to stop. Fatigue was bastardizing his mind. Yet something was amiss. Intrigued, he returned to the Egyptian's file. The Cardinal from Alexandria was an enigma. Focusing strictly on his childhood, Morgan read several pages and suddenly froze.

Mosef Qadesh was placed in a Cairo Catholic orphanage as an infant. At age ten he was selected by Bonito Firelli.

Bingo! The two boys were raised in the same orphanage and adopted by the same parents. Coincidence?

Stunned by the revelation, he noted the Egyptian's age. Qadesh was approaching his fifty-fifth birthday.

The two are pretty close in age. They had to know each other.

Suddenly, his newfound enthusiasm waned. The Firellis moved to Milan. Yet Mosef remained in Cairo and attended a Catholic prep school.

Did distance end the boys' friendship? Are they still close? Enzo remained a Firelli but not his brother. Why did Qadesh retain his Egyptian name?

As the questions mounted, he pondered the boys' relationship. *Were they ever close? Were they blood brothers or mere acquaintances?*

Doggedly, Nash researched Mosef's genealogy. After several paragraphs, he sat dismayed. The Cardinal's lineage traced to 1600 B.C. The date preceded Pharaoh Akhenaten. Frustrated by the time gap, he stopped. Nothing about the Alexandrian made sense.

Why did the Firellis adopt him? His lineage predated the revolutionary king.

Curious, he scanned new pages. Catching his eye were faint scribbles and question marks in the margin. All referenced Amenhotep II.

Someone else posed the same question.

Then it struck him. The Amenhotep family tree was extensive and lengthy. Amenhotep IV didn't change his name until after self-deification.

Bingo! Everything ties to Akhenaten's lineage. Mosef is also royalty. That explains his adoption.

Suddenly, he hesitated. *But why is lineage so damn important? Is bloodline relevant or exaggerated?*

Returning to Mosef's file, he came across another shocker. The introverted Cardinal was pictured with numerous world leaders, including Anderson and Allday. Newspaper articles praised him as the "Silent Saint."

Wearied by the late hour, Morgan motioned to his protectors. A late-night drink was well-deserved. Entering the dining hall, he abruptly stopped. Nestled by the cozy fireplace was his Irish nemesis.

"Well, have you uncovered the Vatican villain?"

"Nope. You were right. The Cardinals are holy men of God."

"Lad, be careful within these walls. A wee leprechaun could easily vanish. This place is not magically delicious." Lightheaded, the Irishman chuckled.

Flashing a faux smile, Nash chugged his drink, waved goodnight, and headed to his room. With a splitting headache, he was ready for bed.

An hour later, he was back at work. His overactive mind made sleep impossible. Too many questions remained unanswered. Scribbling notes, Morgan processed the day's information before dozing off.

CHAPTER 36

Friday, February 19

Arriving for an 8 a.m. breakfast, he was stunned. The Guards' dining hall was virtually empty. Then Nash remembered. Anthony was conducting a special mass. After consuming a meager meal, he was escorted to the archives.

Ever stoic, the taller of the Swiss Guards retrieved the documents. Eager to continue, Morgan fixated on the Camerlengo. Suddenly a small photo caught his attention. After scribbling several notes, he closed the file.

Does the Pope really trust this guy?

Next on the list was Benito Firelli. At age seventy-three the family patriarch was still prominent in Italian politics. His wife of forty-five years was a homemaker. The couple had three daughters. The third had been adopted after her parents were tragically killed in an auto accident. The twelve-year-old Swiss lived with the family for six years before relocating to Boston. Aided by her uncle's wealth and connections, the international banker traveled the world as an influential socialite.

The eldest Firelli daughter relocated to Paris, became a noted artist, and married France's Minister of Finance. The younger sibling roamed Europe as a socialite before marrying into the aristocratic Goetz family. Residing in

Berlin, her influential husband was a member of the German government. Closing the file, Morgan reflected on the Kennedy-like family. The information was prolific. Yet there were gaps. Anthony's input was needed.

Uncertain, he returned to Dietrich's file. Instantly, his eyes focused on an overlooked zippered pouch containing photos. Of interest was the German's picture with the ubiquitous O'Reilly. Another shot had him posing with President Hyatt and Vice-President Anderson. Scanning a new page, his eyes popped. Young Franz had accompanied his father to Egypt on numerous occasions. An amateur archeologist, the German had actively participated in numerous digs. Scribbling several notes, Morgan placed a second red check by Dietrich's name. Then he stopped.

Ambitious Cardinals seldom become Pope. Sleepers often win. Who fits into that category?

Without hesitation, he grabbed the Spaniard's file. At age fifty-six the European had the youth and energy to help RE reshape the world. Scrutinizing every detail, Nash discovered a key fact. The Cardinal was not as arrogant as first noted. A second red check was placed by his name.

As the hours ticked away, he lamented the passing of time. The lunch hour was fast approaching. Yet new revelations were emerging. Unexpectedly, Nash remembered one of Dawn's favorite Biblical passages. It was about the meek inheriting the earth.

Okay, who among you is humble and pious?

Invigorated, he fixated on Cardinal Varza. Growing up in nearby Sienna, Antonio's father was a small-acreage farmer. A devout practitioner of St. Francis, the youthful Italian was well respected by both peers and people. But there were red flags. The Cardinal was tight with the German, the Egyptian, and the Brazilian. Plus, he was pictured with world leaders, including Anderson and Allday.

Antonio, you're my dark horse. Are there others?

Thirty minutes later, he summoned the Guards. Hunger was overpowering thoughts. Entering the dining hall, Morgan grimaced. With mass concluded, the room was overcrowded. Eager to avoid O'Reilly, he zipped through the buffet and ate alone. To his chagrin, the Irishman plopped next to him.

"I didn't see you at mass. Has your day gone well?"

"It's been interesting but not productive."

"Are you any closer to an arrest?"

"Tim, I don't think he's here."

Instantly the joviality vanished. "Agent, dig deeper." The Bostonian's eyes were hard-set and piercing. "Do not be deceived. The Vatican is a treacherous place."

"I appreciate the warning. But I trust my protectors. Well, it's back to work."

With an abrupt exit, Morgan vanished from the dining hall. A call to the surly Camerlengo was pending. To his relief, a 2 p.m. meeting with Anthony was set.

Apprehensive about the Papal session, he fretted. The smallish private room felt claustrophobic. Immediately his fears heightened as the Holy Father arrived in a surly mood. Deciding on a direct approach, Nash quickly summarized his findings and concerns, specifically highlighting the German, Spaniard, and Italian.

"Agent, I appreciate the report. But everything is circumstantial. Am I truly in grave danger?"

"That's my belief. I can make a strong case against numerous Cardinals."

Expressionless, the frail Catholic leader pushed back in his chair. The deep wrinkles in his brow were etched with concern. Another critical moment of truth had arrived.

"So, it's down to a single question. Is there a next step?"

"My answer is yes. But it's complicated."

"I note the conflict in your eyes. You desire to remain but cannot."

"You're very astute. Mackenzie has been cleared to travel. So, I have to leave ASAP."

"Yet, you have unfinished business."

"That's my dilemma in a nutshell."

With an understanding nod, the Pontiff handed Morgan a small card. "This is my private number. Call me. Talk to no one else. Leave a message if I do not answer."

"Thanks."

"Is Cardinal O'Reilly returning with you?"

"Sir, I hope not. Tim's a rather nosy fellow. Can you find something to keep him busy?"

Flashing a genuine smile, the Holy Father chuckled. "Our Irishman has a rather intrusive nature. I was in the process of sending an envoy to Croatia. Cardinal O'Reilly has just been selected."

"A Pied-Piper among Croatians should be entertaining. Tim's a good man with a real gift of gab."

"That's why it's virtually impossible for a Leprechaun to become Pope. Mass would become non-ending. Beer would become the new sacrament."

As the Catholic leader flashed a mischievous grin, Nash smiled. The aged Holy Father was a decent man.

"Thank you."

"No. Thank you, my son. Though blemished, the Holy Church must be saved."

"Amen. Can you sneak our group out of Rome? An early evening flight would be perfect."

"That I can. Wait fifteen minutes and then exit through that private door."

"Luggage?"

"It will be in your vehicle."

Twenty-two minutes later, Nash's black SUV rolled into the hospital's discharge area. Ready and waiting, the American contingent was anxious to leave. Sliding into the back seat, Wilson Senior hesitated.

"Only you? Where's the chatterbox?"

"Our Irish friend is headed to Croatia."

"O'Reilly's a special envoy?" The old man chuckled. "God help the Croatians."

CHAPTER 37

Saturday, February 20

With a dawn landing at Austin International, the customized Boeing taxied to a private hangar. Prior to deplaning, Wilson cornered Morgan. "Son, you've been mighty quiet for hours. Are you okay?"

"Not really. Things have gotten complicated. I didn't say much because Mac needed rest. Later, we have much to discuss."

"Was the research worthwhile?"

"Sir, the details were both alarming and amazing. Numerous suspects have emerged but no hard evidence."

"Well, the trip certainly stirred the pot. We're all in grave danger, including Anthony. You've got my support. But Robby has to disappear."

Overhearing the conversation, Sam Livingston interrupted. "Agent, my work is done. If you need resources, please call."

"Thanks. Stay safe."

As the New Englander's limo sped into the early morning sunlight, the Austin-based trio headed to the safe confines of the Texas Governor's Mansion. The half-hour drive was a welcomed respite from the flight.

Greeted by Mansion security, the team was escorted to their spacious rooms. An hour later, the weary travelers regrouped in a small conference room. Mackenzie's pallid appearance was concerning. The trans-Atlantic flight had been draining. Yet, she had to be briefed. Chomping at the bit was Wilson Senior. Morgan's evasive comments on the return flight had aroused his curiosity.

Wasting no time, Nash summarized his findings.

"Those blood drops in Anderson's secret room symbolize bloodline. The genealogy dates to 1600 B.C. and traces to Pharaoh Akhenaten. The family tree includes Raz and BABA. Surprisingly, it also encompasses an Alexandrian Cardinal and the Camerlengo."

"I knew that mean-looking bastard was guilty," growled the old man. "What about the Egyptian?"

"His name is Mosef Qadesh. He's also a suspect. But that's it. Bloodline is not an admission of guilt."

"What makes lineage so damn important?"

"Bloodline equates to royalty, Mac. The lineage likely includes RE and his inner circle."

"Anything else?"

"The Roman numerals on Anderson's secret clock likely link to Cardinal Xi Li. The connection makes sense. The Vatican's financial whiz is absolutely killing the markets."

"But that's impossible," snorted the rancher. "He should be losing money. There's no way."

"According to Anthony, Li has been absolutely perfect. In November, he liquidated American equities and netted billions. Since early January, he's been betting against the markets. Ecstatic about the financial windfall, the Holy Father has launched numerous feed-the-hungry initiatives."

"Son, perfect investors do not exist. Li is either an inside trader or Vatican traitor."

"Likely, he's both. Capitalize his first name and you get 'XI' or two of the blood red numerals."

"But that leaves the three and five."

Peering first at his boss and then at the rancher, Morgan's eyes were ablaze with excitement. "Folks, our watershed moment has finally arrived. Xi Li has to be the mastermind, a man of many surprises, including a trigger date hidden in plain sight."

"I'm not following." The weak voice of the Dubliner underscored her frail condition.

"The number three indicates month. 'X' symbolizes ten. Add the five and you get fifteen. Ignore the number one. It's likely a ruse. The 'Ides of March' is the trigger date."

With eyebrows scrunched in concern, Wilson Senior wasn't buying. "Son, it's a fool's game to ignore the one. If it's in play, the date changes. Hell, it creates numerous variables."

"But March 15 represents the perfect launch date. It's both theatrical and historical. Caesar's blood red creates an ominous apocalyptic background."

"It's too obvious," countered the billionaire.

"Morgan, are you absolutely sure?" Mackenzie's harried expression reflected a mixture of terror and doubt. "My report to Jameson has to be solid."

Slowly Nash backtracked. "No, I'm not sure. The pieces fit. March 15 is my best guess for the trigger date."

"Okay son, let's play this out," espoused Wilson. "If correct, what happens?"

"I think all hell breaks loose. A series of cataclysmic events triggers the omega's third stage. March 15 ignites dissolution and underscores America's demise. RE is hell-bent on reshaping the world."

"But that's impossible," snapped the old man. "At best, the bastard can create short-term havoc. But that's it. He can't control Anthony or other world leaders."

Nodding in agreement, the Dubliner flashed a terse expression. "Morgan, keep digging. I concur with the date. But without other key pieces, there's nothing tangible for Jameson. Anything else?"

"Yeah. Inform the Director that I plan to kill Anderson."

"WHAT? Dammit, that is not going to happen." Outraged, the Dubliner's fiery temper exploded. "Killing the President is off the table. Forget it. Your ass is toast if you turn rogue."

"Mac, the bastard needs to die. It's the only way to expose RE."

"Morgan, you can't execute a sitting President." As spittle hurtled from the Special Agent's enraged lips, a shroud of gloom engulfed the room.

"Son, you're thinking with that little head again. There are other options."

"I disagree. Killing Anderson is the only logical choice. It disrupts RE's timeframe and eliminates a traitorous minion. The President is definitely not the leader."

"NO! This line of thinking is both idiotic and suicidal."

"Mac, listen. Jameson demands results. You need to heal. I can terminate Anderson and be back within a day or so."

"Son, just what in the hell did you find in those archives?" Intervening, the savvy oilman spoke candidly

"I uncovered a hornet's nest."

"Meaning?"

"RE's network is far more extensive than anticipated. His partners include global adversaries, traitorous Cardinals, and entrenched politicians. Worse, he may or may not be the mastermind. But one thing is crystal clear. Unless we disrupt the schedule, Anthony is dead within days. The Vatican is definitely the epicenter."

"But there's no tangible proof," countered Mackenzie. "Everything is speculative. The Holy Father may or may not be in danger."

"Mac, RE has a timetable. Anthony has to die. A *transitional Pope* has been groomed to take his place."

"Transitional? Son, you're talking gibberish."

"RE needs a short-term bridge to buy time. His future leader is likely not a Cardinal as yet. The long-term Pontiff remains hidden in the shadows."

Instantly reacting, Mackenzie growled. "Let Anthony handle the situation. It's an in-house matter."

"That's impossible. His security is compromised."

"Dammit, I'm not buying. Find me something tangible." Irked, the Dubliner abruptly exited the room. A strong cup of Irish coffee was badly needed.

A short time later, Mackenzie reappeared. Her ashen face and grim expression were telling. "Calling Jameson would have been a waste of time. Instead, I contacted a close friend. Anderson has a private event at his Virginia estate tomorrow evening. You might have a slim chance."

"What about the Secret Service?"

"A small detail will accompany the President."

"Then you approve. The President needs to die."

"No, I don't approve. And I disavow any knowledge of your trip."

"Fine. I accept full responsibility. The faux social gives Anderson an opportunity to chitchat with his boss. Their discussion likely involves us."

"What's your plan?" The curt interruption came from the riled lips of no-nonsense Wilson Senior. "Let's hear it."

"I wait for the guests to leave. Then I evade patrolling agents, enter the house, locate the President, and put a bullet in his brain. Afterward, I dismantle his communication center."

"Son, you are making a huge mistake. You're thinking with that little head again."

"There's no other choice, sir. Any delay means death."

"I reluctantly agree," echoed Mackenzie. "When do *we* leave?"

"Mac, you can't go. You need to rehab."

"And you're dead without me."

"But..."

"Plus, you need a second set of eyes with Secret Service patrolling the grounds."

"Look, I can manage. The President needs privacy. I expect three to five agents at most."

"That's bullshit," countered the oil baron. "A more accurate number is ten to twelve. Morgan, you need to rethink this idiocy."

Unexpectedly, the Dubliner rushed from the room. Two minutes later, she returned with dour news. "Ten to fifteen agents are accompanying the President. You're dead upon arrival,"

"Your source is wrong. Five or less is more accurate."

"Son, you ain't Rambo. Going alone is a fool's mission. My staff can make arrangements."

"Thanks, but forget it. Just chalk me up as suicidal." Miffed by the pushback, Nash steamed out the door.

"Mackenzie, did you notice those hollow set eyes and pulsating neck arteries? Your partner has no intention of returning. I've seen that death look in combat. You've got to stop him."

"How? Rolling the dice is Morgan's only option. Right now, RE is winning."

"Look, your guy needs help. I'm not going to leave him hanging."

CHAPTER 38

Sunday, February 21

Crunching his favorite breakfast cereal, Morgan managed a weak smile as the old man pulled up a chair.

"Son, are you okay?"

"Not really. Has my flight been arranged?"

"Yep. We leave at 11 a.m."

"We?"

"Yeah. Mac and I are your escorts."

Clad in the white service garb of a local plumbing company, the trio boarded a blue service van for the short drive to nearby Georgetown. Switching vehicles, they headed north on I-35 to the Waco Airport. Arriving at a private hangar, Nash was surprised. Security was non-existent. Amused by his expression, Wilson Senior beamed.

"Your cache of weapons was a concern. The Governor pulled some strings."

"Mansion security was extremely generous. Plus, they didn't ask questions."

As the trio entered the billionaire's customized Boeing, Morgan abruptly stopped. Strangers dotted the cabin.

"What the hell?"

Instantly the old man chuckled. "Relax. These men are going with us. They're from my personal security team."

"Dammit, I didn't ask for help."

"Son, thinking with that pecker will get you killed. You'll need help."

"But I don't know these men Are they good?"

"Hell, they're elite. You're looking at six former Rangers and a British commando. All are battle tested and experts in close combat."

"And they have no qualms about the mission?"

"None. They've been briefed." With a wave of his right hand, the oil baron motioned to the nearest man. "Agents, I want you to meet Captain Ben Wilkins."

As his angst slowly defused, Morgan shook the hand of the tall, muscular soldier. With piercing eyes, Wilkins's face reflected both the confidence and the rugged look of a no-nonsense combat veteran. As usual, the savvy rancher was right. Help was needed.

"What's the strategy, Ben?"

"From the shadows, we'll count numbers, match up and sit tight. At the appointed time, we'll strike. No agent will be harmed or killed. A pin light will be our 'go' signal."

"What if a guard hears you?"

"That's not a problem."

As Wilkins returned to his seat, Morgan flashed a wry grin at Mackenzie. The old man was akin to a secret Santa on steroids.

In the twilight of early evening, the luxury jet descended into Dulles International and rolled to a halt inside a private hangar. Within minutes two fully loaded black SUVs were headed to Chantilly, Virginia. Stopping at Wilma's Diner, the team ate a casual supper, played pool, and sipped coffee.

Precisely at 8 p.m., the Dallas agents and Wilkins made the short drive to Anderson's estate. Scouting the perimeter, they noted the festive social event and nine Secret Service agents.

"That extra guard could pose trouble," whispered Wilkins. "He might react before being silenced. Agent Nash, can you help?"

"Certainly."

"What about inside?"

"That's not a concern. The President needs privacy to contact his master. Once the guests leave, Mac and I enter the house."

"I agree," chirped Mackenzie. "Outside is our only concern."

Retracing steps, the trio returned to Wilma's for another caffeine boost. Polishing off dessert, the combat vets were eager for action.

At 9:45 p.m., the team piled into the SUVs and headed to the estate. Cloaked in a dense grove of trees, they donned black outerwear, grabbed weapons, and entered the woods. Led by Mackenzie, the stalkers moved into position and waited. As anticipated, the final limo exited the front entrance shortly after 10:30 p.m. Within minutes, the inside lights were doused. The lone exception was Anderson's study.

On Wilkins' signal, the team crept toward their assigned targets. As anticipated, there were gaps between Secret Service agents. Guarding the spacious estate was nearly impossible for such a small detail. As Morgan crept toward his man, he unexpectedly stopped. His once-stationary target was on the move. Suddenly a black blur flashed out of nowhere and toppled the guard. The dark figure was Ben Wilkins. Embarrassed, Nash unleashed an angry tirade.

"What the hell? I was in position. I didn't need your help."

"Orders, sir. You hesitated. I acted."

As Morgan fumed, Wilkins heard a series of soft clicks. All government agents were down. The path to Anderson was open.

"You're clear, but hurry."

Nodding, Nash flashed a signal into a wooded area. His boss was cleverly hidden in the darkness. Walking at a steady pace, they reached the rear door within seconds. Uttering a hasty prayer, Morgan entered the 'apis' code. As the pad flashed yellow and glowed green, the duo entered the unlocked kitchen door. Moving cautiously through the family room, Morgan snatched a small pillow from a nearby couch. Unexpectedly, the Dubliner held up a hand and whispered.

"Wait. I hear Anderson's voice. He's either on the phone or with someone."

Approaching the closed door, they stopped and listened. With a slow twist of the knob, Nash peered around the edge. Instantly, he flashed a thumbs up. The President was berating a dissenter and facing a window. Uttering a veiled threat, he tossed the phone onto a nearby table and slowly swiveled toward the desk. Suddenly, shock lined his face. Two intruders were pointing Glocks in his direction.

"How dare you enter my office. Dammit, I am the President of the United States." Bristling with bluster, the elitist's voice reflected his lofty position. "Where are my agents?"

Enjoying the advantage, Morgan toyed with the minion. "Your guards are AWOL. Like Vicksburg, they have magically vanished."

"Who are you?"

"We're angels of death."

"That's bullshit. How dare you invade my house and threaten me."

Deflecting the bravado, Mackenzie flashed a cruel smile. “Mr. President, we’re not here to coerce. We’re here to settle a score. Right, partner?”

“Yep. Payback can be a bitch.” Muzzling the barrel with the pillow, Morgan fired. The muted slug slammed into Anderson’s left shoulder. Writhing in pain, the minion glared at the intruders.

“Just who in the hell are you?”

“We’re the exterminators,” quipped the Dubliner. “According to RE, you’re in big trouble.”

“But I haven’t done anything wrong.” The high-pitched squeal mimicked a frightened pig. “I obeyed orders. I made calls.”

“But your people were sloppy. You didn’t kill that nosy bastard, Morgan Nash. You’ve failed miserably.”

“Look, I issued the directive. But some lowlife bumbled the job. That prick should have died a long time ago.”

Instantly, Nash beamed. “That’s very true. But... here I am.”

“YOU!!!”

“Yeah asshole, it’s me. And I don’t bumble things. Your sham presidency ends tonight.” Displaying a wicked jack-o’-lantern grin, Morgan triggered another muted round. The well-aimed shot shattered Anderson’s right wrist. Bleeding from both sides of his upper torso, the puppet pleaded for mercy.

Ignoring the pathetic cries, Mackenzie barked an order. “Take us to your communication center. Obey, you live. Refuse and you bleed out.”

“But there’s no such place.”

“Liar!” Walking to the bookshelf, the Special Agent grabbed the electronic scarab and aimed it at the bull’s forehead. As the panel slowly opened, Anderson’s inflated ego sagged in defeat.

"How did you know?"

"A little redbird told us," quipped Morgan. "You should have been more careful."

"Wait. I can reveal the location. But you must guarantee my safety. You need my testimony. Deal?"

"Sure," replied Mackenzie, "But only if you call RE."

"I can't. It's a death wish."

"Then utter a final prayer."

"No. Stop."

Terrified, the President limped into the secret room and snatched a frame from the small desk. The picture was his photo-op with Anthony. Suddenly, he stopped. With defiant eyes he glared at the Dubliner. Chuckling, Morgan pointed the imposing Glock in his direction. Instantly the faux bravado dissipated. In defeat, Anderson aimed the frame at the clock. The invisible beam trigged a bell toll and soft whirring as an invisible panel opened within the wall.

"Good boy. Now take a seat and behave. This woman kills for the cartels."

Sweating profusely, the President's eyes glazed with fear. Urine dripped from the cuffs of his slacks. Moving swiftly, Nash entered the small cubicle. Vivid frescos and advanced electronics lined both walls. Amazed, he returned to the secret room and eyed the traitor.

"Now make the call."

"No. I can't. I refuse."

Disgusted, Morgan placed the pillow against the barrel. In ultra-slow motion he aimed the Glock at the betrayer's head. Panicked, the minion pleaded for his life.

"Please don't shoot. We can deal. I don't want to die."

"Neither did my wife or daughter." With zero remorse, his trigger finger twitched. The muted bullet slammed into the President's forehead. As Anderson's lifeless body slid to the floor, Mackenzie's apocalyptic anger erupted.

"Dammit, did you have to kill him? He was a key witness. You had a deal."

"I lied. So did Anderson. The bastard would have crunched that capsule before calling RE."

"Now what? We've got a dead President and a huge mess."

"Mac, relax. We take him with us." Deaf to the tirade, Nash returned to the communication center. Trailing close behind was his irked partner. Suddenly the Dubliner's angst transformed into astonishment.

"The frescos are ablaze with color. But I was expecting more equipment."

"For a dumbass like Anderson, less is better. "

"Meaning?"

"RE didn't trust the bastard. Thus, a few simple codes were committed to memory. Files are non-existent."

"The codes could have led us to RE. Plus, Anderson would have talked. But you had to settle a score. Now we're stymied. These new images have to be decrypted."

Deflecting the criticism, Morgan scanned the left wall. Featured along the top was an arcing Picasso-like comet with a radiant yellow head and ominous red tail.

"Mac, note the comet. It ties with March 15."

Intrigued, he edged closer. The comet's tail was oozing tiny droplets of blood. Four dropped onto a small globe. Four landed on bizarre-looking figures.

"Mac, look. That mummy is Osiris. The woman with the feathered headdress is Isis. The other woman must be her sister Nephthys."

"Who's the ugly guy with four animal-looking heads?"

"I have no clue."

"What about the comet?"

"It's prophetic. Blood red symbolizes death. These bastards plan to reshape the world regardless of the cost."

"That explains the frigging map. Note the right wall."

Spanning the surface was an outline of the United States. Flying east to west was a lone red bird accompanied by eight black birds. All were crapping. But the shit was dark, not whitish gray. The red bird's poop was green.

"Morgan, that dark crap represents bombs. But the green is puzzling."

"There must be a code book in one of these rooms."

"But where? Thanks to you, our asset is dead. Let's peruse the far wall and then search. Wilkins is waiting."

Edging toward the back wall, Nash froze. "Mac, look! A tsunami is about to slam New York City."

Churning and swirling along the eastern seaboard were giant tidal waves. Riding atop a white-tipped crest was another wooden boat. The lone passenger was another stick figure clutching an inverted Ankh. An ominous red line extended from the tsunami to the "Big Apple." The notation was chilling: "Dow 5,000."

"That's depression territory," cried the Dubliner. "If that tsunami slams New York City, we're in deep shit."

"Which underscores dissolution. Mac, note the golden vulture."

"The damn thing appears to be nesting on the White House. What's your take?"

"It must symbolize Anderson. He's the master's golden boy...or was."

As the Dubliner studied the images, Morgan removed a camera from his tote bag and snapped a series of pictures. "Okay, that's it. Let's find the code book."

"We're out of time. We have to leave."

"But we need that book."

"And we needed Anderson. But you just had to shoot the bastard."

"Fine. Carry the tote. The President is coming with me."

"That's insane. We don't need a corpse."

"Yes, we do. The Secret Service needs to believe he's alive. A kidnapping scenario buys us time."

"Dammit, Morgan, they're not stupid. We're likely dead before arriving at Dulles."

"I disagree. I think an embarrassed Secret Service covers their ass. A prolonged search works in our favor."

As Nash toted the corpse, droplets of blood followed every step. Outside, the pair located Wilkins. The captain's arched eyebrows flashed surprise and concern. But his lips remained sealed.

"Ben, help me lug this bastard. There's a tarp in the SUV. The President is visiting Texas."

As the vehicles cruised toward the airport, Morgan alerted the billionaire. Enterprising as always, the old man contacted a close friend. Within minutes a coffin and dry ice were headed to the isolated hanger.

CHAPTER 39

Monday, February 22

Shortly after 2 a.m., the team arrived at the Boeing. Other than a casket and Wilson Senior, the hangar was empty. Moving quickly, Morgan cornered the rancher. "Sir, I need access to a large freezer. Some rotten meat needs to be stored for a few days."

"I've made arrangements. A Georgetown butcher and fellow Marine has agreed to freeze the President's sorry ass."

"Thanks. Let's get the hell out of here."

As the sleek jet leveled at 35,000 feet, the billionaire peered at the agents. "Well, you've certainly poked a hornet's nest. We're flying to Waco with a dead traitor and a shitload of problems. Did Anderson confess?"

Upset by the ordeal, Mackenzie was quick to respond. "Not really. The prick revealed the communication center but refused to contact RE. The President might have deciphered codes, but Morgan got trigger happy."

"What about Secret Service?"

"I think they remain mum," quipped Nash. "It's embarrassing to lose a President. Plus, his disappearance creates uncertainty. Is he still alive? Is he dead? Is this a kidnapping gone awry? Without a body or suspects, they track every lead before responding. It buys us time."

"Well, you've certainly created a mess. Did you leave prints or tracks? The President had to be bleeding when you toted him from the house."

"The man was dripping like a stuffed pig," smirked Fallon. "I warned Morgan."

"Hey, I had no choice. Dead or alive, Anderson had to disappear. Now Secret Service has a huge problem."

"Son, we're the ones with the problem," bristled the old man. "You've bought two or three days at most. But then what? Are you any closer to identifying RE?"

"Possibly. It depends on the new images."

"But deciphering takes time. The shit gets deeper by the minute."

Unexpectedly, Mackenzie intervened. "Sir, Morgan and I can handle the job. But we need a safe haven. Is your ranch available?"

"Absolutely not. You're not safe at any of my properties. The bastard has eyes everywhere."

"Then there's only one play," countered Nash. "I need to disappear. RE wants me, not Mac. If I vanish, everyone remains safe."

Instantly the old man gave Morgan a jagged look. "Son, I know that expression. Disappearing is your excuse for travel. What's the destination?"

"Back to the Vatican. There's still unfinished business. With your approval, I'd like to leave this evening."

"Hell son, we're still an hour from Austin. Arrangements have to be made. What about tomorrow?"

"Sir, the Holy Father is in grave danger. Every second counts. I can decipher codes during the flight."

"But the man has security," snapped Mackenzie. "And you're dead upon arrival."

"But there's no other way. RE wants me. You need to heal. The Wilsons need to hide."

"Son, you're taking a ballsy risk. Are you sure?"

"Absolutely. Prominent Cardinals are plotting the Pontiff's demise. Anderson's map was revealing."

"Any identities?"

"Not yet."

"Dammit, you're thinking with that little head again. Without identification, you're walking straight into an ambush."

"I have a plan."

"And it's likely flimsy as hell. Mackenzie's right. Let the Guards protect Anthony."

"Sir, they're also involved. Like it or not, I've got to go."

"Fine. It's your death wish. What's the plan?"

"With Anthony's approval, I set a trap in the archives. Alone, I'm the bait."

"Son, those people have to be expecting you. Without protection, you're dead within minutes."

"Wilson's right," parroted the Dubliner. "It's a setup. Anthony is the real target. Let trusted security do their job."

"Look, you're both right. But I've got no choice. Mac, you saw those birds. Bombs are poised to drop across America."

"But details weren't fully disclosed. There was no timetable or specific targets. Partner, our focus has to be the codes."

"No. We've got to act. Otherwise, we're dead. Look, Anderson was never privy to the entire plan. Nor was America ever the epicenter. The Vatican has always been ground zero."

"Why? Give me one good reason."

"RE has to have a credible leader to cheerlead his global reset. Anthony must be replaced before that can happen. He has a day or so to live."

Reluctantly, the old man nodded. "If Mac agrees, I'll make arrangements. But I will be your escort."

With a sunrise landing in Austin, the weary travelers reconvened at the Governor's Mansion. Baffled by her partner's prolonged silence, the Dubliner finally reacted. "Morgan, you've had your head buried in those damned pictures since D.C. Are the dots finally connecting?"

"Possibly. But you're not going to like the answer. Anderson was both an idiot and *duped.*"

"Duped?" Flabbergasted, the old man expunged a guttural growl. Then the savvy billionaire grinned. "You figured something out, didn't you?"

"Maybe. Check out the map." Grabbing his phone, Nash flashed the image for both to see. "Okay, eight black birds and a lone red bird are scattered across the nation. Flying east to west they're crapping."

"That's ordinance," yelped the rancher. "But the color deviates. Why?"

"I think black indicates infrastructure. It's the most significant color. The green is troubling. Likely it represents a dirty bomb, a type of virus that can spread rapidly, create a pandemic, and kill millions. If so, expect more green droppings on other maps."

"Partner, that's pretty damn grim. Dirty bombs would cripple America, maybe forever."

"That's the goal. Dissolution hastens an altered world."

"Son, can you pinpoint specific locations?"

"Not yet. Either we decipher codes or expose RE. It's a race against time. Plus, the news gets worse. Look at this picture."

As the rancher fixated on America's east coast, his eyes bulged in disbelief. "What the hell? That tsunami is set to crush New York City."

"The tidal wave supersedes the smaller one in the first secret room. The Dow Industrials at five thousand is depression territory. But note the location. The tsunami is still offshore, which buys us time."

"That's unbelievable," growled the rancher. "But this scenario is virtually impossible. No one individual or group can destroy America."

"Sir, it is happening. That's the brilliance of RE's plan. Fed murders destabilize markets. Infrastructure bombs create chaos. Dirty bombs kill millions. Then comes the coup d'état. With America reeling, the bastard plans to *flood* world markets with U.S, greenbacks. That explains the tidal wave and the Dow number. The sell-off devalues the dollar and bludgeons our economy. If RE succeeds, the world changes."

"Dammit. We're in no position to withstand another 2008 recession or worse. Are you sure about this?"

"I'm positive. The tiny eye in the first wave solves the puzzle. Cleverly hidden, it's printed on the back of every one-dollar bill. The foam green tsunami represents greenbacks."

"Son, you're painting a pretty dire picture. But you're right about a global reset. China and Russia have been salivating to seize new territories."

"That's their intent. But there's a caveat. I think they *wait."*

"But why?" Stunned by the revelation, Mackenzie flashed a surprised look. "If this doomsday scenario plays out, there's no reason to hesitate."

"Ah, but there is. China and Russia fear *retaliation*. A nuclear war with America is unacceptable. Thus, they wait until America buckles and General Robison flashes the go signal."

"Robison?" Instantly, the billionaire glared at Nash with hard-set eyes. "Son, that's hard to believe. With Riggs dead, he's the Army's top guy."

"Correct. But the bastard is both a liar and traitor."

"Morgan, that's hard to swallow. Is there proof?"

"Yeah. According to Vatican records, General Robison's birth name was Mario Ernesto Lopez. His Catholic parents were illegal immigrants and pickers. Both were killed by white racists. The young man was raised by his grandmother and radicalized early."

"But that doesn't make him a traitor. Is he going to protect America?"

"The answer is murky, a combined *yes and no*. RE controls the speed of his actions. Likely, Robison obeys the President but drags both feet."

"Son, you've got to report this to Allday and Jameson ASAP."

"I can't, not with a dead President on ice. Plus, Robison's treason is yet to come. That's why my Vatican trip is critical. I need to expose Judas Cardinals and reveal RE's timetable. The bastard is extremely clever. That doomsday clock may trigger in days, not weeks, making every minute crucial, especially with the Secret Service nipping at our heels."

Eying Morgan's pictures, the Dubliner instantly interrupted. "Does the passenger in boat number two play a role in this? Does he link to Anthony?"

"I think he's the *successor.* Those slashes on the block 'T' indicate Asian eyes. If so, Cardinal Xi Li triggers the sell-off of U.S. dollars."

"Is Li transitional or long-term?"

"Likely he's the interim, Mac. I think RE's future Pope is still being groomed. He's well-positioned and exempt from Vatican politics."

As the twilight of early evening cast a dark shadow on Austin, the luxury Boeing rocketed skyward. Nestled in plush recliners, Morgan and the old man sipped drinks. Both were exhausted from the D.C. all-nighter. Uncomfortable about the trip, the billionaire probed.

"Son, your plan to isolate yourself in the archives is pretty damn ballsy. People disappear. Surely you can think of something more realistic?"

As Nash grinned, a mischievous twinkle danced in his eyes. "Sir, have you ever played poker?"

"Hell, I'm from Texas. What's your point?"

"That's my game. Play a card and watch. Any Cardinal that twitches is dead."

"Bluffing can prove dangerous. You might just come across a joker."

"Sir, it's Anthony's house. He sets the rules. Bluster is my only hope."

Unexpectedly, the lone flight attendant interrupted their conversation. "Good evening. I'm ready to serve dinner. Tonight, it's grilled salmon with all the trimmings. For dessert, there's chocolate pie."

"Man, you rich guys travel in style." Chuckling, Morgan flashed a rare smile. His fondness for the billionaire was genuine.

"We're exhausted. So, I made the call. A few perks were in order."

Midway through the gourmet meal, the billionaire unexpectedly gagged. "Aaagh!" "Aaagh!" "Aaagh!"

"That's it, sir. Cough that fishbone out."

"Aaagh!" "Aaagh!" On the eighth hack, the spindly bone finally emerged. Panting and sweating, the rancher sat exhausted.

"Are you okay? You're beet red."

"Dammit, that's the problem with fish. It's those tiny bones." Suddenly his eyes flashed panic. "Aaagh!" "Aaagh!" On the second cough, another spindly bone appeared. "Whew. Those damn things nearly killed me."

"That was never going to happen. I was ready to squeeze it out."

"Well, so much for the fish. "Aaagh."

"What did you say?"

"Nothing. I was clearing my throat."

Suddenly Morgan's eyes bulged in disbelief. "*Aaagh.* Sir, that's it!"

"That's what? Son, how does Mackenzie understand you? You talk in riddles."

"That hacking sound was Raz's final utterance. Though slurred, the word was obviously relevant. The prick died too quickly."

"Aaagh?" So what?"

"His utterance got me to thinking."

"Meaning?"

"There's a similar sounding word. "*Ogdoad.*" Thanks to you this term is suddenly very relevant."

"I'm not following."

"Ogdoad refers to eight. The number references Egypt's initial deities following Amun and RE. More importantly, I think the number links to RE's inner circle and the map's eight black birds. I need to retrieve some notes."

Hustling to his briefcase, Nash ripped through files searching for the specific page. Striking gold, he snatched his phone and returned.

"Sir, I located a helpful summary. Darkness and lifeless waters covered the universe prior to Egypt's creation. Lonely, the King God Amun created the Sun God RE. Later RE birthed Shu, God of Air, and Tefnut, Goddess of Moisture.

Shu and Tefnut procreated Geb, God of Earth, and Nut, the Sky Goddess."

"Morgan, that gibberish means absolutely nothing. How does it relate to the case?" The old man's tone was gruff and to the point.

"The black birds link to Egypt's creation story, which connects to this photo. Take a look." Grabbing his phone, Morgan displayed a baffling image. "This shot was taken in Anderson's secret room. Initially, the four figures were a mystery. Now they're not. Osiris, Isis, Seth, and Nephthys were offspring of Geb and Nut. With the addition of Shu and Tefnut, you have the number eight, or Ogdoad."

"Okay, the number is relevant. What's the connection?"

"The deities were all *descendants* of the Sun God RE."

"That's a symbolic bloodline!" blurted the rancher. "*Ancient* RE links to *modern* RE."

"That was my archival discovery. The *eight* black birds and blood drops are intertwined and link to lineage."

"But how does ancestry help?"

"It exposes motive. If global adversaries rattle sabers... who benefits?"

"That's obvious. Defense contractors win."

"That's my thinking. If true, corporate executives comprise RE's inner circle and not world leaders. That narrows the playing field. We search for eight global titans."

"Son, that's wishful thinking. But there's a flaw. Industry giants don't need RE for contracts. However, if the focus shifts to *small caps,* the list shrinks. It narrows even more if you pinpoint Egyptian or Middle Eastern CEOs."

Intrigued, Morgan peered at the old man. Another critical moment had arrived. "Mr. Wilson, are you sure? I was focused on the global titans."

"Hell, they have lobbyists to create lucrative deals. But numerous small caps are struggling. Russell 2000 companies have the capacity to produce arms but still fly under the radar."

"Invisibility certainly fits RE's style. It's worth a try."

"Wait. We can slice the list even more. Instruct Mackenzie to search for small caps with *recent stock buybacks*. That's our best bet to expose greed, isolate companies, and expose traitors. Tell her to pay close attention to aviation and weapons contractors. Also, research pharmaceuticals and environmental companies. With luck, we can expose traitors, locate ordinance, and prevent delivery. Dammit, those bombs must not fall."

An hour later the two men sat quietly. The call to Mackenzie had gone well. Yet Morgan was pensive. A delicate call to Anthony was pending. A final approval was necessary to set the trap.

CHAPTER 40

Tuesday, February 23

With an early morning landing at bustling Da Vinci International, the luxury Boeing taxied to a private hangar. Idling nearby was a private car bracketed by Swiss Guards. The Pontiff was taking no chances. Within minutes, a parade of black vehicles was motoring toward the Vatican.

~

The impromptu visit caught the Camerlengo by surprise. Fixated on the Americans, his face flashed contempt. Minutes later, a stoic Anthony appeared in the doorway.

"Mr. Wilson, please remain seated. Mr. Nash, come with me." In silence, the frail Pontiff led the weary traveler to his private office. Uncertain about the outcome, Morgan peered into Anthony's troubled eyes.

"Sir, are you having second thoughts about the plan?"

"The honest answer is yes. But evil needs to be exposed."

"What's the latest on the White House? Any new updates?"

"No. The President remains bedridden with a virus."

"That's good. But the clock is ticking. With luck, I can expose the guilty and plant Anderson's body in D.C. Hopefully, the Secret Service blames RE."

"I have prayed for such a speedy conclusion. The omega's trifecta has me deeply concerned. Are you ready for our first guest?"

Fifteen minutes later, an irate Egyptian with bruised ego huffed into the room. "Why have I been summoned? Rumors are rampant about traitorous Cardinals. I have done nothing wrong."

"My dear Mosef, the Vatican grapevine has always overreacted. Mr. Nash has unfinished research about the College."

Noting the Alexandrian's defiance, Morgan eased into the interrogation. "According to the records you were adopted by the Firellis. Yet you maintained an Egyptian name. Why?"

"My adoption is a private matter."

"That's fine. I can research other records. Do you stay in touch with your brother?"

Startled by the question, the diminutive Cardinal tensed. Few knew of his relationship with the Camerlengo. "That information has been sealed. Holy Father, did you reveal our secret?"

"Mosef, Mr. Nash has both my blessing and access to *all* records."

"Enzo and I have talked briefly from time to time. But we were never close."

"You were the stellar academic. Enzo was the stud athlete. But you were special. Your bloodline traced to Pharaoh Akhenaten. Surely the Firellis bragged about your royal heritage."

Unnerved by the confidential revelations, Qadesh's facial muscles twitched as his eyes flashed fear and uncertainty. "You're mistaken. I was never special. Enzo was the attraction. Plus, Akhenaten was forever erased from our history. I have no ties to his lineage."

"The revolutionary king ordered sweeping changes. Your country's entire culture was upended. Was he right?"

"Right about what? Holy Father, is this an interview or interrogation?"

"Mosef, Mr. Nash is actually with the FBI. At my invitation, he's investigating a conspiracy that threatens the church."

"But why am I here? I'm innocent of any wrongdoings."

"Are you?" With snarled lips and guttural growl Morgan struck like a coiled viper. "Didn't you and Enzo agree with Akhenaten? Didn't you plan a new world order?"

"That's not true."

"Liar! Everything changed when you discovered your heritage. You devoted yourself to Akhenaten and reached out to others. A radical ideology became your new religion."

"You're wrong! I've done nothing to betray God or the Church."

As beads of sweat dotted the Cardinal's furrowed brow, Nash upped the ante. "You're lying. For years you and Enzo plotted against the Catholic Church. *Aren't you the chosen one to poison Anthony?"*

"No! That's absolutely untrue."

"Is it? Secret tapes reveal a different story."

"What tapes? Yes, Enzo and I have conversed. But we've done nothing to betray the Holy Father or our vows."

As Mosef fidgeted, Morgan played his trump card. "Initially, you were the Firelli golden boy. Your coveted bloodline overshadowed Enzo's athletic successes. But that changed with an unexpected and hideous discovery. *Enzo was also royalty.* Suddenly, your fragile world crumbled."

"Holy Father, this man is violating my privacy. I refuse to answer."

As Anthony remained mum, Morgan pressed his prosecution. "You had to be furious about the news. No longer were you the special one. How was it possible for a black man to emerge from Akhenaten's loins?"

"You're speculating. You're spinning a false narrative."

"Am I?" Flashing a wicked jack-o'-lantern grin, Nash played a hidden joker. It was time to go all in. "Recruited by RE, *you* became the architect. Lacking papal charisma and Cardinal votes, you agreed to eliminate Anthony and support a transitional Pope."

The Egyptian was stunned by the accusation; rivulets of sweat streamed down his narrow cheeks. Locked in terror, he glared at the Holy Father. "This is absurd. I love the church."

Ignoring the pathetic pleas, Anthony's stoic expression remained unchanged. The high-stakes game had to be played out. Pressing his case, Nash hammered the trembling Egyptian.

"LOVE, MY ASS! You don't love this Catholic Church. It's too archaic. What you covet is power in RE's altered world."

"You're wrong! You're spewing a false narrative. I've done nothing to betray the Church."

With the outcome teetering in uncertainty, Morgan revealed a second joker. "You made one fatal mistake. You accepted Raz's call."

"You're lying! Holy Father, you've got to believe me."

"In a panic, the academic contacted you. RE was hell-bent on eliminating loose ends, which included BABA. But that was unacceptable. Why?"

"Holy Father..."

Raz called because BABA was his son and your blood relative!

"That's not true."

"LIAR! Raz was desperate. He had to warn his only child. But BABA had vanished."

Disregarding the Egyptian, Nash peered at Anthony. "Sir, this man has been plotting your demise for months. I have tangible evidence to prove every accusation."

Glaring at the accused, the Holy Father quietly weighed the matter. The attacks were damning. But everything was circumstantial. Suddenly, his mouth gaped in utter disbelief as the Egyptian twisted and convulsed. Locked in death throes, the Vatican mole gasped, gurgled, and slumped to the floor. As foam crusted around his lips, a hint of bitter almond scented the air.

"Holy Father, death by cyanide was his only way out. The hidden pill has been a RE trademark."

"So be it."

As Swiss Guards stoically removed the body, Morgan heaved a huge sigh of relief. The all-out gamble had paid off. Steeled by the outcome, Anthony shook his head in utter disgust. "Agent, you play a deadly game of poker. The church owes you a debt of gratitude."

"Sir, were you aware of his relationship with Enzo?"

"Yes. Leave the Camerlengo to me. Who's next? Or dare I ask?"

"That is to be determined by my archival trap. A traitorous redbird or two should appear."

"I'll contact security."

"Sir, please don't. I need to go alone. I know the way."

"Such a move could prove deadly. Plus, you need access to the archives."

"That's not necessary. I'm taking notes and a weapon. Exposing myself is the only way. The redbird's identity is still unknown."

"God be with you. Be careful."

Unnerved by the cavernous silence, Morgan questioned his judgment. Posing as the proverbial tethered goat seemed foolhardy. With the Glock nestled on his lap, he randomly flipped through a series of pages. Focus was near impossible as O'Reilly's dire warning bracketed his mind.

After rechecking the area, he took a deep breath and willed himself to think. Surprisingly, a Cardinal from Venice caught his attention. But there were gaps in his ascension to power. According to the files, the Venetian was born into wealth and fast-tracked to his lofty status. Jealous power brokers accused him of selling his soul and ostracized him whenever possible.

So, you're an outcast. True or false?

Intrigued, Morgan read deeper into the file. To his surprise, the Venetian was often praised for his saintly work as Archbishop. He was adored by parishioners, and the Holy Father took notice of his humble service. Suddenly a footnote caught his attention. "Prone to hubris." According to the anonymous writer, the Venetian was both arrogant and rude when away from the prying eyes of the Vatican.

"A great actor...but not worthy. Perfect. You may be my sleeper RE."

Closing the file, Nash placed a bright red check by the Venetian's name. As fatigue dulled his mind, he didn't hear or sense movement.

But... he smelled a distinct odor.

Cautiously, he lowered his right hand and gripped the Glock. The subtle movement was greeted by a deep-throated, authoritative command. "Sit very still. I am right behind you."

That accent. I've heard it before. But where? And the smell?

Then he remembered. *The dining room.*

"Herr Dietrich, how is the summer weather in Hamburg? You enjoy good beer and krauts, ja?"

From the shadows came a sneering laugh. "Ja! Steins are larger than breasts. I have a good life."

"A German lager sounds good."

"Sit very still, Agent Nash. I am an expert marksman."

"I've read about your heroics. But you're not very smart. You have a most recognizable odor. There are soaps that actually work."

"Funny man. Laugh while you can."

"I was hoping you would come."

"Why?"

"I want to join RE's team. That's why I'm here." Morgan baited the German as his darting eyes searched for an escape. Hearing a grunt and shuffle, he froze. Seconds later, Franz Dietrich emerged from the darkness and fronted him. Held tightly in his right hand was a customized Glock with silencer.

"So, you want to trade sides? I'm sure the master would be pleased. But it's too late. You cannot be trusted."

"And you are not very popular. You're much too pudgy to become the Holy Father. Lacking support, you joined RE."

"Pudgy?" Sensitive about his girth, the German tensed and then cracked a smug smile. "You are trying to provoke me. Ja?"

"Frankly, Franz, you're a chubby joke. You lobbied for Anthony's position but failed miserably. The master's offer of power and prestige had to soothe your damaged ego."

"Ah, you are perceptive but wrong. The Catholic Church died years ago. Old men like Anthony have neither vision nor influence."

"And RE does?"

"Ja. World leaders are enamored with his new order."

"So that's your role. You make introductions. I'm sure your fat butt is amply rewarded."

"Ja. I am very rich. As for you, that's not the case. Naughty men simply vanish into the Vatican's darkness."

"You are right. Just moments ago, your Alexandrian buddy disappeared. Mosef pleaded and squealed before dying. But he lived long enough to implicate your sorry ass. Anthony has ordered your arrest and execution. Herr Dietrich, either work with me or you are a dead man. The Holy Father has no tolerance for traitors. Are you going to listen to my offer or not?"

Stunned by the news, the Herman Goering figure hesitated but quickly recovered. "Ha, you Americans are such bluffers. That mousey Egyptian was a nuisance. I have nothing to fear from Anthony or the Guards."

Anticipating a shootout, Morgan repositioned the Glock. Suddenly, both heard grunts and movement in the shadows. The brief scuffle ended with a hideous snap.

Suddenly a terrifying thought flashed across Morgan's mind. "*CAMERLENGO!*"

Emerging from the shadows was the chiseled aide clutching a Beretta with a silencer. The Nubian's eyes flashed hate and contempt. Panicked by his appearance, the German froze and then grinned. The Camerlengo's weapon was aimed at the American's chest.

Then came the unexpected.

With quicksilver reflexes, Enzo swung the barrel toward Franz and fired. The muted slug slammed into the minion's forehead. As the plump Cardinal crumpled to the floor, death veins spread a purplish hue. With eyes fixated on the German, Morgan's response was too slow. The Nubian's gun was pointed at his chest.

"Do not move."

"Go ahead, Enzo. Avenge your brother. I'm here to die. Your hate is evident."

Unexpectedly the Nubian lowered the Beretta and roared with laughter. "Intimidation works well within these walls. I am a trusted servant of the Holy Father."

"What about your brother?"

"Mosef was an American hater and traitor."

"Anthony sent you?"

"I was your shadowy backup. The German was a coward. He did not come alone."

"Was it Li?"

"No. The Brazilian was his backup. Like Dietrich, he too was a pompous ass. Wringing his scrawny neck was a pleasure."

"Thanks. I was expecting a quick death."

"Does the Holy Father require pictures?"

"That's not necessary. Vatican security can clean up the mess."

"Agent, my veins flow with the blood of Christ. I'm here to protect the Holy Father and you."

"I'm most grateful. Can you take me to him?"

Twenty minutes later, a disbelieving Anthony sat dejected and speechless. The betrayals were devastating. After a long pause, he spoke.

"Agent, what is happening? The College is crumbling. Do you anticipate more traitors?"

"I'm afraid so. Xi Li is a likely culprit, plus a mystery Cardinal."

"Mystery? I'm not following."

"Think of him as your short-term replacement. Aided by RE, he steals the election. But his reign is brief. Within a year or so the master's true Pontiff emerges and assumes power."

"Is there a prime suspect?"

"Several names come to mind, Holy Father. But there's no damning evidence. Plus, there's an additional problem. Other traitors may surface as RE resets his Vatican network."

"Other? That creates a huge security problem for the Swiss Guards. I must notify Captain Strader. What is your next step?"

"Hopefully, it's a showdown with RE. For the moment, my Vatican work is done. In my absence, surround yourself with trusted security. Your life remains in grave danger."

"The Catholic Church owes you many 'Hail Mary's. Go with God, my son."

With the meeting adjourned, Morgan headed to the Guards' dining hall to rejoin Wilson. A return to Austin was looming.

In the calm blackness of a Roman night, the customized Boeing rocketed skyward. The long day was finally coming to an end. As Morgan caressed a drink, the billionaire pressed for information. "Son, you haven't uttered a word. What happened in those archives? Did you kill another minion?"

"I got two assists. I bagged one in Anthony's presence. The poor Holy Father was aghast. Unfortunately, more predators are lurking. For the moment, I've damaged RE's network and bought some time."

"That's good. The holy man deserves to live. What's next?"

"That depends on Mac's research. Hopefully, we identify RE's inner circle and stop the bombs. But we need to move fast."

"We may have an extra day," grunted Wilson Senior "According to reports, the President's recovery has been slow."

"That's good. But sooner rather than later, the Secret Service comes clean about Anderson's death. That's when the shit really hits the fan, and Allday takes over."

"Son, there's an old adage. 'Fight one battle at a time.' Get some rest. Then prepare for the next challenge. I need to update the Governor."

Nodding, Nash headed to a private area. Nestled comfortably in a plush recliner, he was asleep within minutes. The arduous twenty-four-hour ordeal was over.

CHAPTER 41

Wednesday, February 24

Arriving in a heavy downpour, the morning travelers were escorted to the Governor's Mansion. Within minutes they were huddled with Mackenzie in a small conference room. Stunned by the revelations, the Dubliner sat dismayed.

"The Holy Father has to be livid about the College. The betrayals are unbelievable."

"Mac, the poor guy was stunned. Anthony has no real faith in anyone, including the Swiss Guards."

"The Holy Father needs to clean house... beginning with the Camerlengo," grumbled Wilson Senior "He may be your hero. But I don't like him. He's a mean-looking son-of-a bitch." Pontificating, the rancher's tone was deep and guttural. "Anthony needs to surround himself with trusted people."

"But who fits that category?"

"Morgan, forget the Vatican," barked Mackenzie. "We need to focus on the immediate. Our window of opportunity is closing."

"Does Jameson know about Anderson?"

"No. I wanted to buy us a few more hours."

"Good. That gives us time to kill RE and unload Anderson's frozen ass. The bastard is accelerating the schedule. All hell is about to break loose."

"But how?" Flashing a dubious expression, Mackenzie posed the query. 'Hell partner, we've been searching for weeks."

"Newly decoded images have evened the playing field. The Vatican library was a veritable goldmine of information."

"That explains the worsening international crisis," lamented the Dubliner. "Whatever you uncovered has RE and friends reeling."

"The mention of global news caught Morgan's attention. "What's the latest?"

"Adversaries are pushing the envelope but not acting. They're claiming 'training exercises.' Russia has transferred two new divisions to northern Syria. Plus, they are moving troops into Belarus to bracket Ukraine. China's massive armada has set sail for the Indian Ocean. Another fleet has edged toward Taiwan. India has added three new divisions to its northern frontier."

"Forget those damn exercises!" decried Wilson. "It's nothing but a smokescreen. Those bastards covet resources. They plan to invade. You can't trust any of them."

"Anthony uttered the same sentiment," added Nash. "His confidential sources are predicting simultaneous incursions. Mac, have any 'training' dates been released?"

"The China-Indo exercises are scheduled for March 15. Coincidence?"

"That's laughable and appropriate. What about your Ogdoad research? Any candidates? We need to move quickly."

"Only two companies have emerged. Both CEOs are Middle Eastern, but not Egyptian. Only a handful of small caps have implemented stock buybacks in this down market."

"Ignore the lineage," quipped the old man. "Name the companies."

"Teffington Environmental focuses on global energy projects. Neptune Industries produces basic materials for construction and roads."

"Dammit. Those companies are irrelevant. They're not in play."

"Sir, I'm not so sure." Unexpectedly, Morgan pushed away from the table. Time was needed to process the information. Several minutes later he spoke. "I think Teffington symbolizes Tefnut. Neptune represents Nephthys. RE thrives on the unexpected."

"And I think you're guessing," growled Mackenzie. "No judge is going to issue a search warrant based on conjecture. What do I tell Jameson?"

"The truth. We're making progress. The Vatican trip was productive. Our list of suspects has narrowed."

With the meeting adjourned, Nash hustled to an unused office. A fresh approach was desperately needed to answer lingering questions. In quick order, he jotted three headings: *Leadership, Charisma,* and *Connections.*

Within minutes he sat frustrated. None of the suspects graded high in all areas. As his angst flared, he tried to relax. Doodling, he scribbled the letter "A." In quick order, he progressed through the alphabet concluding with "K." Pushing back, he mindlessly stared at the letter. Suddenly a bodacious plan began to percolate. He jogged to the conference room, with an impish expression. Instantly the billionaire reacted.

"I've seen that possum-ass look too many times. You're onto something."

"Possibly. I need approval for a kidnapping."

"Who?"

"Xi Li."

"Hell son, we just came from the Vatican."

"He's not there. Anthony's golden goose is conferencing in Madrid."

Irked by the flimsy idea, the Dubliner's apocalyptic temper erupted. "Dammit, Morgan, forget Xi Li. Our focus is here. It needs to be on RE and those bombs. A trans-Atlantic flight is a waste of time. Plus, Anthony would go ape-shit."

"Son, Mackenzie's right. At best, Li is a minion. Think it through. Akhenaten's lineage doesn't include Asians."

"Folks, forget family. Focus on the secret map. That lone red bird is Xi Li. He's the trigger man for RE's flood of greenbacks *and* an insider. The Asian knows locations, timing, and accomplices. Better yet, he knows RE's identity. Hell, he may even be the guy. Either way, Xi Li is our shortcut. A successful kidnapping exposes RE, halts the bombs, prevents the flood, and defuses the timetable."

"What about Anthony?"

"We make the trip and explain later. Yes, it's time-consuming. But Li is our best and only option."

"I vote yes," blurted the oilman. "Play the hand. When do we leave?"

"If my boss approves, you and I depart this evening. That gives Mac additional time to heal. But first, I need to take care of something." Unexpectedly Morgan began pacing the room, checking lamps, pictures, and paintings. Pausing, he snatched a brightly colored ceramic clown from a side table and slammed it against the hardwood floor. The brittle figurine shattered into countless shards.

"Partner, what the hell?"

"Look," cried the rancher. "There's a tiny bug."

Crushing the listening device, Nash flashed a wry grin. “That damn thing was hidden in the bulbous nose by a very clever minion.”

“What tipped you?”

“The ambush in the archives was the final straw. RE was tipped well in advance. There had to be a mole in the Mansion.”

Startled by the revelation, the Dubliner abruptly headed to security. The Governor had to address the breach. With her departure, the oil baron peered at Morgan. His squinty eyes were hard and piercing.

“Son, I need a straight answer. Is there a real plan to kidnap Li? Or is this about protecting Mackenzie?”

“You read me well, sir. The Asian is a priority but not initially. First, there’s unfinished business. While Mackenzie rehabs, we need to move fast.”

“What do you have in mind?”

“We travel north. I think our story begins in New England, spreads to D.C., and then to Europe and Asia. If true, RE is colluding with numerous world leaders.”

“Does the list include Allday?”

“That’s uncertain. Our main priority is stopping those bombs and preventing a national pandemic. We can deal with the V.P. later.”

“When is our actual departure?”

“With Mac’s blessing, we leave tomorrow morning.”

“Destination?”

“Boston. We’re going to visit a charming Irish Leprechaun. Our chatty friend has the cunning and connections to become RE’s next Pope.”

“Will Mackenzie join us?”

“I hope not. This isn’t the big showdown. It’s merely a side trip to flush out two Cardinals.”

CHAPTER 42

Thursday, February 25

Shortly after 7 a.m., *three* passengers boarded the billionaire's Boeing at Austin International. Relaxing in a plush recliner, Morgan glanced at his partner. "Mac, are you sure about going? Your wounds are still healing."

"Wilson said this venture was low risk. But that other destinations were possible. You're dead without backup."

Overhearing his name, the rancher joined the conversation. "Where do we find the chatterbox? Beantown is a Catholic haven."

"The Cathedral of the Holy Cross houses his suite of offices."

"Is O'Reilly a traitor or tale spinner?"

"Boss, I honestly don't know. The man could be innocent. Or he could be the perfect sleeper to replace Anthony."

"But the College never elects an American," countered the old man. "Kidnapping Li seems far more productive."

"You're probably right. But O'Reilly has always been evasive. And RE has a penchant for rewriting history."

"I actually agree," echoed the Dubliner. "And I'm a pretty good profiler. Tim's darting eyes portray him as shrewd, self-confident, and well-connected."

"Add charismatic. The wily Cardinal is a regular Pied Piper," chimed the billionaire "Morgan, is he the mastermind?"

"Sir, that's doubtful. But he makes a perfect *transitional* Pope. The dots connect. RE kills Anthony and replaces him with O'Reilly. Within a year or so, our Irishman meets his demise. Then RE reveals his long-term choice."

"Partner, wait. I thought Tim was in eastern Europe."

"Not anymore. According to his secretary, he's conducting a special mass this afternoon. Holy Cross is the Mother Church of Boston's Roman Catholic Archdiocese."

"I've toured it," chimed the old man. "The cathedral was built in 1860 by an Irish-American ecclesiastical architect. Thousands of faithful worshippers have called it home for decades."

With a noon landing at Logan International, the trio zipped through obsequious security, stepped into a private car, and headed across Boston. Arriving at Holy Cross, they fast-walked into the narthex. A small sign directed them to the Cardinal's suite of offices. Unexpectedly, they heard a litany of shrieks. Numerous female voices were screaming for help.

With Glocks in the ready position, both agents sprinted toward the chaos. Arriving at Tim's office, they abruptly stopped. The ghoulish scene was a Dante masterpiece. Locked in hysteria were five nuns. Crumpled on the floor was the Irishman's ravaged body. A squishy pool of blood ringed the open chest.

Appalled by the butchery, Mackenzie gagged. "Dammit, Morgan, this was a slaughter. Tim's guts are everywhere. Even his heart was removed."

"RE was tipped. Our chatty Pied Piper was likely innocent but knew too much. The man was a fixture within the Vatican grapevine."

Near the body was a disfigured token and tilted scale of justice. The oozing heart easily outweighed the white feather of truth. Panting from the short sprint, the billionaire stopped and gaped.

"What the hell? O'Reilly's been gutted like a steer. But why?"

"His murder was a warning to wavering Cardinals," snapped Nash. "RE has no tolerance for the undecided. Obviously, our Irishman fell into that category."

"I'm calling Jameson. Morgan, this is a fricking nightmare." A blink later, the Dubliner vomited.

~

As scores of FBI and Boston police flooded the scene, the Texas contingent sat quietly in the sanctuary. Occupying a back pew, the old man was livid.

"Dammit. How did RE know? This trip was supposed to be secret."

"It was my mistake," confessed Nash. "I called his secretary. Obviously, the phone was bugged."

"So, what's next? Do we kidnap Li or return to Austin?"

"Mac, Madrid was a ruse to keep you safe. I thought O'Reilly *was* the answer. Dammit, we're running out of time."

"Let's vamoose," snorted the old man. "This place gives me the creeps. We can make decisions on the plane."

As the limo sped to Logan International, Mackenzie's pale face reflected sheer anguish. "Morgan, it was your Vatican trip that expedited Tim's death. Dammit, RE has eyes and ears everywhere. We're next on the list."

"Likely. He's trimming loose ends and accelerating the schedule. Yet, there's still a missing piece. Without it, Anthony dies and RE wins."

"Hold on," boomed the rancher. "Both of you are scared shitless. You're not thinking. O'Reilly was never a loose end or threat to RE. *You've got things all wrong."*

With a confused look, Nash posed a logical response. "Why?"

"Our chatterbox was *Irish.* Tim wasn't *royalty."*

As if sucker punched, Morgan's face instantly twisted. "Dammit, you're right. I've been running scared and looking in the wrong direction. I've got to contact the Holy Father."

As the private car rolled to a stop, the former All-American sprinted up the Boeing's steps. Activating Wilson's secure line, he entered the Pontiff's private number. After eight rings, he sat dismayed. There was no answer.

Is Anthony still alive?

With Madrid the only viable option, the luxury Boeing rocketed into the blackening Atlantic sky. Apprehensive, Nash peered at his partner. "Mac, I'm not sure about bypassing Anthony. Li's kidnapping is pretty damn risky."

"There's no other option. Just pray for answers. Why don't you try Anthony again? Hopefully, he's still breathing."

Moving quickly to the secure phone, Morgan entered the private number. To his relief, the Pontiff answered on the first ring. Yet Anthony's muffled voice registered grave concern. "Agent, I was expecting your call. Cardinal O'Reilly's death was horrific."

"RE has fast-forwarded the timetable. He's been eliminating loose ends."

"How can I help?"

"Your archival files are badly outdated. Are any current records available?"

"I'm not sure. Let me contact Captain Strader. The Camerlengo is Cardinal O'Reilly's replacement in Croatia."

"Sir, please fax any updates. A critical piece is missing. Here's the secure number."

Fifty minutes later, the billionaire's private fax chattered and stopped. As he snatched the five pages, Morgan's darting eyes scanned for nuggets. A section of the third page prompted a return call to the Holy Father.

"Sir, the information is both enlightening and frightening. Once again, I need your assistance."

As he quickly outlined his plan, Anthony hesitated. "Agent, I have grave concerns. Are you absolutely certain about the next step?"

"Yes."

"There can be no mistakes."

"Mac and I will take care of the situation."

"Then so be it. God be with you."

Energized by the plan, Nash quickly rejoined the others. "Sir, we need to return to Boston. RE lives in an upscale neighborhood. It's showtime."

"But there are only three of us. We've got no plan or backup."

"Two of your best men would help. A larger number might spook RE. Instruct your guys to bring Anderson's sorry ass and meet at the hangar."

"Are you positive about the identity?"

"I'm certain and very surprised."

"I'll make the arrangements."

Shortly after 8 p.m., two combat vets and a frozen corpse arrived at Logan International. Eager to end the case, the old man quickly barked introductions.

"Agents, meet Jim and John. They take orders from you."

"Thanks," replied Mackenzie. "The suspect is supposedly home. Let's check it out."

In abject silence, the team headed to a blueblood neighborhood of vintage mansions. As RE's estate came into view, the black SUV rolled to a stop.

"Note the walls," marveled Fallon. "It's a damn fortress. Jim, take John and scout the area. Check for lights, cameras, and movement. Meet us back here."

Cloaked in the frigid blackness of a New England night, the invisible duo scampered down the block. Minutes later, they returned. "We found a gap," reported Jim. "No lights or cameras were evident. Behind the mansion is a small structure."

"Did you note movement?"

"Hell, yes," blurted John. The damn place was lit up like a Christmas tree. People were laughing and celebrating."

"That's unfortunate. Morgan, what do you think?"

"It's likely a private party. I suggest we leave and return around 10 p.m. Hot coffee beats a frozen ass."

Anxious about the outcome, the team returned to the vintage neighborhood. As Jim toted a portable ladder, the black-clad figures darted toward the security gap. Peering at the ten-foot wall, Mackenzie nudged her partner.

"Take the lead. It's your show."

Instantly Nash whispered a soft command. "Wilson and I go first."

"Morgan, no!" The instant pushback was from Mackenzie. "Take Jim or John."

"Mac, he's a combat vet. Plus, I trust him. Stay with your team and wait five minutes. If you hear shots, come running."

"Son, wait. I agree with your boss," chimed Wilson. "Splitting the group is foolish. We may need their firepower."

"Let me clear the wall and check. RE should be alone. Count to fifty and then follow in my footsteps."

"Are you sure about the identity? I wasn't expecting a mansion."

"Mac, trust me. Anthony's latest fax links to BABA's final note. It reveals identity and location."

"But 'RA' pointed to Richard Anderson."

"That was a clever ruse. BABA needed time to exit the country. He didn't plan on dying. As expected, we fixated on 'R-A.' Never did we think about *reversing the letters*. We've known this identity from day one."

Flashing a possum grin, Morgan scaled the wall and hid behind a row of thick shrubs. A minute later, he was joined by the tough-minded rancher.

"Sir, check the structure. It's a fricking chapel."

"But there's no light or movement. Do we hold position or storm the house? It's freezing out here."

"Ignore the cold. We wait for the high priestess to enter her lair."

Twenty minutes later, the old man's angst had intensified. "Morgan, I've got icicles hanging off my balls. Are you ready to call it a night?"

"It's still early. We need RE out of the house and isolated."

As if on cue, flickering lights within the chapel cast an eerie illumination. "Look, sir. There's a faint glow. Wait sixty seconds and then follow."

With his Glock chambered and ready, Morgan moved through the shadows, opened the unlocked front door, and hid behind a wooden pew. Peering around the edge, he relaxed. The rectangular room was empty.

This damn place is a replica of Akhenaten's tomb. Shit.

Dotting each side wall was a maze of colorful hieroglyphics depicting Egypt's storied pantheon. Dividing the small chapel was a narrow red carpet. Ten rows of pews lined the left side. The right quadrant showcased ancient statues and artifacts. Ranging in height from two to ten feet, the antiquities were crafted from pure gold and silver.

Divine metals.

Three steps led to a raised altar. Prominently centered was a hand-carved communion table complete with golden chalice. An imposing three-foot silver obelisk with a golden tip resided within arm's length. Elevated behind the table was a large wooden sarcophagus. Perched on two-foot risers, the coffin's colorful exterior depicted Egypt's glory years. On the wall behind the sarcophagus were two vertical frescos. One featured a Picasso-like rendition of Pharaoh Akhenaten and Queen Nefertiti. Pictured with elongated necks, protruding lips, pouched stomachs, alien heads, and feminine features, the couple was reaching in adoration to the Sun God RE. Both were gripping Ankhs, symbols of eternal life.

The other fresco depicted the Sun God RE. The brilliant orb was showering an array of golden beams onto a recognizable blonde woman and unidentified short man.

The height is deliberately exaggerated. He's definitely not Anderson.

As Nash fixated on the frescos, a shuffle from behind caught his attention. Whirling in panic, he noted the old man. Easing back on the trigger, he smiled. The billionaire's face was twisted in bewilderment.

"Morgan, what the hell? This is a fricking tomb."

"Welcome to "AR's" lair. Note the left fresco. Recognize the face?"

"You're joking. Hell, I've danced with *her* at galas. I've read about *her* in socialite magazines. Are you sure?"

"It's a stunner. Our blueblood socialite is an Islamic terrorist."

"Lady Arabella Rothschild is the ringleader?"

"Yep. Her elitist status offered a perfect cover. Our feared mastermind was adopted and radicalized by Bonito Firelli."

"But why?"

"The patriarch was hell-bent on creating a sleeper cell in America. Arabella was relocated to Boston and groomed. Financed by blueblood relatives, she skyrocketed to fame. In her lust for power Lady Rothschild has been both ruthless and influential."

"Who's the short guy?"

"I don't know. The height could be exaggerated."

"Did Arabella ever marry?"

"No. But there were rumors of a royal affair with Prince Richard of England."

Suddenly a whirring ended the whispers. Entering from a hidden door and striding to the altar table was the dreaded RE. Clad in a priestly robe of white satin, Lady Arabella Rothschild cast a mythical, erotic sight. Atop her head perched a white conical crown, symbolic of kingship.

Reaching for the golden chalice, the renowned socialite took several long sips. As the opioid solution soothed her extremities, a wry smile appeared on her lips. Gracefully pivoting to the sarcophagus, she extended her arms in adoration, chanted an ancient prayer, and rhythmically danced across the altar. Returning to the table, the priestess took another long sip, grabbed a nearby sistrum, and vigorously shook the toy-like rattle. Overwhelmed by sheer ecstasy, Arabella shrieked and screamed as if appealing to the gods.

"Morgan, what the hell?"

"That drink contains opioids. The bitch is delusional, mimicking an Egyptian priestess. The crown represents Upper Egypt."

Fronting the sarcophagus, the socialite chanted another prayer and bowed in devotion. Taking advantage of the distraction, Nash edged toward the altar. Lagging five steps behind was the old man. Sensing danger, RE whirled and faced the intruders. Flashing a satisfied smile, she calmly stepped to the table and punched a hidden button. Instantly the right wall revealed three small holes. Seconds later, the floor began to squirm.

"Snakes," yelped the rancher.

"Shit, they're asps. Deadly."

Sensing heat and fear, the Nile vipers slithered rapidly toward the two men. Panicked, Wilson triggered two wild shots. The third attempt wasted the closest serpent.

Waiting patiently, Morgan allowed the remaining asps to squirm closer. Suddenly his trigger finger twitched twice. The movements abruptly stopped.

"Damn, that was close," uttered the billionaire, as beads of sweat dripped from his brow.

"Be very careful, sir. The bitch seems awfully confident."

With eyes fixated on the altar, neither noticed a tiny opening in the lower right wall. Suddenly a soft "whoosh" filled the air as a miniature arrow jettisoned into the rancher's right thigh. Writhing in agony, Wilson released the Glock and tumbled to the floor.

"Welcome to your final resting place, Agent Nash. And forget about your friend. His lifespan is brief."

Whipping around, Morgan stepped toward the rancher and stopped. The billionaire was no longer writhing or in agony.

"It's just you and me," came the silky smooth, confident voice from the altar. "I suggest we chat." Arabella's smug expression reflected supreme arrogance. Standing erect behind the table, she casually sipped her elixir. Riding an opioid high, AR was in no hurry as her eyes fixated on Nash. "I've been expecting you. How did you find me?"

"A whiny redbird chirped before dying."

"Cardinals are plentiful and often pathetic. You were a fool to enter this sacred sanctuary. Contained within these walls are many holy relics and devilish surprises."

"Look, I came to talk." Morgan's calming faux tone was reassuring. "But my friend needs help. He's a rancher, not a cop. Let me call an ambulance."

"Forget the damned fool. The old man is a ghost within two hours. Ask your daughter. Oh, you can't. She's dead. The asp is small but deadly."

"Screw you, Arabella. Or should I refer to you as Lady Rothschild? Or maybe you prefer 'King's Wife' or 'Bride of the Hidden One'?"

"I go by many names." Sipping the magic elixir, the socialite flashed a joker's grin and then weaved about the altar. Suddenly the graceful movements morphed into a scream. "I love my beloved Amun!"

"'King's Wife,' my ass. Your opioid world is sheer fantasy."

"Were the murders fantasy? Were the financial losses fantasy?"

"The FBI knows your sordid plan. Even Anthony knows. Forget Xi Li. Forget the flood."

"Agent, you are such a fool. *Floods upon floods* are approaching. What I've set in motion cannot be stopped."

"Lady, your dream of global domination is toast. That's why I'm here. The FBI wants a deal."

"That's laughable." Seemingly void of fear, the Boston blueblood took another sip and erotically pranced around the altar. Ceasing all movement, she glared at her adversary. The hard-set, squinty eyes reflected sheer hate.

Suddenly the bowels of hell exploded.

As if possessed by Osiris, the socialite shrieked an alien language and viciously clawed at her face. As droplets of blood trickled down both of her cheeks, Morgan stood transfixed in uncertainty.

"No human can stop the aligning cosmos. Forget any offers."

"But you need to listen. Your reign of terror is over. The Ogdoad is no more."

"Fool! Your idiocy is childish. You see but don't see. The hour is much later than you think. Like an evolving dawn... dissolution hovers just below the horizon."

"Ha! Those bombs will never touch American soil."

Amused by the pushback, the socialite flashed a devilish smile. Extending her arms in adoration, she chanted. "Allahu Akbar! Allahu Akbar! Allahu Akbar!"

As the rhythmic adoration grew louder and louder, an evil grin of anticipation appeared on her lips. Ceasing all movement, she spoke more lucidly than ever.

"America will soon weep and wail for a savior. And their cries will be heard. A new messiah will emerge... at the appointed time."

"Are you referring to your golden boy? Hell, I killed Richard Anderson. The whiner was a puss."

"Good riddance. I detest weakness."

"What about Mosef? Was he your savior? Sadly, the "silent saint" didn't make the cut. Neither did the German or Brazilian. Your messiahs are quickly disappearing."

"Fool! You know nothing of the looming apocalypse."

As her lucidity morphed into hysteria, Arabella's eyes popped wide and wild. Locked in a narcotic trance, she grabbed a nearby dagger, sliced her arm, and erotically sucked the blood. As crimson streaks oozed down her chin, she bellowed in a demonic voice. "Unbelievers know the truth! Believe in the Aten or die!"

Unnerved by the erratic behavior, Nash found himself reeling. The situation was quickly spinning out of control. Wilson was either dead or in dire need of help. But none was forthcoming...not while Arabella was still alive. The woman needed killing...but not yet. Answers were desperately needed.

Gripped by indecision, he tried to calm his mind, praying that the rigid disciplines of Uechi Ryu would control his actions. As a quiet peace eased his anger, Morgan edged toward the altar. Speaking softly, he tried to dissuade the bitch.

"Arabella, it's over. You need help. Let's talk."

"Little man, you know nothing. Nor can you stop the omega's fury. The trifecta marks America's demise."

"You're delusional. The accord has zero chance. BABA knew that. Even Enzo rejected you. You're a raving addict."

"You dare taunt me?" As her face twisted in hellish anguish, the socialite roared with an alien-like cackle. "Ha! My brother could snap your scrawny neck with one hand. Killing Anthony is laughable. But why bother? That feeble old man is dead within days. The Catholic Church is a relic."

"You're so wrong. The Camerlengo has vowed to protect the Holy Father."

"Agent Nash, you are such a fool."

"Am I? I owe my life to Enzo."

"My brother obeys orders. But is he loyal? That's the question. Why don't you ask him yourself?"

"What?"

"ASK HIM. ASK ENZO. HE'S RIGHT BEHIND YOU!!!"

Whirling in panic, Morgan heard a loud clap accompanied by a sharp sting. The well-aimed bullwhip ripped his right wrist, causing the Glock to fall harmlessly to the floor.

Clothed only in a loincloth, the Camerlengo's steeled body shimmered with oil.

Suddenly the whip cracked again, shredding Nash's jacket and right shoulder. Flashing a Satanic grin, the Nubian released the bullwhip and circled his prey. Salivating with rage, he shrieked. "Hear me, Akhenaten as I devour the heart of my enemy and drink his blood! I revenge my brother!"

Frantic, Morgan felt helpless. Weakened by numerous injuries, his body stood little chance against the Camerlengo's pulsating, brutish strength. Desperate, his eyes darted right and left. As Enzo edged closer, escape was impossible. Suddenly an unexpected calm replaced terror as the disciplines of Uechi Ryu took control. Repositioning his feet, he prepared to engage the black beast.

Then came a surprise.

Feinting left, Enzo unexpectedly bull-rushed. Aping an enraged linebacker, his muscular body drove the widower to the floor. Landing abreast, the beast's huge fists pounded his adversary's face. With death a certainty, Morgan swung his right elbow toward the Nubian's face. But against bastardized strength, his feeble effort was short.

In the background, Lady Rothschild's maniacal shrieks reached new heights. "Kill him, Enzo! Kill him! Feast on his heart!"

With his life ebbing, Nash played his last card. With an all-out push, he tried to unsettle the ebony assailant. But the attempt failed. The muscular aide was too strong. The game was lost.

Suddenly, a loud clap shattered the chapel's eerie shroud.

Shot in the upper back, Enzo's shoulders arced upward. A second shot blew away part of his skull. Battling the throes of death, the tough-minded rancher had squirmed to his gun and trigged the shots.

"NOOOOOO!!!" As though Ammit's bowels had been ripped apart, the piercing scream reverberated throughout the tomb. In total disbelief, Arabella clawed at her face and howled to Amun.

Fighting blackout, Nash frantically shoved the Nubian off his chest. Rolling right, he groped for the Glock. Unexpectedly, another shot rang out. The bullet slammed into Wilson's right shoulder. Breathing a weak yelp, the billionaire dropped his Glock harmlessly to the floor. Wielding a hidden Beretta, Arabella flashed a smug smile and calmly sipped the opioid.

Partially blinded by the savage blows, Morgan's reached out, his searching fingers finally touching metal. Gripping the Glock, he triggered two shots. Both were wild and high. Suddenly another loud clap rang out. RE's misaimed shot sliced the outer flesh of his left thigh. Instinctively reacting, he rolled right and squeezed off another round. The poorly aimed shot slammed into the far wall.

With the old man likely dead and her nemesis disabled, Arabella calmly sipped her elixir. Soothed by the warming effects, she fingered another shot. The slug ripped into Morgan's left shoulder. Grimacing, he rolled left and fired. The erratic shot was wide.

Cackling like a wild hyena, the Bostonian fingered another round. The slug tore into Wilson's left leg. Yet no sound was heard. Aided by the distraction, Nash wiped at his good eye and squeezed off three rounds. The first two missed badly. The third grazed Arabella's neck. Bellowing an alien-like shriek, she took aim at her enemy's chest.

Suddenly bright arterial blood spurted from her wound.

Weakened by rapid blood loss, Lady Rothschild reached for the altar but missed badly. Off balance and stumbling, she fell into the razor-sharp obelisk, impaling her midsection.

Nauseous and light-headed, Nash crawled toward his lifeless savior. Cradling the rancher's head, he speed-dialed

Mackenzie. His backups were AWOL. Answering on the second ring, the Dubliner's response was confused and raspy.

"Boss, where were you?"

"Bushwhacked."

"Get over here. Wilson's either critical or dead. I can't tell. And I'm hurting."

"Hang on. I'm calling for help and then heading your way."

Minutes later, the Special Agent limped into the chapel. The left side of her face was badly swollen and purplish in color.

"Mac, are you okay?"

"No. Enzo ambushed us. Jim and John are fatalities. I was hammered in the head and left for dead. I just woke up."

"Mac, you need a doctor."

"Later. What's your status?"

"Alive. The old man saved me from the beast. But not before I was beaten and battered."

"EMTs are on the way. I thought Enzo was in Europe."

"Obviously, he deviated. Wilson blasted his head."

"Morgan, your face looks like hell. There's blood everywhere."

"I need patching. But I'm staying. Our answer is here."

"What can I do?"

"Contact Jameson. The old man desperately needs an asp antidote. His window is less than ninety minutes."

"Anything else?"

"Yeah. Inform the Director that RE killed Anderson and stored his ass. None of his agents are to ask questions. We have the evidence."

"What about the bombs?"

"Arabella refused to answer. The bitch ranted and raved but her utterances were pure gibberish. We've got to rip this place apart."

"I'll make the call."

Within minutes a bevy of ambulances and agents arrived on the scene. In quick order, the billionaire was rushed to a nearby hospital. A faint pulse had been detected. Refusing to leave due to the national emergency, Morgan and Mackenzie were treated by paramedics and given a brief reprieve. With whelps on his face and one eye swollen shut, Nash looked like a boxer on the losing end of a prize fight. But he could still see and hobble. His thigh wound was painful but not serious. Neither was the shoulder wound as the slug missed bone and vitals with a clean entry and exit. Blood loss was minimal. A thorough examination at the hospital was pending after the search. .

Mackenzie held an icepack to the side of her face, her head pounding. But like Morgan, she was still functional. The bombs had to be stopped.

During a short break, Nash spoke quietly to his boss. "Mac, find the lead agent. Instruct him to relocate Anderson's body to the chapel. Tell the others to search for hidden seams and cavities. But be damn careful."

"I'm on it."

A short later, the Dubliner returned. "I briefed the senior agent. His people are following orders and not asking questions."

"Good. That solves one problem. But we need to find Arabella's secret lair. Stay close. I need your eyes."

As Morgan perused the sarcophagus, his partner scanned the table. Neither search proved productive. Unexpectedly, they were approached by the lead agent. "We found a hidden door adjacent to the altar. It led to the outside. We're still searching."

"Assign several people to scan artifacts," replied Fallon. "Look for hidden spaces along the wall. Work fast but cautiously."

With the agent's disappearance, the Dubliner focused on the two vertical frescos. "Partner, I recognize the blonde. That's Lady Rothschild. But who's the short guy?"

"That's our mystery man. He's likely the true mastermind."

"But I thought Arabella was RE."

"That was my belief until the chapel. Mac, we've been played. At best, Arabella was an addict and domestic terrorist. Her sole focus was America's demise."

"What changed your mind?"

"It was a specific rant. She babbled about *'floods upon floods.'* The implications were global."

"I'm not following."

"The selloff of greenbacks simply marks *the beginning of dissolution*. It's the *first* of numerous worldwide catastrophes. We need to find her plans ASAP."

Stepping to the far wall, both were mesmerized by an array of colorful hieroglyphics. Even with blurred vision Nash recognized the more notable symbols. Catching his attention was a bulbous "Eye of Horus." The raised pupil appeared to be looking in all directions.

"Mac, am I seeing things? The eye looks three-dimensional."

"Hell, that's no pupil. It's a button. Push the damn thing."

"Wait. It's too obvious. The eye could be a trap."

"But it's worth the risk. There's no time." Throwing caution to the wind, Mackenzie boldly pressed the rubbery center. Suddenly both heard a soft whirring as a narrow panel opened. Hidden in the montage of hieroglyphics, the seams were practically invisible.

Moving gingerly, the Dubliner entered the doorway, trailed by her half-blind partner. The smallish cubicle was ablaze with color yet lacking in equipment and furnishings. Abutting the left wall was a small table and transmitter. Positioned next to the doorway was a wooden desk and chair.

Depicted on the back wall was another glorious fresco of Pharaoh Akhenaten. The revolutionary leader was clutching Ankhs in both hands and reaching skyward in adoration.

The short right wall was both puzzling and troubling. Tucked in the left corner was another clock with Roman numerals. Spread across the surface was an outline of the United States. A huge flock of black birds was flying east to west.

Squinting, Morgan edged closer and immediately yelped. "Mac, it's those damn black birds again. The flock is massive."

"But they're smaller in size, a hundred or more. The lead birds are larger...and hideous."

"Describe."

"Four have female heads. Four have male heads."

"That's eight. The leaders represent the Ogdoad. The grotesque heads symbolize deities. Can you pinpoint a starting point?"

"No. The birds are spread out and headed west. They're all crapping. Dammit, we've got to find dates and targets."

"Wait. Where's the lone red bird? Am I missing something?"

"No. This map is different."

"That explains Arabella's arrogance. *We can't stop the motion.*"

"I'm not following."

"It's another rant. *Motion* implies a double meaning, referencing both *floods and formation.*"

"So, RE wins. How do we stop simultaneous strikes *and* floods?"

"Mac, the answer is right here. It's in these images. Start with the flock. Describe it."

"The smaller birds are similar in size and identical. Spanning the nation, they're flying east to west."

Instantly, Morgan tensed. "Bingo! That's it. Size symbolizes aircraft. *Small* planes release the bombs."

"What about the eight lead birds?"

"They imply leadership. The Ogdoad houses the bombs and coordinates the attack. But without dates and targets, nothing connects. What about the fuzzy clock?"

"It's smaller than the one in Anderson's room. But does size matter? It's also puzzling."

"Why?"

"The numbers are askew. Nine Roman numerals are black. Two are green with one red. The number four has been deleted and a duplicate six added. Several numbers have been repainted. Their coloring has a different look. Someone did a sloppy job."

"Mac, that's it. It's a *rush job.* The revisions reference RE's accelerated timetable. But deciphering the changes is problematic. Ignore the black numbers. Describe the primaries."

"The greens are "II" and "VI." Another "VI" has been painted red."

Stepping away from the map Nash paced the room. Suddenly, his face morphed a ghostly white. "Mac, what's today's date?"

"It's February 25. But it's almost midnight. Why?"

"What's the exact time?"

"It's seven minutes 'til twelve."

"Dammit. We're screwed. We are so screwed."

"What do you mean?"

"Mac, those bombs fall *tomorrow*! Green symbolizes month and day. February 26 is the launch date. Green for go.

Red indicates time. The birds fly at six. But does that mean 'am' or 'pm?' And does 'VI' reference take off or bomb release?"

"It's definitely 6 a.m.," cried the Dubliner. "Friday morning traffic would be absolute hell in metro areas. Bombs across America would wreak havoc."

"The formation indicates simultaneous bombings. That means 6 a.m. east coast and 3 a.m. west coast. You need to contact Jameson."

"Not yet. We need cities, targets, and ordinance. Keep searching. Take the desk while I scan the equipment."

CHAPTER 43

Friday, February 26

Shortly after midnight, the Dubliner's high-pitched yelp was ecstatic. "Morgan, I found a lever. It was practically hidden in the seams."

"Check it out. But be careful."

With trepidation, Mackenzie pulled the handle. Unexpectedly nothing happened. "Dammit, it's fake. Arabella is screwing with us."

Suddenly, both heard a soft whirring coming from the far wall. Transfixed, both turned and watched as a faux panel revealed a hidden cavity.

"Morgan, it's the files."

"Files don't wiggle."

Squirming through the narrow opening was an angry, pent-up viper. Reacting to the motion, Nash screamed. "Boss, shoot! It's an asp."

Blindly fingering his Glock, he triggered three rounds. But with his distorted vision, the shots were high and wild.

Sensing fear, the viper veered toward the Dubliner. Panicked, Mackenzie squeezed off four quick shots. The first three were wide. The last round severed the asp's midsection. Emptying her clip, the hail of bullets peppered Cleopatra's serpent of choice. Sweating profusely and badly shaken,

Mackenzie's rosy cheeks pulsated scarlet. "That was close. That damn thing was tracking me."

"The bitch warned about surprises. But we have to keep looking. We're out of time."

Frustrated after an extensive search of the small table, Morgan sat dismayed. RE was winning. Unexpectedly his volatile, pent-up anger exploded. Snatching the lightweight chair, he slammed it against the wall. Shattering on impact, the wood splintered into hundreds of pieces.

"Feel better?" The Irish sarcasm was followed by a wry smile. Suddenly, Mackenzie's face flashed amazement. "Partner, look! There's a packet protruding from that hollow leg."

Snatching the tightly rolled paper, he eagerly unveiled the contents. But the flimsy sheets with small print were unreadable. "Mac, I can't see. Take a look."

Thumbing through the pages, the Dubliner beamed. "Jackpot! These are financial reports. All are small-cap companies."

"How many?"

"I count seven."

"But that's wrong. There should be eight."

"Then a critical piece is missing. Dammit, the bitch keeps winning."

"That's not going to happen. We beat Arabella at her own game."

"How?"

"We compare the seven names with Egyptian deities. That's a start. Is there a company that begins with the letter "G?"

"There's one. Gabe Gibbons runs Gibbons Agriculture and Produce."

"That's likely a winner. Gibbons juxtaposes Geb."

"Morgan, that's pretty damn thin. Hell, it's just a guess. I can't report this to Jameson."

"Trust me. Who's next?"

"Wait. There's scribbling in the margin. But it's in tiny letters."

"Read it."

"Dammit, I'm trying. Wow! Gabe Gibbons is an alias. The CEOs real name is Fatima Hussein."

"That's Jameson's confirmation," bellowed Nash. "Executives from the Middle East operate these small caps. These financials reveal RE's inner circle."

"Plus, all seven companies would benefit from the bombings, especially the pharmaceutical. If that virus spirals into a pandemic, an available vaccine would be worth a king's fortune."

"Greed is their end goal. But there's still the missing company. With nothing recorded, it's likely the key. Mac, recheck the bird fresco. Does any minute detail pop out? Knowing RE, the answer is in plain sight."

"I'm not seeing anything." Suddenly, Mackenzie tensed as her eyes fixated on an aberration. "

"WINGS!"

"Morgan, the *wings* on the smaller birds are different. They've been altered."

"How?"

"They're oddly shaped."

"Mac, that's it. Helos! The alteration represents choppers."

"That's possible but not definitive. They sure as hell can't be military."

"At least it's a lead. Tell Jameson to research small cap aircraft manufacturers. Maybe the wings symbolize a mix of small planes *and* choppers."

"Morgan, get your blind ass over here." The command was curt as the Dubliner's fiery green eyes sparked in anticipation. "There's a unique symbol on the lead bird."

Edging next to his boss, Nash stared at the fresco. "It's too fuzzy. I can't make out details. What's up?"

"There's a *tiny cross* imprinted on the head."

"Cross? But a Christian reference makes no sense. That's not Arabella's style."

"Forget theology. It's more like Red Cross or...."

"Bingo, boss. "HOSPITAL!" Cross symbolizes *care flights.* That's the missing component."

"I'm calling Jameson. His people can research chopper companies and investigate the Ogdoad seven. Let's hobble into the chapel for better reception."

"Instruct him to move fast. Hell is about to unleash its unbridled fury."

Awakening the Director from a peaceful slumber, Mackenzie quickly provided an in-depth summary. Listening intently, the veteran agent sat stunned. "Mac, you're talking apocalyptic. Are you sure about the CEOs?"

"Yeah. All identities are aliases."

"Okay, I'm ready with pen and paper. Give me the list."

"Ari Ramsesh is CEO of Osi Pharmaceuticals. Next is Cataya Yemweh of Isishe Chemicals. Geba Faruseh heads Seth Meyers Advanced Weapons. Fatima Hussein runs Gibbon Agriculture, followed by Marah Raptaof Neptune Materials and Mining, Moustafa Faqua of Shuh Investments, and Arish Kamen of Teffington Companies."

"What about the eighth?"

"The identity is unknown. Tell your people to research small cap aircraft companies that manufacture transport choppers."

"Are you referring to care flights?"

"Correct."

'Good work. That's a start. I'm calling my people. Expect an update within the hour."

"Hurry. Either ground those choppers or waste them."

"Have any targets been identified?"

"Not yet. Focus on infrastructure sites like power grids, dams, water supplies, agricultural storage, and bridges. RE plans to create chaos as a prelude to the pandemic."

"What about cities?"

"No specific locations have been identified. The birds were widely scattered. Logically, they have to be metro areas."

"You indicated dirty bombs. How many? What type?"

"That's uncertain. Here, talk to Morgan."

"Director, the virus is likely ancient, rare, and lethal. The bitch ranted about an avian strain that goes airborne and spreads rapidly."

"What about a vaccine?"

"Apparently, one is available. That's the Ogdoad's golden goose."

"Are you positive?"

"Yeah. Avarice trumps demise. But patience is their game. I think they wait until millions die. Then the formula magically appears along with a stockpile of vaccine. That benefits their greed as well as Russia's and China's intentions. Tell your people to scrutinize the Ogdoad pharmaceutical and chemical companies. But remember, RE loves surprises. Any of their companies could house the vaccine."

"Thanks. Give me a few minutes." Instantly, the line clicked dead.

Twenty minutes later, a harried Jameson was back on the line. "Mac, put Morgan on speaker. Canut Industries manufactures 'Life Flight Helicopters.' It's the leading chopper company. The CEO is Martha Cooper."

"That's an alias," snapped Nash. "Tear that fricking place apart. Canut contains "Nut," an Egyptian sky goddess."

"Agent, it's not that simple."

"Why?"

"Canut has delivered hundreds of choppers to care centers, hospitals, fire stations, and so on. I've instructed the military and law enforcement to locate and disarm, or destroy the grounded Canut helos. All airborne Canut choppers are to land immediately or be torched. But we're behind the eight ball. Anything else?"

"Yeah. Arrest General Robison ASAP."

"Dammit, Morgan, I can't do that. He's the Army's top dog and a distinguished four-star general."

"Which makes him the perfect mole."

"That's insane."

"Director, Robison has been colluding with RE. Thanks to Anthony and his confidential sources, I've collected the evidence. Have agents search his home and office."

Instantly Jameson hedged. "That will take some doing. The Secretary of Defense will likely not cooperate. I'll converse with the Vice President and get back with you." With a click, the line went silent.

Instantly Nash peered at his boss. "That's it for us. Let's head to the hospital for exams and then check on our hero."

"That sounds good. Hopefully, the case ends with a soft whimper and not some apocalyptic bang."

"Everything hinges on Jameson eliminating the choppers. None of the aggressors want a nuclear war against a healthy, angry superpower."

"Then, that's it. Until daybreak, we sit, wait, and pray."

Rechecked at the hospital, the battered duo was cleared for light duty. Hobbling to intensive care, they were dismayed. The old man was back in surgery and listed as critical.

"I'm contacting Robby," replied Morgan. "I sure hope Wilson pulls through. Without his heroics, I'm dead and RE wins."

"Make the call. That gives me time to text Nick. Hopefully, we can start planning our wedding."

Camped in the waiting room, the pair brooded. Words were inadequate. At 4:30 am, the Director called with a mixed update. Raids were being conducted on the eight Ogdoad companies. Yet, locating hundreds of choppers was problematic. As the line clicked silent, a weary surgeon trudged into the waiting room.

"Agents, the news is grave. At best, Mr. Wilson's condition is critical. Overcoming the combination of snake bite, GSWs, and age is challenging. But he's a hardened rancher. The next twenty-four hours are critical. We need him to stabilize. After that, he might make it."

"That man needs saving," gushed Nash. "He's a true American patriot. Take good care of him."

Nodding, the surgeon exited.

At 7:57 am, a grim Jameson reported with an update. "Three CEOs were arrested. But they never made it to interrogation. The bastards chose hidden cyanide pills. Sixty-seven Canut choppers laden with bombs have been seized. All were carrying five-hundred-pounders."

"That leaves thirty-three unaccounted."

Instantly, the Director bristled. "Morgan, I wasn't finished. The military shot down twenty bomb-laden helos, creating spectacular mid-air explosions. Thirteen escaped detection and released ordinance."

"Damage?"

"Mac, initial reports are sketchy. Ten bombs destroyed infrastructure. Flooding and blackouts are being addressed. Unfortunately, three were dirty, creating an apocalyptic scenario."

"Locations?"

"Manhattan, Oklahoma City, and San Diego were hit. The virus-laden bombs exploded in dense population areas. Loss of life has been extensive. Stricken people are panicking, collapsing, and dying."

"Sir, you've got to locate those other CEOs," snapped Nash. "They have access to the vaccine."

"That's not going to happen."

"Why?"

"The remaining five are dead. All committed suicide before we arrived."

"What about CDC? Any progress?"

"They're working around the clock to identify the virus."

"But developing a new formula takes years. A proven vaccine is housed at one of those companies."

"Agent, I know my job. Dismantling facilities takes time and manpower." Instantly, the line went dead.

Shortly after 8 a.m., Jameson's angst was evident. "Agents, we're on the brink of collapse. We have not located the formula or the vaccine. Now, world markets are being flooded with U.S. greenbacks. The sell-off has crushed our currency. Both allies *and* adversaries are involved. Any explanation?"

"The bombings triggered the sell-off," replied Mackenzie. "A traitorous Vatican redbird orchestrated the transactions."

"That makes no sense." Stunned by the revelation, the Director's mind was spinning. "Anthony has always sidestepped politics. And England, Germany, and France have been reliable allies. These actions are unthinkable."

"Director, they're being coerced," chimed Nash. "They have no choice."

"Blackmail? By whom?"

"Russia. The Europeans are dependent on Soviet energy, especially Germany. Given our problems, we're in no position to assist allies."

"But the bomb damage is fixable. America is still a force."

"Not anymore. Not if that virus spreads into a national pandemic and kills millions. Without a vaccine, we're only days away from that scenario."

"You're talking end times...the destruction of America."

"Director, that's RE's goal. Plus, the news gets worse. As America withers, Russia plans a takeover of the entire Middle East. With a stranglehold on oil and gas, the Soviets can coerce our allies at will."

"They certainly have a shitload of firepower stockpiled in Syria, mostly armor supported by a couple of divisions. But they've been hesitating. Any reason?"

"Like China and India, Russia has no desire to tangle with a healthy America. Collectively, they're monitoring the virus. If it spreads into a national pandemic, all three are launching invasions and gobbling resources. We've got to locate that vaccine and formula."

"Is there any good news for Allday?"

"Yeah. The dollar sell-off has an end in sight. We've identified the European influencers and traitors."

"That's a start."

As the line clicked dead, Morgan peered at his partner. "I need to contact Anthony. It's regarding a delicate matter."

"Care to share?"

"The Holy Father has identified RE's moles in France, Germany, and England. But he was dubious about the sell-off and bombings. Thus, he refused to act without proof. Now he has it. These traitors have to be eliminated."

"But Anthony has no jurisdiction outside the Vatican."

"That has been his dilemma. The betrayers are high-profile and well-placed. Without concrete evidence, an international firestorm wasn't worth the risk."

"Who were the culprits?"

"The Firelli daughters were two of the instigators. They duped their high-profile husbands and government leaders into dumping U.S. greenbacks. Hopefully, both couples have been eliminated. That was Anthony's promise."

"What about the third?"

"Not a Firelli, this mole was dicey at best. The Holy Father was to visit with the Queen of England regarding the elimination of a crown jewel. But Anthony may have hedged on the call. If so, I have to act."

"Morgan, you're talking British royalty. Anthony has zero authority. And you..."

Instantly, Nash interrupted.

"Mac, it *is* a church matter. The crown jewel is RE's pope-in-waiting. Anthony wants her majesty's permission to proceed."

"What if the Queen says no?"

"Then I throw caution to the wind and kill the bastard. I owe it to Anthony."

"That's insane. Is he the map's lone red bird?"

"No. Our blueblood is currently an iconic black bird, which muddies the water. His promotion to Cardinal comes next week. Groomed from an early age, he is well-positioned to control the Catholic Church."

"But I thought a future Pope was already in place."

"That was my mistake and another RE surprise."

"I'm not following."

"Anthony's death triggers the election of a *transitional* Pope. But his reign is brief. Likely, he succumbs to poison.

Once the crown jewel gains acceptance and rises to stardom, he's elected the Holy Father."

Quizzically, Mackenzie peered at her partner. "How do you know these things?"

"Anthony's latest info was extremely revealing. Prominent Cardinals have sold their souls for power and prominence."

"What's next?"

"We likely travel to London. Then, it's a return to the Vatican. Hopefully, we don't deviate to France or Germany. We need to protect the Holy Father."

"When do we leave?"

"That's uncertain. Our timing depends on Anthony's actions. Ideally, we fly late this evening."

"That soon? But your face is a holy mess. Your wounds need to heal."

"Mac, there's no time and plenty of unfinished business. Plus, the swelling is slowly subsiding. Just blame my facial appearance on an auto accident. Look, my right eye is fine. I can shoot, especially at close range. Let's check on Wilson before leaving."

Moving gingerly, the pair ventured to intensive care. To their dismay, the billionaire's condition was unchanged. With heads bowed, they exited in a state of prayer.

"Robby's on his way." The passive utterance reflected Morgan's somber mood. "That should cheer the old man."

Unexpectedly, his ring tone jangled. The caller was Anthony. The French and German traitors had been eliminated, but not the London target. The Queen had reluctantly approved the assassination but with a stipulation. The hit had to be carried out by the Vatican with no English involvement.

"I've been given the green light. We're headed to London."

"God help us."

CHAPTER 44

Saturday, February 27

Descending through grey clouds and light drizzle, Wilson's Boeing touched down at London Gatwick and taxied to an isolated hangar. Idling nearby in the dense morning fog was a black limo.

"You ordered a limo?"

"Mac, have you ever driven around London? I splurged. Plus, the driver has been vetted by Anthony."

Easing into the backseat, Mackenzie was surprised to see an early edition newspaper. Glancing at the headlines, her eyes popped.

VATICAN FIRE KILLS THREE CARDINALS

Scanning the article, she sat stunned. "Morgan, you didn't reveal much about your Vatican escapades. Those Cardinals were high-profile. Did you kill all three?"

"Nope. I didn't touch anyone. One committed suicide. The Camerlengo bagged the other two. The assist gave him great cover. Afterward, I scratched him off my list. That was a near-fatal mistake."

"Okay, we're here. But you've been super secretive."

"That was Anthony's idea. The crown jewel has a rather high profile. The Holy Father has no desire to involve you or disrupt your wedding plans."

"Who's the target?"

"The Archbishop of Westminster."

"What? Dammit, Morgan, that's insane. The guy is a British rock star and religious icon Hell, he's untouchable."

"It was Anthony's call. So, here we are. This madness has to end."

"But he's a national celebrity."

"Yep. According to British tabloids, our crown jewel has a greater following than Princess Di or the Beatles. Bookies have him favored as a future Pope."

"Dammit, let the Queen do her own dirty work. It's a family matter. Prince Richard is the guy's best buddy. Hell, they play polo on the same team."

"Look, it's Anthony's decision. I owe the man. Without his help, RE wins."

"And we lose. Killing David Beckham is a better option. Think about it. The archbishop leads the Roman Catholic Archdiocese of Westminster. Plus, he's President of the Catholic Bishops Conference in England and Wales. And even more impressive, he's the de facto spokesman for the Catholic Church in Great Britain."

"Bravo, you're well read. We have a date with the future Pope at 1 p.m."

"Have you and Anthony weighed the ramifications? The Queen's approval was likely tepid. You're about to trigger an international scandal."

"That's the goal. We need to unsettle the master and disrupt his plans."

"Is this another flimsy-ass scheme like Cairo? Or is there an actual plan?"

"Mac, it's simple. We waltz into the archbishop's office and make introductions. That's your only involvement. Then I shoot him. Afterward, we drive to the airport."

"You're crazy."

"Likely. But things will work out."

"Dammit, Morgan, this is Scotland Yard's home turf. There's no Anthony or Jameson to protect us. The Queen is a non-factor."

"Relax. It's going to be okay."

"Okay? Hell, it's more like a death wish. Look, I want to get married. This is insane."

"Boss, calm down. Trust me. Let's peruse the cathedral. Afterward we can break for lunch. By the way, your name is Christine Riley from San Francisco. The archbishop is expecting a huge check to preserve the historic Catholic Churches of London."

Amused at the simplistic idiocy, Mackenzie cracked a wry Irish grin. "You're certainly generous with my money. And I haven't been to mass in months."

Promptly at 1 p.m. the pair entered the iconic Westminster Cathedral. Halting a nun, they requested and received directions. Meandering down a long hall Nash spoke candidly.

"Mac, we need to separate. The receptionist is expecting a Christine Riley. Just introduce yourself and flash that Irish charm."

"Where are you going?"

"I need to plan our escape before reappearing."

Greeted by an obsequious receptionist, the Dubliner was promptly introduced to the British icon. As the pair chatted, Morgan slow-walked the hallway. Spotting a nearby exit he breathed a sigh of relief and instantly headed to the archbishop's suite. To his delight the receptionist was on break. Exuding an air of confidence, he strolled into the private office. Irked by the intrusion, the icon flashed a hideous scowl. Noting the heinous expression, Mackenzie quickly soothed the troubled waters.

"Sir, meet my personal secretary. Theodore records my *substantial* transactions. The poor soul is recovering from an auto accident."

Overwhelmed with greed, the minion's focus quickly returned to the benefactor. A minute later his eyebrows arched in consternation. Something was terribly wrong. Instantly his face twisted in horror.

"YOU!!!"

"Yeah, it's me. My picture seems to be very popular." With a quick draw, Morgan waved his Glock at the stunned jewel. "Sit very still. Blink and I shoot."

"I'm calling security."

"That's not a good idea."

"Why?"

"I bring a message from Anthony."

"The Holy Father? But..."

"It's about your parents. Anthony wants to protect them."

"I don't know my parents. The Holy Church is my family."

"LIAR! Your real name is Charles *Richard* David. Does that middle name ring a bell?"

"But..."

"Hell, you're no orphan. You're royalty, the *bastard* son of the Prince of Wales."

"That's not..."

"And your whorish mother was also blueblood."

"Was?"

"Yeah. Lady Rothchild's reign of terror is over. Unfortunately, that ends your blackmail money from Richard."

Ambushed by Morgan's accusations, the archbishop's mouth gaped in disbelief. "You're lying. Anthony has no proof."

"Ah, but you're wrong. According to secret files you were both *illegitimate* and *unwanted*. Richard wasn't about to forfeit the crown. Panicked, he dumped your sorry ass in a Catholic orphanage. But the stunt didn't sit well with your socialite mother. Arabella retaliated and coerced the prince. Together, they plotted your ambitious future. Since childhood, you've been fast-tracked to Archbishop. Next week you're to be elevated to Cardinal."

"How do you know these things?"

"Your bitch mother enlightened me. You were no ordinary bastard child. You were the crown jewel and future leader of the Catholic Church."

"You're bluffing. I've never heard of this Lady Rothschild. I have to contact Richard."

"You're not touching that phone. For years the prince treated you like royalty and covered your butt. You're awfully young to be a redbird, not even forty."

"How dare you. I'm making the call."

"I wouldn't do that."

Deliberately breaking eye contact, Morgan side-stepped to a sofa and snatched a small pillow. Emboldened, the icon snatched a letter opener and bull-rushed Mackenzie. Anticipating the move, Nash muzzled the barrel and fired. The muted bullet slammed into the archbishop's temple. With lifeless eyes, the royal puppet crumpled to the floor.

As the Dubliner stared in stunned disbelief, Morgan flashed a mischievous grin. "Well, I've bagged my limit."

"Dammit, you *are* crazy. You're kill-happy."

"Mac, the bastard had to die. We were losing England's alliance because of his control over Richard."

"But you didn't have to shoot him."

"Why not? Cyanide was his other option. A bullet was more fun."

"Well, you've certainly stoked the fire. We're knee-deep in shit and about to be hunted like wild dogs. What were you thinking?"

"Mac, calm down. What time is it?"

"It's almost 1:20 p.m."

"Good. Anthony is to update the Queen at 1:25 p.m. At 1:30, the Holy Father releases a statement lamenting the archbishop's death in a *Scottish* hunting accident. Vatican Security is currently disabling the hallway cameras. The body vanishes once we leave."

"Dammit, why wasn't I informed?"

"It was the Holy Father's call. He wanted to protect you if things went awry. Any guilt was going to be pinned on me."

"That's thoughtful. But I'm still your boss. Look, the secrecy ends now. Understand?"

"Yep."

"What's next?"

"We deviate to Milan."

"Why?"

"I have to eliminate a very troublesome elderly couple. Bonito and Nita Firelli are the targets. Their radicalized children have fueled this entire mess."

"Did Anthony agree?"

"Yep. It was his decision. The Pontiff handed me their address with an attached smiley face. Since Rome, I've been waiting for the right time."

Arriving in the blackness of a wintry night, Mackenzie overpaid for a frumpy-looking driver and dented car. Shortly after 9 p.m., the vehicle rolled to a stop at the Firelli residence. With the confident ease of a veteran salesman, Morgan sauntered to the front door and rang the bell. For late dining

Italians, the time was relatively early. Concealed behind his back was the imposing Glock.

"May I help you?" The homemaker's greeting was laced with surprise. The nighttime stranger was American.

"Mrs. Firelli, I'm an envoy from Pope Anthony. It's about Enzo. I'm afraid the Camerlengo is in serious trouble."

"Please step into the hallway. Bimbi is in the kitchen preparing supper."

Irked by the interruption, the patriarch stormed into the family room. No visitors were expected. Instantly, his face flashed a quizzical expression.

"You are from the Holy Father?"

"Yes. It's about Enzo."

"Is something wrong? But Anthony would... *never send an American.*" As recognition vaped to shock, the patriarch yelped. "IT'S YOU!!!"

"Yeah Bimbi, it's me in the flesh... and not a RE photo." Flashing a twisted smile, Nash revealed the Glock and triggered two rounds. A third slug hammered the hysterical wife. With a sly grin and no remorse, he slow-walked out the door and entered the dusty vehicle. Awaiting him was a volcano of anger.

"Dammit, partner, I'm not deaf. Neither is the driver. Three shots and hysterical screams make a lot of noise."

"Boss, chill. Milan is the murder capital of Italy. Think South Chicago. Tip the driver well. You know, this is actually enjoyable."

"You're disgusting."

As the rusted sedan entered the airport, the Dubliner breathed a huge sigh of relief. The duo had not been arrested or shot. Once Mac had bribed the frumpy driver with a generous tip, the non-descript Fiat vanished into the night.

"What's next?"

"We grab a snack and wait until pre-dawn. Anthony needs his rest. The flight to Rome is brief. After that, it's showtime."

"Does that mean more notches on your gun?" Spewing sarcasm, the Special Agent's unbridled temper had not abated.

"That's to be determined. I'm not sure what to expect."

"What about Xi Li?"

"The wily Asian is definitely in the crosshairs. But is he the true mastermind?"

CHAPTER 45

Sunday, February 28

Shortly after sunrise the weary travelers sipped coffee with the Holy Father. A bevy of Swiss Guards stood watch outside the private office. Acutely aware of the late hour and the Pontiff's haggard appearance, Morgan quickly summarized the Milan visit.

"Sir, the Firellis have been terminated. What about the Germans and French? How are they reacting to the daughters' and their husbands' deaths?"

Totally distracted, the Holy Father's eyes darted to Mackenzie. "Ms. Fallon, I owe you a huge apology."

"Why?"

"My overriding desire has been your protection. Agent Nash was ordered to secrecy."

"Morgan explained everything. Initially, I was furious. But you were right. My wounds were a liability. And, I have a June wedding. But going forward I have to be included."

"You will be involved in all future decisions."

Eager to continue, Nash quickly intervened. "Sir, the U.S. dollar has been decimated by a worldwide sell-off. The dumping was triggered by the Vatican Bank."

"So, I heard. The news was a surprise."

"Who makes your financial recommendations?"

"The Finance Council sends me transactions for my approval or denial. A traitorous act of this magnitude is unthinkable."

"Excluding Li, who makes up the committee?"

"Council members include New York's Cardinal Kurita, Italy's Cardinal Rossi, Argentina's Cardinal Renaldo and Poland's Cardinal Woznik."

"Kurita? Is he Asian?"

"Yes. His parents were Japanese immigrants. Raised in New York City, Kurita attended Catholic schools. An American citizen, his ministry among Asians has been phenomenal. Scholarly and quiet, Kurita has been most prominent."

"Interesting. My focus has been on Li."

"Maybe Kurita is our man," quipped Mackenzie. "Those block T slashes might point to him."

"That's my thinking. If so, the initial Roman numerals reference a trigger date and not Xi Li. Holy Father, can you summon Kurita? I know it's early. But we desperately need answers."

"Agent, can't this matter wait? I'm extremely tired."

"Sir, it's a matter of grave importance. The airborne virus is spreading. The death toll is rising. It's urgent that we see Kurita."

Acquiescing, Anthony roused the slumbering Asian. Obedient, he reluctantly agreed to attend the hastily called meeting.

Fifteen minutes later, the New Yorker was a no-show. Irked by the tardiness, Anthony made repeated calls. The attempts were fruitless.

"Holy Father, something's wrong," barked the Dubliner. "Check with security."

"I'll make the call."

As the trio chatted, Anthony's private phone jangled. Answering immediately, he listened and nodded. Suddenly, his pallid face twisted in unbelief. "Agents, Cardinal Kurita committed suicide. Crusted foam was laced around his lips. Most likely, he had something to hide."

"That's bull," countered Morgan. "Kurita's death is a little too convenient. Holy Father, can a bank official circumvent the council and track the sell order? We need verification."

"Massimo Verismo can access bank records from home." Without hesitation, the Pontiff's nimble fingers punched a five-digit number.

Within minutes, the fawning banker returned the call. Following a brief conversation, Anthony hung up. "Cardinal Kurita authorized the massive sale. Apparently, he acted alone."

"Sir, that's impossible. Other Cardinals should be involved."

"Agent Nash..."

Rudely interrupting was the shrill ring tone of Mackenzie's phone. The Director's deep voice quivered with fear and uncertainty.

"Mac, is Morgan with you?"

"Yes."

"Put him on speaker. The news is grim."

"The Holy Father is also with us."

"We have not located the vaccine or formula. Agents have dismantled the Ogdoad facilities but found nothing. Stricken people are collapsing everywhere, overwhelming hospitals and dying in droves. Authorities in the infected cities are trying to control the mob-like atmospheres."

"Any word from CDC?"

"Yeah. And it's bad, Mac. This particular strain destroys the immune system and prevents clotting. Uncontrollable bleeding leads to organ failure. Atlanta believes it's a rare form of avian virus. The death toll is already in the thousands and rising. Once airborne, the damn stuff spreads rapidly. It's a killing machine."

"What about Dallas and Nick? Is he okay?"

"At last report, North Texas has not been affected. But without the formula or vaccine, we're in a shitload of trouble."

"Check Lady Rothschild's holdings," blurted Nash. "Look for distribution outlets. According to her, the vaccine *is* available for delivery."

"But that woman was delusional. Morgan, are you sure?"

"Absolutely. Money was her almighty god. The woman was an addict but shrewd. Her people have been sitting on the vaccine, just waiting for the death toll to reach *one million*. Their asking price was a whopping *a hundred billion dollars*."

"That's insane."

"Director, it's smart business and relatively cheap when compared to millions of deaths and absolute chaos."

"Dammit. A full-blown pandemic will destroy America. We'll keep searching." Instantly, the call terminated.

"That mercenary bitch." Instantly Mackenzie caught herself, embarrassed by the outburst. "Sorry, Holy Father. The treachery makes me livid."

"Agent Fallon, at this moment 'bitch' seems very appropriate."

"Remorse certainly wasn't in her vocabulary," quipped Nash. "That vaccine..." Suddenly he hesitated, his eyes bulging in disbelief. "Boss, get Jameson back on the line."

"Why?"

"I've overlooked a crucial point."

Answering on the first ring, the Director's response was curt. "Make it fast, Mac. Our situation is spiraling out of control."

"Morgan might have something."

"Put him on speaker."

"Director, Lady Rothschild was a micromanager. Have your agents comb storage facilities and warehouses within a twenty-five-mile radius of Boston."

"That's impossible. The area is densely populated."

"Then narrow the search to small pharmaceutical and chemical facilities. Think labs and such."

Labs! That's it!

"Director, wait. Focus on *private* labs within a ten-mile radius of RE's chapel. Check for CEOs with Egyptian names and isolated locations."

"Will do. I'll update you within the hour."

As the Vatican trio focused on suspects, Jameson called with an update. "We've identified six small labs. Morgan, are you listening?"

"I'm here."

"The names are Xerxes, Wassum, Kaly, Ramsish, Balman and Mun."

"Ramsish? Who's the CEO?"

"George Campbell."

"Location?"

"New Haven."

"No. That doesn't fit."

"What about Balman?"

"Baal was an ancient deity but not Egyptian."

"What about Mun?"

"What's the full name?"

"The corporate listing is Cyrus A. Mun and Associates. The CEO is Nat Enberg."

"I don't..." Suddenly, Morgan's lips twisted as his mouth gaped in utter dismay.

Could it be that simple? Connect the letters?

"Director, that's it! Nat Enberg. The name contains "N-a-t-e-n" as in "Akhenaten." Where's the location?"

"Kingsway, Maine. It's on Hathorne Street."

"Spell the street name."

"H-a-t-h-o-r-n-e."

"That's the location. Forget the last two letters. Hathor is an Egyptian goddess."

"Are you positive?"

"Yes. Cyrus references Osiris,' judge of the living and dead. 'A' and 'Mun' equate to Amun or King God."

"Good work. I'm sending choppers from Boston. It's about a twenty-minute flight." Instantly, the line clicked silent.

~

An hour later, Jameson's voice quivered with disappointment. "We raided the lab but found only *trace* amounts of vaccine. Either this was a test site, or they've relocated the shipment. Morgan, you were right about availability. Now we're stymied."

"What about CDC? Given traces, can't they replicate the vaccine?"

"Mac, it's not simple. Testing takes time. Approval stages could take weeks or months."

As the all-too-familiar shroud of doom descended on Nash's shoulders, he sat dismayed. "Director, I've screwed up big time. I've wasted both time and manpower."

"I'm not following."

"Like Arabella, I was duped."

"How?"

"I convinced myself that she was RE. But the bitch wasn't trustworthy. Arabella was never the mastermind. Nor was she privy to the entire plan. What you uncovered was a *final testing*. The vaccine was never created in quantity or stored in that lab."

"Then we're doomed." Instantly the line clicked silent.

"Morgan, Arabella had to know," cried Mackenzie. "Hell, she was a Firelli. Are you sure?"

"Yeah. She was manipulated like the rest of us."

"Then we're screwed. Without that formula..."

Deaf to her desperate plea, Nash rudely interrupted. "Mac, I *know* the location."

"Where? This is no time for speculation."

"It's right here. The Vatican *is* the epicenter, home for both the formula and mastermind."

"Who?"

"It has to be Xi Li."

Unexpectedly, the deep-throated jangling of Anthony's private phone interrupted. Listening intently, the Holy Father nodded twice and then terminated the call.

"Agents, an ominous cloud has befallen the Holy Church. The bodies of four leading Cardinals have been discovered. According to security, all ate an early breakfast and died from food poisoning."

"Sir, that's nonsense. Where?"

"They were found in a small chapel, Agent Fallon. I've instructed Captain Strader to launch an investigation."

"Food wasn't the problem," blurted Morgan. "Those men were poisoned. Cyanide was the culprit."

"If so, the Holy Church has truly become a nest of vipers. These were saintly and irreplaceable men."

"You have our deepest sympathy," proffered the Dubliner. "Who were the victims?"

"Two were Italians. There was also a Pole and Venezuelan. Spiritually gifted, all were prime candidates to be my successor."

"Who's next in line?"

"Agent Nash, that's unanswerable. Likely, it's a Spaniard, an Argentine, or an Italian. Cardinal Li is a dark horse at best."

"Sir, can Strader be trusted?"

As Anthony hesitated, Mackenzie's shrill ring tone interrupted. The caller was an emotionally distraught Jameson.

"Bad news, sir?"

"Mac, we're descending into an apocalyptic hell. Thousands are succumbing to the virus. Now we're on the verge of a global war. Allday unexpectedly authorized a launch of tomahawk missiles."

"Why?"

"The aggressors were disrespecting his warnings. So, he got pissed. Aping Harry Truman, he wanted to send a strong message."

"Targets?"

"Airbases in Syria and the South China Sea were slammed. The Russians and Chinese are livid. India has been cautioned to stand down."

"Those bastards won't listen," chirped Morgan. "With a rising death toll, reduced military, and zero vaccine, his threats are meaningless. The President has zero leverage."

"That's why I called. Allday is hell-bent on pushing the envelope. If the new Axis alliance refuses to stand down, he plans to up the ante."

"Director, without that formula, he's a damn fool. An all-out war against three global adversaries is absolute suicide."

"That was the Pentagon's response. As a result, he's softened his stance and given the aggressors twenty-four hours to withdraw. After that, we're in uncharted waters." Instantly, the call terminated.

"Agent Nash, is this the prelude to a third global conflict?"

"Doubtful. It's more like diplomatic poker. No one wants a prolonged or costly global conflict. That includes Russia and China."

"Will they stand down and negotiate?"

"No. Instead, I think they exercise patience and wait. With no formula or vaccine, time is their ally. If America collapses, they dictate terms and seize prized territories at their leisure. A chaotic superpower without allies represents little threat."

"So, the stakes get higher."

"That's about it." Suddenly, Morgan flashed a wicked jack-o'-lantern grin. "Sir, poker expediates our search. With your approval, it's time to separate the rats from the mice."

After approving a flimsy hail-Mary plan, the Holy Father summoned the first player. Entering the private office was a smallish, sleepy-eyed man. Leary of the two Americans, Xi Li remained defiant and silent. In attack mode, Mackenzie fired the first question. "Why did you authorize the sale of American dollars?"

"I didn't."

"But such a massive transaction required your authorization. You had to know."

"I did not."

"Why have you aligned the Vatican Bank with Russia, China, and India?"

With glaring eyes, the financial whiz stiffened and countered. "Many nations have accounts with our bank. But I did not authorize the massive sale of your currency. Nor have

I made arrangements with other nations. When contacted by bank officials, I investigated."

"Why didn't you alert Anthony?"

"There wasn't time."

"What did you find? Was a rogue council member involved?"

"No."

"Then who triggered the sale? Was Kurita the culprit?"

"No. Covert operatives from the dark web initiated the transactions."

"That's unbelievable and unacceptable." Irked by the Asian's cavalier attitude, Mackenzie bristled.

"It's true."

"Liar! You have bragged incessantly about your impenetrable firewalls."

"Hackers often find a way. Ask your corporate titans."

Unexpectedly, the solemn Pontiff interrupted. "Li, I have to know. Were you involved?"

"No, Holy Father. My firewalls failed the test. Assailants took control and initiated the transactions."

"Who else has access to these accounts?" Fixated on a guilty verdict, Mackenzie glared at the Asian.

"The short list includes the finance council, vetted bank officers, and Swiss Guard leadership."

As uncertainty shrouded the prosecution, Anthony did the unexpected. With a wave of his hand, he dismissed Li. Aware of the agents' disbelief, he flashed a wry grin. "Vatican IT can identify the perpetrator. New traps can be set. Li is not going anywhere."

"Sir, did the deceased dine in the chapel?"

"No, Agent Nash. They ate in the main dining hall as per their customary habit."

Unexpectedly, the Pontiff's secure line jangled. Answering immediately, Anthony listened, nodded, and terminated the call. Unexpectedly, tears trickled down his wrinkled cheeks.

"Agents, my heart has been shredded. Cardinal Baroni's body has also been discovered. Seeking solitude, he dined in his quarters. My closest friend was not aware of the chapel deaths."

"Was Baroni a leader?"

"Oh yes, Agent Fallon. Both popular and charismatic, Antonio had broad support."

"So that leaves the Argentine, the Spaniard, and the Asian as our prime suspects. Is that correct?"

"Yes. But expect another Italian to emerge."

"Sir, who controls the dining hall?"

"The Swiss Guards have operated our food services for decades, Agent Nash. Surely, you're not suggesting their involvement."

"Do Guards intermingle with Cardinals?"

"No. They oversee the kitchen and preparation. The Cardinals partake shortly after daybreak. Then the Guards appear at staggered times."

"Has Captain Strader been here for a while?"

"Yes. Both he and Lieutenant Schass arrived about six years ago. Their records are impeccable."

"Are they well compensated?"

"Agent Fallon, these men are humble servants. Forsaking lavish salaries, they're attracted by prestige and loyalty."

"May we speak with them?"

"Certainly." Grabbing the phone and punching several buttons, the Holy Father issued the order. "Both should arrive shortly."

Twenty minutes later, two casually dressed men entered the private room. Surprised by the Americans, Strader bristled. "Holy Father, why have we been summoned at such an early hour?"

"My guests have questions about the chapel deaths."

"Sir, I am well aware of Agent Nash. But this is the Vatican. The investigation falls under my jurisdiction."

"Captain, the Holy Father has expanded the search. These murders are likely linked to American killings."

"Who are you?" The tone was icy and steeled.

"I am Special Agent Mackenzie Fallon. Agent Nash and I work together."

"This is not America."

"True. But it *is* a joint investigation."

As tension gripped the room, Morgan's eyes darted to Johann Schass. Of Swiss-German heritage, the Lucerne native was a poster boy for the Guards. His sky-blue eyes and white-blonde hair were pure Arian.

"Captain, may I interrupt?"

"Agent Nash, you've been a disruption from day one. You have a penchant for creating trouble."

"The Lieutenant and I have met before."

"That's not true," clamored the Swiss. "This is our first meeting."

"Let me rephrase. I recognize your face."

"How?"

"A certain photo was prominent in the Firelli home. I noted it during a recent visit. It was a picture of you and Enzo."

"The Camerlengo and I are friends."

"Correction. You *were* friends. That relationship has changed."

"What are you saying?" The poster boy's quizzical expression was revealing. News of Enzo's death had not circulated via the Vatican grapevine.

"Your buddy is dead."

"No! That can't be."

"Does that make you sad?"

"Yes. We had a great relationship."

"That's putting it mildly."

"I resent that tone."

"Your partnership ran much deeper. You were friends with *benefits.* In fact, you were *lovers.* Enzo twisted your loyalties."

Blindsided by the bombshell, the Swiss Guard sat aghast. "Holy Father, this is untrue. I deny these accusations."

Ignoring the pathetic plea, Morgan pressed his attack. "That cozy beach photo was telling. The Firellis had to be thrilled with your romantic relationship. But unfortunately, they too are dead. I shot them both."

"You what?"

"The Firellis were traitors. But you knew that. Johan, when were *you* radicalized?"

"What are you saying? I've never betrayed the Catholic Church."

"Liar! Your sole loyalty was to Enzo. The Camerlengo turned *you* against the Holy Father, gave *you* access to Vatican accounts, and ordered *you* to poison the Cardinals."

"Holy Father, he's lying. I am a faithful believer."

"But what's your theology? Do you worship God or RE?"

As beads of sweat dotted Johan's brow, Nash's eyes darted to Anthony. "Sir, meet your Vatican betrayer. Enzo's blonde beauty is your assassin."

Enraged by the kangaroo court, Strader's glared at Morgan with hard-set eyes. "Agent, you are totally out of line. You're condemning an innocent man with nothing but mere accusations. Johan has performed his duties admirably. He's been faithful to the Holy Father."

"Captain, check his accounts. Check his texts. Check his whereabouts in the kitchen. Proof is readily available."

"And check his molars," blurted Mackenzie. "Only the guilty carry a cyanide capsule."

Seething with anger, the muscular Swiss Guard clenched both fists and stepped aggressively toward his accuser. Anticipating a brawl, Morgan tensed. Suddenly Johann stopped, flashed a wild-eyed look, flipped a false molar, and defiantly screamed: "Allahu Akbar...Alla..."

Locked in the throes of death, Schass twisted in agony and then slumped to the floor. Heaving a huge sigh of relief, Nash waxed philosophical. "The lieutenant folded way too early. The man held aces high."

Instantly Mackenzie stared at him in disbelief. "You were bluffing?"

"It was my only play. I had to gamble on his weakness. Without his black beast guardian, Johan wasn't so brave. Unnerved, he took the bait and swallowed the easy way out."

"Were you aware of the hidden capsule?"

"Yes, Captain. It exposes the guilty. These radicalized minions would rather die by cyanide than reveal their master."

Wringing his hands in utter disgust, Anthony sat with slumped shoulders. "What has happened to my beloved church? Even a loyal Guard has betrayed me."

"Well, I'm outraged," blurted Strader. "I knew Johan and Enzo were friends. But an intimate relationship was not on my radar. Nor did I believe a colleague was capable of murder."

"Captain Strader, recheck the credentials of every Guard. I want no further surprises from Vatican security." With the mild rebuke, the Holy Father peered at the agents. "I owe you another debt of gratitude. Is there a next step?"

"Sir, you can help to resolve a delicate issue," replied Mackenzie. "Can you authorize the repurchase of U.S. dollars in the amount sold?"

"Absolutely."

"Can you bypass the finance council?"

"I can."

"Good. Trust no one until we find answers."

"Anything else?"

"Yes," quipped Morgan. "We need access to four private offices. Does Xi Li work here or at the Vatican Bank?"

"His executive suite is adjacent to the Argentine's and nearby. These particular areas underscore their council ranking."

"What about the Spaniard and the leading Italian?"

"Both have private offices down the hall. Captain Strader has keys and access."

Moving quickly, the trio entered the Spaniard's office. Surprisingly, the cubicle was plain and compact.

"Carlos is a very humble man," remarked the Swiss. "Despite his lofty position as World Care Chairman, his office is rather Spartan."

Wasting no time, Mackenzie barked instructions. "Captain, search the left side of the room. Morgan, take the desk. The right side is mine." Within ten minutes, the tidy office was in shambles. Disappointingly, nothing of interest was revealed.

"Dammit," grumbled the Dubliner. "I guessed wrong. This guy was my sleeper."

Suddenly a plush black bull caught Nash's attention. The Spaniard was from Pamplona. Vastly oversized, the stuffed animal sat on the floor.

"You're fixated on that bull," quipped Mackenzie. "Any reason?"

"Anderson and Carlos both ran with the bulls. The animal's markings are identical to the apis. Captain, are you carrying a knife?"

"Of course."

"Upend the bull and cut the belly. Check the stuffing for hidden objects."

Working quickly, the Swiss sliced the soft covering, ripped through layers of padding, and then sighed. "I've found nothing."

"Dig deeper. That bull is more than a showpiece."

Dubious about the outcome, Strader repeatedly jammed his hand into the soft stuffing. Suddenly, he flashed a wry grin. Buried deep within the recess was a small plastic object.

"That's a remote," yelped Mackenzie. "Point it at the bookcase."

With eager anticipation, the Swiss responded, yet nothing happened. Frustrated, he aimed the remote at other sections. Nothing clicked, creaked, or whirred.

"Try that hanging crucifix," barked Morgan.

"But it's too small."

"Humor me, Captain."

As the invisible beam linked with Christ's agonized face, a soft click was heard. Unexpectedly, the abdomen sprung open. Rushing to the crucifix, the Dubliner noted a two-inch cavity. With slender fingers she carefully removed a tiny bag. The contents were revealing.

"Diamonds!" yelped Strader. "What the hell? All five are two carats or larger."

"And they're likely without blemish," observed Mackenzie. "Has the good Cardinal been pilfering Vatican museums?"

Suddenly, Morgan flashed a twisted smile. "Mac, these are blood diamonds. They're a payoff. Carlos was not worthy to succeed Anthony. But RE needed his services."

"I'm ordering an immediate arrest."

"Captain, wait. We can deal with the Spaniard later. The formula is our priority. Take us to the Italian's office."

"Follow me. It's next door."

An avid practitioner of St. Francis, the Italian's cubicle was also small and sparse. After a lengthy search, the trio gave up. Nothing of value had been uncovered.

—∾—

As the trio approached the Argentine's executive suite, the shrill of Mackenzie's ringtone shattered the cavernous silence. The frantic caller was Jameson.

"Mac, have you found anything? Things are getting out of hand."

"We've narrowed the search but located no formula yet. Several suspects have been eliminated."

"That's helpful. Anything else?"

"Anthony has agreed to repurchase U.S. dollars in the amount sold. He has also encouraged European allies to do the same."

"That's a start. But it doesn't offset the massive dumping by Russia, China, and India."

"Have any launched invasions?"

"Not yet. The Russians and Indians are poised but hesitating. Likely, they're waiting for the Chinese. Beijing's two main armadas have merged. But they're moving out to sea and very slowly."

"Destination?"

"That's a real unknown and extremely problematic." Abruptly the line clicked off.

"Morgan, Jameson is scared shitless."

"Hell, we're all feeling the pressure. A viral pandemic and unwinnable war are terrifying prospects."

"Then we've got to find that formula."

—∾—

The South American's plush suite featured wood paneling, ornate ceiling, and double chandeliers. A two-tiered bookcase sat atop a long row of lower cabinets. Showcased in the center of the rectangular room was an elaborately carved wooden desk.

"Morgan, peruse the desk. Captain, take the left. The right is mine. Man, this guy loves animals. Look at these babies."

"The Argentine hails from a small farming community," remarked Strader. "His adoring people send a constant stream of toys and plush animals. Think of him as a Latin Pied Piper."

Twelve minutes later, the Dubliner's yelp was aflush with excitement. "I've found something. There's a lever in this book. The Latin may be our guy."

"Mac, check it out. But be damned careful."

Buoyed by the discovery, the Special Agent cautiously pulled the faux spine. To her dismay, nothing happened.

"Try again," encouraged Morgan. "That damn thing triggers something."

As three sets of eyes fixated on the mechanism, no one noticed a tiny crevice opening atop the bookshelf. Emerging quickly and scurrying along the edge were six tiny creatures. Veering left, two leaped. Both landed softly on the Dubliner's shoulder. Instantly, Morgan growled.

"Mac, don't move. For God's sake, don't you dare move."

As two waxy scorpions edged toward Mackenzie's open neck, Nash whipped out his Glock and swatted them to the floor. Stomping the pair with his shoe, he noted additional movement. The four remaining scorpions were on the carpet and sprinting in separate directions.

"Quash 'em, Strader! Kill the little bastards!" Moving swiftly, the two men quickly ended the threat.

"Damn, that was close," muttered the Dubliner. "I've been stung before. It wasn't pleasant."

"Boss, these babies are lethal. Raz mentioned them. They're imported from the Sahara Desert."

Convinced of the Argentine's guilt, Strader quickly interrupted. "Do we arrest the Cardinal now or later?"

"Later," grumbled Mackenzie. "We need a definitive link to RE. The scorpions could be the Argentine's security. This place may be holy but certainly not safe. Keep looking but be damned careful."

After a thorough search, the frustrated trio glanced at each other and shrugged. No damning evidence had been noted. Inadvertently, Nash's eyes locked on a ceramic blue heron.

Could it be that simple? A union of deities?

"Captain, point the heron at the falcon. See what happens."

Flashing a quizzical expression, the Swiss acquiesced. Suddenly, a slight humming reverberated within the bookshelf, but there was no movement.

"It's another ruse," lamented Fallon. "The damn thing is a dud."

"I'm not so sure. Captain, aim the heron at the bull."

"But that makes no sense."

"Just do it." A blink later, the trio stood transfixed.

"Morgan, look! That green frog is glowing."

"Meet Heket. Strader, rotate the goddess. Let's see if anything hums or opens."

As Strader twisted the deity; nothing happened. Peering around the room, Nash's eyes locked on the agonized face of Jesus. The mounted crucifix was more ornate than the Spaniard's.

"Mac, check the crucifix."

"Why?"

"Christ's agony pulsates wealth, not life. The cross is silver. And the thorns..."

Intervening, the Dubliner completed the sentence. "And the thorns are gold. Divine metals?"

"That's my guess. It's an oxymoron. Captain, tilt the frog toward the crucifix."

Nodding, Strader rotated the goddess. Unexpectedly, the bookshelf hummed and creaked as the mid-section opened.

"Look," cried Mackenzie. "It's another secret room."

Eager to explore but leery of surprises, the trio slow-stepped into the Argentine's lair. A small overhead light revealed frescos of vivid colors. Overwhelmed by the tomb-like images, Strader's eyes bulged in astonishment. "What the hell? It's a burial chamber."

Instantly Morgan chuckled. "Welcome to tomorrow's Catholic Church."

As the Swiss gaped, the Dubliner barked. "Partner, look. There's another crested wave. But it's much larger. Hell, it's gigantic."

"Stop," yelped Strader. "Tell me what I'm seeing."

"Captain, meet *RE's transitional Pope*. That's him in the wooden boat. Adorned in full regalia, he's standing tall, riding the giant wave and praising the Sun God. The crowded beach represents his adoring people."

"But Anthony would never allow such sacrilege."

"The Holy Father won't be around. Within a day or so he'll be dead."

"Who's the woman in the boat?"

"Mac, that's the goddess Isis. Revered as the guardian of kings, the Egyptian beauty is protecting RE's short-term minion."

"Wait. Something's amiss. This tsunami is brown, not foam green like Anderson's room. Mistake?"

Puzzled by the poignant query, Morgan stepped away. The color variation had to be significant. But what? Totally frustrated, he slammed his right fist into a wall.

"Feeling better?" Amused at her partner's idiocy, the Dubliner flashed a sardonic grin. "Hell, that hand is likely broken. It may need pins."

"PINS!"

"Boss, that's it. Color equates *linchpin*. It's another in a series of disastrous linchpins targeting the United States."

"Care to explain?"

"Ecru is the true color, which makes this particular image both troubling and surprising. RE plans to flood South America with Middle Eastern terrorists. Skin tone is both the common denominator and linchpin trigger."

"Morgan, tell me you're wrong. You've got to be mistaken."

"Mac, Isis represents a cleverly designed *double meaning.* The goddess is not only protecting the Argentine but also *ISIS, the terrorist group.* RE is set to unleash a veritable tidal wave of steel on the Latins."

"But that's insane. An ISIS presence in Latin America would prove horrific."

"That explains Arabella's smugness. Her rants about *unstoppable floods* extended far beyond sell-offs and bombings. I sure as hell didn't connect floods with terrorists streaming into Latin America."

"This is a frigging nightmare. What about the inland golden dome? The damn thing shimmers."

"It's another iconic *double meaning*. For radical Muslims, the dome represents a Latin Jerusalem. For local Catholics, the shimmering symbolizes a prosperous future. The image is a blend of half-truths and falsehoods."

"That actually makes sense. But the Argentine can't be the mastermind. No transitional Pope is going to penetrate RE's inner circle."

"I agree. That's why we focus on Xi Li. Captain, take us to the Asian's office. We can deal with the petty traitors at our leisure."

"Follow me. It's nearby."

~

The financial guru's wood-paneled suite replicated the Argentine's. Numerous investor plaques adorned the walls. Mounted behind the ornate desk was a magnificent crucifix. Nearby was a framed picture of a previous Pope. Numerous gifts from adoring fans were carefully arranged on an extended two-tiered bookcase. The featured attraction was a ceramic rearing cobra. An elongated plush snake stretched across an eight-foot section of shelf.

"You know the drill," barked the Dubliner. "Search but be careful."

Approaching the desk, Morgan was stunned by the massive size and neatness of the desktop. Carefully positioned to the right was an ornate pen set. Nearby was an imposing twenty-inch bronze statue of a seated man wearing a skull cap and grasping a rolled papyrus. To his left were two computer screens. Both were turned off. The keyboard rested on a hidden pullout. Scanning through numerous files, he noted monthly statements, recent investments, and economic reports. Nothing of note caught his eye.

Working the right bookcase, Mackenzie examined the ceramic cobra. Curious, she aimed it at various objects. But nothing whirred or creaked.

Deviating to the framed Pope, Strader peeked around the wooden edge. Suddenly, his eyes bulged with anticipation. "Hey, there's a faux panel behind this picture."

"Take a peek," yelped Mackenzie. "But be damned careful."

"Acquiescing, the Swiss cautiously opened the small door. Suddenly, an unexpected "whoosh" shredded the silence as a small dart rocketed from the opening and slammed into Strader's throat. Crumpling to the floor, the Guard writhed in agony.

"Mac, check him while I call Anthony." Whipping out his cell Nash punched several buttons. Eager for an update, the Holy Father answered on the first ring. "Agent, I hope you bring good tidings."

"Sir, Strader has been struck by a poisonous dart. The damn thing has lodged in his throat. We're in Li's office."

"Vatican medics will arrive ASAP." Instantly the line clicked silent.

Six minutes later, numerous paramedics converged on the scene. Watching pensively, Nash nudged his partner. "Mac, I've got a bad feeling. That gooey substance must be venom."

"Are you thinking asp?"

"Yep. The damn stuff is filthy."

"That panel was pretty obvious. Was it another safeguard like the scorpions?"

"That's a real possibility. This place is definitely not safe. Li could be innocent."

With the arrival of a lone ambulance, Strader's limp body was rolled through the door. The selected hospital was eight minutes away. As paramedics faded into the hallway, the Americans resumed the search. A short time later, both sat frustrated.

"Partner, there's nothing obvious. Li might not be our man."

Unexpectedly, Morgan's fragile emotions exploded. "Then dammit, who is? Someone is orchestrating this shit. And it isn't the Argentine."

"Are you sure about Arabella?"

"Mac, the woman was an addict. Plus, Wilson was right. Lady Rothschild wasn't that bright. Li has to be our guy. We're out of suspects."

"Then we keep digging. Recheck the desk while I peruse the walls."

Doggedly, Nash scrutinized every inch of the surface. After a futile search, he stopped. Joining him was the distraught Dubliner. "It's hopeless. The Asian isn't our man."

"Dammit!" Irked by another failure, Morgan slammed his fist into the hard wood. As his face contorted in anguish, Mackenzie flashed a wry grin.

"Satisfied? That had to hurt."

Ignoring the sarcasm, Nash stared blankly at the bookshelves. As the all-too-familiar shroud of doom cloaked his shoulders, he peered at his boss. "Mac, did Strader ever contact Vatican IT? Was the hacking ever verified?"

"I don't remember any calls or updates. Why don't you take a look?"

Sliding out the keyboard, Nash switched on the dual computer screens. Immediately, his interest spiked. "These screens were never opened. IT never deciphered the password. Knowing Li, it has to be a bitch."

"You decoded apis. Any ideas?"

"Are you kidding? Anderson was a clueless idiot. Plus, I had the magazine photo. With Li the possibilities are limitless, including Chinese characters."

"I disagree. If he's guilty, the password is likely Egyptian."

"That's possible. But a gamble at this late stage could prove fatal." Dubious, Morgan scanned the room for clues. Suddenly his eyes fixated on the lower bookshelf. "Mac, note the plush snake. Asians revere their history *and* vipers. That baby is at least eight feet or longer."

"Meaning?"

"The password could be Apophis. The giant serpent guards the underworld."

"Take a chance."

Uncertain, Nash cautiously entered the seven letters. Instantly, the password was rejected. "Dammit, no luck. But there has to be a clue somewhere in this room."

As two sets of eyes scanned the suite, nothing popped. There was no black bull to save the moment. Suddenly, Mackenzie fixated on the bronze statue.

"Morgan, did Raz ever mention the seated man?"

"Maybe. If so, it's vague."

"Then think. The little guy may be important."

Pushing away from the desk, Nash stared at the ceiling and reflected. Several blinks later, he flashed a twisted expression. "It was something about pearls."

"But Egyptians never wore pearls. Are you sure? The reference had to be symbolic."

"Possibly." Pausing, he began rapping his fingers. Suddenly a wry grin appeared. "Mac, that's it. Pearls symbolize wisdom. Give me a minute."

Searching for a connection, Morgan's eyes locked on the bronze statue. *Wisdom ties to scroll. No. Papyrus doesn't think. But... a wise man does. What's his name?*

Ewok?

No. More like Iwop.

Wrong. Shit.

Ihob. Ipop. Ihoe. No.

After fifteen agonizing minutes, Mackenzie intervened. "Morgan, the clock is ticking. Any luck?"

"I can't remember his name. Give me a few more minutes. The answer is likely in plain sight."

Was this little guy a reminder? Or did Li rub his head for luck?

As the Dubliner paced and fumed, Nash reflected. "*Hojo. Hoto. Hoteb. Hotek.*"

Possibly. Sounds like "hotek." No. "Hotep." Ivan? Evan? No.

Think, dammit. Push yourself. Remember the...

"Mac, I've got it."

"Are you sure?"

"Yeah. *Imhotep* was revered for his "pearls of wisdom."

"Excellent. Give it a try. But be careful. I'm stepping away."

With Mackenzie safely in the background, Morgan timidly entered the letters. To his delight the word "Accepted" flashed across the moss green right screen. A blink later the left screen glowed sky blue as a series of scrambled letters appeared.

"Mac, we're screwed. Imhotep was right. But the bastard has a *second* password. Scrambled letters are the problem."

"Let me look." Edging closer Fallon hovered over her partner's shoulder. "It's like a scrambled word search. Seven letters can be a bitch."

"With hundreds of deities, that's an understatement. "k-m-t-s-e-h-e."

"Partner, wait. Something's not right. I sniff a trap."

"I agree. But we need answers."

As both studied the letters, Morgan noted the Dubliner's trembling fingers. With a mischievous grin he tried to break the tension. "At least the characters aren't Chinese."

"You are not funny. The odds are stacked against you. Hell, they're incalculable."

"Which means our financial wizard was lying. His accounts were well protected. Vatican IT never had a chance."

"Do you?"

"Possibly. According to Raz, the number seven was a symbol of '*perfection*' for ancient Egyptians. But the bastard didn't elaborate."

"Then it's a crapshoot. Worse, it's a race against time. Just do your best. I'm stepping back."

~

Locating a pen and pad Nash rearranged the letters to form words. Twenty minutes later he threw up his hands in disgust. Egyptian gods and goddesses had bizarre names. Worse, some had no vowels.

"Mac, this is insane. There's a shitload of unpronounceable deities. Even with a correct answer, the spelling is impossible."

"Try your cell phone."

"I did. But most of the deities weren't listed."

"Forget the minor ones. Focus on the best known. That's your only chance."

Pensive, Morgan scribbled a series of strange-looking names. Within minutes the list numbered twenty-seven. Unexpectedly, he grinned.

"Boss, Sekhmet is the password."

"Are you sure?"

"Yeah. A lion-headed protector makes *perfect* sense. Thus, seven is "perfection." But I'm unsure about the spelling."

"Go with your gut."

Typing his top choice Nash quivered as his finger lightly touched "Enter." Instantly the right screen changed color as another set of scrambled letters appeared on an ecru background.

"Mac, Sekhmet is right. But there's another jumbled word."

"How many letters?"

"Six. "h-h-t-u-a-e."

"Keep working. You can do it."

Working feverishly, Morgan sighed as he reflected on thirty-one possibilities. Yet after twenty-five agonizing minutes a gut-wrenching decision had to be made.

"Mac, I think the answer is Hauhet. A snake-headed goddess associated with the "primeval flood force" seems very appropriate. But the spelling is iffy."

"Take a chance. There's no Plan B."

Ignoring the beads of sweat that peppered his brow, Nash reluctantly entered the six letters. As "Accepted" appeared on a radiant purple background, he heaved a huge sigh of relief. Suddenly, his eyes popped in disbelief.

"Dammit Mac, there's a new set of scrambled letters. I can't keep doing this. It's a losing proposition."

"How many letters?"

"Eight. It's likely the final password and a reference to the Ogdoad. But the answer is likely some remote deity."

"I'm coming."

Peeking over his shoulder, Mackenzie stared at the jumbled letters. "Unbelievable. It's "w" city. "w-t-w-e-w-a-p-e." Just take a deep breath and think. It's doable." With a pat on the back, she backed away.

~

Forty agonizing minutes later, Morgan slammed the desk in disgust. "Mac, I've got two pages of fricking possibilities but no viable answers."

"What triggered the possibilities?"

"The letters likely symbolize the "Opener of the Ways." It's appropriate. But a correct spelling is virtually impossible."

"Then pick your best option and hope. But hurry."

Reluctantly, Morgan selected a possible and touched "Enter." Suddenly all hell broke loose as "Invalid Password" pulsated on a scarlet background, triggering a deafening alarm. Forty seconds later, the high-pitched screech waned. As both relaxed a soft whirring was heard.

"Boss, listen. There's movement." Suddenly Morgan's eyes widened in fear. "Mac, look! There's an opening.... SHIT! DUCK!"

As both reacted, a "whoosh" shattered the silence, followed by a thud. Activated by the invalid password, a small arrow jettisoned from the bookcase and embedded in the desk chair.

"Dammit, that was close," muttered Morgan. "That missile was perfectly aligned with my chest and the chair."

Removing the arrowhead, the Dubliner noted the sticky substance. "It's the same goo as Strader's. Li must be our man."

"Likely. But the bastard could claim protection and argue circumstantial evidence. We need a definitive link to RE."

Cautiously, the pair rechecked the office for more hidden surprises. Noting nothing, Nash resumed work. Abruptly, he stopped. His entire body was shaking.

"Mac, it's useless. There's too much pressure. I don't know names or spellings. And I sure as hell can't outguess a genius."

"Then stop. RE wins, millions die, and the world changes."

"That's not fair."

"Work fast, but be ready to duck."

"That's not funny. Duck rhymes with fuck, which perfectly describes my dilemma."

"Morgan, trust those instincts."

"That's unfair. You sound like Dawn. Okay, let's try option number two."

With one eye warily fixated on the bookcase, Nash tentatively entered "Wepwewat." A blink later he sat dumbfounded as nothing happened. Suddenly, the screen flashed scarlet. As the alarm blared and "Invalid Password" pulsated, he yelled "DUCK!" Yet, no whirring or creaking was heard. As the screeching halted, the room remained eerily silent. Carefully scanning the walls, both stared in bewilderment.

"Morgan, is it safe?"

"How the hell should I know?"

"Then keep working. We need that formula."

"Mac, it's not that simple. Try unscrambling eight foreign letters. It's virtually impossible. Plus, this guy loves surprises. Focus is a joke."

"Then walk away. Add another failure to your list."

"Dammit, stop. Quitting is not an option. But I sure as hell don't like the odds."

As Nash fixated on his list, the Dubliner stepped away. Neither saw nor heard movement from *behind.* Slithering stealthily through a small opening was an eight-foot king cobra. As the black harbinger of evil twisted closer, Morgan sensed motion. Instinctively turning, his eyes popped in sheer terror.

"MAC, DON'T MOVE! FOR GOD'S SAKE, DON'T MOVE!"

With eyes glued on the viper, he fumbled for the Glock. Unnerved by the warning, the Dubliner shuffled two steps and then stopped. Aroused by the movement, the cobra hissed and rose into a defensive posture. With neck ribs forming a classic hood, the devilish black head elevated and swayed at the back of Mackenzie's thighs.

As Morgan eased the gun into position, his partner panicked. Instantly reacting, the cobra lashed at her exposed hamstring. Two hollow fangs drove deep into the tough flesh. As Mackenzie screamed, he triggered three quick shots. Mortally wounded, the viper slithered toward the hole. Two more shots obliterated the menace.

With the Dubliner writhing in agony, Nash whipped out his cell phone and tapped the screen. Answering immediately, Anthony uttered a single word.

"News?"

"Sir, it's bad. Send paramedics to Li's office ASAP. A cobra just struck Mackenzie." Instantly, the line clicked silent.

"Mac, did the fangs penetrate?"

"Yeah. They stung like hell."

"Hang tight. Help is coming."

"Text Nick. Reassure him that I'm okay."

"I will. Plus, I'll order a case of Irish whiskey to aid your recovery."

"Funny man. Just pray the hospital carries the right antidote."

Within minutes a parade of EMTs arrived. Working quickly, they placed the Dubliner onto a stretcher and rolled her to an idling ambulance. An antitoxin was available at Strader's hospital.

Wasting no time, Morgan took a deep breath, texted Nick, and returned to his daunting task. Unexpectedly, an imposing shadow appeared in the doorway. Much to his surprise, a grim-faced Anthony entered the room.

"Holy Father, be careful. This place is extremely dangerous."

"We're in good hands. Trusted security and first responders are nearby. I've come to assist."

"But it's not safe."

"My presence is God's will. Plus, I bring information. A cobra's venom affects both vision and the nervous system. Within minutes swallowing becomes difficult, making breathing and speaking virtually impossible. Untreated, the venom leads to respiratory failure and death."

"Damn. Will Mac and Strader make it?"

"That's my prayer. The captain is temporarily on a respirator and in grave condition. The arrow's location is the main issue. However, the news is positive. If a victim receives the antitoxin within thirty minutes, the survival rate is good."

"Then it's going to be close."

"Cobra de capello."

"What?"

"It's Latin for hooded snake. But you need to refocus. What's the challenge?"

"It's an eight-letter password."

"Have you made any attempts?"

"I've failed twice. The wrong answers triggered a poisonous dart and the black cobra."

"I note your list. It's very impressive. Obviously, you think the answer is Egyptian."

"Ancient deities were the first two passwords."

"Let me take a look. The number three implies a heavenly opening. It's likely your last hurdle."

"And virtually impossible to solve. The Egyptian pantheon is massive. Spelling is a nightmare. Sir, this room isn't safe. Surprises spring out of nowhere."

"Agent, I'm fine. My passion is ancient history." With darting eyes, Anthony scanned the lengthy list of possible answers. With a wry smile, his spindly finger pointed to a scribbling. "That's the word. This spelling is correct."

"Are you absolutely sure?"

"Have faith, my son. Wepwawet was Egypt's "Opener of the Way."

"Holy Father, please step outside. The password could be a trap."

"Agent, type the letters. Trust me."

As Morgan touched "Enter," the dual screens immediately turned black. As both tensed the left screen flashed "MAPS" in pastel yellow. A blink later, the right screen blinked "PLANS" in tranquil teal.

"Good call, sir. But can you trust either screen?"

"Click on "Maps." Obliging, Nash repositioned the cursor and punched "Enter." Instantly both heard a muted whirring.

"Duck, sir!"

"Look! Moses is parting the Red Sea. That bookshelf is dividing. It's a divine miracle."

"The overlaid paneling perfectly concealed the seams. Like always, the answer was right in plain sight."

Cautiously, the duo entered the narrow doorway. The smallish secret room was square and sparse. Attached to the far wall was a world map laden with colorful arrows.

Suddenly Morgan gulped. In front of him was hell's unbridled fury. "Sir, we've entered Satan's den. Clearly defined are the aggressors' invasion routes. Were you aware of this room?"

"No. These suites were remodeled before my time."

"Who cleans these offices?"

"A night custodian works Monday through Saturday."

"Have him eliminated."

"May I ask why?"

"Your custodian is a RE minion. He's a keeper of snakes and scorpions."

"So be it."

Mesmerized by the maze of crisscrossing lines, both men edged closer.

"Dammit," uttered Morgan. "I can identify routes. But there's no timetable. The invasions may be staggered. That's problematic."

"Have faith, my son. We have just begun."

"I hope God is listening. Simultaneous invasions would overwhelm American capabilities and forever change the world."

Deflecting the concern, Anthony immediately fixated on a bold blue arrow. "My sources were correct. India's government has deliberately misled the Vatican. Their military exercises along the Pakistani border are not peaceful. They have bold plans to invade both Pakistan *and* Afghanistan."

"It's a power grab, sir. India salivates for Afghanistan's lanthanum and other rare earth materials, plus the drugs. With America neutralized, they can succeed with air power and minimal ground forces. If RE succeeds, they win."

"That would destabilize the region, which must not happen. Note the Middle East. Multiple red arrows crisscross in numerous directions. Can the Soviets succeed?"

Edging closer, Morgan studied the details. Suddenly his eyes bulged in disbelief. "Absolutely! Perfectly timed incursions by Russia and Iran would be unstoppable. Hell, just a few armored divisions coupled with airstrikes would do the trick. Plus, there's a surprise. Breaking their NATO alliance, *Turkey* also wants a piece of the action."

"Can you decipher the myriad of arrows?"

"Possibly. Russian troops in Syria delay movement, *join axis allies,* and then blitzkrieg into Iraq to seize oilfields."

Suddenly he hesitated. "The plan is pure genius."

"Why?"

"A military union of Iran, Russia, and Turkey creates a regional powerhouse. Plus, the conflict expands into neighboring countries. Note the map. Russia secures its Iraqi targets and then invades Lebanon and Jordan. Iran and Turkey capture Baghdad and surrounding regions and then roll into Kuwait, Qatar, and the Emirates. The trio rejoins forces in a pincher movement to overwhelm Saudi Arabia. Iran then launches attacks against Israel. It's a replay of Hitler's lightning war; a series of small-scale attacks that reap huge rewards."

"The end goal?"

"Russia wants to be the world's gas station. They want a stranglehold on European and Middle East energy. If successful, they can bully and threaten our allies at will. Turkey and Iran gain coveted Middle East territories and oil revenues. Plus, Iran gets a strategic staging area for incursions into Israel. Their radical leadership salivates at the thought of obliterating the hated Jews."

"Surely the United States has enough weaponry to prevent this apocalyptic scenario."

"That's questionable. Everything depends on the virus. If millions die, America stands alone. That puts Taiwan and South Korea at risk. That smallish purple arrow indicates China's intent to send a well-armed armada in Taiwan's direction. But that's stage two and a later date."

"What about Japan. Can't they help?"

"Not without America's help, Holy Father. Otherwise, they stand down. Plus, it gets worse. That smallish green arrow underscores North Korea's invasion into South Korea. Dammit, none of our allies can survive this onslaught."

"Can the Israelis mount a successful defense?"

"Temporarily. Their firepower can certainly stop initial attacks. But it's not enough to offset the combined military assets of Russia, Iran, and Turkey. The global scope of these invasions really spreads our military."

"I assume the bold purple arrows represent China's primary intent. But I'm surprised. The massive "exercise" fleet is deviating from India."

"Yep. And Pentagon officials are going to shit Dixie. Those warships and troop transports are bypassing Africa and steaming toward *the Americas.*"

"A surprise?"

"Totally. Military brass predicted a Taiwan invasion and possible incursions into South Africa or Southeast Asia. Their raw materials and natural resources are desperately needed by the Chinese. Obviously, Pentagon officials were wrong."

"But why would China target Venezuela and Mexico? Southeast Asia is much closer."

"True. But Latin America is the crown jewel. The Chinese covet control over our southern hemisphere. A monopoly gives Beijing total energy independence. Plus, it creates an endless supply of raw materials, agricultural products and cheap labor."

"But most Latin countries are poverty-stricken. Human suffering has risen tenfold."

"Holy Father, the Chinese don't give a damn about people. That explains Beijing's collusion with an arch enemy. If India controls Afghanistan, drugs flow non-stop into China's new Latin America. Asian triads replace Mexican cartels."

"But I would vehemently protest these moves. I would urge the people to resist."

"Sir, your voice won't be heard. You'll be dead."

"When?"

"Within days. The Argentine betrayed you. RE bribed him with a truth and a lie. The truth was straightforward. The Latin was promised your position."

"The lie?"

"It was twofold. He wasn't told about his pending demise. Nor was he privy to China's true intent. The only thing he heard was bliss. Chinese occupation would bring peace, prosperity, and stability."

"That explains his recent arrogance. If successful, would the Chinese invade North America?"

"Doubtful. Their leaders are greedy but not stupid. Like Russia and India, they're content to let the U.S. wither on the vine and descend into a vassal state."

"This is unbelievable. What about the yellow arrows?"

"More surprises. In a secondary move, Iran launches multiple attacks to overwhelm Turkmenistan, Azerbaijan, Uzbekistan, and Kazakhstan. Later they cross the Black Sea to seize Bulgaria, Serbia, Croatia, and Romania. From Belarus and other staging points, Russia ignores NATO threats and moves on the Poles, Latvia, Lithuania, and Estonia."

"But why?"

"It's a recreation of the old Soviet Union plus Poland. That explains Russia's earlier incursion into Ukraine. Moscow gains coveted territory and assets like neon gas. Unknown to most, this gas is critically important to the semiconductor industry. Ukraine is also the agricultural breadbasket of Europe."

"But Poland is a major NATO country."

"Forget NATO. It's toast. Russia needs Poland in order to squeeze Germany. Later, they target Finland, Sweden, and Norway. Without U.S. intervention there is no European deterrent. And the news gets worse. Once the Nord Stream 2 pipeline is functional, black gold flows freely and vastly enriches the Soviets."

"What about the gold arrows? Turkey wouldn't dare."

"I beg to differ. With the Middle East secured and Eastern Europe in chaos the Turks steamroll into Greece via the Cyclades Islands. Santorini, Crete, and Athens become prime targets as well as shipping and fishing lanes of the Aegean Sea."

"That same greed triggered the ancient Persian-Greco wars. Persia attempted three invasions into Greece during the 490 B.C. era and failed."

"That won't happen this time. Turkey's minor incursion will soon become a major invasion. Russia will supply their every need."

Suddenly Anthony hesitated. The scope of the invasions was beyond belief. "If the Turks actually succeed, western Europe is surrounded and screwed, including the Vatican."

"Yep. That's the apocalyptic scenario. The world is forever altered."

"Agent, this madness cannot take place. We must find that formula. These traitorous acts forever alter the world, expand the teachings of Allah, and doom the Catholic Church. That must not happen."

"Sir, the answer is here. That's RE's style. It's likely in these frescos."

"Then we must move with haste. Note the golden vulture. The shimmering scavenger appears to be nesting on Washington D.C."

"I think *scavenger* is another play on words. That same image is depicted in the Argentine's secret room. It likely represents Richard Anderson, RE's deceased golden boy. But I could be wrong."

"What about the nearby obelisk and stream? Is this a reference to the Washington Monument and Potomac River?"

"Possibly. But nothing connects."

"Then we keep searching. Should you contact the Director regarding the invasions?"

"Not yet. We need the timetable… and formula. Please instruct your Guards to rip this room apart."

"But dismantling takes time. Every wasted minute offers the alliance a *golden opportunity.*"

"You're exactly…" Suddenly Morgan's eyes popped as his grim expression twisted into sheer terror.

"NO! IT CAN'T BE! IT CAN'T!"

"What can't be? Agent, talk to me. What is happening?"

"Suddenly, the pieces fit. Golden *represents RE's coup d'état*. It's a final, devastating surprise."

"I'm not following."

"Forget the divine color. *'Shimmering'* is the key. That vulture is nesting on a small nuclear device. RE plans to vaporize D.C. and plunge America into darkness. Dissolution is the end goal as the omega accord comes to full fruition."

"But the device hasn't detonated. Why?"

Stunned by the simple logic, Morgan hesitated. "Bingo! The device triggers when the death toll reaches *one million*. According to Arabella, there's a golden number. That's it. One million triggers the Ogdoad's massive payout as one of their labs magically appears with the formula."

"Agent, this is unbelievable...surreal."

"It gets worse, Holy Father. With D.C. decimated, there's no Federal government. Contract negotiations with the Ogdoad stall. The delay slows production, which adds millions to the death toll. Meanwhile, our aggressors continue to seize prized resources with minimal efforts. The golden number explains their patience. A withering, leaderless American poses zero threat."

"What's the current death toll?"

"It's well beyond a hundred thousand and accelerating. Likely the device detonates within twenty-four hours."

"But D.C. is a metro area. That bomb could be anywhere."

"But the location is somewhere right before our eyes. It's in these images. I feel it."

"Then we must solve the riddle. Obelisks link to Egypt's creation story. They stand tall. But white is the standard color, not *silver.* Is that important?"

Stymied by the query, Nash hesitated. Suddenly he flashed a sly grin. "God bless you, sir. Forget structure. Forget divinity. Forget theology. Color is literal, not symbolic. Silver indicates location."

"What about stream?"

"It too is literal."

"Silver stream?"

"Sir, that's the answer. *Silver Springs, Maryland is the location*. It's nearby and well within the killing zone."

"Can you pinpoint an address?"

"No. But the vulture offers two additional clues. An Ogdoad facility houses the device. And the company's name mimics the goddess Nekhbet. It's time to call Jameson."

Whipping out his cell, Morgan quickly updated the Director. Stunned by the revelation, the veteran agent quickly took notes and terminated the call.

"Was Jameson aware of the threat?"

"No. The poor man was stunned. But at least his people have a viable lead. Sir, we've got to find that formula."

"But where? You've searched Li's suite."

"But we didn't tear it apart."

"My Guards can solve that problem."

After decimating the room, the Swiss quietly exited. No damning evidence had been discovered. Dismayed by another failure, Morgan slumped in the desk chair. Overwrought, tears welled in his eyes.

"A penny for your thoughts, Agent Nash."

"What thoughts? God is refusing to listen."

"Our Master often works in mysterious ways. What you seek is likely within sight. But your troubled mind blurs your vision."

"Holy Father, we've shredded this place. That formula had to be here. Li was my last suspect."

"Do not despair. Keep praying and searching."

As Anthony rummaged through the rubble, Morgan mindlessly perused the desktop. Catching his attention was the bronze statute.

Little man, you're supposed to be wise. What have I missed?

Interrupting his blackened mood was a call from the Director. "Agent, we've identified two small-cap defense contractors near Silver Springs. Both have the capacity to assemble and activate a small nuclear device. The companies are Neimeyer and Nebert."

"Who are the CEOs?"

"Norman Bailey and Nickie Beth Moore are the CEOs. They're likely aliases."

"Nickie Beth juxtaposes Nekhbet. That's your target. Dismantle it."

"Will do. Choppers and vehicles will be underway within minutes."

Glancing repeatedly at his watch, Nash sat paralyzed. As he prayed for divine intervention, his darting eyes scanned the room for a tiny clue. Suddenly a single word flashed across his mind.

Scroll! That could be it!

Enthused, he waved at Anthony. "Sir, you were right."

"I'm not following."

"Imhotep's scroll has always been front and center." Snatching the bronze god of wisdom, Nash felt along the edges of the narrow cylinder. Near the top was a slight indentation. "I think the cap pops open."

"Flip it."

"I can't. It's sealed. I need a knife."

Stifling a chuckle, the Pontiff uttered a soft command to a nearby Guard. Whipping out a genuine Swiss knife, the soldier handed it to Morgan. With eager anticipation, he wedged the blade into the indentation. The seal refused to budge. Exerting more pressure, the cap finally popped. Instantly, he turned the statue upside down. But nothing dislodged. Peering into the tube, he noted a thin, tightly wound piece of paper.

"Sir, I see something. But I need tweezers."

Opening the center drawer, his fingers slashed through numerous pens, clips, and business cards. Finally, his eyes fixated on a slender pair of tweezers. With the delicacy of a surgeon, he carefully manipulated several tightly wedged sheets of paper. After several attempts, the tightly rolled thin slips tumbled from the hollow tube. Suddenly, he beamed.

"The print is tiny. But these calculations and data must unlock the formula."

"Praise God. If accurate, is there a timetable for the vaccine rollout?"

"It could be within a short time assuming President Allday cuts red tape, grants manufacturer immunity, and pushes production." Suddenly Morgan hesitated. "But everything depends on the FBI. If that device explodes, all hell breaks loose."

"Agent, trust God. Evil never prevails."

"Amen, Holy Father. The strength of your faith is amazing."

"Let God guide you, my son. The end is near. Director Jameson is most capable."

"Mackenzie feels the same way. The Director is a tough SOB, but smart. I believe in his people."

"Assuming the best, does 'short' mean days or weeks?" Fixated on the vaccine rollout, the Holy Father locked eyes with Morgan.

"My gut says weeks. If so, the death toll could exceed a million. Hopefully, Allday encounters no political interference. 'Never let a good crisis go to waste' is a favorite D.C. slogan.' The President's opposition may try to slow the process and tamp his success."

"Then your government needs to forgo politics and act swiftly. I can make some confidential calls."

~

Ninety minutes later a jubilant Jameson was breathing a sigh of relief. "We've located *and* disarmed the nuclear device. CDC and pharmaceuticals are validating the formula. No timeframe has been projected."

"Keep us updated."

As the line clicked silent, the Vatican duo sipped coffee and enjoyed snacks in a secure private office.

"Sir, the news is positive. CDC is analyzing the vaccine. Allday is rallying allies and confronting aggressors. The global crisis appears to be waning."

"Praise God. Later today, I will expose the 'faux exercises.' The world will know the truth."

"Amen."

"Thank you, Agent Nash. The Vatican is in dire need of spiritual leaders, not traitors. "Damnatio memoriae."

"You've damned a memory?"

"No. *Numerous memories have been damned.* The Judas Cardinals have been eliminated from all Vatican records."

"It's only fitting. But there's still unfinished business. I need to visit the Argentine and the Asian."

"Do you seek mercy or vengeance?"

"Holy Father, that's unfair. I'm a Christian believer. But at this moment, I lean toward the Old Testament."

"An eye for an eye? You seek justice for your family?"

"Absolutely. But payback is unlikely. I expect both Cardinals to commit suicide."

"So be it. Security will escort you to their quarters. Afterward, they will clean up your 'Texas roadkill.'"

Moving swiftly, the well-armed Swiss contingent led Nash to the Argentine's quarters. With key in hand, the team leader quietly opened the door. As anticipated, RE's transitional Pope was asleep. Edging to the bed, Morgan prodded his foot with the Glock. Rudely awakened, the Latin blinked and then screamed.

"YOU!!!"

"Yeah, it's me."

As the Argentine's face twisted in sheer terror, the revenge-seeker flashed a smug grin and slowly squeezed the trigger. The perfectly aimed slug slammed into the Cardinal's forehead. Two more shots shredded his heart.

One for Dawn. One for Erin. One for me. Three for Texas.

Nodding at the leader, he barked a soft command. "Send someone to take out the trash."

Ten minutes later, the team silently approached Li's sleeping quarters. Stopping, Nash sensed a trap. Using hand signals, he repositioned the Guards and tested the handle. As anticipated, the door was unlocked. In a whisper, the widower uttered the magic word.

"SHOOTER."

Quietly he added: "I'm going alone. This is my show."

As the team stepped away from the field of fire, Morgan twisted the knob and pushed. As the door swung open, three shots immediately slammed into the hallway plaster. Countering, he dove low, spotted movement along the far wall, and triggered two rounds. The first hammered the Asian's left shoulder. The second shattered a night lamp.

Frantic, Li fired again. But the misaimed slug shredded the doorframe. Returning fire, Morgan unleashed two more rounds. Both ripped into the betrayer's chest. Stepping to the lifeless body, he aimed the Glock at the Asian's forehead and squeezed the trigger.

Winking at the unreadable Guards, he stepped away. The final shot had been both memorable and gratifying.

Twenty minutes later, he rejoined Anthony. "Sir, your betrayers are no more. But suicide was not their demise. I've come to confess my sins."

"Agent Nash, our Lord is both merciful and forgiving. I'm sure He understands. My stomach churns when I ponder the abominable treachery. I must guide the remaining faithful toward an infusion of the Holy Spirit and Christ's teachings."

"You're the perfect man for the job."

"That is to be determined. I owe you a backlog of gratitude."

"Nonsense. Hopefully, you've made a new friend. With your permission, I have to check on our patients."

"I'll make the arrangements."

In the tranquil twilight of a Roman evening, Morgan chatted with intensive care nurses. Strader's news was positive. He was breathing independently, his condition improving. The report on Mackenzie was also good. But no visitors were allowed. Walking to a nearby waiting room, he quickly updated Nick. Next on his list was a call to Robby. The news on the old man was favorable. The billionaire was returning to Austin within a week.

Unexpectedly, his solace was interrupted by Jameson. "Sir, how's it going?"

"Great. The aggressors are withdrawing. The bastards aren't willing to wage an all-out war against an improving America and angry allies."

"What about the virus?"

"Not so good. CDC estimates two hundred thousand casualties before the vaccine can be distributed in quantity. It's terrible. But an end is near."

"That's too bad. Even in death, RE wins."

As the line clicked silent, Nash kicked back in the hospital waiting room. The grisly ordeal was officially over. Within minutes he was fast asleep.

CHAPTER 46

Wednesday, March 3

Shortly after 3 p.m., a procession of black SUVs exited the Vatican and motored to the hospital. As his vehicle rolled to a stop, Morgan flashed a huge grin and waved to his boss. Enjoying the outside air and bright sunshine, Mackenzie appeared more than ready to exit her wheelchair and leave Rome. Managing a weak smile, the Dubliner's pallid coloring was telling.

"Mac, let's head home. Nick wants to see you."

"That sounds heavenly. Is the case really over?"

"Yep. We can talk on the way to Beantown."

"Boston?"

"Yeah. We need to visit the old man. Thankfully, he's doing well."

As the luxury Boeing rocketed skyward from Rome's Da Vinci International, Nash relaxed in a plush recliner. Glancing at his partner, he noted trepidation.

"Mac, are you okay? You're shaking."

"Sorry. It's that damn cobra. I keep picturing those beady eyes and swaying head. I wake up in a sweat."

"Overcoming trauma takes time. Believe me. But this ordeal is over. Your viper is dead. RE is dead. The news is mostly good."

"Mostly?"

"CDC estimates two-hundred thousand deaths from the virus. But the number could go higher. The formula is being fast-tracked into production."

Instantly the Dubliner's fiery green eyes darkened. "So, Arabella keeps on killing. The death toll is outrageous."

"Yep. Deep within the bowels of hell, Arabella Rothschild is smiling. But the case is over."

"What about Allday? How is our new President doing?"

"The man has done remarkably well, imposing stiff economic sanctions on the aggressors and repositioning military where needed. He's rallied the people, sidestepped politics, and pushed the CDC. Robert Anderson's presidency would have destroyed the country."

As Mackenzie napped, Morgan peered out the window. Flying at 35,000 feet, he observed that the radiant blue sky was crystal clear. In the distance, he noted a solitary cloud. Suddenly, a foreboding thought bastardized his mind and panicked his soul. As beads of sweat dotted his brow, he tapped the Dubliner's shoulder. The angry response aped a guttural growl.

"Dammit, I was trying to sleep."

"Mac, I desperately need to talk."

"Why?"

"The case *isn't* over. There's a final piece."

"Dammit, no. This sordid mess is finished."

"But you need to listen."

In total disbelief, Mackenzie rubbed her puffy eyes and glared at her beleaguered partner. "You're sweating...and trembling. Are you sick?"

"No. Terror has that effect."

"But we're done with the case. You're finally free, a man without a care."

"Not anymore. A cloud changed everything."

"Cloud? Good god, Morgan, what the hell?"

"Do you remember that all-seeing eye hidden in a puffy white cloud?"

"Yeah. It was featured on several frescos."

"That's the missing link. It *symbolizes* Arabella's marriage to Amun. What I'm picturing is apocalyptic."

"No! That's utter nonsense. Cloud prophecies don't exist. Nor can a raving lunatic marry a mythical deity. Pour yourself a stiff drink and get some rest."

"I can't. The image is horrific."

"Hell, you sound like me. Okay, let's hear it." Mostly skeptical but somewhat empathetic, the Dubliner's mood lightened. Her longtime partner was obviously suffering from a form of PTSD.

"What's the deal?"

"In one of her final rants, Arabella raved about her blissful marriage to the "Hidden One." Amun was the cloud image. But I dismissed the theatrics and focused on Wilson. Since Boston, a critical gap has bugged me."

"Meaning?"

"Every key player was linked to Pharaoh Akhenaten by bloodline. Lady Rothschild was the exception. Our dreaded adversary wasn't royalty nor the mastermind. Neither was Xi Li."

"Partner, everything points to the Asian. He's the real deal."

"Is he?"

"Yeah. That's my take."

"That was my belief. But not now. In our haste to indict Li, we overlooked the real culprit. Cloud images were everywhere. But our fixation was RE and the formula."

"Morgan, stop. Those symbols were fiction."

"Really? Would you agree that even in death RE still surprises?"

"Yeah. The virus is still killing people."

"Well, I think there's a final surprise. In fact, it's the *granddaddy of surprises*. Our case is about to come full circle."

"Dammit, no. We're done with this mess."

"Not yet. Do you remember the short guy in the chapel?"

"Yeah. He was greatly downsized. But the fresco was pure sarcasm."

"That was our mistake. The image wasn't a joke. Neither were Arabella's maniacal rants. That short guy was her husband, the true orchestrator of the global crisis."

"Morgan, you're fantasizing, desperately trying to hang onto the case. Li and Rothschild were the masterminds. BABA and Raz were credible witnesses."

"Both were duped. Hell, we've all been duped. That puffy white cloud has always been in plain sight but never our focus. Only Arabella was aware of the 'Hidden One's' true identity."

Exasperated, Mackenzie's apocalyptic temper exploded. "Dammit, that's more than enough. You could make the same argument with any hieroglyphic. This discussion is over."

"Doubtful. The bloodline remains intact. Amun represents a very real danger."

"Forget it. It's a great theory but with no factual basis."

"I'm more right than wrong."

"Partner, listen very carefully. Your mind is screwing with you. It desperately wants this case to continue. Without it, what's left? Subconsciously, you think there's nothing. But there is life after death even for an avowed loner like you. That's a promise."

"You think my life is empty?"

"Absolutely. Your out-of-control imagination is creating a false narrative. But this mental paralysis is only temporary. In time you can find a new purpose. Relax. This cloud crap is pure theater."

"I'm not so sure."

"Dammit, give it a break. Your mind flip-flops between psychotic madness and intellectual brilliance. It keeps me guessing."

"Fine. You win. Go back to sleep. The 'Hidden One' does not exist."

"That would be copacetic."

"Yeah. We need good insurance."

As Fallon grinned, Morgan winked. "Boss, sometimes you can be so damned obsequious. Copacetic, my ass."

"You knew all along?"

"Yeah. Dawn would have never married a dumb jock."

"You called me obsequious."

"It's Irish for copacetic. Maybe I should accept Wilson's offer and buy a ranch."

"You can't. The Director is grooming you for my job."

"What if I don't want the responsibility?"

"You have no say in the matter. I promised Jameson that everything would be copacetic."

"Well, it's not."

Unexpectedly, Nash's shrill ringtone interrupted the playful bantering. On the line was a jubilant Wilson Senior.

"Is everything okay?"

"Everything's copacetic. I'm calling to say thanks."

"Let me put you on speaker. Mac is with me." With a quizzical expression, Morgan glanced at his partner. "Sir, you're very gracious. But you saved my life. You were the real hero in that hellhole."

"I'm not calling about the chapel. I want to express my gratitude for the *surprise gift."*

"Sir, Mac and I haven't sent anything. We've been rather busy. Any gift had to be from Jameson or Anthony. Or it was from the hospital administrator. After all, you are a billionaire."

"Well, I have to thank someone. I've never seen anything so amazing."

"That's terrific. Describe the serendipity."

"It's a miniature figure of Robby. The damn thing is a perfect likeness."

Immediately, Morgan tensed. "Is it a wood carving?"

"Yeah. Little Robinson stands about a foot tall or so. The artwork is incredible. It's a spitting image. But the head doesn't bobble. That's too bad."

"Was there a note?"

"No. Only the words "Carpe Diem" were scribbled."

"Seize the day?"

"Yep. It's one of my favorite phrases."

"Was there a signature?"

"Nope. There was just a smiley face hidden in a puffy white cloud. Honestly, the gift has been a godsend. These past few days have been really tough."

"Sir, the gift sounds perfect. I'm anxious to see it."

"You're coming to Boston?"

"Yep. We're on the way."

"Great. We have much to discuss."

"That's an understatement. Stay safe."

As the call ended, Morgan tossed his phone and stared out the window. Visibly upset, his mind was racing. The case had a new beginning.

"You're troubled. Why?"

"Mac, that was no gift. That likeness was a damn shabti."

"A what?"

"It's a *funerary* figure. A shabti performs hard labor for the deceased in the afterlife. Amun is targeting Robby."

"Amun? Dammit, you've got to stop this nonsense. Imaginary demons are lurking everywhere. That gift was likely sent by a very shrewd administrator."

"A shabti? Who sends a shabti? It's a funerary figure."

"Morgan, relax. Likely, it's an overzealous work of art. Once in Boston, we can figure things out. The Director can run background checks if necessary. In the meantime, get some rest. Enjoy a smooth flight."

Ninety minutes later, the Dubliner's peaceful slumber was shattered. Irked by the unexpected call, her fiery disposition quickly softened. The love of her life was on the line. "Hey Nick, what's up?"

"I wanted to check on my girl. How are you feeling?"

"Great. The doctor prescribed lots of relaxation and you."

"That's wonderful. I can't wait. By the way, thank your partner. His surprise gift is both thoughtful and unique."

"What gift?"

"It's a wood carving of me in a tux. It's a perfect likeness and wonderful wedding gift. But the head doesn't bobble. That's a shame. The artistry is likely Italian and very exquisite."

"Is it about a foot in height?"

"Yeah. That sounds right. The figure is definitely a showpiece."

"Did my partner include a note?"

"No. There was just a puffy cloud, smiley face, and 'Carpe Diem.' A small shamrock and Irish verse were imprinted at the bottom."

"Interesting. Read the verse."

Make a wish.
Spin a tale.
Drink a pint.
Then run like hell.
Rub the head for good luck

"The message is very Irish and Morgan-like. Note that it ends with *Rub the head for good luck."*

"That's my eccentric sidekick. The man loves surprises."

"Should I make a wish and drink a pint?"

"Does the carving appear safe?"

"Mac, it's just an exquisite piece of wood. The artistry is pure genius."

"Then rub it. Make a wish for both of us."

"Okay. I wish for unending love and happiness. And I wish for June to get here faster. I am so ready."

"Me too."

"Well, here goes. I'm rubbing my head for goo..." Suddenly, hysteria replaced bliss as chokes and gasps crammed the line. In Dallas, something was terribly wrong.

"Nick, talk to me! Nicky! Say something. Baby, what's happening?"

Hearing nothing but fuzzy static the Dubliner raced to her dozing partner. "Morgan, get the hell up. Nick is in real trouble. He can't breathe."

"Where?"

"Home."

"I'm on it." Whipping out his cell phone Nash punched a special number and barked orders.

"Paramedics are on the way. What happened?"

"He called about your surprise wedding gift. Then all hell broke loose. I heard horrific chokes and gasps followed by silence."

"But I didn't send anything."

"That was my thinking. But he was so excited. The wood carving depicted him in tux. It was a perfect likeness. For luck, he rubbed the head and then choked. That was it."

~

Forty minutes later a dejected Jameson confirmed the worse. Mackenzie's love was dead, a victim of cyanide poisoning.

"Morgan, this is unbelievable. It's surreal." As the Dubliner grieved, he held her tightly. The tragic suddenness was overwhelming and beyond comprehension.

"Partner, I'm so sorry. It's a damn shame."

"But why? Why did this happen? Why in God's name was Nick targeted?"

"The 'Hidden One' seeks revenge. That cloud symbol is real. Amun is targeting our loved ones and friends. I need to warn Wilson."

Following a hasty call, he exhaled a deep sigh of relief. "Robby's okay. The bureau is retrieving the shabti. Likely the wood is a minefield of sharp pricks. If coated in cyanide, any rubbing creates skin penetration and kills the victim. That's the only answer."

Unexpectedly, his cell phone flashed Anthony's private number. "Holy Father, this is a surprise. What's up?"

"Agent... Agent, can you...?"

"Sir, speak louder. I can barely hear you. The call is breaking up."

"Agent. Agent, is that you?"

"Sir, I'm losing you."

"Is this better?"

"No. Your voice is faint. Is everything okay?"

"No. I'm calling to..."

"Sir, I can't hear a word. Sir."

"What about now?"

"It's faint but getting stronger. What's up?"

"My shroud of woe continues. Strader is dead."

"What? Was it the dart?"

"No. The captain was murdered at the hospital. He ingested a pill laced with cyanide. My people are investigating."

"I'm so sorry."

"Agent, you must warn your partner. She's in grave danger."

With a quick glance, Morgan panicked. Releasing the phone, he chopped Mackenzie's wrist, sending an array of colorful pills in various directions. The painful blow was met with an icy fury.

"Dammit, that hurt. I needed those pills. What the hell?"

"Mac, Strader's dead. A little pain is better than death. One of these pills is laced with cyanide."

"Agent Nash! Agent, can you hear me? What is happening?"

"Your call saved Mackenzie's life. Those pills were clutched in her hand."

"Thank the Lord."

"We are most grateful, Holy Father. Unfortunately, her fiancée suffered Strader's fate."

"Cyanide?"

"Yeah."

"Was he Catholic?"

"Yeah. Nick was a decorated police officer but not real active due to a wacky schedule."

"That doesn't matter. Reassure Agent Fallon that I'm coming to Dallas in the near future. I plan to conduct a special mass for the fallen officer. Your partner is in my prayers."

"Thanks. Mac will be pleased."

"Agent, why has this happened? I thought the case was over."

"It's not. The nightmare continues."

"But why?"

"The true mastermind seeks revenge. The 'Hidden One' is no longer hidden."

"Amun?" Instantly, Anthony tensed. "That means Arabella's husband is real."

"That's my take."

"Then we must fight fire with fire."

"Amen to that. Pray for a speedy conclusion."

The End

ABOUT THE AUTHOR

A White House honoree, author and speaker Steve Edwards has a successful background in ministry, healthcare and business development. A recognized authority on eldercare, he has made appearances on national television and radio, and has been featured in newspapers and magazines. In recognition for his innovative eldercare initiatives, President Ronald Reagan honored Mr. Edwards in a Rose Garden ceremony. He also received similar awards in his native Texas.

In addition to *The Omega Accord*, Mr. Edwards has authored *Off and Running*, a lauded church stewardship program and the *The FamilyCare Organizer*, praised as a "must have" book regarding family preparedness.

In his off time, Mr. Edwards enjoys golf and travel with his wife and family.

Connect with Steve Edwards at:

omegaaccord.com

www.ingramcontent.com/pod-product-compliance
Lightning Source LLC
Chambersburg PA
CBHW020418030726
47495CB00006B/1556

* 9 7 8 1 6 1 1 5 3 4 7 2 6 *